D0897518

FREEDOM SOLDIERS
Katherine Williams

HARDBALL

PRESS

MONROEVILLE PUBLIC

OCT 5 2019

LIBRARY

MONROEVILLE PUBLIC LIBRARY

4000 Gateway Campus Blvd.

Monroeville, PA 15146

Copyright © 2018 by Katherine Williams
All rights reserved.
Library of Congress Cataloging-in-Publication Data:
Williams, Katherine
Freedom Soldiers
1. Underground Railroad —Fiction. 2. Elgin Settlement. 3. Slavery. 4. US History. 5. Racism in America. 6. Katherine Williams.

No part of this book may be reproduced or transmitted in any form or by an electronic or mechanical means, including photocopying, recording or by any information storage and retrieval system, without the express written permission of the publisher, except where permitted by law (fair use).
Cover art by Anna Usacheva
Book design by D. Bass
Set in Palatino Lino.
Published by Hard Ball Press, Brooklyn, New York
ISBN: 978-1-7328088-5-0

www.hardballpress.com

DEDICATION

This book is dedicated to my children and grandchildren,
whose loving hearts and kind actions make this world a
better place and make me proud.
To the people of the Elgin Settlement and the
Underground Railroad.
To their descendants who have kept their genius and
triumphs alive,
And to all of us in every corner of this beautiful world who
strive to obliterate the chains of oppression and create an
egalitarian world.
May we remember that destiny is in our hands, and that we
have the intellect and the power to create a new world.

The Escape ~ February 1840

As twenty-year-old Abiah looked over her shoulder she felt panic rising in her belly. Unable to speak, she grabbed the young Conductor's shoulder so hard that her fingers dug into his skin. He pulled away and turned to her in alarm. When the Conductor saw the wild look in Abiah's eyes, he whipped around to see what caused it. There on the snow-glazed hilltop silhouetted by the flame colors of the setting sun, he saw two riders not even half a mile behind them. Then he saw one of the riders point in their direction and heard a distant shout. By now the other escapees were also looking at the riders. They froze in fear as they watched their pursuers begin galloping down the hill.

The Conductor was a youth who had collected a small band of runaway slaves that morning from a safe-house just south of the Ohio River in Virginia: Abiah, her baby, and an older man with two teenage sons. He had guided several groups before, but this was the first time slave catchers had found him.

"We have to split up," he said, his tense voice unnaturally high. "They can't go five directions. If we split up, the most they can catch is one of us." His eyes jumping in every direction, he added, "I'm sorry, but it is now every man for himself." His eyes came to rest on Abiah, holding her two-year-old daughter. The young woman's gut turned over at the pity she saw in his face. Harriet, sensing her mother's fear, clung tightly to mama's neck with chubby little fingers.

The father and sons, unwilling to separate, took off running along the riverbank to the left. The pursuers now had only three directions to choose from. Abiah hesitated only a moment. She knew that she and little Harriet would be the ones the horsemen would catch. Fear was so thick in her stomach that she nearly vomited. Hugging Harriet tightly to her, she fought down the panic. No! They would *not* catch her.

She looked at the Ohio River just below them and the patch of ice stretching partway across. She would rather they drown in that slushy, slow-moving river than face what awaited them if the riders caught them. Better that Harriet died than grow up enslaved. A tight sob escaped from her throat.

Squeezing the little girl tightly to her hip, she took off running, sliding down the steep bank as fast as she could, using her free hand to balance herself by grabbing at the leafless branches and dead grass. She paid no attention to the young Conductor, who ran away from the river into the woods he knew so well.

Abiah skidded down the icy riverbank, her feet nearly coming out from under her. The rough voices of the men on horseback came closer: coming for *her*. Burdened by Harriet, she was the slowest of the group and the least able to put up a fight.

She heard the horses clatter to a stop at the top of the bank where she'd just been standing. The riders jumped off.

At the river's edge, a sheet of ice nudged the shore and extended far out onto the water. Gasping for breath, Abiah launched herself onto it, praying it would not give way beneath her. The momentum of her descent down the bank propelled her into a long slide, and she threw her free arm into the air trying to maintain her balance. She failed. As her feet came out from under her, she rolled to protect Harriet from hitting the rock-hard ice, folded her knees and skidded along on her side.

As she was sliding she saw the men reach the edge of the ice and stop. One of them put his heavy boot out and brought it down heavily to test the ice. When it did not give way, he stepped cautiously out to pursue her.

Time drifted into dreamlike slow motion. Abiah could hear the men arguing about whether the ice would hold them. Whether to wait for her to get stranded and give up. Meanwhile, the ice skidding by under her was tearing through her clothes. She thought, *tomorrow I'll be all bruised and scraped.*

Tomorrow, she mused. *Will there be a tomorrow?*

She watched herself scrambling to get upright as if she were outside herself, observing her actions.

A loud, sharp crack startled her back to real time.

She looked at the men, flinching and expecting to see a gun, reflexively turning so her body shielded the child. But no bullet tore into her flesh. She saw no gun. Instead, she saw the man who had stepped onto the ice jumping as if someone were shooting at *him*. Abiah could see no gunman.

A wave of dizziness came over her. She began to lose her balance. The world was heaving. She sat down hard. Harriet whimpered and wriggled, and the young mother realized she had been squeezing her baby so hard the child could barely breathe. She loosened her grip slightly and kissed Harriet's forehead. The dizziness did not go away.

She looked at the riverbank, where the men were again talking to one another. They were rocking up and down as if they were on a boat. With a shock, Abiah realized there had been no gunshot, the crack had been the sound of the ice breaking. It was she that was swaying up and down as the broken chunk of ice beneath them floated lazily down the river.

She watched the men run back to their horses, intent on chasing the other members of her little band of fugitives. They had given her up for dead. Abiah put her arm over her eyes, feeling a flash of relief that was immediately chased away by terror. Had she chosen death over capture? Would she now watch herself and Harriet die in the freezing river?

3

She looked down at Harriet's eyes, innocent and frightened. As the thought of her child being swallowed by the icy waters crushed her heart, tears leaked out the corners of her eyes.

They stayed in silent embrace as their icy craft heaved and rolled slowly down the river, the bank gliding past Abiah's unfocused eyes as she grew numb in body and mind. They drifted closer and closer to another chunk of loose ice until they juddered into it. The impact jolted Abiah out of her numbness.

She felt the ice they were on tilt and instinctively moved to balance it. She would not give in to despair. She would not give up! Cold was digging at her where the ice had ripped open her clothes. Though her feet were numb and her hands ached, she still clutched Harriet, who clung tightly to her neck. Looking around, Abiah realized they had come close to the Ohio side of the river. She began to search the bank frantically for someplace she could chance a jump off and make it to shore. She stood up on legs shaking from cold and fear, feet spread wide apart to balance the ice floe beneath them like a raft.

Her breath was coming in deep, rasping heaves. Their ice was about to bump into another, larger chunk wedged against a tree trunk that had fallen into the river. With no time for hesitation, Abiah leaped recklessly from their accidental ferry. Harriet began slipping out of her arms at the sudden motion, and the ice floe under her feet slid away faster than Abiah expected. As the top half of her body fell heavily onto the wedged ice, Harriet slithered out of her hands, gliding a few feet ahead, leaving Abiah's legs and hips submerged in the icy water.

Panic clutched her belly once again. Abiah kicked furiously while clawing at the rough ice, fingernails digging and breaking, inching her forward toward her daughter. Little Harriet clambered to her feet. Seeing her mother half in the water flopping on her belly, the child began to cry loudly and toddle toward Abiah. Flesh tore off Abiah's fingers, but she didn't feel it. A strength she didn't know she had dragged her body forward until her hips were on the ice. Her legs didn't seem to have any feeling in them, but her hands still pulled her, pulled her until she was fully out of the water. She reached Harriet and gathered the whimpering baby into shaking, grateful arms.

Mother and child lay motionless for a moment. Then Abiah pulled herself to a sitting position and used the inside of her cuff to wipe the tears from Harriet's little face. The baby pulled away, her fear replaced by irritation at the rough cloth scratching her freezing cheeks. The ordinariness of Harriet's response brought an absurdly out-of-place smile to Abiah's face.

But she didn't have time to be grateful. The impact of their sudden bodies had dislodged the ice from the log. It began to slowly tilt away from shore—so close!—and toward the current. Abiah scrambled onto wobbly-jelly legs and gathered Harriet back up. Somehow she stumbled across this new piece of ice and launched herself off of it just before it came completely loose. Her motion pushed the ice out into the river behind them. For a moment she felt suspended in mid-air, then her feet were back in the icy water and finding the bottom below. Every muscle in her body strained to keep her upright and holding Harriet high. As she started to fall forward, one numb leg somehow moved ahead of her and she regained her balance.

Dragging half-dead feet, she reached the shore and began to climb. Part way up, her strength gave out and she slid to the rock-hard, frozen ground.

A wild, hysterical laugh gurgled up from her shattered lungs. Turning over, she set Harriet down beside her. The little girl, hearing the unfamiliar sound her mother was making, began laughing uncertainly. Abiah looked across the river and saw no trace of the slave catchers. She sent a hasty prayer that they would fail to catch her traveling companions. Then she took a deep, croaking breath and rolled back over until she was lying prone on the Ohio earth.

"Thank you," she whispered. Then, louder, with tears in her voice, "Thank you, Jesus, thank you, thank you!"

Little Harriet was confused at this rapid change from laughter. But eager to imitate, she rolled over and sprawled out on the ground, too. With her eyes on her mother, she threw her arms out to either side of her plump little body and in her high little voice cried, "Fankoo, Desus! Fankoo, Desus!" She was delighted when her mother started laughing in a familiar way.

Abiah sat up to settle her breathing. She looked around at countryside that appeared just the same as that on the other side of the river. Was it really possible that it could be so different a land? Was it really possible that this precious child beside her would not know slavery? That Harriet would grow up in a life Abiah could barely imagine? With her heart filled to bursting, Abiah hugged Harriet to her chest and covered her with kisses. She felt Harriet shivering and realized that she herself was shaking like an autumn leaf about to break loose from its twig. They would have no life at all if she didn't quickly get them somewhere warm.

The winter sun had set, and darkness was thickening on this cold land of freedom. She stood up and began a faltering, heavy-footed trudge toward the flickering light in the window of a distant farmhouse, praying to God it contained a warm hearth and a kindly stranger.

Another Escape

A few years after Abiah crossed the frozen Ohio river, many miles to the south and east another family ran in search of freedom. Nine-year-old Thaddeus Childs felt his arm nearly come out of its socket as his mother plunged into the warm, still water, dragging him behind her. When his face momentarily dipped into the water, he heaved himself upright, gasping and coughing. But his mother didn't turn or slow down, so he shoved his legs under him to push off the muddy swamp-bottom to keep up with her.

The slow, drawn-out baying of the bloodhounds came closer and closer, and Thaddeus felt fear pucker his scalp. He vividly remembered when the men brought Uncle Timothy back to the plantation after the bloodhounds caught him. The dogs' long teeth had made tatters of him. The plantation owner had forced everyone, even little children like Thaddeus, to see Uncle Timothy brought home. The vision of that torn and bloody body was burned into Thaddeus' memory: one arm gone and a bloody, ragged stump at his shoulder, strips of skin hanging loose, and deep bite-marks all over his naked legs and torso. Uncle Timothy lived for three days after he came home, and for all three of those days, Thaddeus heard him moaning and crying, praying for death.

Thaddeus pushed harder through the muck and water until he was keeping up with his mother and no longer felt her pulling his arm. His mother's other hand was clamped to that of the man he knew was his father, and Thaddeus' little sister was clinging to the man's back, her hands clutching deep into his hair, her face tight with fear as he bounced and sloshed under her. Thaddeus quickly glanced over his shoulder and saw the bloodhounds lope out of the woods and reach the water's edge.

"*Mama!*" Thaddeus screamed. His father glanced back and then launched himself forward as if bee-stung, dragging his mother, who in turn pulled him. Her hand wet and slippery, he nearly lost her.

The dogs hesitated at the water's edge, awaiting the signal of their minders. Men soon ran out of the woods behind them. Thaddeus heard their voices like dry corn on a grater, and a chill went through his body.

Just ahead of the family, the bank of the swamp took a sharp turn to the left. A large cypress tree hung out over the water at the turning.

The slave catchers ordered the dogs down and raised rifles to their shoulders. Thaddeus heard two explosions behind him and the thwack of the bullets as they slammed into the cypress tree just beyond his father's head. His father plunged forward like he was possessed, and the extra pull from his mother's hand lifted Thaddeus off his feet. He was dragged, floating, kicking, struggling to keep his face out of the water as they reached the cypress tree and turned the corner.

The slave catchers didn't finish reloading before their targets disappeared from view.

Eight Years Later . . .

The Spirits Who Touched This Place ~ September 1850

The horse burst out of the woods in a dust-raising gallop, seventeen-year-old Thaddeus leaning forward until his face was nearly on his mount's sweat-slick neck, his sinewy legs wrapped tightly around the bay's midsection, his fingers entwined in its mane.

At that moment a slender, dark-skinned girl with lively eyes was sitting, unwilling on the doorstep at the back of her house, leaning against the doorframe. She was holding the darning her mother Abiah had just thrust into her hands. To her mind, it was far too nice an afternoon to be mending clothes. Just getting used to the discipline of sitting still at school all day, her soul rebelled against sitting still some more. She wanted to run, to go play jackstraws or hopscotch with her friends, or at least go tend to their horse. But her mother had caught her the minute she changed out of her school clothes and pushed the darning into her hands, saying, "Harriet, you better sit your skinny butt down and fix this shirt before the weather gets cold. I don't want to hear you crying to me about you're cold when you feel that icy-sharp wind ride right through those holes like a hawk, you hear me?" Harriet knew protest was not an option, so she sat down in the doorstep, careful not to get a sliver from the raw wood of the newly-built house.

Today was warm, but the nights were coming colder. The frosty fingers of autumn would soon feel their way into Canada West. The leaves on the trees were turning yellow, the garden was full of red tomatoes and beans drying in their pods. The shirt Harriet was supposed to be mending was made of rough wool—the off-white color of the sheep that had surrendered their own warm coats to the settlers' spinning wheels and looms last spring.

In the few short months between March, when her family had moved here to the Elgin Settlement, and July, when the long days made the evenings warm enough to store it in the cedar chest, Harriet had worn holes in the elbows and frayed the cuffs. The shirt now draped uncomfortably warm and itchy across her lap as she reached for the small ball of yarn, reluctantly trying to thread its fuzzy end through the eye of the darning needle. Looking wistfully across the field to where blackberries dangled sweet and juicy near the edge of the woods, she took in a long breath and nearly let out an even longer sigh, but caught herself. Her mother was close by in the kitchen, and Harriet didn't want to hear what she thought of a long sigh.

The sudden, urgent sound of galloping horses was an excitement. When her mother turned toward the sound, Harriet twisted from under her mending, carefully setting it on the step as she darted around the house to peek from behind the front corner. At first she could only see a cloud of dust rising from the woods. Then two tall horses, dark with sweat, riders on their backs, broke out of the trees along the row of wooden houses. Reaching their yard, the riders drew the horses up so sharply at the front gate that their hooves slid in the dust. At the same time, she heard her mother's piercing call out the back window.

"Whooo—*eee*, Tho-*mas!* *Come!*"

The carrying power of that hooting voice! Harriet imagined the cows in the far field pulling their wet noses up out of the grass, abruptly halting their chewing to turn their wide heads to look.

Her mother reappeared at the front door. As the horses stood heaving, the two riders dropped stiffly to the ground to politely greet her. Harriet saw that the one that had arrived first was actually a boy in his teen years, still scrawny in his body, but with shoulders that were broadening into a man's and muscles that spoke of hard work. He had prominent cheekbones on a smooth, oval face, his ebony skin now covered in sweat and road dust, his dark eyes deep, liquid, and shining with intensity.

"Harriet!" her mother turned back toward the house to call her. Abiah looked momentarily startled when Harriet stepped immediately from around the corner to her right. "Come take the horses. Cool them down, give them some water."

Harriet came through the gate. Peeking shyly at the lanky youth, she collected the reins from both riders. She recognized the older man: her parents knew him. She led the horses around behind the house. Usually happy for any task with horses, this time she was impatient with curiosity. She saw her stepfather striding swiftly to the far side of the house, where he disappeared from her view: she knew he would be shaking hands with the tired, dusty travelers, then inviting them into the house.

The horses' flaring nostrils blew warm, wet breath onto her neck and head, dampening her head-wrap as she skipped forward to keep her bare heels out of the reach of their heavy hooves. As their breathing settled, their sweat beginning to dry, she wondered who the strangers were, particularly the young one with the eyes that drew her into them. Why had they arrived in such a dramatic fashion?

The two riders appeared behind the house, stopping beside the washstand a few feet from the door where Harriet had been sitting. She watched as each poured water in turn for the other to wash the road dust off his hands, face and the back of his neck. First one, then the other used the piece of sackcloth hanging from a nail to wipe the water off before stepping carefully over Harriet's abandoned darning and proceeding through the back door.

Finally she was back on the doorstep, after tying and watering the horses and washing her own hands. She pulled her long skirts down over bare legs and spread the shirt on her lap again, angling her body so she could see inside. The back door opened right into the room where the grown-ups were now seated around the table, the visitors eating chunks of bread topped with slabs of the butter she had helped churn early that morning. Harriet's mother turned to fetch drinking water from the stoneware urn that was always kept filled in the corner of the room. Seeing Harriet, Abiah's eyes cut meaningfully to the girl's motionless hands, cocking one eyebrow. Harriet quickly picked up the darning needle, bending over to thread it, relieved that her mother had not shooed her away.

"You going to stay the night with us, Walker?" her stepfather asked.

"Thank you, no," said the older rider, who was about the age of Harriet's parents. "We're grateful for the food and drink. But we've got to carry word about the new law to the church meeting in Chatham tonight. This Fugitive Slave Act will create an emergency for a whole heap of folk south of the border. We'll have to plan how to prepare for them. Thaddeus is going to stay with Gunsmith Jones in Chatham to help, I'll go back to Windsor tomorrow."

Harriet's mind strayed from the voices. "Church meeting" sometimes meant another sort of meeting. For weeks there had been a flurry of talk amongst the adults. It was something to do with the increasing dangers on the freedom road, a trip she and her mother had taken too long ago for her to rightly remember. She didn't know what the new law was they were talking about, or why it created an emergency, but she knew she would find out by eavesdropping on her parents the next few days.

The other piece of information that registered was that the boy with the eyes like deep pools in the forest shade

– Thaddeus – was moving to Chatham, ten miles away. Harriet's family had just moved from Chatham last March. They often traveled back there now that they had the mare Meldy to pull a little buggy they shared with other settlers. Maybe she would see the boy again.

Harriet's fingers stopped moving as she drifted away from the conversation into a daydream about the Jones' house in Chatham: about Gunsmith Jones—Uncle James—herself sitting at his feet to listen to stories about his father the African, about Auntie Emily, who had tutored her from the books they had brought from the college in Oberlin, Ohio, where they had lived before moving to Chatham, about the warm stove that always had a pot of something smelling wonderful on it. Now the youth Thaddeus would be there, too.

Chairs scraped loudly as the men in the kitchen rose to leave. The sound startled her out of her daydream. Harriet's elbow hit the doorframe, sending pins and needles to her fingers. Rubbing her arm, she jumped up to go fetch the horses.

<>

North Buxton, Ontario, 1975

The year is 1975. A man bearing Thaddeus' last name sits on the same doorstep where Harriet sat more than a century ago. With silent reverence, the man strips layers of paint from the doorframe, restoring the old cottage on the museum site. He rests his hand on the bare wood and shivers as goose-bumps come up on his arm. His heart flutters. Spirits dwell in this place. Listening to the empty kitchen behind him, he hears the whispered echoes of conversation: the long-silent voices of his ancestors. These walls bore witness when fire still crackled in that old brick fireplace. They have lessons to teach. He will help give them voice. Leroy Childs bends back to his work.

A restored house from the Elgin Settlement, like one Harriet's family would have lived in.
Courtesy of the Buxton National Historic Site and Museum

4

Silent Stories Reverberate

"That was uncalled for," Walker said in a cold voice as he and Thaddeus rode away from the Ingrams' farm. Thaddeus knew Walker was talking about the wild gallop he had led in the last half-mile to the Elgin Settlement.

"You're young: that's why they chose you for courier. But it's not going to work if you're young *and* stupid, too."

Thaddeus' ears began to burn.

"Truth is, this Bloodhound Law is about to swamp us. Now any black person in the northern states can be taken as a fugitive and not allowed to defend himself in court. And any and every white person is required by law to help catch us. Our people will soon wash into Canada like a tidal wave,and it's our job to provide for them! We've got to step up our organizing, strengthen our support network, and communication has got to be tight. That's where you come in."

Walker shook his head in disgust. "But you know all that already," he continued. "Why am I even talking to you?"

Thaddeus was silent. He reached out his hand to pat his fatigued horse on the neck. Walker kept talking, a note of tiredness in his voice.

"Look, boy, it's an important job you're taking on. You're going to be back and forth on this road more times than you can count. You think you can be misusing your horse like that? You swore into the Order. You're supposed to know better than that. You got some demons inside that you think running can chase away?"

Walker's words were so well aimed that Thaddeus flinched. He was proud that the secret society had the confidence in him to give him this new assignment. This tongue-lashing implied Walker had lost that confidence. Thaddeus couldn't excuse his mistake. Shame rode heavy in his belly. He sent a silent apology to the horse.

Walker didn't talk for the rest of the two-hour ride to Chatham, but his remark about demons hung in the air.

Thaddeus' mind drifted back to that night in North Carolina when he was nine. He and his little sister Charlotte each held one of his mother's hands, tiptoeing into the hushed silence of the night forest. He figured they were going to see their father, so his body grew tense. These meetings did not happen often, but with his mother constantly looking behind them, Thaddeus was always scared until they got back home. He felt nervous around Joseph Childs, with his deep, slanting eyes, his broad, powerful shoulders and thick body striped by long, raised scars. That night his mother grabbed onto Joseph as if she were drowning. Joseph whispered fiercely, "That man's not gonna lay another hand on you, Sarah." With those words, the family set out into the night forest, the little boy who had his father's eyes tagging along with a rapidly beating heart.

The nights of endless walking were vivid in his memory: Thaddeus working his short legs until they ached and cramped, Charlotte on her father's back. They slept during the day. The memory of the ghostly baying of the bloodhounds still crawled under his scalp sometimes when Thaddeus lay in his bed on a quiet night.

He felt again the terror of the race at the end, his hand slippery in his mother's clawed fingers, his face in and out of the water, spluttering for breath.

When the dogs and slave catchers disappeared behind them, they continued sloshing, panting through the swamp until they reached muddy ground that was defended by bushes with teeth nearly as vicious as a bloodhound's. A husky voice from behind the bushes startled them: "Hey there—this way!"

A weathered old man appeared through an opening in the

bush above them. He reached down to pull them up with rope-muscled arms whose strength belied his white hair. As daylight retreated before a night made darker by enclosing forest, the wiry man led the family, dazed and shaky, to a cluster of sleeping houses. They had arrived at a place the slave catchers didn't dare follow. Thaddeus would learn that neither money-lust nor fear of their employers could lure bloodhound men to follow their quarry into the Great Dismal Swamp. Those few who tried rarely came out alive.

Thaddeus woke up the next morning on a straw pallet in a corner. Until they ran away, he had never seen more of the world than the fields surrounding the one-room house in the barracks where he'd been born. There, he and everyone he knew had dragged their tired bodies from sleep before the sun, resentment and fear saturating their movements as they readied themselves for work. Here, when the little boy awoke, the sun was already glittering through the trees. People he didn't know were moving easily and boisterously about their morning tasks. They shouted greetings and scolded one another with sly words that triggered hoots of laughter.

Thaddeus wanted to tell them to hush. He looked for his mother—she would warn them! But when he saw her, she was leaning against the open door, smiling shyly at something or someone outside. Sunlight lit her face and she wore a clean, pretty dress Thaddeus had never seen before. She must have bathed, for he saw none of the mud that stiffly coated his own legs. A brightly colored headscarf made her look like Christmas. Had they landed in a different world?

As he pushed himself to a standing position, dried mud crumbled and fell from his knees and ankles. "Where are we, Mama?" he murmured shyly, sidling close to her.

"It's freedom, baby!" his mother laughed. She threw her head back so he could see her long, graceful neck. "There's no white man here, Thaddeus, no boss-man! We're going to have to work hard to make our life, but it will be *our* life, can you imagine?"

Thaddeus couldn't imagine, but when some boys his age ran over and grabbed him, she nodded, smiling for him to go off with them. Peewee, it turned out, had been born in this place and never seen a white person or a whip.

"You mean you all don't have to work in the fields?" he later asked.

"You mean in the farm? Of course we do! How else we going to get our food?" Peewee looked at him amazed. How had Thaddeus gotten this big without knowing such an elementary fact?

"I mean," Thaddeus stammered, "I . . . there's no Big House around here? You don't have any boss man?"

Peewee shook his head with impatience at the ignorance of this new boy. "No, boy, this is *our* place. 'It belongs to the black man,' that's how the grown folks say it. But you got to be careful." He clearly enjoyed his role of instructor. "Don't be going yonder past that big tree." Peewee thrust out his arm, pointing far across the field made up of vegetable gardens behind the houses. "We've got sentry-men minding the edge of the Swamp, but you don't want to go close because the bloodhound men could catch you." His voice was hushed now. "And there's snakes in the water, and quicksand will swallow you up. And bears in the woods, too. And at night"—his voice was down to a whisper now—"at night, the rolling calf is out there with his fire-eyes and chains clanking, and the black-heart man, too: he'll cut out a child's heart and eat it if he catches you by yourself!"

Peewee had seen snakes and bears, but as to the other creatures, he was repeating stories the old folks told. He wasn't so sure they were true, but he surely enjoyed the shiver that went through Thaddeus when he spoke.

Within days Thaddeus was tolerating dripping humidity and clouds of mosquitoes to roam the wilderness with his new friends. They taught him to make bird traps. He practiced with his slingshot, climbed trees to capture their fruit and fished in the interior waters of the Swamp. He began to contribute fish, birds and fruit to the family meals, only he had to listen to Charlotte complain that he was allowed to do all sorts of things she wasn't.

◇

Soon Thaddeus' mother's belly began to grow. At night he could hear his parents talking, their voices pressed out like a dog squeezing under a gate. Sometimes he was sure the muffled lumpy sounds were his mother crying. In the daytime he looked for the tracks of her tears and studied his father for a clue to what he had said to make his wife cry. The boy knew he was supposed to love and respect his father. His mother told him this over and over again when he shied away from the man and leaned close against her evenings after supper. Something about Joseph Childs felt hard and unforgiving to him.

A few months later when the baby was born, the muffled nighttime conversations became loud public arguments. Many of their neighbors contributed firmly voiced opinions. Thaddeus suddenly understood the words his father had said to his mother the night they left home: the baby boy was the color of sand, with loosely curled brown hair and green eyes. Joseph wasn't the father of this baby. Sarah looked at the newborn and cried. She refused to nurse him for two days until Thaddeus heard her say her breasts were so painful that she had to.

On the day of the birth, Joseph left the house and stayed gone for hours.

"Go find that man and get him back here," one neighbor ordered her near-grown son. "This is no time for him to run off from his responsibility. He has to take care of his wife! What's wrong with him? He thinks she chose this?"

Thaddeus and Charlotte huddled in a corner of the

kitchen, listening to the confusing words and the comings and goings, frightened by the drama of the birth and then their mother's tears and father's disappearance. But before night, Joseph came home. Thaddeus was grateful when he gathered up his children with unexpected gentleness, fed them and got them to bed, telling them they would have to be extra helpful to their mother now. Joseph stayed, a household rhythm was established, but the arguing erupted now and again. His mother seemed sad and drawn into herself. Joseph didn't hold the new baby for nearly a week. Sarah didn't argue with him, but the neighbors had no trouble voicing their feelings.

"Man, that baby doesn't know who his father is! A baby's a baby, born pure and innocent into this world, and blessed in the eyes of the Lord. Far as he's concerned, you're his daddy. You better quit that moping, you know Sarah had no choice in that matter!"

Joseph wouldn't respond to their talk, but when the family was alone, Thaddeus heard him muttering bitterly, then Sarah shouting, "How could you even think that, Joseph Childs? I could just as much turn him away as you could turn away that whip that marked up your back!"

Then Joseph would apologize over and over again and hug her, but she looked more like a board in his arms than the soft pillow she was when she enfolded Thaddeus.

Thaddeus hated his father for making his mother cry. But he also felt a void growing between him and his mother. The baby's birth brought back memories of the loud, mean white man with tomato cheeks and bloodshot eyes who came to their little one-room dirt floor house three times in the weeks before their flight to the Swamp. The first time he came, the man had picked up Thaddeus and Charlotte by their ears to toss them into the gravel yard, shouting at them to leave the place. Both of them had landed flat out, scraping and bruising themselves on the hard ground. Thaddeus cried. But his mother didn't defend them, didn't pick them up and see to their injuries. Instead, a neighbor woman had grabbed them and pulled them inside her room until the white man left. Later his mother, tears in her eyes, told them that there was nothing she could do, she had to do what the master said. She told them they would understand more when they got bigger, but he only felt hurt and ashamed, he didn't think he'd ever understand.

But now the little boy suddenly knew—and wished he didn't know—what the red-faced man with the green eyes was doing in their house. To their mother. To *his* mother. And the thought of it, the image of it, made Thaddeus feel more than hurt and ashamed, it made him angry. It also made him feel a revulsion toward his mother that completely confused him.

Joseph and Sarah named the baby Nathaniel after the rebel Nat Turner from neighboring Virginia.

<>

The Great Dismal Swamp, North Carolina, 2010

The year is 2010. The ghost-echoed voices of the Swamp lure a new generation. Careful shovels expose discolored soil: the remnants of a cook-fire where long ago children listened to stories that made them clutch tight their mothers' skirts. Lying heavy in the hand of student volunteer Malika Childs is a musket ball. She closes her fingers around its pitted hardness and feels the determination of the once-enslaved, never to surrender their freedom. Her soul senses her own people in this consecrated ground. The voices of these secret people: their heroism, their love and grief, their hardship and labor, their songs and stories—all were buried in the moist, devouring earth of the Great Dismal Swamp when her people were finally able to make their exodus. Her fingers tighten around the object in her hand, her eyes shut. She listens as the silent stories reverberate.

5

Departure

As Thaddeus and his companion Walker neared Chatham on their tired mounts, his mind jumped to when he was sixteen, just a year ago. His muscles had grown tough as the vines that ran up the trees, and he and Peewee were both working with a crew that cut cypress wood and hauled it to the edge of the Swamp several miles away. The wood was highly prized for making shingles. There was a lively market for it along the canals that bordered the Swamp.

The business community on the canals operated under its own rules, which were enforced by those who traded there: white, black and Indian. It was a neutral zone, no slave catchers were allowed in, which protected what the traders called "the hidden people" of the Swamp who supplied them with cypress. And it was true: each time Thaddeus' crew finished selling their wood and buying supplies, they disappeared without a trace. Only the people who lived in the Swamp knew the secret pathways to their communities from the canals.

◇

One day while his crew was waiting for business to be negotiated, Thaddeus noticed a small group of tattered people coming off a boat, led to an open-fronted shack by a young man wearing tall leather boots. He pointed them out to Peewee.

"Underground Railroad," Peewee said. "They must be on their way north."

Thaddeus had heard of the network whose mission was to conduct people from slavery to freedom, but this was his first time seeing it in action. The neutral zone was also a safe stopover for the "railroad."

Curious, Thaddeus decided to go talk to them. "Howdy. Where are you all heading?"

The boots man stepped in front of the others and answered: "Do you live here?"

"Not far," Thaddeus replied, gesturing back toward the Swamp. "We're just delivering cypress."

"You used to be a slave?" the man continued.

"Yes, sir," Thaddeus replied slowly, nodding at the tired people sitting behind him. "Just like your friends here, I imagine."

The man in the boots relaxed, smiling. The people he was escorting—for he was a Conductor for the Underground Railroad—looked at Thaddeus with interest. A woman spoke up. "We're heading north to freedom!" Her voice held anticipation and excitement. "But how come you can be free and living in North Carolina?"

Thaddeus gestured again back toward the thick swamp forest. "Slave catchers can't follow us in there. You'd be surprised, we've got our own little country up in there," he said proudly.

"Matter of fact," added boots man, "there are free black communities in the swamps all the way from here down to Florida. But..." He looked at Thaddeus now, "Up north is more secure. Slavery is against the law in places like New York and Massachusetts and Connecticut. Black folks can own their own farms, get jobs, work just like white folk. We can't vote for the government yet, but we're working on that. The black conventions have been meeting and planning, and the black press is pushing loud and strong for real equality. There's a pretty strong movement to abolish slavery in all the states, too. We've been holding meetings that hundreds of people attend, black *and* white."

The man nodded sharply at Thaddeus, clearly happy to

show off his knowledge and experience. Thaddeus would have laughed at his attitude, but his mind was spinning too fast with what he had just heard. Live and work among white folk as a free man? He shook his head. Nothing in his experience gave him any desire to live close to white people. He couldn't imagine feeling free or relaxed around them.

But all the same: to live in a place that was not surrounded by swamp, not infested by snakes and mosquitoes, not surrounded by hostile people ever alert to an opportunity to capture you and send you back to slavery? To be a part of mass meetings and a movement to free his people from bondage? He imagined himself riding in on a fiery, snorting horse, brandishing a sword, liberating the friends he had left behind on the plantation, children he had grown up with, played with, suffered alongside: his aunties, uncles and cousins, and laying waste to the green-eyed man and his family. A great sense of pleasure accompanied that daydream. Peewee's shout brought him back to reality. Time to go home.

"Well, I have to say goodbye to you all. Safe journey, now."

On the way home, he and Peewee talked about the North.

"Yeah, I know about the Underground Railroad," said Peewee. "Sometimes I think about going to live up north, see some wide open spaces, and all that. But man, I don't know about being around white folks. I can't see how I could feel safe, and I *know* I won't feel respected! Why put up with it? And besides, I hear the slave catchers follow people north and catch them and take them back. No, man, I'm happy staying here so far."

Thaddeus smiled. "And Peaches is here. You know you're not about to walk away from her!"

Peewee grinned with embarrassment. Their conversation ended, but it stuck with Thaddeus like a fly with its feet caught in honey, the thoughts just wouldn't give up flapping in his head.

He noticed he was isolating himself from his family more

and more. He was tired of the times he had to defend his little brother from other young boys who taunted Nattie as a "white boy." And he was confused at the times he found himself pushing Nattie away because when he looked at him, he saw that man going for his mother. He still hadn't forgiven his mother, though he knew that was childish. And in all these years, he hadn't come any closer to his father, who remained hard and distant. The one he had a soft spot for was Charlotte, but nowadays she was usually busy with her girlfriends.

It was just easier to be away from home, so he spent more time on the cypress crew.

On one trip to the canals, Thaddeus and Peewee sat down beside a group of men and women eating lunch under a tree. One of the women, wire-slim and very dark, was talking about Canada, a land beyond the United States: a place where slavery was illegal, where once a person set foot there, no slave catcher could follow. A place where freedom was guaranteed by law. But most important to Thaddeus' spellbound ears, she mentioned growing communities of escaped slaves working together to build a new life. Were there really places like his Dismal Swamp community that were surrounded by freedom, not by slavery and danger?

According to the woman, these communities were building schools where young and old would learn reading, writing and the mechanical arts. They were building sawmills and farms and churches. He questioned the woman repeatedly, wanting to know every detail, until she finally motioned him to one side, away from the ears of others. Peewee nodded as he walked off with her. Watching Thaddeus closely, she told him she was a Conductor on the Underground Railroad, and that if he met her there the following week, she would be happy for him to join the small group she was gathering from a nearby plantation to guide on their way to Canada.

"The first part of the trip will be dangerous," she explained in a low voice. "But once we cross into the Northern states, we will travel more safely. You don't need a pass to use the roads in the North, and we have many safe-houses where we stop to rest and eat. You would be a help to me, because this group will include three young children."

Thaddeus responded so fast he startled himself. "Look for me, I'll be here." Had he really said that? He looked at the woman's eyes and felt breathless, his heart beating in his ears. He suddenly saw a path before him that led away from his confining family, from his brother's green eyes, from his father's hardness, from the roil of confusing feelings toward his mother. He saw a road to escape, to adventure—even, possibly, to revenge.

The next night after clearing up from supper, Thaddeus told his parents. They listened quietly, and he saw pain in his mother's eyes. He felt a flash of sadness. Was he right to leave? Yet he knew that he would leave even if his parents opposed him. His father surprised him.

Joseph said, "Son, you're old enough to make your own choice now. If you want to go, you go on. When you arrive, you just send a message and tell us if the woman spoke the truth about the place. Maybe we will even follow you, who can say?"

Sarah only nodded, her eyes watery and shining. Thaddeus felt his own throat block up, realizing that his mother didn't trust herself to speak. Nattie looked confusedly from one to another, but at eight, Charlotte was old enough to know if Thaddeus left she might never see her brother again. Her eyes dilated with fear, she threw her arms tightly around his midsection, flattened her face into his chest, and began to sob.

That night as he lay in his bed in the dark, Thaddeus wondered whether he was about to be a traitor or a hero. An ache of impending separation invaded his heart, fear drew his neck and shoulders tight. But anticipation outran all the other emotions.

A few days later he left the Swamp with his parents' blessings. And felt guilty for their blessings.

6

Underground Railroad ~ 1849

The trip to Canada was exhausting, mostly done at night. Often, he bore the children on his back, like his father had carried Charlotte all those years ago. But the Underground Railroad was well maintained, its "machinery" well oiled, its "stations" well prepared. Pauline, the slim woman who started them on the trip, handed the group off two days later. Through the journey they went from one Conductor to another every few days.

Thaddeus was surprised to find that while most of the people who took care of them were black, some of these Conductors were white. A few of the stations, mostly barns, attics and cellars, were even owned by white people. His first reaction was fear and distrust, but he soon understood that the black Conductors trusted these people completely. This was a breed of white people unlike those he had known before. They fed and hid him and his fellow passengers with care and sympathy, and he knew that they risked themselves and their families to do it. It was a wonderment to him, puzzling, but his weariness made him leave it until later to figure out. Aside from a few tense moments, the trip went without incident.

On the last night, the little group arrived in Detroit, where only a wide river separated Thaddeus from the free soil of Canada West and his new home in Windsor. They were taken into the basement of a church to rest for the daylight hours, away from outside eyes. The people he had been traveling with were to stay in Detroit for now, to be taken to their new homes that night. Only Thaddeus was crossing the river.

Too excited to sleep, Thaddeus waited for night to fall. When finally it did, he was led to a boathouse along the riverside. There a group of men had him recite the code words Pauline had taught his group before she left them. These were the words that let each Conductor know they were passengers.

The man who seemed to be in charge motioned Thaddeus toward a small rowboat. His breath catching in his throat, Thaddeus whispered, "I want to become a part of your organization. What must I do?"

The man looked him up and down silently and raised one eyebrow. He paused, then nodded. "Someone will contact you after you have settled in."

Thaddeus' heart bounced into his throat, so he only nodded in reply and whispered a strangled, "Thank you, sir."

◇

When Thaddeus woke up that first morning in Windsor, the first thing on his mind was to make good his promise to send a message to his family. He had met his landlady, Mrs. Settles, the night before. Her skin was brown with a reddish cast to it. She had a round face and a rounder body than anyone was able to achieve in the Swamp. Her hair was pulled back and knotted into a frizzy, wavy bun. Thaddeus thought she probably was part Indian. He had seen that combination of features in the Swamp, too.

Isaac, the boatman, had brought him to her door. Mrs. Settles called them to open it, then turned from her stove to greet them, wiping her hands on her apron. Moving quickly to get back to her cooking, she showed Thaddeus to his room with a warm smile, promising a plate of food shortly. She was older than his parents, and her presence radiated a calmness that relaxed Thaddeus. He had barely managed to eat before he fell asleep, weeks of tension draining from his grateful body.

Now that he was awake and dressed, he went looking for

Mrs. Settles to write a letter to his family. He found her in the yard.

"Morning, ma'am," he murmured.

"Well, good morning, young man. How do feel this morning? Did you sleep well?"

"Yes, ma'am," Thaddeus replied. "Thank you. I wonder if you could help me write a letter to my family: let them know I arrived safely."

"I'll be happy to. But first, breakfast." She turned to the woodpile beside her. "Split a few of these logs for me, I don't have enough wood to finish the cooking."

Later, wood split, breakfast eaten, Mrs. Settles sat beside him at the long wooden table in the kitchen, brought out writing implements, and helped him find the words for what he wanted to say.

Windsor, Canada West, 16 August, 1849.

Dearest Mother and Father, Sister and Brother,

I hope this letter finds you, as I am, blesst with Happiness and Health. After a long and Eventful trip, during which I was helped along the way by many Beneficent people and had not a few exciting Moments, I have safely arrived. I am happy to inform you that I am now living in a comfortable room to myself in a Large, white-painted, rooming house own by a kind Lady of our own Race who is writing this letter for me. My landlady also Cooks meals for me and the other people who live in this House. I have a bed with a soft, warm Quilt, and a shelf for my things. My Rent will be due at the end of the month, and today I will go seek a job. When I am able, I will seek out the Black Settlements of which I have been told. I will write again soon. Please accept my most heartfelt affection. I will keep all of you in my heart as I live in this new land, under protection of the British Lion.

Your truly, son and brother,
Thaddeus Childs
Windsor, Canada West.

Mrs. Settles assured Thaddeus that she would send the letter with Isaac that night. The next Conductor to go south from Detroit would carry it in reverse direction along the track he had just followed. The Swamp already seemed a distant place, where the air's soft, damp touch and the smells of familiar food cooking were only memories. He had little idea how long it would take for his message to reach there and wondered whether his family would really decide to follow him. Meanwhile, he was on his own.

Stepping down from Mrs. Settles' porch, Thaddeus was confronted by a new world for the second time in his life, this time alone. His landlady had told him which way to walk to find a man who ran a logging operation, so he moved along the wide, unfamiliar street hoping he looked more confident than he felt. The air was warm, sunshine filtered between the leaves of large trees. He walked past people going about their business, nodding and saying a polite good morning to each of them. He soon saw that no one took any particular interest in him. They assumed he belonged there and knew what he was about. It was a new and exciting feeling. For the first time, he was a man in his own right, making his own way in the world. His chest swelled. He held his head high.

The days turned to weeks. Thaddeus was doing the familiar work of cutting and splitting wood. Although the weather was still hot, he was told that winters in Canada West were long and cold, so each household and business needed a vast stack of firewood. The only strange thing about the work was the money that came from it. He learned the currency, how to count to make sure he'd been paid the right amount. He used it to pay his rent, buy food for Mrs. Settles' kitchen, and have shoes, boots and clothing made to prepare for winter.

A month after he arrived, Isaac found him and led him to meet the man he had spoken with in Detroit. In time, the Order initiated him, assigning him to be a second boatman for those nights when Isaac was not available. Pulling the oars through slushy water in wintertime, he watched exhaustion and hope contend in the faces of his secret, night passengers. By the time spring came, he also began to carry messages, the Order providing a horse and teaching him how to find his way through the forest along the rutted country roads between villages. In this way he added boatmanship and horseback riding to his list of skills. Sometimes he remembered his original conversation with the slim, dark woman under a tree and could barely believe he was now actually a part of a movement he had then only dimly imagined. He vowed to prove himself worthy of the trust the Order had put in him.

But alongside that passion, Thaddeus also began to notice a growing yearning for his mother and the rest of his family. In the icy depths of winter, his head buried in quilts, dreams carried him to the familiarity of the Swamp and his people, which time and distance had redrawn using only the colors of warmth and love. He longed for a message from them. Despite his many letters, he never received a word in return. Had his letters not arrived? Did they not know where he was? Or were they on their way to join him? In daydreams he would imagine rounding a corner and seeing them there on a street in Windsor, holding one another's hands, looking lost and awestruck.

And so, the galloping hooves in the dust the following September when he first met Harriet: his sudden fear, with passage of the Fugitive Slave Law, that his mother, his father, Charlotte and Nathaniel were at that moment reliving the panic of slave catchers and bloodhounds as they made their perilous way to him through the places he had passed un-pursued a year ago. He began to fill with dread.

Had he selfishly led them into destruction?

<>

Freedom Soldiers

Greensboro, North Carolina, 1960

Charlotte searches her green eyes in the mirror over the sink in the North Carolina dormitory. She recalls the colorless eyes in the faded photo of her mother's near-white grandfather, Grand Daddy Nat, who died an old, old man thirty years ago. And she wishes, once again, that her eyes were not the pale legacy of whichever man had raped her great-great grandmother.

She hurriedly brushes back her hair and clips a barrette into it, smiling ironically. I'm dressing myself up to go to jail, she thinks. Another glance at the mirror: someone else's eyes look back at her. Her breath catches. 'Step forward today,' her great-grandfather's eyes are telling her, 'as I did in my time.' Her eyes widen, then her reflection is hers again. She shivers. Her back straightens.

On the green in front of the dorm, she joins a small group of students. They walk the few blocks to the Walgreen's store, open the door, and take their seats at the lunch counter, their heads high, their hearts thumping like drums, the strength of their generations within them.

7

Abiah's Story ~ 1850

After Walker and Thaddeus had mounted their horses and rode away, Abiah sat with her elbows on the table, her chin resting on her hands. Mr. Walker had been right, the Fugitive Slave Act would cause an emergency for thousands of people. People who had escaped from slavery and now lived in the North of the United States would no longer be safe from slave catchers. She was sure that many, many people would choose to flee to Canada, where slavery had long been made illegal and slave catchers were not allowed to operate. She thought of the crisis that would hit so many families, and it made her remember her own escape from the slave catchers.

When Abiah had stumbled from the riverside to the farmhouse ten years ago, she was half-frozen. A white man opened the door. He stood and stared at her in silence until his wife appeared at his side. The woman nudged her husband aside and grabbed Abiah's arm, pulling her and Harriet into a blessedly warm room. The woman sat them beside a stove that had a well-fed fire burning in it. The warmth soon put Harriet to sleep, as Abiah's lips finally thawed enough for her to murmur her gratitude.

The farmers were a young couple, as yet without children. They understood immediately what had brought Abiah to their doorstep. They warmed and fed the refugees that night. The next morning, Abiah watched the man hug his wife before she wrapped herself in coat and scarf and walked up the road through the snow. She returned several hours later.

"Someone will come for you tomorrow." She smiled warmly to Abiah, then glanced at her husband, who nodded. "The man who is coming knows the route to get you to a safe place. You will be all safe with him. Sleep well. I will fix you some food to take on your journey."

These words brought a confusing mix of fear and hope to Abiah. Oh, how she wished Jacob were with them! Jacob, whom she had left—was it possible?—only days ago, in the forest at the edge of the Quarles plantation. From the time they parted she'd been possessed by the fear that she had lost Jacob for good. She knew the Underground Railroad had a system for moving letters to people on the plantations from their loved ones who had escaped, but when she lost the Conductor, she and Harriet had fallen off the rails. Now her heart jumped in hope that the man coming tomorrow was a part of that Railroad. But another part of her wondered if she could really trust these people. The woman had used the word "safe" too many times.

She couldn't sleep. Lying in the cold dark room, she wondered if she should take Harriet and steal out of the house. But she had no idea where to go in that empty, icy landscape. The couple had been so good to them that, really, it was hard to believe they would be sending them back to slavery. Staring at the night-blackened roof of the cottage, listening to the rustlings and pokings of mice trying to find crumbs to sustain themselves, she waited for morning and hoped.

Abiah looked at Harriet beside her, sleeping peacefully in the security of her mother's presence. She imagined how innocent she herself must have been as a small child, playing with her little friends in the dirt track alongside the slave quarters, gazing across the far fields to the endless woods beyond them. How quickly her innocence and peace had gone! She was put to work pulling weeds in the kitchen garden for the Big House before she was five years old. By the time she was eight she was working alongside the grown-ups in the near fields for all the hours of the day, and the energy and curiosity of childhood became displaced by exhaustion and resentment.

Early one morning before work started, she heard

Mistress Quarles call for Abiah's best friend Louise. Abiah walked out, curious to see what Mistress wanted, because Louise worked in the fields and had little contact with the Mistress. Astonished, Abiah watched the white lady from the Big House, dressed in layers of puffy white fabric like a pile of cottonwood fluff take a firm hold of Louise's small hand and lead her toward a carriage that stood near the end of the verandah. Suddenly, Louise's mother bolted past Abiah, an unearthly wail coming from deep in her chest. Abiah came up in goosebumps. Abiah's mother grabbed her into her skirt, holding her so tight Abiah had to struggle to turn her head to see.

Unfamiliar white hands were reaching down from the carriage to lift Louise up into it. Louise was squirming, looking to her mother, who was now shrilly, hysterically screaming her name over and over again. One of the overseers grabbed the sobbing mother around her waist and held her back. Louise started screaming for her mother, reaching her hands out, her cries echoing her mother's, louder and louder, more and more panic-stricken on both sides.

An icy fear shot through Abiah. She looked up desperately at her mother, but any question died in her throat when she saw her mother's distorted face. The carriage door slammed shut behind Louise. The driver whipped up the pair of grays, jolting the carriage forward into the lane, the little girl's sobbing growing fainter as the carriage drew farther and farther away. Louise's mother's screams continued until the overseer threw his arm across her mouth, smothering the sound. Then she fainted in his arms and he dropped her to the ground, where she lay still.

"Mama?" Abiah squeaked in panic.

Her mother hurriedly dragged her back to their one-room house. Abiah could see her shaking. She grabbed her mother's skirt and clung to it like she was two years old again. After a few minutes Abiah's mother pried her fingers off the fabric, wiped the tears off Abiah's face with a corner of her skirt, and held her daughter's hand tightly as they walked down the lane to the field, unsteadily trying to act like it was just another day.

Abiah remembered that moment now as she snuggled her sleeping daughter closer in the crook of her arm. With hot tears wetting her face, Abiah thanked God that Harriet was here safely by her side. Abiah prayed for her mother and everyone else she had left behind. Especially Jacob.

Memories continued to tumble around her sleepless mind.

On the day Louise was taken away, something changed in Abiah. A deep anger at her captivity and an aching to be free aged her beyond her eleven years. As she grew older, many experiences fertilized those feelings. She saw others sold, she saw people whipped or locked into hot boxes for punishment. She endured many blows herself as her bitterness made her less cooperative. She saw friends forced to submit to the desires of the master or his violent son, dreading the day one of them would turn his attentions to her.

Then she met Jacob Roberson. When she was seventeen a crew of men, including Jacob, was transferred from the far fields to the quarters where Abiah lived near the Big House. As naturally as a bird settling in his nightly roost, Jacob settled into Abiah's heart. He was tall and graceful, his movements smooth as a cat's. He had skin like rich, strongly brewed coffee before you added the cream, with wide, powerful shoulders and the most hypnotizing face she'd ever seen. His eyebrows accentuated the almond shaped eyes, turned down at the outside corners in a way that made him look perpetually thoughtful and sensitive. His nose was broad, sitting atop a thin, black mustache that framed his sensuous lips, which, when they opened into a smile, bewitched her, made her weak.

And smile at her he did, for Abiah caught Jacob's eye and captured his heart just as surely and naturally as he did hers.

Jacob became her hope and her happiness.

Soon the darkness after the workday couldn't come quickly enough for Abiah. No longer was it just the time to fight off mosquitoes, to try to get comfortable on her pallet of straw on the floor near her mother and sisters. Now it meant secret (or so she imagined) meetings among the old hickory and black walnut trees behind the quarters, the touch that inflamed her whole being, the whispered plans and dreams.

From talking to Jacob, Abiah began to think of freedom as a real possibility rather than just an acid hunger. Four men had run away from the far field a few days before Jacob's transfer. That was the reason for the move: the master had not found the runaways. Now he was afraid that the rest of the crew knew the escape route, so he switched them with a crew from the near fields.

Jacob told Abiah about something called the Underground Railroad. It was the reason the runaways hadn't been recaptured. He described a network of Conductors who helped runaways to move from one station to the next—hiding places on the route to the North, where they would be free. All of this was new to Abiah, and it aroused her imagination as vividly as Jacob had enflamed her heart. The thrilling eagerness of her love for him mingled with frightful anticipation at the thought of fleeing to freedom. It became one unrelenting, breathless agitation.

When Abiah became pregnant several months later, it reinforced their secret pact to escape. They would leave this life and create one for themselves in a place where they could be a family. When baby Harriet was born, Abiah felt the fierceness in Jacob's repeated promises that they would soon be free. But it was difficult to contact the Underground network from so close to the center of this vast plantation, and they knew that there were always people who would betray them in exchange for favors from the master.

When contact came, it was in an unexpected form. The

master was hosting a white man by the name of Mr. Ross, who was traveling the country studying birds. Master Quarles assigned Jacob to be his guide as he explored the woods and fields of the plantation looking for rare species. A few nights later, Jacob visited Abiah and drew her and Harriet away from the slave quarters to talk in the privacy of the woods.

"Mr. Ross is not who he appears," Jacob whispered, barely holding back his excitement. "He is an agent of the Underground Railroad!"

Abiah caught her lower lip in her teeth and looked into Jacob's glittering eyes. Could this be true?

"He is going from plantation to plantation, finding people who are ready to escape. He has given me a satchel of provisions, and tomorrow night I will take you and Harriet to the assigned place to meet the Conductor."

"Oh, Jacob! Can it be true?" Abiah bounced on her tiptoes, holding Jacob's forearms tightly in her hands. "Can it be real?"

"But, Abiah my love," Jacob continued, "I will not go with you. I will have to follow you on the next journey."

"What? No!" All the happiness drained out of Abiah in an instant. She gripped his arms until Jacob grimaced in pain. "I can't leave without you, Jacob!" A sob came into her voice.

"Sweetheart, I will be a great loss to the Master now that I am a wheelwright. He will certainly search for me very hard, and if I go with you and Harriet, we will not be able to move swiftly enough to evade him. No, you must go without me. He will not notice you missing as soon as he would me. You will have a better chance without me, and I will join you very soon, do not fear!"

Abiah heard the confidence in Jacob's voice and knew the reason in his argument. Her next cry of "no!" was softer and more resigned.

Jacob continued to reassure her. "Mr. Ross is certain that

we will be able to communicate with one another until we are reunited. Please, baby, please take this opportunity. Nothing will stop me following you!"

As Abiah looked down at Harriet, her mind flashed to the memory of Louise struggling as she was put into the carriage. She decided she would have to be stronger than her fear. She would have to leave everything and everyone she knew and trust herself and her baby to a complete stranger in an unknown world. She caught her breath, then nodded.

When the time came, she arose hours before dawn, gently lifted the sleeping Harriet and went to Jacob, who led her to that forest beyond the far fields that she had gazed on as a little girl. It was a cold night. They could see the cloud-puffs of their breath. Abiah had put as many clothes on herself and Harriet as she could, even taking some of her sister's things. Her mother and sisters were asleep when she crept out of their room. She hadn't told them her plans, hadn't said a last goodbye to the people she had lived her whole life with: the fewer people who knew, the better.

When the Conductor came for them, three men from another plantation were with him. "Try not to worry," the young man whispered to Abiah. "You will be able to write to one another until your man can come join you. We have a good system for delivering letters."

Abiah swallowed with a dry throat, nodding silently. She and Jacob clung tightly for a long moment. The Conductor shuffled one foot in the leaf litter, and Jacob pulled back. His eyes brimmed with wetness as they fixed on his sleeping daughter, limp on her mother's shoulder. With her heart squeezed by fear at their separation, Abiah let go of Jacob's hand, turned and slipped into the woods behind the other four, beginning the trip that had taken her to this farmhouse on the north bank of the Ohio River.

Morning finally came, and Abiah's memories disappeared into the sunlight. A white man with a long, brown beard drove up to the farmhouse in a wagon, wearing the clothes that Abiah would learn to identify with members of the Quaker faith. He listened in silence to the story of Abiah and Harriet's escape. He assured her that he was also a part of the Underground Railroad network, that he would continue her on her way to freedom. There was something in his gentle manner and soft voice that made Abiah trust him, especially when she learned that he knew the young Conductor that she had parted from on the bank of the river.

Abiah and Harriet continued their flight. They were delivered from one house or barn to another for several exhausting, confusing weeks, until they arrived in a town where they could stay under the protection of the local Vigilance Committee, a network of black residents who kept watch for slave catchers. They were to live with an older black couple, and Abiah was instructed to tell people she was their niece moved from Pennsylvania to help them in their old age. From here, Abiah was able to send word to Jacob. She was delighted to receive letters from him in return as promised. Strength and hope came back to her as she began a new life.

This arrangement lasted for a few years. Abiah helped the elderly couple. She also began to take in washing, earning money for herself. Then, in a stroke of bad luck, someone arrived from the very Pennsylvania town where Abiah was supposed to have lived, so she and Harriet were forced to travel once more. This time the journey landed them across the Canadian border into the Chatham home of the Lovejoys.

Diana Lovejoy was white: a plump woman with a round face flushed from constant activity. She had curly brown hair streaked with gray and lively gray eyes. She and her husband were part of the Vigilance Committee, which here in Canada West provided warm beds and material support for new Underground Railroad arrivals until they got on their feet. The items of clothing and food were gathered by an extensive organization connected with several churches that raised money throughout Canada West and into the northern U.S. Unlike their counterparts in the U.S., Canadian Vigilance Committees rarely had to concern themselves with hiding or defending escapees from slavery.

Abiah and Harriet stayed with Mrs. Lovejoy when they first arrived in Chatham, and Abiah came to have great respect for this hard-working woman, who seemed to constantly go from one meeting to another, and had conversations around her kitchen table late into the night to convince neighbors and visitors of the equality of all God's children, of the obligation each person has to look out for others. Sometimes as Abiah watched her, she remembered Mistress Quarles handing Louise into the carriage and wondered at the difference. Wondered what caused it and how deep it went.

Although Abiah only stayed with Mrs. Lovejoy for a week before moving into her own rooms, the two women stayed in contact. Abiah laundered and pressed the clothes Mrs. Lovejoy collected for new arrivals. Mrs. Lovejoy helped Abiah write letters to Jacob, getting them sent along to Virginia.

Gradually Abiah built up a clientele for her laundry business until she could soon take care of herself and Harriet without any aid. She also planted a small kitchen garden and preserved her vegetables for the long winter months when little fresh food was available. Sometimes she looked at those rows of jars on the shelf and looked at her hands in wonder. *These hands have done all this,* she thought. Looking around the cozy room, taking in Harriet sleeping peacefully in her warm bed, she said: "I have done all this for us!" From somewhere in the middle of her chest a joyous ache grew and settled. Her eyes rested on her daughter, whose life contained no pain or heartbreak. But Harriet would never know the grandmother or the aunts Abiah had torn them from, the family whose absence Abiah could feel from her center to her fingertips. And what about her father? Will she only have me?

43

Alexander Ross, who helped Jacob set up the escape for Abiah and Harriet in the novel, was a real agent of the Underground Railroad. This plaque stands in Chatham, Ontario.

8

The Letter

It had been years now that Abiah and Jacob had been apart. Harriet had no memory of her father. Since they had arrived in Chatham, Abiah had heard from him only twice, but now nearly a year had gone since his last letter. He had written that he had fallen out of favor with Master Quarles, who from the first suspected him of helping Abiah escape. When she tried to picture Jacob's life on the plantation, it seemed far away, like looking at the landscape through a long tube: small, distant, fuzzy. But his letters had always made Jacob seem close and connected. As the months since his last letter slipped past, her mind fell on him with an unsettling sense of dread.

When communication finally came, the ground she stood on seemed to fall from under her. Abiah had taken a package of laundry to Mrs. Lovejoy, and from the moment her friend opened the door, she could tell something had happened. There were lines of distress on Mrs. Lovejoy's normally jovial face.

"Something wrong, Diana?" she asked, anxiety rising in her chest.

"Please sit down, Abiah," responded Mrs. Lovejoy. "Let me get you a cup of tea."

Abiah sat at Diana Lovejoy's kitchen table, her fear growing. She fingered the edge of the orange gingham tablecloth and watched her sponsor's back as the older woman attended to the teakettle. Finally, Mrs. Lovejoy turned a pained face toward Abiah as she poured the steaming tea into a china cup, setting it in front of the younger woman. She spoke quickly in a shaky voice, avoiding Abiah's eyes.

"I've gotten a letter from the Quarles plantation. I am *so* sorry to have to tell you this. They have sold Jacob."

Abiah gasped, her hand sweeping to her mouth. "No." Her voice was high and thin. "No, it must be a mistake." Her desperate mind invented hope. "Maybe he ran away, and they're saying that to cover it!"

"I'm so sorry, Abiah," Mrs. Lovejoy said again. "I'm afraid it's not a mistake. Here's the letter." She picked a paper up from the sideboard and passed it to Abiah. Having learned to read a little, Abiah searched the letter but her eyes were blinded by tears.

Mrs. Lovejoy put a gentle hand on the young woman's shoulder, saying: "The Conductor talked with several trusted people from the Quarles plantation, including your Jacob's brother. They told him. Mr. Quarles always suspected Jacob of helping you and Harriet get away, so he kept him under close watch. It took years, but when Jacob finally made his escape, it seems someone betrayed him. He was caught not a day after he had left."

In her mind, Abiah saw her little group scattering as the riders galloped down the hill. She shuddered. Diana continued. "The Conductor went back for a second try six weeks later. His contacts on the plantation told him Jacob had been sold. They've been trying to find out where he's been sold to, but so far they don't know. It wasn't anyone they recognized."

Abiah felt as though she were floating, as though the floor was no longer there. She thought her head would burst from the pressure. Her heart pounded in her ears until she didn't think she could hear, but still the sounds of the kitchen were piercing—the cup clinking on the saucer as she tapped it, Mrs. Lovejoy's chair scraping against the floor as her friend sat down. Abiah clapped her hands over her ears, dropping her head to the table. She didn't know if she was repeating "no" aloud or only in her mind. After a while, she felt Diana reach across the small table and take her hands off her ears, covering each with her own.

"I'm so sorry, Abiah," she repeated. "They will continue to check at Quarles and will send back any information they get."

But months went by. The only other word that ever got to Abiah was that Jacob had been sold to a broker and had gone on the auction block. No one knew where he had ended up.

One day followed another, as they do, regardless of heartbreak and loss. Abiah's days were taken up with survival and with Harriet, who was growing and thriving, untroubled by the loss of a father she didn't know. The little girl was now helping her mother with small tasks. She also had a life of her own that filled Abiah with amazement and, in spite of everything, happiness: a child growing up carefree and curious, without the cloud of slavery heavy in her sky. Harriet made friends, played hopscotch and jacks on the street—she was even asking about school.

As time passed, Abiah's grief went into hiding. For years she had clung to her love and loyalty for Jacob, but now he was lost to her. Seven months after the arrival of that fateful letter, over a year since her last communication from Jacob, she bumped into Thomas on her way to deliver laundry. She had thought love was in her past, a lost feeling, something she would have to live without. But when Thomas' eyes met hers, her heart jumped, a spark ignited. *No*, she thought, *I don't want to be alone forever!*

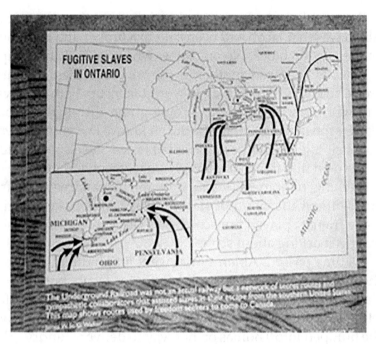

Map showing the main routes fugitives from slavery took to
get to freedom in Canada along the Underground Railroad.
Drawing by Timothy C. Walker, on display at Uncle Tom's
Cabin Historic Site, Dresden, Ontario: by permission.

9

Sweet Pea ~ 1841-1850

Harriet remembered very little of her flight to freedom in her mother's arms. Although she had no memory of the place they ran from, that night on the frozen river left dream-like memories. Or maybe the memories came from hearing her mother describe it: moonlight on white patches of ice with black water snaking between them, her mother's breath coming fast and hard as she ran and jumped, her mother's arm squeezing her too tight around her chest, threatening to cut off her air, wetness, a cold so deep even the memory made her shiver.

She had slippery memories of a house where they had lived with affectionate people she called Granny and Grampy. Then there was a long, uncomfortable trip in a boat across a lake so big that she lost sight of land. She was cold and sick the whole crossing, repeatedly leaning over the side of the boat to vomit. She remembered that! And then a few wooden houses appearing from the water, completely surrounded by a dark forest that went on as far as she could see along the shore. The houses grew until the boat bumped to a stop next to a wooden pier.

A narrow road laced its way from the lake into the marshy woods in three rutted lines, two cut by cart wheels and one by horses' hooves. They followed the three-striped road, bouncing on planks in the back of an open wagon for twenty teeth-jarring miles, weaving around massive trees and splashing through streams until they reached the big town: Chatham.

Harriet liked the snug new rooms she and her mother had all to themselves. She was allowed on the street to play, and quickly made new friends. She was also now big enough to help her mother. She liked sloshing clothes in the soapy bucket, watching rainbow bubbles slide across her hands and burst.

After some time, Thomas Ingram began appearing at their home. At first, he would come on a Sunday afternoon, knocking at the door holding his hat in his hands, his peppercorn hair neatly trimmed and combed, his face clean-shaven but for a pencil-line moustache and a chip of beard under his bottom lip. He smelled like soap. His eyes were round and kind, with corners creased from squinting in the sun and set into a round and friendly face.

Thomas was a big man. Much bigger than Harriet's small and slim mother. She could see powerful shoulders and arms beneath his loose-fitting shirt. When Abiah ushered him through the door, Thomas would unfailingly reach into his pocket for a sweet wrapped in a twist of paper. With a quick look at Abiah for her approving nod, he would hand the sweet to Harriet, who would briefly come out from behind her mother's skirts before ducking into the corner of the room with her prize, but not before she had (sometimes with a sharp reminder from Abiah) spoken a proper "thank you."

Harriet didn't know then that Thomas had recently arrived on the Underground Railroad. She just knew he was a woodcutter. After a while he began showing up on days other than Sunday, sometimes coming directly from work. On those days, his clothing was stained and in need of mending, with clinging chips of sawdust that had resisted his attempts to brush them off.

Small, coiled shavings were even in his hair. Harriet would watch her mother stand behind him, gently pulling them from his wiry curls while he gratefully drank soup at the table. Sometimes after he had eaten, he would pull a fife from his workbag to play tunes for them. Abiah would grab Harriet and dance around the room, laughing.

At first Thomas felt like a foreign presence, but soon Harriet found herself looking forward to his visits. Sometimes instead of a sweet, he would pull out of his pocket a toy he had carved for her from small bits of wood left over at the sawmill. One time it was a toy gig that was so perfectly formed that it spun nearly forever if she started it on a level surface. Another time it was an amazing thing shaped like a maple seed that turned in circles and floated down when she threw it up in the air. And then he began bringing little wooden people that she collected, playing with them endlessly. What little girl can resist a good-looking man who is kind to her and makes her toys?

After a time he moved into their home. Harriet noticed the lines around her mother's eyes soften. The sharp impatience that was sometimes in her voice when she got vexed with Harriet relaxed. She smiled more. Harriet was happy to have Thomas living with them, but his presence in the house made her wonder about her father. She wanted to ask her mother about him, but when she did her mother gave her short, quick answers, then changed the subject. Harriet knew she had his name, Roberson. Her mother told her that she looked like him, that he had loved her very much, and that he had not been able to come with them. He was still a slave in Virginia or somewhere. Her mother told Harriet she would never see him, but she didn't believe that. She wondered what he looked like and how his voice sounded. Sometimes she weaved fantasies about him coming to find her.

Meanwhile she basked in the warmth of a father's attention from Thomas. Thomas called her "Sweet Pea." Sometimes she noticed him looking way off into the distance when he called her that.

One day Thomas was playing with Harriet and the little wooden people. Harriet moved one of the little people closer to the rest.

"This is the daddy," she said.

Thomas smiled. "Right, Sweet Pea." He put his hand on her head and stopped talking. Harriet looked up at him and saw that he was looking out the window. His eyes looked shiny.

"Who is Sweet Pea?" she asked, looking steadily at his eyes. He didn't say anything. "Who is Sweet Pea, Daddy Thomas?" she repeated, pulling on his sleeve.

Thomas blinked and looked at her quickly. He took her face gently between his two hands. "You are, baby! You are my little Sweet Pea." With that he returned to playing with the little people. "Do you think they want to eat now?" he asked her.

10

Sanctuary

With two people working, Abiah and Thomas were able to keep a comfortable home, and soon Zach was born. Life fell into a rhythm. Harriet spent many hours taking care of baby Zach, often at the Jones' house. She would play with Zach and the Jones children while Mrs. Jones cooked. When the little ones napped, Mrs. Jones would sit with Harriet and teach her to read and do her numbers. Harriet was excited about the lessons and learned quickly. She only wished that she could go to a real school.

One afternoon when Harriet was at home, her mother returned from delivering laundry excited. She grabbed Thomas' hands and pulled him to sit at the table.

"Did you hear about Reverend King and the new settlement?" Her eyes danced with intensity.

"Seems like I heard some of the men talking," Thomas said, looking at her with a question in his face.

"They're starting a settlement for black people down by Buxton. They call it the Elgin Settlement. A minister from Scotland named Reverend King and a set of his late wife's freed slaves are coming up from Louisiana to settle there. Reverend King has formed an association that is selling fifty-acre plots only to black folks. Offering mortgages and everything. They're going to start farming down there and run their own place. Oh, Thomas, how I would love to get out of this town and have something for ourselves! Do you think we can make the down-payment?"

Thomas's eyebrows rose near his hairline. "Whoa, girl, slow down! You want to move? You want us to be farmers?"

"Well, we'd have to clear the land first, and build a house, and then we could plant and . . ." Abiah was nearly breathless.

Thomas put his hand on top of hers. "Okay, okay, slow down. Let's find out exactly what it's all about. How much land, how much money, what the situation is."

The conversation drifted into words Harriet didn't understand about earnings and savings and mortgages and down payments and acreage and backers.

Meanwhile, Thomas had forgotten about his usual time to play with Harriet. She lay on her bed staring at the ceiling, hearing her parents go on in the background. It was boring. Anyway, she was already feeling unhappy and out of sorts.

Lately Harriet didn't see much of the friends she had played with when she was littler. They were going to school while she was going to the Jones house. After school hours sometimes Harriet went outside, but then only Faith, who lived in the next street, was around. Faith would bring her schoolbook and slate to show Harriet everything she was learning. Harriet constantly pestered her mother to be allowed to go to school. She knew she was learning as much from Mrs. Jones as Faith was learning in school, but she yearned for her own slate and books. She wanted to carry a lunch pail and take her place in the schoolhouse beside the other children. Her mother said she was working on it, but nothing seemed to come from her repeated trips to the school beyond furrowed brows and whispered evening conversations with Thomas. Sometimes Thomas' whispering sounded angry and her mother had to calm him down after she told him whatever secrets it was she came home with. When Harriet pressed her for explanations, she was told to mind her manners and stop interfering in grown people's business.

Harriet had a suspicion that the color of her skin was a problem. Some of the children she used to play with didn't come around anymore. Abiah, who knew their parents, had told Harriet that some white people had a problem and didn't want to be around black people. Then one day, as Harriet went out to meet Faith, who was coming home from school, her friend stayed on the other side of the street with two girls that Harriet had never seen before. Faith waved to Harriet but did not come across, instead turning up her own street, laughing and chatting with her new friends.

When Harriet saw her the next day, she was glad that Faith was alone. But instead of her usual smile, Faith said stiffly, "Why are you always dirty?"

"*Dirty?*" Harriet was shaken. She knew that her mother never allowed her to go out of the house without washing and making sure her clothes were what she called "presentable." She looked at her fingernails and unconsciously touched her face.

"I'm not dirty!" she blurted, angry and confused.

"Your skin looks like mud," Faith replied, her nose wrinkling, her eyes looking at a pebble she pushed around with her shoe.

Harriet was stunned. She felt her face grow hot. Not knowing what to say, she just stood and stared at her friend.

"My friends don't like you. They won't play with me if I'm friends with you. I can't play with you any more, Harriet. I'm sorry." Faith's face had turned bright red. She rushed through these words, and once they were out she twirled on her toes and ran away across the street.

Harriet didn't tell her mother when she came inside: she felt too humiliated. She was also afraid that her mother would chastise her for being dirty—that happened often enough as it was. Was she really dirty, or was it that Faith's new friends didn't like dark-skinned people? She had a miserable feeling in her belly, with no one to play with now if she went outside. She didn't want her mother and Thomas to know how alone and unlikeable she had become.

Harriet took to finding excuses for not leaving the house at the time she would ordinarily go out to play with Faith. When her mother wasn't satisfied with her explanations, she would just shake her head and retreat to her bed and the little wooden people, avoiding her mother's eyes and the squeezed-up eyebrows that met one another at the exclamation mark above her nose. She was lying there now, idly turning the little dolls over in hands, staring at the ceiling, lost in sad feelings.

Something in her parents' conversation brought Harriet back to the present and made her listen again.

"Before we think about all the rest of it, I'll make a trip out there to see what the place looks like. It's no use planning to change up our whole life if the place isn't suitable."

Harriet sat up.

"Can I go too?" Her voice startled the two adults, who had almost forgotten she was there in the corner bed.

Abiah smiled. "No, sweetie, that trip is too long and hard for you. It's ten miles!"

But her voice didn't sound decisive. In truth, she was surprised—and relieved—to see something motivate her daughter, whose low spirits were troubling her. Thomas didn't say anything, but later that night when she was falling asleep, Harriet thought she heard the two of them whispering about it.

A few days later, the dawn brought a warm, sun-shiny, mid-summer's day. Harriet sat up in bed and rubbed her eyes. Then her heart leapt: her mother had set out clothes and food for both Thomas and her! She was skipping with excitement. With her hand in her stepfather's the two of them set off on their great adventure, leaving little Zach with Abiah.

Harriet couldn't remember ever walking so far. The road was mainly flat. At first she kicked stones, watched the woods and fields with interest, her keen eye out for birds and small animals. Now and then they passed a farm with cows and horses. Harriet imitated a horse's whinny and laughed with delight when two horses looked up and then ran toward the roadside to investigate, sniffing the air in confusion when they didn't see another horse. But after a few hours, her energy deserted her, her footsteps slowed. Thomas had to repeatedly urge her to catch up.

The last part of the journey was through woods. Every time they saw a break in the trees, Harriet would ask Thomas, "Are we there now? Is that it?" When the woods opened up onto a meadow containing an old barn, Harriet finally heard the longed-for words, "Well, Sweet Pea, looks like we're here!"

A man and woman were out in front of the barn. Both of them had dark skin and more lines in their faces and white in their hair than her mother or Thomas had. The woman was cutting potatoes and carrots on a rough plank table. The man was setting a cooking fire, arranging two logs on some burning sticks. As Thomas called out to them, they both looked up in surprise. Wiping their hands, they walked forward to meet their unexpected visitors. Their faces looked friendly to Harriet. She saw behind them the heads of three young boys, each one higher than the one below him, peering out from behind the barn door. Thomas extended his hand, while Harriet shyly held onto his other hand. He introduced himself to the welcoming couple, named Isaac and Catherine Riley. It turned out they were the first residents of the Elgin Settlement.

Thomas sat down by the table and started talking to the grown-ups. Meanwhile, the three boys gathered around Harriet.

"Come, we'll show you the barn," said the oldest one, about her own age. "We're staying here until Reverend King comes and then we're going to build our own house!"

He grabbed one of Harriet's hands, the middle boy grabbed her other one, and they pulled her eagerly through the barn door. Her fatigue vanished as she followed them up the ladder into the hayloft.

"Come on," said the littlest boy, looking back. He was the first up the ladder. "We sleep upstairs. Wait 'til you see our tunnels!"

Harriet saw that the barn had stalls that the family was using for storage, and a big one that had never been used for animals where Mr. and Mrs. Riley made their bedroom. She followed the boys up the ladder. The hay was fresh and smelled wonderful. Each boy had a blanket stretched out on it and a small, neat pile of clothing. It was true what the smallest boy had said: the hay was so deep that they had made tunnels in it! The boys disappeared one at a time into a hole. Harriet crawled into the narrow space behind them, thrilled at the warm, sweet-smelling darkness. They came out of the tunnel near the edge of the loft. One after another, the boys jumped down to the main floor. Harriet looked down at the thick pile of hay strategically placed to cushion their landing and hesitated.

"Come on!" they shouted at her. Taking a breath to calm her fear, she slipped under the railing and dropped into the soft pile.

Laughing gaily, they helped each other pick hayseeds off their clothes and hair.

"Come on, we'll show you the farm." They ran out the barn door, leading Harriet in a small circuit around the meadow, always staying within sight of the three grownups. At the edge of the forest the boys had already found patches of wild raspberries and blackberries, plus an old apple tree from the original farm site. The children feasted on jewel-red, juicy raspberries and checked the progress of the blackberries, which were still hard and white, with only a thin blush of pink to foretell their sweet, purple-black promise. They tasted and spat out green, tongue-puckering apples. Harriet already loved this place. It held endless adventure and discovery. Here she had friends to play with who were not going to tell her she was dirty or wrinkle their noses at her. She wanted to burrow into the hay in that hayloft and stay there forever.

The sun was getting lower, and Catherine Riley was keeping a close eye on the four children, who were now chasing each other in a wild game of tag through the fresh-cut field.

"You all come back here now, before one of you hurt yourself!" she called loudly.

Reluctantly, the children trooped back, panting and sweating. Mr. Riley sent the boys to fetch water for washing. Weariness suddenly flooded back over Harriet. She sat on the bench beside her stepfather, leaning against his shoulder. Soon she ended up with her head on his lap.

As he wiped beads of sweat from Harriet's forehead and gently picked grass stems and hayseeds from her sleepy head, Thomas listened to the Riley family's stories of traveling the Underground Railroad from Missouri. Harriet barely paid attention as they spoke of how they had lived and worked in Windsor, Detroit and St. Catherine's before hearing about Reverend King's proposed settlement. But she heard the excitement in their voices when they described helping to start the Elgin Settlement.

"It will be a model of self-sufficiency," Mr. Riley was saying. "Black folk can live together in peace, take care of our own, grow our own food, build our own farms, not worry about who accepts or doesn't accept us, and send our children to school so they can have a better life than we've been able to. Reverend King plans to start a school first thing." Harriet's eyes popped open when she heard the word "school."

She looked at Isaac Riley's craggy face, full beard and eyes that were both tired and excited, and noticed that Thomas was listening closely as the older man recited the rules of the new settlement. Harriet's eyes closed themselves again, and she drifted off to sleep hearing words about acres and money, size and placement of houses, the prohibition of alcohol and the richness of the soil.

Thomas woke Harriet up to share the Rileys' food. Later they climbed into the hayloft along with the boys. They slept the night there, crushing some of the tunnel network in the loft. Harriet whispered apologies to the boys about destroying the tunnels, but they whispered back that she mustn't worry, they would just build new ones tomorrow. Harriet fell into a deep, contented sleep.

The next morning while they were eating breakfast, Harriet put down her spoon and asked, "Can I stay here with the Rileys until you and Mama and Zach come?"

For some reason, this caused Thomas, Isaac and Catherine to laugh merrily. Harriet felt embarrassed and the boys looked disappointed. Finally, Thomas smiled broadly.

"I don't think your Mama would take kindly to it if I came home without you, Sweet Pea! But I'm with you, child," he continued. "I think we'll be back here with the Rileys soon as we can."

Thomas' words soothed Harriet's disappointment. He liked it here! They were going to come back forever and ever!

As they walked the long road back to Chatham, Harriet was full of questions, and she and Thomas made the miles pass imagining what their new home would be like. Yes, they probably could have a horse, he said. They would have to build a barn. But a house for the people came first! Yes, they could have chickens, and yes, Harriet could be in charge of collecting the eggs. Also a cow for milk, though Thomas had to admit that he didn't know how to milk a cow, and didn't know whether Abiah did either. But he was sure that among their new neighbors would be someone who could teach them. In fact, among the neighbors would surely be one person or another who knew everything they would need to know.

"Remember, it won't just be us, Harriet. It's a whole community of folk and we'll all be helping one another build a whole new life for all of us together. I can teach woodsman skills and we will push back this big old forest, use it to build our houses and then plant the new fields we make. Your Mama doesn't only know washing and sewing, she knows farming, too."

Harriet chattered about how she imagined their new life. Thomas smiled happily at her. The walk home seemed shorter than yesterday's.

◇

North Buxton, Ontario, 2010
Angie and Malcolm grab one another and scoot closer in the dark so they can feel the comforting warmth of the other's body. An eerie hooting comes from the graveyard again, and they both shiver. Their parents sit nearby on the long metal bleacher but do nothing to reassure them. The children know it is a play, but that knowledge does not calm their tremors. Soon, a young girl floats, ghostlike, out of the graveyard into the circle of light cast by the bonfire, wearing a white bonnet and a rough, white dress that flows all the way to the ground. The silence of the onlookers deepens.

"I am Eloise, and I am buried behind you in the cemetery." The sudden loudness of the thin, young voice coming through the sound system startles Angie and her little brother. They both jump, then squeeze even closer to each other. "I came to visit you tonight to tell you my story so that you can remember where you came from. I can never forget the sound of bloodhounds chasing my mother and me as we ran through the woods..."

The voice continues hypnotically, and ten-year-old Angie is transported to the past, feeling a chill at the doleful thought of the bloodhound's baying. The real Eloise was her great-great-great grandmother. They visited her grave that afternoon as soon as they arrived in North Buxton after the long car ride from their home in Tennessee. They take this trip nearly every Labor Day weekend. Angie has always looked forward to the picnics and parades and softball games, barely listening to her parents' boring lectures about ancestors and slavery and all that old stuff.

But this year is different. This year, the spirit of Eloise glides out of the graveyard and lodges in Angie's soul.

THE BUXTON SETTLEMENT 1849

In 1849 the "Elgin Association", founded by a Presbyterian minister, the Reverend William King (1812-95), purchased 4300 acres of land in this area on which were settled freed and fugitive Negro slaves. Under King's direction the settlement prospered, and in 1851 Buxton post office, named after Sir T. F. Buxton, the British emancipator, was opened. By 1864 the community contained about 1000 persons, a combined saw and grist-mill, a brickyard and other small industries. During the U. S. Civil War seventy Buxton settlers served in the Union forces. Following that conflict a number of the settlers returned to their former homes in the United States, but descendants of those remaining still live in this region.

Archaeological and Historic Sites Board of Ontario.

Visitors to the Buxton National Historic Site and Museum today can see several buildings that were there when Harriet would have lived there.
Courtesy of the Buxton National Historic Site and Museum

11

Invasion of the Despised ~ 1849-1851

"So Larwill says we're lazy, dirty and uncivilized! We're invading their territory and threatening their morality. Their morality must not be very strong!"

The people laughed roughly, all of them assembled in Gunsmith and Emily Jones' kitchen. Harriet, who had sat herself on the floor behind the kitchen door to listen, heard anger in the laughter.

"He says the property value in Chatham will go down if too many of us move into Reverend King's new settlement," said another voice, adding scornfully: "That white folk will move out when we *invade*. The man is too full of himself. Look at him: member of the Township Council, member of the Legislature, and Commissioner of Education! As if that's not enough, he's also editor of the paper and can spread whatever lies and scandals he wants to spread! The man makes me sick." The voice was kindled with enough heat to start a fire. Harriet made herself smaller.

Although she didn't understand everything, the words she did catch made her uneasy and confused. Was it true that just being around black people made white people want to run away? She turned her dark coffee hand over to consider the lighter skin on her palm and sighed, imagining how it would be if the rest of her skin were that color. Maybe then Faith, with her pink skin and straw-colored hair, would still be her friend.

Then a woman spoke up, sounding just as angry. "And he says we should post a bond to stay in Canada West, just like where I came from in the States! And pay a poll tax to vote! And he doesn't want black children to go to school, either. I can't get the school to take in my Molly nor Alexander!" The woman's voice rose with each injustice she recited.

Harriet's back stiffened. That was the reason her mother wasn't sending her to school? A little fire started smoldering deep in her belly and the corners of her mouth turned down. Harriet knew she was smart—all the grown-ups said so. She was already reading more than a little from the things she had learned from Auntie Emily. *I don't care if my skin is purple or green, I'm supposed to be able to go to school!* The burning moved from her belly to her chest. Tears of pain and anger sprang to her eyes, and flames licked at memories of Faith's scorn. Faith's treachery should be grounds for not being allowed in school, if anything was. If black people living at Elgin made white people leave, it wouldn't bother Harriet one little bit. Especially Faith!

"Okay, folks, time to make our plan to organize everyone we know to come support Reverend King when he debates Larwill next week," Harriet heard Aunt Emily saying.

<>

When debate day came, Abiah, Thomas, Harriet and Zach were among the black portion of the crowd of hundreds standing in the mud of King Street. Some of the audience—all of them white—stood on the strip of boardwalk to either side of the hotel and craned their necks to look up at the speakers, who had stepped through the four tall windows onto a narrow balcony that was fronted by a white wooden railing.

Reverend King stood flanked by two other men on the right side of the balcony. Larwill and his men were on the left. Reverend King spoke first. As he began speaking, many of the white people began to boo and hiss.

Harriet pulled Thomas' arm sharply. "Pick me up, please? I want to see! *Please?*"

With an easy motion Thomas swung the slim girl onto his shoulders. The Reverend in his black coat and ministerial collar ignored the booing and continued smoothly in loud, firm, measured tones. Harriet stared at him, trying to memorize his face. His lank, brown hair started far back on his pale, pink forehead and came down to his earlobes on both sides of his head. His eyes looked intensely out from under deep brows and bushy eyebrows. His lips were so narrow they almost weren't there.

Harriet didn't really understand most of his words, but she felt the deep determination and courage in his voice. People standing near her periodically shouted "amen!" and "tell it!" Their intensity was contagious, and Harriet bounced with excitement on Thomas' shoulders until she felt a firm jerk from his hands on her ankles. Now sitting quietly, Harriet silently pledged, *I am with you, Reverend King. Whatever you do, I will be with you, I promise!* A secret smile played on her lips.

When Larwill began speaking, much of the white crowd burst into raucous cheering. Thomas lifted her down from his shoulders. She leaned against him, impatient and uneasy.

After the debate, Harriet's family and many other black people in the crowd followed Reverend King to the Presbyterian Church, where white parishioners asked him questions. Harriet realized that some white people didn't support Larwill.

"I want to do this, Thomas," said Abiah, with a spark in her eyes. "If we stay in Chatham, we'll always be living around people like Larwill. We'll have to depend on them for our livelihood. And Harriet and Zach might never go to school."

Thomas nodded. "Plus they have to walk the street and deal with the taunting and fighting. Yes, 'Biah, I've had enough being around hateful people! I want better for the children. I want to grow my own food, take care of my own family, and live amongst people we can trust to give our children love and confidence and hope, not hatred and hostility."

"And they can go to Reverend King's school," Abiah said. "He said the school will be the first thing he does. Larwill and his people might attack us, but both of us have dealt with worse before. Let's catch Reverend King right now and arrange to purchase a lot. If they stop the settlement, I think we can trust him to repay us."

Harriet was on pins and needles as she minded Zach while her parents went to find Reverend King. When they returned wearing the biggest smiles Harriet had ever seen, she started jumping up and down, which caused Thomas to grab her arms and spin her in a circle, laughing out loud. As they walked home, Harriet danced along daydreaming about jumping off haylofts into soft piles of hay, oblivious to the rapid-fire conversation being conducted over her head about savings and payments and cooking pots and fireplaces and chopping trees.

And separate bedrooms!

◇

When the Elgin Settlement was approved, the family planned their move for early the next spring. The Settlement would be a Presbyterian mission, so Abiah and Thomas decided to get married that winter. They held a small, private ceremony at the Baptist church they sometimes attended. As Harriet watched her mother and Thomas stand before the minister holding hands, she felt proud that Thomas was now officially her stepfather. Her mother was now an Ingram, like Thomas and Zach. But Harriet was a Roberson, daughter of Jacob Roberson. *I wonder where he is now,* she thought. *What is he like: is he like Thomas or different?* The thought made her feel a little like a traitor, but she wanted to know. She promised herself to ask her mother about him again, but not right now. She would have to choose her time wisely, because her mother's face always closed down when she mentioned him. Besides, Harriet was afraid to hurt Thomas' feelings.

12

A New Kind of Life ~ 1850

The early spring of 1850 was cold and wet. When the big move came, it was more than a disappointment to Harriet. They lived at first in a quick-built wooden A-frame shelter while they worked with other settlers to clear land to build houses. Their temporary home did little to keep out the elements. It was damp, dark, uninviting. Bundled in layer upon layer of clothes and wrapped in bedclothes, Harriet felt chilled and frightened at night. The tall trees of an ancient forest surrounded them. There was only one road and no shops. It was so dark and so quiet that Harriet wished she were small like Zach so she could snuggle in between her mother and Thomas. She longed for a real home with a fire-place to chase away the damp, with windows to invite in the sun and furniture to keep her off the cold ground.

This new life they had chosen certainly wasn't all sweet-smelling haylofts, juicy berries and warm sunshine.

"Nothing good comes easy, Harriet," her mother reminded her until she was tired of hearing it. "We want a life here, we just have to bend our backs. It's no use asking a cow to pour you a glass of milk."

Harriet didn't mind the work, though. The bustle of day-time was a relief. All the new settlers felt the same urgency to chop trees and raise houses. They worked with the cheer-ful spirit that accompanies a shared undertaking. Harriet was nearly twelve now, able to be a real help. While some people were cutting, trimming and pulling logs to build the house, others labored with forks and spades to dig gardens, or chopped, kneaded and boiled to prepare big pots of food every day. Some evenings and early mornings, the men and boys went hunting to put meat into the cooking pots. Harriet envied them, wishing she knew something about slingshots and snares, rifles and shotguns. She and the other children were put to work collecting firewood for cooking, weeding the new gardens, fetching and carrying, minding younger children—doing whatever jobs they could manage. Still, they found plenty of time for exploring and playing among the log piles, the unfinished construction and in the edges of the forests. But they never strayed far into the forest itself.

As long as the sun was out and they were working, they stayed warm, but it was good to sit around a big fire after the sun's warmth sank behind the forest. A motley collection of bowls, plates, mugs and gourds held each person's share of whatever was in the pots. Afterwards, there was usually someone with enough energy left to tell stories, and the children would struggle to keep heavy eyelids up and stay awake to hear them. They laughed and clapped to stories about Brer Rabbit outfoxing Brer Fox, and hugged close to their parents when the stories were the scary ones that jumped to mind when they were tempted to stray into the dimness of the forest. There were songs, too. Thomas was frequently called on to play his fife to accompany singers, and two or three other men had banjos or found something to knock for a drum.

> *Follow the drinking gourd,*
> *Follow the drinking gourd,*
> *For the Old Man is a-waitin'*
> *For to carry you to freedom,*
> *Follow the drinking gourd.*

Harriet's sleepy eyes searched the stars in the black sky to find the Big Dipper and see the North Star her mother had shown her. She and her new friends fell asleep around the fire many a night to the songs that had kindled their parents' spirits during the dark days of slavery or helped them find their way North when their time came to ride the Underground Railroad. Finally, fathers and mothers carried weary children to their makeshift beds without hearing a murmur of resistance.

<>

The days of communal work and play soon changed for Harriet. School was about to open! Several days each week her family had been helping to put the finishing touches on the new church, which would double as schoolhouse. Most of the nearby settlers helped, plus some white people who lived alongside the settlement. These were farmers who had joined Reverend King's church and wanted their children to go to his school. Harriet's mother was talking to one of them one day—a woman in a long, gray dress whose daughter was the same age as Harriet.

"Tell me something, Miss May, you don't have a problem with your child going to school with colored children?" Abiah asked bluntly.

Harriet slipped behind a big tree so she could listen, feeling her face get warm.

"No, Miss Abiah, I certainly don't. I think it's purely evil, the practice of one human being enslaving another one." Harriet had to listen carefully because the woman talked so funny it was hard to understand her. "We came here from England after my husband and my brother were put out of their jobs in the mill. We nearly starved the year before we came here. I have a sympathy for any soul misused by another human being. I teach my children to treat everyone with respect. We heard that Reverend King is an excellent teacher and will give our children a strong education."

Abiah nodded. "Well, I believe you're right about that, and I'm glad to hear you say it. My Harriet is itching like she's got into poison ivy for this building to finish so she can go to school! I guess your Allison feels about the same way."

May nodded, and the two women moved off to refill their cans with whitewash. Harriet looked over at Allison, who had also been listening to the mothers talk. Allison gave Harriet a shy smile. Harriet smiled back, but she felt herself hesitate. Would Allison be like Faith?

And then, one cool but fine spring morning when the breeze carried a sharp smell of winter's leaf mold mixed with the smell of sun-warmed earth and new grass, Harriet's mother woke her up and scrubbed her until her skin tingled and she had goose-bumps from the cold water and the brisk air. She put on the long apron dress her mother had sewed for her and a crisply ironed headscarf over her tightly braided hair.

Thomas had already left the house. She knew he had to work some days on his old job so they could buy food, nails and other supplies, but he didn't usually leave so early. Harriet was disappointed to miss his presence on the day she had wished for for so long: her first day of school. Her stomach felt as if something was flapping around inside it and her breakfast porridge sat funny in her belly.

Harriet's heart beat a rapid rhythm as she walked along the verge of the road until she was standing in front of the new church-school. Soon there were sixteen of them gathered there: thirteen other black children, including her friends the Riley boys, and two white children: Allison and an older boy. All of them were scrubbed and starched and nervous as they filed quietly into the new schoolroom, girls to the pews on the left, boys to the right. Reverend King himself was there and led them in prayer. Then he introduced a white man, much younger than Harriet's parents, as their teacher, Mr. Rennie.

Harriet was standing beside Allison. Allison smiled shyly at Harriet and they reached for each other's hands as Mr. Rennie led them in a psalm. Harriet's heart sang along with her voice: she was finally truly in school! For a quick moment she imagined her real father watching her from some distant place with pride filling his chest.

◇

That night when her parents thought she was asleep, Harriet discovered the reason Thomas had disappeared that morning, as she overheard his low voice relating the story to Abiah.

Before dawn, along with most of the men and older boys of the growing settlement, Thomas had quietly filtered into the woods along the road from Chatham. They were armed, carrying whatever weapons came to hand, including guns, knives and farm tools. Unknown to the children, their parents had learned that a mob of Larwill's people planned to attack the school on opening day.

"We had the youth high up in the branches. Just when we could hear the children singing in the church, they gave the birdcall to signal that horses were coming. We men came out into the road, both sides and across it, holding our weapons. Larwill's two scouts came round the corner. Girl, you should've seen how fast they stopped those horses when they saw us! No one spoke, either side. The scouts looked terrified. Several dozen black men and boys, all fully armed. They could see it in our eyes that we meant business. They could tell we were not only ready to defend our children, we were actually kinda hoping for a battle. The two horses felt how nervous the riders were and began to prance and spin. Then the men just looked at each other, turned the horses back the way they had come and galloped off without saying a word. We jumped and shouted and clapped one another on the shoulder. But we weren't sure they wouldn't return, so we stayed in the woods, the youths stayed in the trees, and we waited the whole day until the children were safely home from school." Thomas' voice was husky with pride and happiness.

Harriet shivered in her bed as she heard the story, but it was the pleasurable shiver of a child who feels safe under the covers with her father nearby. And she realized something: learning wasn't just something she wanted, it was something her parents were ready to fight for. She resolved to study hard and make them proud.

<>

Rural Mississippi, 1957

Fourteen-year-old Jimmy Ingram lies on his belly just behind the ridge overlooking the sawmill, his head peeking up between those of his uncle, his father and four neighbor men. They look silently down on the road linking their farms with the sawmill and behind it the gristmill where they grind their corn at the end of every summer. His heart thuds with excitement, but he holds the squirrel gun steady. Rumor has it that nightriders are coming. Tonight is the first time Jimmy has been included on patrol.

Jimmy has grown up nourished on a diet of stories about the long line of freedom fighters in his family going back to an enslaved Ingram who fled to Canada and later came home to his family after the Civil War: freedmen forging a life in this fertile bottomland. Stories of the white nightriders who destroyed what his forefathers had built, murdering many: those riders the granddaddies of the men they are ready for tonight.

His daddy and his granddaddy and all of the others did what Jimmy is doing now, protecting family and what they've built. He feels manhood pulsing in his veins.

"Here they come." An urgent whisper, and Jimmy sees a pickup truck approach. They wait until it is very near. His uncle rasps: "Now!" Jimmy and the other men fire their guns. He sees the bullets kick up dust on the road thirty yards in front of the pickup. The brakes squeal and send up a cloud of dust that obscures the truck's body as it executes a gear-grinding three-point turn and races back the way it came.

13

Women Are the Foundation of the World

Harriet was an eager learner, and the lessons she had received from Emily Jones prepared her well. She was soon near the head of her class. One day, Mr. Rennie announced that he would give a special class for the study of Greek and Latin after school hours. Harriet appealed to her parents excitedly for the fee to join it.

"Harriet," her mother looked at her sternly. "You are not joining that class. Greek and Latin are for boy-children. Mr. Riley and Mr. Abbott will send their sons to study to be doctors and solicitors, but for you that class is like hat feathers. There's no money in this house to spend on decoration. We need you at home."

"But Mama, why can't I do the same as the boys? I could be a teacher, maybe even a doctor!" Harriet's eyes filled with tears, startled that her mother wasn't supporting her. "I *want* to study, Mama," she spluttered, not knowing what to say.

Thomas was standing with arms folded, and Harriet appealed to him with her eyes, knowing better than to ask him to overrule her mother. But Thomas' face, though kind, revealed no sympathy.

"Harriet," her mother's voice was softer now, seeing her daughter's distress. "You can still be a teacher if you want. You don't need Greek and Latin for that. Listen, baby, it's not for women to be doctors and lawyers and such. You're going to grow up and marry and have children for yourself. University is expensive, child! Thomas and I don't have anything to even think about sending a child to university, much less a girl child. And right now we've got nothing for extra classes either."

Harriet put her tear-stained face down onto her arms on

the table in silent, defeated despair.

Thomas finally spoke up: "Harriet, Sweet Pea, look at me."

Harriet looked up.

"You know your mama and I are proud of you. We want you to continue school and continue to do well and make us proud. We also want you proud that you're a woman. You've got no need to follow a man's path! Women are the foundation of the world, you don't know that? Woman is the creator of life. Tell me before God, what higher calling is there than that?"

Harriet could tell Thomas was talking from his heart.

"Without woman, man's got no strength," he said. She lifted her head just enough to be respectful. "Imagine the strength of your mama here, finding her way in the wilderness with you in her arms! We wouldn't have gotten anywhere here in Buxton without the women! Maybe you can't see it yet, but you're a very important part of this family right now, baby-girl. We need you right here."

"No more crying now," Abiah said, the firmness back in her voice. "And no more argument."

Harriet sat up straight and wiped her tears with the back of her hand. She gave no more argument. Though Thomas' words made her feel some measure of strength and pride, she still didn't see why a girl couldn't do what a boy could.

A kernel of bitterness sat inside her. *If my real father were here, he'd let me join the class,* she thought defiantly. *It's not fair!*

She set out to learn how to hitch horses and oxen to pull logs, how to ride horseback as well as any of the boys, if not better, how to drive a buggy and a hay wagon. She even watched the men carefully to learn carpentry skills. When the school started a homemaking class for girls, she refused to join.

14

Outrage

One Sunday morning Thomas was chopping trees to clear a field a little way from their newly built house and Harriet was behind the house with her mother washing clothes while Zach played nearby. The earth began to rumble and when they looked across toward the main road, Abiah and Harriet saw five young men cantering toward their house on horseback. They were white. Harriet recognized only one of them, the son of one of the white farmers who lived just outside of the Elgin Settlement.

Abiah turned abruptly to Harriet and said urgently, "Take Zach, go inside, and you all be quiet!"

The young riders were barely slowing their horses as they approached the house. Harriet grabbed Zach's hand and dragged him protesting into the kitchen. She stood where she could see out the window, sitting him on her hip. The boys came to a skidding stop near her mother. One of the horses stepped on some of the clean clothes they had laid out on the grass. Harriet gasped angrily, biting her tongue to keep from shouting at the boys.

"Now, that one looks nice, don't she boys? She looks like a tasty morsel." One of the youths belted out an ugly laugh. Smarting with anger, Harriet cringed at the disrespect in his voice. She saw her mother stiffen and curl her hands into fists.

"Shut up, Georgie! Control your mouth!" shouted one of the other youths. George didn't say anything more.

"Hello, ma'am, how you doing this morning?" asked a third youth, but the closeness of his prancing horse belied his respectful words. "We're just taking a Sunday morning ride, see what you folks do on a Sunday."

The other boys grinned at one another.

"Come on, let's go," said the one who had chastised the loudmouth George. "You have a good day, ma'am." He spoke over his shoulder as he turned his horse abruptly. The others followed, digging heels into their horses, making them jump forward, kicking up clods of earth, several of which flew onto the clothes, and one of which landed square on the yoke of Abiah's apron, speckling her face with dirt.

Harriet crept quietly back out the door. Abiah brushed off her apron, her hands shaking as she wiped her face. Harriet slipped around behind her and began lifting up the carefully washed clothes, now spattered with mud or marked by deeply ground-in dirt in the shape of a horse's hoof. Her mother stood for several more long minutes, hands on her hips, fighting for self-control. Finally she turned to nod at Zach, who was uncharacteristically quiet.

Harriet gathered her courage. She spoke in a thin and shaky voice: "Those boys have no respect, Mama! Look what they did to the washing! Now we have to wash all over again."

"You're right, Harriet girl, they've got no respect. Bunch of heathens. And to think they're out on the Lord's Day behaving like that. Reverend King needs to hear about this!"

The next afternoon when Harriet came home from school, Reverend King was sitting at their kitchen table along with Thomas and her mother, plus several more people. Harriet stood quietly outside to listen. Thomas was speaking.

"We thank you kindly for coming, Reverend. Several of us have concern about the behavior of a group of white boys that rode through our yards yesterday. It was the Lord's Day, but they were rude and disrespectful and behaving in an un-Christian manner. They had no business with anyone, just cavorting through people's yards, looking into people's windows. Their horses kicked dirt over my wife's washing. We are asking you to talk to them, tell them not come here any more."

Harriet could hear the anger simmering in Thomas' carefully controlled voice. The others around the table nodded and murmured agreement.

Reverend King responded: "It does sound like those young men should have been more careful and respectful. I would prefer they had been in church, but I guess we all know how boys can be when they are not properly disciplined. However, I must tell you that the result of their exploration yesterday was very positive indeed!"

Harriet's eyebrows bunched together in confusion at this unexpected statement. She peeked and saw several of the adults sit back abruptly against their chairs as Abiah's and Thomas' eyes meet.

The reverend continued, "After church yesterday, I was at the home of some of the white people who attended services. Those boys had gone home and reported how quiet and peaceful it was in our settlement. They told their people that they looked through the window and saw Mrs. Riley kneeling in prayer with her children. They gave a very good impression of the piety and Christian nature of our colored settlers, and that has reassured their families about the character of their new neighbors. It is just the kind of impression you all want to make to encourage good relations with your white neighbors."

Harriet listened for her mother to tell Reverend King what the boys said to her. But Abiah was silent. She was looking down at the table, her fingers gripping each other so tensely that her knuckles grew tight and shiny.

Finally, Mrs. Riley broke the silence, speaking in a slow and precise voice: "Reverend King, I'm happy to hear that good came of it. However, I can tell you it was not a pleasant experience to see five white boys ride their horses roughly into my yard and look through my window at me and my children. As you know, Mr. Riley was in church yesterday morning, and I was alone at home with the children because the smallest one was poorly. My children were frightened, and I have to admit that I was, myself. I beg you to strongly discourage the young men from behaving in such a way again."

Reverend King nodded solemnly. "I will let them know that their behavior frightened people and was out of order. I hope that they are merely curious and that if I have a quiet word with them, they will respond properly. If I were their parent or teacher, I would discipline them, but unfortunately, that I cannot do."

These words were greeted with another silence, which extended so long that Harriet began to fidget. At last, Mrs. Riley stood up and said she needed to go home. Thomas stood and thanked Reverend King for coming.

"My pleasure, Thomas. I'm happy that you came to me with this problem. I wish all of you a good evening." He smiled and nodded at the little gathering. Harriet skittered from the doorway as she saw him approach it.

"Thanks to you, Reverend, good evening to you, too," came from a variety of polite voices, ushering the man out the door.

It remained quiet for a while after he left, people standing and watching his back through the window as he walked down the road toward his home. Then there was head-shaking and angry grumbling that the good reverend was taking this too lightly.

A man who had recently moved to Elgin spoke up, outrage in his voice. "I still think we should go find those boys and teach them a lesson. The way they talked to Mrs. Ingram— we can't allow it!"

"Give Reverend King a chance first, Clarence," responded Abiah quickly. "We are in a delicate situation here. We don't want to start warring with our neighbors. If he doesn't handle it, we'll talk again."

The man called Clarence shook his head and the anger

drew his neck tendons tight, but he didn't say anything more. Mrs. Riley had put her hand on Abiah's shoulder and nodded. After some scattered small conversations, the rest of the people left. Thomas was standing still and silent, his arms crossed, his brow wrinkled.

As Harriet changed out of her school clothes, she pondered what she had heard, remembering what the men of the Settlement did on the first day of school. She wondered what they might do if Reverend King failed to control the boys. She felt nervous, but then she told herself she was well protected. Those boys on the horses would be dealt with. She didn't need to be afraid of them.

15

Plans ~ Summer 1851

"...find plenty clay when we're digging the drainage ditches," a man's voice filtered through the open window of the church. It was a warm, bright summer evening, and Harriet was tending Zach on the church lawn while their parents attended a meeting inside. "Both of us know brick-making," the voice continued: one of the new settlers. "Only thing brick-making needs is plenty clay, plenty wood, and plenty hands. If we've got nothing else, we've got plenty clay, plenty wood, and plenty hands! You all ought to let me and James here start us up a brick-making factory."

"Amen, brother!" shouted several voices. "Yes, sir, sounds great! Let them do it."

"Reverend?" This was the voice of Abiah's friend Ruth Little. It was followed by the deep voice of Reverend King, which seemed it could carry for miles, though his tone was gentle.

"Yes, Sister Ruth, speak your mind."

"It hurts my heart every time I see a bonfire in a field. Look at all this good, good lumber just going up in smoke! It's a sin! If we're going to be self-sufficient like you all say all the time, why we don't start cutting our own board instead of burning up what logs we don't need? We could be selling it, and people could work right here making lumber instead of working out for someone else. Seems like we're sitting on a gold mine and just watching all the gold wash away down the river."

Excited voices greeted Ruth's suggestion, but Zach had grabbed Harriet's hand and was pulling her away from the church, so the voices began to meld and mix up. Then he started getting cranky and she had to take him home.

Hours later when Thomas and Abiah returned home, Harriet learned that in the meeting they had agreed not only to the brick factory suggestion, but also to build a sawmill, a grist mill to grind their own corn, a pearl-ash factory to make fertilizer from the ashes of the burnt wood, and a general store. All of these would go up not far from where Harriet lived, in a square near the church and Reverend King's house. As she got ready for bed, Abiah and Thomas were buzzing about a hotel, a post office, a shoe shop and a carpenter shop. Harriet tried to imagine a village where now stood only woods and pastures.

That summer Harriet was taken up with the work of tending the farm, helping new arrivals, and filling her lungs—and her soul—with the air of excitement that had settled into Buxton like the heady scent of lilacs in spring.

16

It Was the Women Who Put an End to Him ~ May 1852

One late afternoon in the spring of the year she would turn fourteen, Harriet walked through Buxton's town square on an errand for her mother. The day that Thaddeus first galloped up to her house came suddenly into her mind, and she stopped and leaned against a big tree to follow her thoughts. Mr. Walker's prediction of a flood of new arrivals had come true. Black people were no longer safe in the North until they crossed the border out of the United States. Since the Fugitive Slave Act passed it seemed every house in the Elgin Settlement pulsed with a rhythm, stuffing new settlers in with families that already lived there, making the few rooms bulge while more forest became fields and fresh houses grew, then expelling the guests into their new homes for a breather before engorging once more with a new influx of fleeing humanity.

The dark, hardwood beams of the church roof looked down on earnest men and women huddled in lamp-lit meetings week after week. Harriet often fell asleep on her loft bed above the murmur of late-night planning sessions at her kitchen table. Days were thick with work while cauldrons of food bubbled ceaselessly over outdoor cook-fires. Life was never boring.

Harriet roused from her memories and looked around her. There sat the new sawmill, an uneven squawking of saws and enticing scent of sawdust drifting from it. Nearby the steady knock of hammers and shouts of workmen announced the erection of the gristmill. Across the way sat the pearl ash factory where her mother now worked some days, its sweet, wood-smoke aroma floating over everything, turning trees from the new-cleared Elgin fields into fertilizer. Beyond it there were the shops and the general store. Harriet gazed at the hotel site, spotting the stacks of waiting bricks fresh from the new Buxton brickyard that squatted a short distance up the new road from the church. Plans were also in the works for their very own post office.

Harriet harked back to a vivid memory of the seemingly endless nights shivering in a cold, damp A-frame two years ago: listening with vigilant, skeptical ears to the forest's furtive night sounds. How recently her feet had trod no roads, only the paths of woods and fields!

Harriet felt certain that the Elgin Settlement was not only a rebirth for its settlers, but an achievement that would make history. The thought made her pulse surge. She had heard that people all over Canada West and even below the border were talking about what was happening at Buxton. Why, black folk in a far-distant place named Pittsburgh had sent them the handsome bell whose dulcet toll called them to school each morning. She was a part of something important. She was more than just a child!

When Harriet got home, Abiah scolded her about her lateness. Her homework still awaited her, and when she finished eating and finally got to it, the wavering candlelight soon seemed to make the words flow over one another like water over rocks in a stream. Her mother glanced over as she rubbed her eyes.

"Looks like bedtime for you, sweetheart. I'll wake you up early to finish your work."

Harriet nodded silently, gathered her slate and books into a neat stack, and dragged herself sleepily up the ladder. She was about to enter a dream, her head under the covers, when Reverend King's voice brought her wide awake. She crept to the top of the ladder, where she could peek down on what was happening below.

Both of her parents were at the front door, their backs to Harriet.

"Of course, of course. Welcome, brother, welcome, sister," she heard them say simultaneously. They backed up and stepped aside, and Harriet could see Reverend King outside in the dim light, one hand raised in a good-bye-and-God-bless gesture, and in front of him, a pair of strangers who stepped into the house, looking worn and tired. Her parents called her to meet William and Eliza Parker, and Harriet knew that their house would be home to two more people for a while. She hoped they liked children.

<>

William Parker was a slim, muscular man whose body and spirit seemed constructed of tough, springy hickory wood. He was several years younger than his wife, younger than Harriet's parents, too. Eliza had arrived exhausted in mind and body, but as the weeks went by, the haggard hollows of her face gradually softened to reveal a hidden strength that drew Harriet to this new Auntie.

One evening, Mr. Parker told a story Harriet would never forget. Eliza listened with a flickering smile and spirited eyes, occasionally adding pieces or reminding her husband of a detail: "I grew up in Maryland, near Fred Douglass. I knew him when I was a little boy, before he escaped, and by the time I was ten, I knew I had to find a way to get free, too. I couldn't tolerate the way I had to live. My master was considered one of the 'good' ones, but how can someone who owns other people be good? He sold my best friend Levi when I was thirteen. I was seventeen when I claimed myself and flew.

"I had to break someone's arm in the process: some kidnappers ambushed me. I think I went nearly insane when they came at me, and I laid into them with a tough branch I was using as a walking stick. I shouted, 'I'd sooner die or kill you than let you take me back!' And it was true.

"When I got to Pennsylvania I thought I'd reached heaven. I couldn't believe I was truly a free man! But it wasn't long before I realized that I wouldn't be content with my own freedom while kidnappers were on the loose, capturing my brothers and sisters and taking them back to slavery. A few of us got together and set up an alert system, so when kidnappers came around we could organize ourselves quickly and go after them. It was a successful system. We freed quite a few people, and if some kidnappers ended up dead in the process, that was only justice! A few times we also had to deal with traitors: our own colored neighbors who told kidnappers where to find their prey. That was harder, in a way, than dealing with the kidnappers themselves. I think I was more outraged at a black traitor than even a slave catcher. We nearly killed one of them. We were in the process of meting out justice to him when we were interrupted. But believe me, he learned his lesson—he was never a problem to us after that!"

Hearing this, Harriet's eyes widened. Her eyes turned from Mr. Parker to Mrs. Parker, expecting some disagreement, but she was surprised to see only pride in Eliza's eyes as she nodded her head. Harriet was shaken. This man who was living in her house, who had chopped the wood now burning in the fireplace, hauled water to the kitchen, helped his mother chop onions for dinner: this man sitting calmly at the table talking to them had killed slave catchers in the course of freeing their captives. That was difficult for Harriet to imagine, but it at least seemed justified. But he had conspired with others to kill a black man as punishment for his betrayal: could that be God's will?

Mr. Parker had more to tell: "We had a lot of support from our neighbors, both black and even some of the whites. Once we severely wounded a group of kidnappers in the process of fighting to release their prisoner. The doctors in our area refused to treat them. Two of the men died, and we got word later from Maryland that another few had bones that were never properly set, and at least two more died after they got home."

Harriet gasped. Doctors refused to treat dying men? *White* doctors? A chill crept down her spine as a realization began to dawn on her in a way it had not before: the Parkers' story was not like some of the other tales she had heard of death-defying flights from slavery. Theirs was a story about a war.

"There was one white innkeeper who made it known that his place was available to any slave catchers who came our way," Mr. Parker said. "One night, his inn mysteriously burnt down while my friends and I looked on. He changed his tune after that: sang only songs of freedom for the fugitive."

Mr. Parker laughed. Harriet blinked at the fiery image his words had conjured of the burning inn. Again she looked at Aunt Eliza, whose eyes were also twinkling, trying to understand the woman who had aligned her life with that of this tough, angry, dangerous man. Some of the iron that was in him must be in her soul as well. And yet, the Parkers she knew by day were warm, loving people who laughed easily and were kind to her and her brother.

"Then I met Eliza." Mr. Parker paused and Harriet saw love in his eyes when he looked at his wife. It was followed quickly by a flash of shadow that made Harriet think of the Parkers' three children left behind in Pennsylvania. He blinked and continued. "A few years after we got married, we settled in Christiana. I was still involved in work against slave catchers, we both were, and last September we started hearing rumors that they were coming for me. I'd been threatened so often that I just laughed it off. But it turned out this wasn't an idle rumor, the human bloodhounds really were on my track.

"I don't know if you all know about this up here, but in Philadelphia there's an amazing organization. It's called the 'Special Secret Committee,' and its business is to spy on the slave catching network and disrupt it. They figure out who the kidnappers are and who aids and abets them in each part of the state. Plus, they know about these gangs in Virginia, Maryland and Washington. If it weren't for them, I wouldn't be here telling you this story tonight.

"The men who were coming after me were Edward Gorsuch, his son and his nephew. They said they were chasing horse thieves, but the Special Committee knew they were after some fugitives who were staying in our home. The Special Committee sent a man named Williams to travel in the same coach with Gorsuch's group on their way to Christiana. Williams eavesdropped on their plans to capture the 'horse thieves,' and then he got off the coach at one of its stops and took a shortcut to get to us. That's the only reason we were prepared for what happened next.

"It hurts my heart that Williams is now languishing in jail along with thirty-odd others who participated in the events I'm about to describe. Thank God for the Special Committee! It is taking care of them in prison, and of their families, too—legal counsel, food, clothing, whatever they need. I'm so thankful for them, I have no words."

Mr. Parker's voice had become husky and soft. He took a moment before continuing to speak. Harriet saw Eliza squeeze his hand.

"It's a good thing my friends took Mr. Williams' story seriously when he arrived in Christiana, because I still laughed at it as rumor. Some of my friends insisted on staying the night in my house as lookouts, and just before daylight on September 11, one of them left to go home. A moment later, he burst back in and ran up the stairs to the rest of us. He was shouting 'kidnappers!' and sure enough, several white men followed him through the door. I jumped out of bed—well, I guess we all did!— and went to the top of the stairs to look down at them.

"One of them stepped forward, said his name was Kline

and identified himself as a United States Marshall. I remember exactly what I said to him. I told him, 'If you take another step, I will break your neck. I don't care about you nor about your United States!'

"This backed them up, but my brother-in-law whispered that we should give ourselves up, since he was sure they would take us in the end. I answered him out loud, so Kline could hear me: 'He hasn't taken me yet. Don't be afraid. Don't give up to any slaveholder. Fight to the death!'

"Gorsuch looked me in the eye while he poked Kline in the shoulder and told him to go upstairs with him to get his property. That 'property' was two of the men in the room behind me. Kline read out the warrant he had with him for taking the men. 'You're welcome to come up for them,' I said, with a smile on my face.

"They wisely refused the offer, and we went back and forth until they threatened to set fire to our house. 'Go right ahead,' I told them. Eliza stood by me and took my hand as I said, 'Before we give up, you'll see our ashes blowing in the wind.'"

Harriet felt a chill at those words. Where were their children, she wondered? Weren't they in the bedroom, too?

Mr. Parker kept talking: "The sun was coming up then, and Eliza whispered to me that she was going to blow the horn to call for support. She went to the window and blew the horn—that was the way we had in our community to call for help. Everyone would come when someone blew a horn.

"Kline was no fool, he knew what the horn meant, so he ordered his men to shoot at Eliza." Harriet saw Eliza's back straighten as she held her husband's hand. "Two of them climbed trees and fired at her, but they missed. The house was made of stone, and she was on her knees below the window with the horn on the windowsill. They fired blast after blast, but the horn kept sounding. Finally, I stuck my head out a different window to try to talk to them, and Kline fired his pistol at me and broke the glass just above my head. I grabbed a gun and shot at Gorsuch, because he was the instigator, but my brother-in-law grabbed at my arm, so the bullet only grazed Gorsuch's shoulder.

"Then Gorsuch lost his patience and started up the stairs. His son was up in a tree where he could see through the upstairs window. He saw us moving toward the landing with our guns, swords and corn cutters. He screamed at his father that we were heavily armed and would kill him. The old man went pale as a ghost and backed down in a hurry.

"Then Kline shouted for Gorsuch's nephew Joshua to go bring a hundred men from Lancaster. I shouted that he'd better bring five hundred.

"My brother-in-law got cold feet and started talking again about giving up. I told him if he tried, I'd have to blow his brains out. My wife stood there with a corn cutter in her hand and I'll never forget what she said." Mr. Parker glanced at his wife, who was still holding his hand, her back even straighter than before. "She said, 'I will cut off the head of the first one who attempts to give up.'"

At this point in the story, Harriet's mouth fell open as she stared at Eliza Parker. Mrs. Parker looked back at her and spoke an answer to her silent question. "I doubt I could have done it if it came to that, he was my kin, but it made him quit his whining."

Mr. Parker continued. "By this time, the neighbors had gathered, black and white. The white ones were Quakers, peaceful people who refuse to engage in violence for any reason. Kline ordered them to help him capture us. According to the new Fugitive Slave Law, they were required to help him, but they told him, 'If Parker says they will not give up, you had better let them alone, or he will kill some of you. We're not going to engage in battle.' And they walked away. Some of them are in jail along with Williams right now for making that stand.

"I went out into the yard at that point and walked up to Gorsuch, who had a pistol in each hand. Several armed men stood behind me. I put my hand on his shoulder and told him if he didn't leave I would break his neck. Even Kline tried to get him away then, but he kept insisting on having his 'property' back. He was a stubborn old man! Then Kline offered to withdraw his men if I'd withdraw mine, but I told him it was too late for that. We had about ten men, and we faced thirty or forty white men, but I figured our men were ready to go down fighting and theirs were a bunch of cowards. You could see it in their faces.

"Then Gorsuch's son got indignant. He asked his father 'if he was going to take this from a nigger.'

"I looked straight at him and said, 'If you repeat that, I will knock your teeth down your throat.'

"The son fired a wild shot at me and missed. I ran up and knocked the pistol out of his hand. He ran, one of our men hit him with a shotgun blast, and he stumbled into the corner of the cornfield and collapsed.

"I turned around and saw that Samuel Thompson was talking to Gorsuch. Thompson was one of the men Gorsuch considered his property, and Gorsuch was actually standing there insisting that Thompson should come with him! Thompson grabbed the shotgun from my brother-in-law and knocked Gorsuch to his knees with it. The old man signaled his men and they opened fire. We rushed them. It was really too close for shooting, so we clubbed them with our rifles. Old Gorsuch was the only brave one there, just as I thought. The rest of them threw their weapons down and ran, but not the old man, and sometimes three of our men were on him at once. Samuel Thompson beat him with the gun until it bent.

"By the end of the fighting, the old man was dead, his son was dying in the cornfield, his nephew was badly wounded—he hadn't left for those reinforcements when the fighting broke out. Only two of us were wounded, neither seriously. I discovered that two paths had been cut through my hair by bullets, but there was no blood.

"Some people want to say that Gorsuch's slave shot him to death, but that's a lie. His gun was bent so it couldn't fire. He struck the first few blows, and three or four others added theirs. But the truth is it was the women who put an end to him."

Harriet once again stared intently at Eliza Parker, whose eyes seemed turned inward. She was gazing at her hands. Harriet realized that when Mr. Parker said, "it was the women who put an end to him," the emotion that made the hair stand up on her neck was pride. She was shocked at herself.

Mr. Parker said: "After the battle, we scattered. Eliza had to hide, and we left the children with her mother. Officers were looking for me, and my friends told me I should leave. I tried to go home first, but I met several female friends on the road who told us that there were dozens of armed men at my house. I did manage to see my children before I set out for Canada. That was harder than the battle itself. I felt I would rather die than be separated from them. But it had to be done."

William Parker's eyes filled with tears at this point in the story, and Harriet felt a lump in her own throat. The children still had not arrived at Buxton, and she felt anguish at the thought that they may never see their parents again. They had been separated now for several months. Harriet had heard Eliza confiding to her mother her desperate fears that they would not be reunited.

A few nights later, William Parker continued the story. "The Underground Railroad guided Pinckney, Johnson and me to Rochester. The last segment of the journey we were in a coach with several white men. They were discussing a one-thousand-dollar reward being offered for my capture. At first, Pinckney and Johnson wanted to get off the coach at the next stop, but I knew those men didn't know who we were. One of the white men in fact became very friendly with me. Just before we got to Rochester, I asked him what would happen to Parker if they caught him. I'll never forget what he said.

"He told me, 'I don't believe they'll catch him. I think he's in Canada by now. At least I hope he is, because I think he did right. I'd have done the same in his place. I think Parker is a brave man, and all you colored people should honor him. He is a man who wasn't fighting for a country. He wasn't fighting for personal glory. He was fighting for freedom. He only wanted freedom, just like any man does. You colored people should protect him and remember him as long as you live.'

Harriet felt goose bumps arise on her skin when she heard these words, and knew she would do just as that man had said.

Mr. Parker described the rest of his trip—his stay in the home of Frederick Douglass in Rochester, who sent him safely on to Canada, the trials of life in Toronto trying to find work and barely finding subsistence; his tortured emotions at hearing rumors that his family had been sent back to slavery, followed by his ecstasy at learning that his wife was on her way to Detroit, his decision to meet her in Detroit and come to make their future in the Elgin Settlement.

Mrs. Parker did arrive in Detroit, but without the children. It was true she had been captured—twice—and freed by the Underground Railroad and Vigilance Committee members. They arranged for her and the children to leave Pennsylvania for Canada, but a third capture was attempted the day before they were due to leave and she was forced to flee without the children.

Mrs. Parker never told the story of her early years. She only shook her head later when Harriet asked. Behind her eyes was a wall that did not allow emotion to cross it.

Many nights Harriet lay in her bed pondering the Parkers' story. In the daytime she found excuses to be near them, to help them with their work or just be in their presence. How lucky she was that Reverend King had brought them to her house! The Parkers were steadily, if unconsciously, replacing Reverend King as the model against whom she measured herself, especially Eliza Parker. She wondered if she would someday take her own place on the field of battle, like Mrs. Parker. The thought made her shiver with trepidation and anticipation.

17

I Left My Family There ~ May 1852

It was Thaddeus who had delivered the Parker family to Buxton the night Reverend King brought them to Harriet's house. Since his move to Chatham he had traveled the road to Windsor almost every week, guiding one branch of the river of fugitives that had become a flood with the passage of the Fugitive Slave Act. The stories he heard could fill a book and made his own journey from the Swamp seem easy. Thaddeus knew the Order was straining to safely send across the Detroit River these travelers who arrived with only the clothes on their backs and find connections for them in the towns, villages and settlements of Canada West. The Canadian Anti-Slavery Society had organized support networks for the new arrivals, scraping to find housing, clothing and work for the never-ending human torrent. He watched the black population of Chatham swell rapidly and the Elgin Settlement see the start of new homes almost weekly.

The previous autumn, at about the same time that the Parker family was battling slave catchers in Christiana there was a Black Convention in Toronto. Thaddeus had voiced a strong desire to attend, but the Order did not send him. They told him he was needed to guide travelers, but he also suspected that they considered him too young and uneducated for the discussions and debates expected to happen there. He had to admit that they might be right.

Thaddeus had put himself under the tutelage first of Mrs. Peggy Settles in Windsor, and later of James and Emily Jones when he moved to Chatham. He'd felt desperate to learn to read and write properly. Illiteracy had weighed on him like an opponent in a fistfight sitting on his chest. It was a constant source of shame and inadequacy. When he joined the

Order, it became vital to him to catch up with his brothers' and sisters' knowledge, so he could understand the great debates going on about the future course of black people and the struggle to bury the system of slavery. He struggled to read Fred Douglass' paper, the other abolitionist literature, and later Henry Bibb's *Voice of the Fugitive*. Henry Bibb lived in Windsor and had officiated at the Black Convention. As he learned to read and grew less embarrassed about himself, he began to seek out Mr. Bibb during his brief stays in Windsor.

On a cool day in late May, evening was approaching, as was a group that he was to guide from Windsor to Buxton. The Order in Detroit was sending them to Mr. Bibb, but they hadn't yet arrived. Thaddeus went to the Bibb house in the afternoon to wait for them, walking the short distance from Miss Peggy's along streets bordered by young apple trees that danced above either side of the road like clouds tinged by a soft, pink sunset, amid a chorus of birds frantic to out-sing one another. He felt the quickening of life around him. Henry Bibb and his wife Mary were on the porch with several other people in lively discussion. From what Thaddeus could catch, it had to do with black settlements in Jamaica trading with black settlements in Canada. The term "self-sufficiency" flew from one speaker to another.

"The North American Agricultural League will organize the settlements in both countries and the trade between them," Bibb said. "Black people will not only be creating their own self-sufficient communities in both places, but also demonstrating that products made by slave labor are not necessary to a successful economy. And we won't be dependent on white companies and organizations and charities for our livelihood."

Thaddeus sat on a porch step watching this intense man in fascination. Bibb's back was ramrod straight, his dark eyes flashing with intensity. Thaddeus took in the light brown skin, the soft waviness of his hair, the sharpness of his nose, the thinness of his lips, and it struck him – not for the first time – that Bibb must have more white than black in his ancestry. With a jolt, he saw his brother's face appear before him. Nathaniel's skin was the same color as that of the man talking with such conviction. Shame seeped through Thaddeus' veins. How could he so admire the man in front of him and yet be embarrassed by his own brother?

The conversation ended, the group on the porch drifted away. When Mary went into the kitchen, Bibb invited the youth into his living room, smiling in welcome.

"So, young man," he said, "tell me about yourself! I have seen you these many times, but don't know your story. I know you have one."

Thaddeus felt himself relaxing in the presence of the man's warm smile and fatherly manner.

"I came here from the Dismal Swamp," Thaddeus said. Then to his own surprise he added, "I left my family there." A lump entered his throat. "My mother, my..." The lump closed off speech. His eyes begged Bibb to allow him to stop.

Bibb merely nodded and said softly, "I know, son," and waited for Thaddeus to continue.

Thaddeus swallowed to make space for his voice. "I...my old master was so evil." Thaddeus had never talked with anyone about these memories. They had remained locked up tightly inside him as he had gone about creating his new life in Canada. What was it about this man that made him spill himself out? His voice came out low and hoarse. "He come to our shack and tossed me and my sister out in the dirt. He picked us up by our ears. You wouldn't do that to a dog!" Thaddeus felt tears fill his eyes, but he couldn't stop. "He threw us in the dirt and went in to my..." He stopped. "She had a little boy..." Again he couldn't go on. His head dropped between his knees, his eyes shut, squeezing tears out the corners, and his hands came up to cover his ears as if he could blot out the memories that way. His shoulders shook.

Bibb pulled his chair close enough to put a hand firmly on each of Thaddeus' shoulders.

"Okay, boy, okay. I know. I know. There's no shame in crying about it." He waited a few moments, and then said, "Lift your head up, boy. Tell me about the Swamp. I always wanted to know about that place."

Thaddeus lifted his head, wiped his eyes with his handkerchief and told Mr. Bibb stories about life in the Great Dismal. Bibb got excited about the economy the people there had created, the trade in shingle wood, and talked again about self-sufficiency. Speaking about it lifted some of the pain from Thaddeus' heart. He was gratified to be able to share with Bibb something the man didn't already know.

Bibb said, "Thaddeus, I'm going to tell you a story now. I want you to listen close and understand me well."

Thaddeus nodded.

"My father was a senator from Kentucky. Senator Bibb." His smile now was a sneer. "I never met the man. My mother and your mother had the same experience. Same as so many of our women." His eyes hardened now and flashed. "Same as my first wife." He paused.

Thaddeus heard the stoppage in Bibb's throat, and knew the older man was struggling to control harsh emotions. Thaddeus felt his heart beating faster. He listened as if there were no other sound in the world than the voice of this man who sat opposite him leaning forward, his elbows on his knees, hands clasped tightly in front of him.

Bibb collected himself and started again.

"I saw all of my six younger brothers sold. Each one sold was a sadness to me and a dagger in the heart of my mother. But somehow I grew up. I married a beautiful young woman, Malinda, a light-skinned woman conceived in this world in the same way I was. We have a daughter, Frances." The catch came back into Bibb's voice. Thaddeus had to look away from the pain in his eyes. He realized what it was costing

Bibb to tell this story and felt compelled to focus his mind so he would be sure to understand what the man was telling him. Bibb cleared his throat.

"Frances," he repeated softly. There was another long pause. "I left them. I left the two of them, my beautiful wife and my beautiful daughter. It was the hardest thing I've ever done, and I've done many hard things in my life. But it was the only way I saw that I could eventually lead them to freedom. Malinda and I stood before each other, she with the baby in her hands, both of us with tears in our eyes. I found my way to freedom, and six months later I went back for them. I will not try to tell you the story in detail, only to say that we were captured and sold to a man in Mississippi whose cruelty is not to be imagined. We escaped again, but our way was blocked by a pack of wolves, and again we were recaptured. They whipped me until I nearly died."

Bibb's shoulders unconsciously pulled back as if feeling the whip once more, and Thaddeus cringed. Bibb let out a long breath.

"I escaped again, and several more times I tried to get my dearest family to safety." He paused again. When he spoke, his voice came out thick and gravelly. "I never succeeded."

Bibb paused once more, his head hanging for a moment. Then he lifted it, looked Thaddeus in the eyes, and spoke now with bitterness on his tongue.

"Nine years ago, a planter bought my wife to be his mistress. I was finally forced to accept my failure. That's when I came to Detroit, and then here. God gave me another chance at happiness when I found Mary. But it seems He abandoned Malinda." Rancor had crept into Bibb's voice with that last statement. He shook his head. "God forgive me, I don't mean that." He paused before continuing, again looking directly into young Thaddeus' eyes.

"Thaddeus, this I want you to hear, and hear it well. A poor slave's wife can never be true to her husband contrary to the will of her master. She can neither be pure nor virtuous contrary to the will of her master. She dare not refuse to be reduced to a state of adultery at the will of her master."

Thaddeus stared fixedly at the floorboards between his feet, willing Bibb to stop pouring acid over his heart. The pause continued, forcing him to look up. He found Bibb watching him patiently, an unwavering directness in his gaze. Thaddeus couldn't turn his eyes away.

"Thaddeus, your mother had no choice. You must not judge her. And you certainly cannot blame your little brother." Bibb smiled ruefully at this point. "We none of us choose our parents. I certainly would not have chosen my father!" His smile broadened. "Your brother—you never know, he may turn out like me!"

At this point, Bibb laughed, and Thaddeus smiled with him, but inside his emotions were as mixed up as scrambled eggs.

"I got some advice from a wise old woman when I was going crazy with grief after my wife and daughter were sold. She told me to take all that grief and anger and turn it to working for our people. I'll offer that same advice to you. Thaddeus, right now we are in an historic moment. We have the world of slavery to destroy, and we have the world of freedom and equality to birth and grow. Take your anger and dedicate it to those two tasks, those two sides of one coin. You're on the right road now, keep on going!"

Thaddeus knew he had received a gift. He was grateful and humbled that this man, so highly respected, chairman of the Black Convention, had taken the time and paid the emotional price to grant it to him. He blurted his thanks awkwardly and accepted the firm, warm handshake Bibb offered, realizing that it would take some time for him to untangle his reactions so he could absorb the story and decipher what it meant for him.

But it would be a while before he had the leisure to attend

to that task. At that moment, the sound of numerous pairs of feet clattered heavily up the steps and onto the porch. The party from Detroit had arrived, including Mr. and Mrs. Parker.

Christiana House
Home of William and Eliza Parker in Christiana, Pennsylvania,
where the battle with Gorsuch and his men took place
Courtesy of the Buxton National Historic Site and Museum

In 1850 the "Fugitive Slave Law" was passed to appease slave-owners by making it illegal for anyone to help in the escaping or hiding of runaway slaves. The penalty for this such crime was a $1000.00 fine or six months in jail. Although no one could help the runaways, United States Marshals could demand anyone to help in the capture of any runaway slaves or be tried for treason. At this time Blacks were not allowed to testify in their own defence.

On Sept.11.1851, Edward Gorsuch, a Maryland slave-holder, accompanied by United States Marshals and 15 to 20 other men, rode to the home of William Parker in Christiana Pennsylvania. They had come to recapture four of Gorsuch's slaves whom William Parker was giving refuge in his home. As Gorsuch approached the house, Eliza Parker, William's wife sounded a horn to summon help. Neighbours had gathered in Parker's defence. A fight broke out and in the end Gorsuch was killed, his son was critically injured and Parker and the escaped slaves were on their way to Canada. Parker settled in Buxton, Canada West.

Not only did this incident hold the largest treason trials ever held in United States history but it also challenged the Fugitive Slave Law and unofficially helped in the beginning of the Civil War.

Courtesy of the Buxton National Historic Site and Museum

18

Truly a Man

Mary Bibb reached the porch ahead of her husband. She smiled and opened the door wide as Henry joined her. Simultaneously, the two said, "Welcome to our home, brothers and sisters."

Five weary travelers faced them on the porch: four men and a woman, their faces haggard from their long, hazardous journeys. Their clothing showed the signs of having been worn for several days, crowded into bruising coaches with no time for rest. Their eyes were sunken from fatigue but nonetheless reflected sparks of gratitude and hopefulness. Watching them from the parlor, Thaddeus vividly remembered when he stood on Miss Peggy's doorstep in the same condition.

The Bibbs showed their guests where they could wash and rest their weary bodies. Because they were expected, food was ready for them. Temporary clothes were provided, and Mary Bibb collected their clothing and sent it to be washed by others in the Vigilance Committee network. By the next day, the travelers would be clean, refreshed, well fed, and feeling the return of strength and confidence that comes from being supported and cared for.

Thaddeus was introduced to his new charges, including Mr. and Mrs. Parker, whom he would soon escort to Buxton, where they would find their temporary home with Harriet's family. Then he went back to Miss Peggy's, where memories, images and emotions tumbled and bounced through him like swift-running water swirling and splashing around rocks. Snatches of his conversation with Henry Bibb surfaced and disappeared, along with glimpses of the deep feelings in the worn faces of the newcomers he would guide tomorrow:

people struggling to accept the possibility that they might no longer need to protect themselves from capture and brutality. Sleep did not come to Thaddeus easily that night, nor flow smoothly once it came.

When Thaddeus returned the next morning, Bibb was in private conference with William Parker. Mrs. Bibb opened the door to the room they were in, said something to her husband, then beckoned Thaddeus into the room and shut the door behind him.

"Thaddeus, you met William Parker."

Thaddeus nodded politely to the slim, dark brown man with penetrating eyes who sat to Mr. Bibb's left on a yellow wingback chair embroidered with climbing roses.

"He came to Detroit from Toronto to reunite with his wife Eliza, and as you know, they and the others are on their way to Chatham. I have just arranged for the four to travel by coach, for this reason: there will be a meeting tomorrow and the next day in Detroit, which Mr. Parker will attend. He will relate the story of the events in Christiana, and we will discuss several other matters of importance. You will then take Mr. Parker to rejoin his group in Chatham, and continue with Mr. and Mrs. Parker and Mr. Johnson to Buxton, where they intend to settle. I would also like you to attend the meeting in Detroit."

Thaddeus had been nodding calmly throughout Mr. Bibb's explanation and instructions. The last sentence sent a burst of excitement through his body, setting it tingling. Only a few months ago, he had wanted to go to the Toronto Convention and been rejected. Now, here was the Chairman of that convention inviting him to a secret meeting on the other side of the border. He restrained his excitement and merely nodded again, murmuring, "Yes, sir, I'm honored."

Bibb and Parker left to collect money to pay for the coach. Thaddeus stayed in the kitchen with Mrs. Bibb and Mrs. Parker, laying a fire in the hearth for Mrs. Bibb to cook dinner.

Mrs. Parker told the older woman about the Christiana Riot and the several times she had subsequently been captured by slave hunters and escaped. Thaddeus had heard something of the so-called riot and listened with sharp attention. Mrs. Parker's voice was firm and proud as she described the events, but her speech became halting and broken when she began to talk about the three children she had been forced to abandon when she escaped the last time. Mrs. Bibb had been listening carefully, nodding and encouraging Eliza to go on, but at this point, she interrupted with passion in her voice.

"Sister Eliza, listen to me well. The story you are telling about your family: most of the black people you see in Windsor and in Detroit can tell variations on the same story. We have a very strong organization both sides of this river, and in the next two days it will make plans to retrieve your children and bring them to you at Buxton. Your husband will give them all the information they need. Sister, ease your mind and rest assured that the party they send for your children will not fail in its mission. The action your family took has been a call to arms in our battle against the bloodhound law and the entire evil system of slavery. Our people take it as a sacred duty to make sure that the agents of the devil don't succeed in separating your family. Go to Buxton with clear heart and mind! Choose your lot and start your building. Your children will soon join you in your new life."

Mrs. Bibb gathered Mrs. Parker into her arms and held her tight. Thaddeus saw tears on the newcomer's cheeks and a shaky smile on her lips. His heart wrenched with his own memories, and he yearned for the Parkers' children to be reunited with their parents.

By evening, Bibb and Parker had returned with a purse of five dollars. Parker divided this with the other travelers, and the next morning, his wife and the three others climbed into a wagon drawn by two horses. Thaddeus spoke with the driver to get the name of the boarding house where he would find them in Chatham when he and Mr. Parker followed in a few days.

Having seen them safely off, Thaddeus, Bibb and Parker walked down to the river and boarded a ferry to Detroit. Henry Bibb knew Detroit well, having lived there for several years until the Fugitive Slave Law passed, when he decided it was safer to make his home across the river. There was still a man in Mississippi who regarded him as valuable property, and he would always look over his shoulder if he remained in Detroit.

Thaddeus had been back and forth several times in his capacity as courier, so many of the streets were familiar to him as well. When they disembarked from the ferry they made their way to Fort Street and the hall that housed the Second Baptist Church.

In front of the door stood two young men at military style attention. As Thaddeus, Bibb and Parker each spoke the correct code words, the men nodded and stepped aside to allow them to enter. Thaddeus noticed shotguns leaning against either side of the door within easy reach of the two sentries. There was a window on each side of the hall. At one window stood a young woman, eyes steadily on the watch, with another man in a similar posture. Bibb gestured for Thaddeus to sit while he guided Mr. Parker to a seat at a table beside the pulpit.

The meeting opened with a prayer led by Reverend Monroe, followed by the assembled singing several of the songs of the Underground Railroad. The tingling up and down Thaddeus' spine continued throughout as he listened to the exhortation of the minister to continue God's fight for the freedom and equality of all mankind and then sang the words that had helped guide so many of his fellow human beings to the land of freedom. But nothing would compare to the excitement of listening to William Parker tell the story of the events in Christiana. Thaddeus' imagination formed pictures to go with the words, and by the time Parker finished talking, he felt as if he had been by the man's side during the fight.

After Mr. Parker spoke, several of the assembled stood to hail him and their companions as heroes of the war against slavery, while the sentries at doors and windows never strayed from their watchfulness. Thaddeus noted and admired their discipline. How difficult it must have been for them not to look at William Parker as he told his story!

Next, Henry Bibb spoke from the front of the hall about the progress in implementing the decisions of last September's Convention. Meanwhile, Reverend Monroe and several other men disappeared into a small back room with Mr. Parker. Thaddeus realized that this must be the committee whose mission it would be to fetch the Parker children. He said a silent prayer for their success.

That night, Thaddeus and his companions stayed at the home of William Lambert, a deacon at the church and head of the Detroit Vigilance Committee. Thaddeus knew Lambert as lead organizer of the African American Mysteries, the secret Order that he had sworn allegiance to. Conversation went on into the night. Thaddeus listened until his head was buzzing like a swarm of honey bees come back to their hive at the end of the day.

The next morning the household arose and ate a breakfast of eggs, fresh bread and tea before heading back to the church hall. As they walked near the river's edge, they noticed a flurry of activity at a docked steamboat. When they saw several Sheriff's officers at the center of the crowd, they paused to look more closely. Lambert signaled the others to stay where they were while he walked down to the crowd. The officers had disappeared onto the boat, and soon reappeared surrounding three raggedly dressed black men, their shoulders slumped and heads down. Lambert hastily returned up the bank to where they stood.

"They say they are arresting three horse thieves," Lambert reported breathlessly with heavy emphasis on the word "say."

Thaddeus was standing next to William Parker and felt the man's body tense. "Those are no horse thieves!" Parker's voice was sizzling hot, but carefully quiet, giving voice to what they all knew. "Those men are fugitives! I'm sure of it!"

"I'll go to the telegraph office and find out what message the Sheriff's office received," Henry Bibb said, his voice also urgently quiet. He turned and walked off swiftly.

The rest of them joined the growing crowd that was now beginning to surround the officers and their captives as they moved away from the river toward the city jail. The three men were taken inside the jailhouse, but the crowd refused to disperse. Comments and speculation burst and flew like popcorn on a hot stove.

By the time Bibb returned, word had spread and most of the people expected for the meeting at the Church had instead rushed to the jailhouse. Lambert pulled Bibb and Parker aside, along with Thaddeus and about a half dozen other men and women. Their heads close to one another, they spoke quietly.

The young woman who had watched at the window yesterday and one of the sentries who had been at the door were sent running to alert one of the boat captains who ferried passengers on the Underground Railroad across the river to Canada. Thaddeus knew where the captain docked his boat. Then Bibb turned to Thaddeus.

"We'll go confront the Sheriff and distract him. You watch the door and first opportunity you see, go in, take the prisoners and run them to the boat. Cross the river with them, you won't be safe this side after that. Take them to my house, we'll join you tonight."

Thaddeus' heart banged against his chest. Bibb's voice

expressed confidence in the success of this bold and simple plan, and even though Thaddeus knew it was extremely risky, the man's assurance infected him. He didn't hesitate. He nodded and strolled away from the group to lean against a tree not far from the jailhouse door. He crossed his ankles and his arms, trying to appear nonchalant and uninvolved, and he probably succeeded to outside eyes. But inside he felt like a stranger to his own body. His entire being was vibrating, his gut felt hollow, his mouth was dry and bitter and his breath came fast and shallow through his open mouth. All his senses were on high alert, his eyes pinned on the Sheriff and the door behind him, waiting for the moment that would call him to action.

The rest of the little planning group meanwhile rejoined the crowd that had now swollen in numbers. The Sheriff stood in front of the door. Parker moved close and shouted, "Let them go! They are not horse thieves! They are fugitive slaves and you are doing the dirty work of the men who claim them as property! How much are they paying you?" Following his lead, the crowd began to yell menacingly at the Sheriff. Parker stepped closer until he was nearly in the Sheriff's face.

"If you get any closer, I will arrest you," the Sheriff spoke loudly and threateningly, not backing down.

"Go ahead," Parker returned hotly. "See me here?"

Thaddeus watched the enraged face of this man who had only two days ago been reunited with his wife and only yesterday sent her off to Chatham in expectation of joining her tomorrow. This man was now risking his freedom without a second thought in the interest of freeing three fellow men held in captivity by this Sheriff. Parker's fearlessness was contagious. Thaddeus watched eagerly for his chance to act.

At that moment, the door was opened from the inside, possibly in anticipation of the Sheriff bringing Parker inside. Thaddeus slipped through it, nodding to the deputy as if he had business there. The deputy looked at him in confusion, but stepped outside to stand alongside his embattled boss. The three prisoners sat on a bench, their hands shackled. On the other side of them was a gate that opened to the back of the building. With the deputy at the front door, momentarily no one was watching.

"Come!" Thaddeus whispered hoarsely. The three jumped up without hesitation and all four men ran through the back gate. Thaddeus led them headlong, twisting and turning down alleys and between buildings toward the riverbank, hoping against hope that the two sentinels had found the boat captain and the boat would be ready and waiting.

Soon they heard loud shouting that told them the prisoners' disappearance had been discovered. Thaddeus knew his brothers and sisters would be doing their best to slow down the pursuit. He picked up speed, and the four men, their breath coming now in deep whines, slid down the riverbank beneath an old willow tree.

A small, wooden dock stood in the shade. A wide rowboat alongside it equipped with two sets of oars bobbed gently in the peaceful river. The captain stood on the dock, holding the rope that had moored the boat. The young man and woman who'd been sent to find the captain emerged from behind bushes and handed the captives into the boat, Thaddeus jumping in last.

"Can you help row? Do you have the wind for it?" asked the young sentry. "This is a lot of weight for one oarsman."

"I can do it," croaked Thaddeus, gasping. He knew that right now he had the strength and kick of three mules.

The youth nodded, and he and the girl stepped into the water to give the boat a vigorous shove into the current. Quickly untying the only other boat at the dock, they also shoved it, sending it floating harmlessly away from shore. Then, hearing the approaching pursuit, they took one another's hands and began strolling slowly along the riverside, heads bent close, to outside eyes a pair of lovers so absorbed in each other that they were unaware of the world around them.

The boat captain ordered the three fugitives to lie flat in the bottom of the boat, while he and Thaddeus bent themselves, rowing with all their strength. As he pulled the oars, Thaddeus could see the Sheriff and his deputies, surrounded and impeded by the large crowd, arrive at the riverbank to look on helplessly as their craft receded from the Detroit side of the river and slowly but surely approached the free soil on the other shore.

<>

It was fully dark when Bibb and Parker pulled open the door and stepped into the Bibb home where, for the second time in three days, fugitives were being tended to. The sound of the door barely disturbed Thaddeus, who was asleep on a chair at the back of the room, the hint of a smile pulling at the corners of his mouth. He jumped when Bibb put a hand on his shoulder. Embarrassed to be found dozing, he stood up quickly, struggling against the weakness of a body whose energy had drained like water from a washbasin when the plug has been pulled. But Bibb was smiling broadly and clapped him on the back.

"Well done, Thaddeus! You're a fine soldier, son!"

With those words, Bibb embraced him tightly. Energy burst back into Thaddeus' body and he came fully awake. He straightened his back and shyly returned the hug. What reward could be greater than the sense of victory he had felt when they reached the Windsor side of the river and he helped the three freed men clamber out of the rowboat? And yet, this hug meant the world to him.

When Thaddeus arrived in Buxton late the next day at Reverend King's farm with Mr. and Mrs. Parker, he stood in the front yard and introduced the new arrivals. King welcomed them into his home. Thaddeus said his goodbyes as the couple walked into the house behind the Reverend and Mrs. King. William Parker was the last one through the door, and Thaddeus watched the man's slim, straight back and broad shoulders.

"That is truly a man," he thought to himself. "Truly a man."

<>

2005
Chatham, Ontario

When Auntie Gwen asked what she was learning in history class, fifteen year-old Brenda Childs spoke enthusiastically about the abolitionists William Lloyd Garrison, the Quakers, John Brown and Reverend William King. Auntie Gwen snorted about mis-education. "You and I descend from heroes, Brenda. You owe it to yourself to learn about them before you go off to college. I didn't go to college, but if they teach you that we didn't author our own liberation, I don't need it!" The intensity in her voice gave Brenda chills.

Today, she has come to the two-room Black Historical Society for the first time. She is stunned. On the wall are photographs of people who can only be her great-grandparents. She doesn't know how long she stands before the photos in reverie, but she now moves into the next room: cluttered, lined with shelves of books and binders filled with typewritten pages. She starts reading.

A secret, armed black society. Black men like DeBaptiste who together with John Brown planned the raid at Harper's Ferry. (Why have I only heard John Brown's name?) Osborne Perry Anderson's report about the raid. William Lambert and the Underground Railroad. Mary Ann Shadd Carey. J. C. Brown. Henry Bibb. Eliza and William Parker. Gunsmith Jones and his daughters: right here in Chatham!

She grows angry. The stories of these people and their struggles have been kept from her. She stares at her unruly pile of documents. Why are white people in the history books while black people are on photocopied pages on a shelf?

Francis Parker, son of William and Eliza Parker, with his wife
Isabella, around 1910.
The Parkers' descendants still live in the Buxton area.
Courtesy of the Buxton National Historic Site and Museum

19

Who Should Preside? ~ Summer 1852

The Parker children arrived! Harriet ran upstairs and cried when she saw the long-hidden fear that was revealed by Eliza's screams, William's squashing hugs, the children's tears and laughter. That night there was a celebration in the Ingram house, complete with a fresh-baked cake.

Everyone worked even harder now at clearing, planting and building the Parkers' place. Harriet was put in charge of the children: the oldest was twelve-year-old Ezekiel, only a year and a half younger than Harriet, who was now fourteen. Harriet and Ezekiel were old enough to be useful to the clearing work, and they towed the younger children along behind them. While the men were cutting trees and the women were quilting, cooking and collecting the necessary items to start a household, Harriet and Ezekiel used corn-cutters to chop the smaller limbs from the felled trees. The younger children dragged the branches into a pile at the middle of the clearing for burning. Harriet showed Ezekiel how to put the mare Meldy into harness and drag the logs to the building site. Meanwhile, she filled him in on what he and his brother and sister had to look forward to when school started back in the fall.

At midday, everyone stopped their work and came together in the shade to eat.

"Tell me about Reverend King," William Parker said after the food was gone and the group was resting for a while before getting back to work. "When he came out this morning and did some chopping with us—he usually do that kind of thing?"

"Yeah, pretty much. When he's not gone to Toronto or Chatham looking for money for the school, he's around a lot."

"I noticed white farmers live along the road he lives on," Mrs. Parker put in.

"Yes ma'am," answered one of the men. "That road was settled before the Elgin Association bought land around here, and most of the white farmers stayed. Reverend King bought one of their farms. They didn't mind a white minister moving in, but there was conflict at first about the back lots behind the white farms. Some of the white farmers didn't want black folk moving in behind them. They tried to buy up the property but couldn't, because it was Elgin Settlement land."

Thomas spoke up, "I got a chance to see Reverend King work with them. That first year—one time when King was gone somewhere, Brother Harris arrived and took up his piece. We all started doing just what we're doing here now. A gang of us chopping trees to put up a log house for him, and John Rowe—that's the white man who owns the front lot—he shows up with a musket in his hand, telling us get the hell off his property or we won't like what comes next."

A couple of the other men who'd been there nodded and made noises of agreement. Harriet had never heard this story and listened closely. She noticed that Ezekiel had balled up his fists, and she imagined him for a moment standing in the room behind his father when the slave catchers were in their house. How different his reaction was from hers: he was expecting to hear a story about a fight, while Harriet fully expected that Reverend King had solved the problem peacefully.

"Well, Harris wasn't about to be intimidated. He takes his location ticket out his pocket and shows Rowe that he's got every right to be there. Rowe doesn't even look at it: says he bought the lot and if we don't leave peaceful, we're going to leave by violence. Got to hand it to Harris, the man didn't even flinch. Just looks Rowe in the eye and says, 'Well, I know I'm within my rights. I know this is my property. But since as how Mr. King is not here, we're going to leave for now and wait for him to come back come settle this.' We just tipped our hats to Rowe like it was a conversation between friends, turned around and left him standing there.

"When the Reverend got back, he called a meeting with Harris, Rowe, and a few more of us. Turned out Rowe had given some earnest money to some white guy who told him all the back lots behind white farms were for sale. Reverend King listened to him quiet-like, then asked to see his deed. Of course Rowe didn't have one. Then, calm as you like, Reverend King goes in his pouch and pulls out the title to the property. 'Mr. Rowe, sir,' he says in a soft voice, 'you have been cutting wood on that back lot to sell. I'm afraid you've been cutting wood that doesn't belong to you.' Mr. Rowe commences to looking kind of peaky now, eyes shifting backwards and forwards. 'I'll tell you what we can offer you, Mr. Rowe,' says King. 'We would be willing to let you take the wood you've already cut and do what you want with it.' At this point Mr. King looks at me and the other settlers, and we give him our nod. 'We will also overlook you driving the lawful owner off the land and won't bring the law into the matter.' We nod again. 'I'll be happy to help you try to get back your money from the con man who took it. But for your part, you will have to give us your solemn promise and oath before God that you will not go on the land again nor harass the owner or his friends.'

"By now, anybody could see that Rowe is plumb scared. He knows now he's been swindled, and worse, he's in the wrong before the law. I guess he's just happy to get that wood off there. Anyway, he agreed to Reverend King's proposal and that was the end of that."

William and Eliza Parker were quiet. Harriet, feeling pleased that she had correctly anticipated the end of the story, watched them, thinking how impressed they must be. What Mr. Parker said next surprised her.

"So, tell me something," he broke the silence. "Is Reverend King the judge and jury for all the conflicts in the settlement? Or do you all settle your own problems between yourselves?" One of his eyebrows was cocked up. There was a touch of hardness in his voice as he asked questions which Harriet did not understand. Did Mr. Parker think there was something wrong with what Reverend King had done?

Thomas spoke up: "Some of both, Brother William. There's a lot of things never reach as far as Reverend King we settle amongst ourselves. There's some things we know he just won't understand, you know what I'm saying?" The others nodded and looked at Mr. Parker. "We have something called a Court of Arbitration. Reverend King presides, and four of us settlers are on it. But there's plenty times he's not here, and then we conduct court ourselves. We never have police nor sheriff come on the Settlement. One thing Reverend King is really good at, though, and that's taking the piss and vinegar out of the white folks around here. Sometimes it's truly hard to take his advice and cool down in face of some of the stuff they pull." Thomas shook his head uncertainly. "Truth is, I don't know the right way of it. But so far, this way is working. And so far, we've been taking care of the conflicts we know he can't handle."

William glanced at his wife, and she at him. They shook their heads slightly. Ezekiel was still tense. There was silence for a long moment.

"Well," Eliza finally spoke, "we're newcomers here. Got a lot to learn and don't want to be putting out an opinion about something we don't know yet. I have great respect for Reverend King. But I've got to say, I would feel better if we weren't leaning on a white man to be in charge. I'll close my mouth for now and just keep my eyes and ears open. William and I are more accustomed to fighting than talking. This here is a new world for us." She sat back and smiled.

Harriet was quiet the rest of the afternoon, that conversation turning round and round in her head. She loved Reverend King. From that day years ago when she watched him stand up to the crowd in Chatham she felt like he was someone she could depend on to defend what was right. When Reverend King preached in church or led prayer in school, she always felt a warmness toward him—and more: a sense of loyalty. A determination that she would strive in every way to live up to the standard of righteousness and courage that he set.

The story of how he solved the dispute between Mr. Harris and the white farmer only reinforced her confidence in his commitment to truth and justice, his calmness and power as a man of God. But when she heard Thomas talk about things Reverend King "wouldn't understand," about things we "settle amongst ourselves," she was confused. And Mr. Parker's phrase "judge and jury" caught her up short. Three people whom she also revered had hesitations about Reverend King. There were things they would not confide in him, times when they would not choose to depend on him. Even further, the Parkers, who had quickly become her new heroes, seemed to think Reverend King was holding himself above them. She had heard some people refer to the Reverend as "the king." Now she began to wonder, just a little, if that was respect or something else. Did the Court of Arbitration need Reverend King, the only white man in the Elgin Settlement, to preside over it? She had never asked herself that question before.

As she trudged back home after work was finished, she pondered how frustrating it was to feel yourself growing within reach of adulthood and still not understand adults.

20

What Then Is a Neighbor?

On the first day of school in September, the Parkers were still living with the Ingrams, and Harriet and Ezekiel both awoke in a state of high excitement. They rushed through morning chores, washed themselves thoroughly and put on clothes they had carefully prepared the day before. Eliza and Abiah could barely get them to eat breakfast.

The scene at the schoolhouse was in sharp contrast to the day it first opened. Back then just over a dozen children waited for the doors to open, and none of them knew what to expect. This morning, there were six dozen children of all sizes, including more than a dozen white children. The noise level echoed their excitement. While many of the older children stood as if at church, clutching their bibles and slates close to them, their lunch pails dangling from crooked elbows as they chatted with friends, many of the younger ones left their possessions scattered carelessly on the ground while they chased each other boisterously, climbed trees or taunted one another. Not a few children, when they finally filed in to start the day's studies, had grass stains on their carefully laundered clothes and bits of twigs or flower petals sticking to their hair.

Harriet and Ezekiel were among the dignified ones, and Harriet wondered what Zeke was thinking. Back in Christiana he had been tutored along with some other black children in the home of a neighbor. The white school there did not accept black children. Like Harriet, he was highly motivated and had learned quickly. He was clearly eager for his first school experience, his eyes darting to and fro, taking in everything.

Finally the huge bell that had been donated by black

supporters in Pittsburgh started tolling loudly, the doors opened, and Teacher McLachlin stood at the top of the stairs. The playing children quickly ran panting to collect their belongings and line up. Two little boys, one white and one black, tussled with one another in front of Harriet and Zeke, jockeying for position in line. Harriet glanced at Zeke.

"You two! Behave yourselves!" Harriet hissed at them. The two little boys looked up at her, then glanced at Zeke, whose hands appeared ready to grab them. They settled. Harriet took one by the shoulders and placed him squarely behind the other one without protest.

"I've got to admit, this is definitely strange to me," Zeke whispered to her. "Black and white children together without distinction!"

Harriet smiled with more than a drop of pride. "I know. The common school is having trouble keeping its students. Everyone knows the teaching at our school is better. Our teacher makes no distinction, all children are treated the same. Except the ones who misbehave!"

Zeke shook his head in wonderment. The line started moving, the children filing into the schoolhouse. Here Harriet and Zeke separated, Harriet going to the girls' side of the room and Zeke to the boys'. They took their places, the smaller and less disciplined ones finding plenty of hiding space for squirming and poking behind the tall backs of the wooden pews. But everyone grew still as Reverend King stood in the pulpit and led them in prayer. Then he left, and Teacher McLachlin led them in song. Finally, he had them open their bibles for an oral recitation. Harriet knew the chorus of their young voices could be heard for a long distance from the little schoolhouse.

At lunchtime Harriet and Zeke sat together under a tree.

"Teacher McLachlan isn't managing too well," Harriet commented with some disappointment. "We've had different teachers every year, and I hear a new one is coming soon to replace him. He can't manage misbehavior. He doesn't even understand half of what the colored children are saying. I don't know why he doesn't put his foot down and make the children be still! Those children don't behave that way in church. When Reverend King comes into the school, they all behave."

Zeke munched on an early fall apple, nodding. "Yes, so I notice. But those who want to learn will learn. Man! Those boys reading Latin! That's impressive! I want to join that class."

Harriet willed herself to avoid cringing at the thought of the Latin class. Zeke's excitement made her happy. She'd been worried he would find fault.

<>

After dinner, Harriet sat with her bible, studying the lesson Mr. McLachlan had assigned. She started to read aloud, and Zeke joined her. Their parents listened.

"Then one of them, which was a lawyer, asked him a question, tempting him, and saying, Master, which is the great commandment in the law? Jesus said unto him, Thou shalt love the Lord thy God with all thy heart, and with all thy soul, and with all thy mind. This is the first and great commandment. And the second is like unto it, Thou shalt love thy neighbor as thyself. On these two commandments hang all the law and the prophets."

The room fell silent. Ezekiel's brother sat on the floor, legs folded, listening, but his little sister and Zach had both climbed the ladder and were murmuring in sleepy, muffled voices upstairs.

"And what do you learn from that lesson, Harriet?" Eliza asked quietly.

"Well, ma'am," Harriet started hesitantly, "I understand the first commandment. The second one..." She paused. "I don't think I understand what it means 'on these two commandments hang all the law and the prophets.' If the law says that, how come there could be slavery? If one must love one's neighbor as oneself…"

"Good question," William said. "Zeke, what do you make of it?"

"Umm…" Zeke looked self-conscious. "Umm, I don't think they're obeying the law, then, are they?"

"Whose law is it?" Abiah asked. Harriet looked at her mother and realized this was a thought question. She looked back at the Bible and searched it silently.

"It God's law!" she suddenly blurted, a thought birthing in her mind. "So the law of man and the law of God aren't the same thing?"

The adults smiled. Eliza said, "I think you're on to something there, Harriet. There is evil in the world, the work of the Devil, some say." Thinking of the white children in the schoolyard and the white Quakers who had helped hide her from the slave catchers, Eliza added, "I say white folks— well, not *all* of them, but plenty of white folks seem like they are the Devil himself. They make laws that directly defy the Word of the Lord right there."

There was silence for a moment as the children thought. Harriet asked, "Then what is a neighbor? Is it only the person who lives by you, or does Jesus mean everyone?"

All the adults laughed out loud at that one, and Harriet's ears got hot with embarrassment.

"Whoa, this one's a thinker, isn't she?" blurted William Parker, a look of fatherly affection on his face. Harriet was still confused, but beginning to feel better. "That's the real question, that one there. Zeke, you see that question? That's the difference between reading the word and reading the meaning. Give respect: you can learn from Harriet here!"

Harriet glanced rapidly from her mother to Thomas, who both had broad smiles on their faces. Her mother, seeing

Harriet's eyes glitter as she glanced at Zach, spoke quickly and softly.

"Now Harriet, don't you succumb to the sin of pride, you hear?" She looked back and forth at the other adults. "Time you children got ready for bed. Don't forget you've got school tomorrow, too. Off you go!"

Harriet was only too glad to exit the limelight and avoid responding to either Mr. Parker or her mother. But she carried the glow of Mr. Parker's words with her as she clambered up the ladder.

The bell that black residents of Pittsburg donated to the Elgin
Settlement and that called children to school.
Courtesy of the Buxton National Historic Site and Museum.

21

The Order Needs Another Courier ~ March 1853

"I still hope," Thaddeus said, but his was voice not hopeful, and he turned away from Harriet's gaze. They were sitting on the wall along the road in front of the Jones family yard in Chatham where Thaddeus lived and where Harriet's family was visiting. The blustery March weather was just sunny enough to take the chill off the stones beneath them, but the two young people were huddled close against one another, bundled in their coats and hats against the chill air, their hands tucked up under their armpits. Harriet flinched, realizing her mention of his family had caused him pain.

"I know," she responded quickly, in what she hoped was a reassuring voice. "We've got to have hope. And thank God for each day no bad news comes." Her mother had told her recently about the day she had learned Harriet's father had been sold. She shivered, then shook loose the memory. "I'm sure they heard about the Bloodhound Law before they started and decided not to risk it," she went on, repeating the thought Abiah had used to quiet his fears over the years. "They know you're safe, and if they stay in the Swamp, they're safe too."

Thaddeus saw the genuine sympathy in Harriet's eyes. Something made him keep talking. "Every time I'm in Windsor I look for them, you know. And Isaac always checks for me in Detroit. They tell me that when any Conductor goes near the Swamp, they don't find anybody who knows my family. Everything's more dangerous now, but..." His voice trailed off. Thaddeus had never revealed to Harriet the growing fear and flashes of shame he felt. He hadn't told her about Nathaniel's father, he hadn't shared the images seared into his memory of his mother and the white man. Those images only appeared to him rarely now. Occasionally he would notice that and feel grateful—and then guilty. Henry Bibb's story about going back for his wife and daughter had made him feel ashamed about leaving his family, but at the same time he was proud of the life he had made for himself and the work he was doing for the Order. It was too confusing to talk about.

"The Order needs another courier." Harriet deliberately changed the subject. She could see that Thaddeus was done talking. "I heard Uncle James talking about it and I asked him to recommend me." She suddenly felt embarrassed. Her boldness in talking to Mr. Jones almost felt childish to her. Why did she tell Thaddeus?

"Harriet, you're a girl. That work is too dangerous for you!" Thaddeus' mind still turned into itself and he spoke without really thinking, so her abrupt reaction startled him.

Harriet jumped off the wall and turned to face Thaddeus, her eyes sparking with anger. Suddenly, her hands weren't cold anymore, her whole body was boiling.

"Too *dangerous?*" she shot back fiercely. "More dangerous than my mother jumping across the Ohio River on chunks of ice with me in her arms?" The anger mixed with embarrassment. Why was she using her mother to defend herself? She paused to collect herself and control her shaking.

Thaddeus paused and stared at her. "What are you talking about? That really happened?"

"Yes, I'm not making it up! Me and my mom were part of a group coming north, and then the slave catchers got close just when we came near the river. Mama tells me the Conductor separated the group so they would have to choose who to follow, give the other ones a better chance. I wasn't even three years old. I've got no idea how my mama carried me and ran too. All I know is, we reached the riverside and she saw them coming after us. I guess we were the lucky ones they chose to follow," Harriet snorted and looked into Thaddeus' face. His eyes were pinned intently on hers, but he was remembering the feel of his own mother's hand gripping his in the swamp water.

"The only choice was, try to cross," she went on. "It was February, can you imagine? And the river was frozen, but not all the way across. Mama says the three other people in our group pulled foot running down the riverbank the other direction. But my mama, she just grabbed me up and ran out onto the ice, then jumped from one chunk of ice to another, all the way across. She squeezed me so hard I could barely breathe. I remember that. God must've been watching over us for real! Mama told me she would've jumped right into that freezing river if they came after her, because she couldn't bear to think of me growing up to the life she had." Those last words came out softly, with a quiet wonder. Harriet heard Thaddeus letting out his breath. She shook her head, took a breath and continued, speaking more slowly and calmly now.

"We were both covered in ice when we got across. Mama says my hair looked like somebody broke glass in it, all sharp and shiny like. But when she looked back cross the river, they weren't coming—those men weren't about to risk their lives on our account!" Harriet laughed hollowly. Thaddeus shook his head, his eyes still drilling into hers, his chest hollow in the memory of being pulled through the water, around the corner, hearing the crack of rifles.

"So, what—why didn't you both die from the cold and wet? February? Damn, girl!" Thaddeus knew he had to respond.

"She wasn't sure we were gonna make it either. She went right up to the first house she came to, figured couldn't anything worse happen than if we stayed outside and froze to death. It was a white man opened the door. He just stood there and stared at us. I guess we were a sight, too. Then he called his wife. Mama says the woman took one look and pulled us in through the door, put Mama on a chair as close as possible to the stove. We started to melting. Must've been a sight. Mama's dress, Mama's face and little me all started to dripping, but Mama's back was still covered in ice. Then the woman made her take off all our clothes, and put a big, dry blanket around us. Gave us hot tea to drink and hung the clothes on a line over the stove. I was just as warm and cozy wrapped up inside that blanket watching the steam come off the clothes, and I fell asleep. Mama says she couldn't rightly tell if she was asleep or awake, alive or dead, she was that numb, inside and out. But those white folk put out the word, and don't you know a Railroad Conductor came, and Mama carried me the rest of the way to where we lived for a while in Ohio."

"Whoa, Sister 'Biah did all of that by herself? Dang, I never knew that. She seems so, I don't know, quiet and sweet."

"*Sister* 'Biah?" Harriet nearly exploded with indignation now. "Who the Sam Hill do you think *you* are, Thaddeus Childs? You're not old enough to be calling my mother 'Sister.' *Aunt* Abiah to you, *boy!*" She spat the last word in her anger.

Despite her outrage, Harriet knew in the back of her mind it was natural for Thaddeus to call her mother Sister, he was nearly twenty years old, a trusted agent of the Order, and he attended the same meetings her parents did in Chatham. In those meetings, everyone called one another Brother and Sister.

Thaddeus started to smile down at the feisty fifteen-year-old, but one look at her flashing eyes erased the smile and made him rear back and raise his eyebrows.

"Yes ma'am, Harriet. You're right."

Calling Harriet ma'am only made matters worse. He could see she thought he was making fun of her.

"And if you think my mama is 'quiet and sweet,' you haven't seen her in action, nor heard her mouth. And you better not *ever* call *me* '*soft*,' you hear? You think I'm some fainty little rich white lady?" She sucked her teeth. "I can ride a horse good as you any day. You think I can't be a courier? You'd better think again, Thaddeus Childs!" Harriet's face felt like it was on fire, and she could hear her blood whooshing explosively in her ears. Pulling in a breath past a catch in her throat, she wheeled around and walked as fast as she could without running: away from Thaddeus, away from the Jones house. She felt tears pop into her eyes and blinked hard to keep them from dripping out.

Thaddeus sat paralyzed. Harriet's story was a knife in his heart. He still felt his mother's hand squeezing his, felt his panic as the water surrounded him, and the sound of the bloodhounds—so close, so close—even now the hairs on the back of his neck were standing up.

His mother's face seemed to be in front of him. He shook away the vision and ran his hand along the rough stones to remind himself he was safe, sitting on a wall in Chatham. Then he realized Harriet was moving quickly away from him down the road.

Harriet had been a child when he first met her, but this year something made him stop and pay attention to the spirited girl, now growing into a young woman. He had found himself looking forward to her family's visits to Chatham. The two of them had begun taking walks together, or volunteering to wash plates together. And now he had belittled her and she was storming away from him. He jumped off the wall and jogged after her.

"Harriet!" he shouted.

Harriet heard a little jump in Thaddeus' voice. She hesitated in her step, then resumed her pace. Let him run after her if he wanted to, she was aflame with righteous anger, though she felt it start to cool when she heard him coming. Then she smiled to herself, replaying that instant when he saw the look in her eye – when the smiled disappeared from his face. She had just started to slow down when she felt a hesitant touch on her shoulder and heard his breath coming fast. She stopped and looked up at him, challenge in her eyes, hands propped on her hips, arms akimbo.

"Harriet, I'm sorry, baby-girl," Thaddeus panted. "You're right. I know you can ride. You want me to talk to Brother Jones for you?"

In an instant, Harriet's anger was transformed into an equally burning gladness. She threw her arms around him and buried her face in his chest.

Thaddeus felt relief wash over him, infinitely grateful that he had managed to say the right words. He hugged this precious, sweet being, planting a soft, hidden kiss on the top of her head, holding his lips in contact with her tight braids and rocking gently back and forth. What was he getting himself into?

22

A Telltale Glow ~ October 1853

As spring and summer passed, the flood of refugees kept Thaddeus busy. Harriet was consumed by the work of the Elgin Settlement. Though they barely saw one another, one evening in October found both of them waiting outside a large wooden house in Chatham, its windows glowing with yellow-orange lamplight as a meeting went on inside. The subject of the meeting was a slave who had been captured on Canadian soil. The slave catchers had crossed into Canada to catch the man and carried him back to the United States. In Detroit some men from the Order had managed to release the man and get him to Chatham, but the Americans then went to court, and the captive was arrested pending the court's decision. Tonight's meeting was making plans for the court case and for the possibility of having to break the prisoner out of the jail if the court decided for the slave catchers.

When the meeting was over, Thaddeus was to ride to Detroit to share the plans with the brothers and sisters at the Second Baptist Church. Harriet was waiting with him for the meeting to end. Dried leaves rustled under the restless feet of the tall, chestnut horse tied beside them. The smell of autumn's sweet decay was in the still-warm air.

With Harriet's parents in the meeting, her family would sleep at the Jones' house, where they had left Zach. Tomorrow they would do some shopping and pick up the mail before going home. She had come out with them to the meeting secretly hoping Thaddeus would be there. Her parents hadn't objected, which surprised her.

Standing with them was Ezekiel, now fourteen years old. William Parker had brought his son to keep him company on the ride home that night.

Zeke still looked like a young boy, Harriet was taller and already more a woman than a girl in her body. Zeke's short, wiry body and crackling voice embarrassed him, and in vain he tried to hide his crush on Harriet. Harriet was fond of Zeke, but in an older sister sort of way. She also found herself pricked by envy of his every day, routine access to his parents, especially Eliza. She had been forlorn when they moved out of her house.

To make matters worse, Ezekiel always talked as if he had actually been old enough to bear arms in the Christiana battle just because he handed his father a pitchfork to wave at Gorsuch and Kline from the landing. He had been in the upstairs rooms behind where his father confronted the slave catchers and been witness to the events, a fact for which Harriet found it difficult to excuse him. Although he was younger than Harriet, she knew his parents included him in their evening conversations about the news from the anti-slavery movement in the States. They subscribed to several abolitionist newspapers, which her own parents sometimes borrowed from them. On those occasions, they often called on Harriet to read articles aloud to them.

Now Zeke was going on about something he had learned from those newspapers and his parents' conversations.

"They get most of their money from free black folks, but you think any of us are making any decisions?" Ezekiel's indignation was nearly a visible steam coming off his body. "Frederick Douglass, Henry Bibb, Sojourner Truth: those are the folks out on the stump, inspiring the audiences, raising the money, and Garrison doesn't even have a black boy working in his office to empty the garbage. No lie!" Harriet suspected Zeke of repeating his parents' words from memory. But his words still provoked her to think. "Thing is, the white abolitionists, they're mostly interested in saving their souls. *We're* mostly interested in saving lives—we're after *freedom* and *respect* and *human dignity*," he emphasized heatedly.

"I hear you," Thaddeus said, winking at Harriet as he let the boy know he took him seriously.

"You hear about the Liberia thing?" Ezekiel switched to a new topic.

"What Liberia thing?"

"You know Liberia's a country in Africa, right?"

"Man, who do you think you're talking to?" Thaddeus laughed at the boy. "Liberia is where the American Colonization folk want to send all the free blacks so the only black folk in America would be slaves."

"Yeah, but..." Momentarily deflated, Ezekiel, paused, then continued, "but there's also black folks talking about moving over there. The Black Conventions talk about it all the time. Man by the name of Martin Delany is one of them. *Smart* black man." He tilted his head up slightly. "I want to go to Africa," he added. "It's our homeland."

Now that's Zeke's own idea, thought Harriet. No way William and Eliza would be thinking about deserting the fight against slavery!

"Homeland? Man, Africa's none of my homeland! The Dismal Swamp is my homeland, if I've got *any* homeland." Thaddeus paused and glanced at Harriet, who was looking at him quizzically, hearing the hot passion in his voice. She'd never heard him talk about the Swamp as home, he'd only talked about it as a place he'd been glad to leave behind. Come to think of it, he had talked very little about his life there. As to herself, she had no question: the Elgin Settlement was *her* homeland!

"If free black folk want to move out," Thaddeus continued with urgency, even anger in his voice, "why they don't move here and join the Order, contribute to the cause? How are you going to want to leave your people in slavery and just bail yourself out? No, man, my loyalty goes to the black man here and now. Black folk"—he glanced at Harriet again—"free and equal right here, right now!" Then he softened his voice, looking at the hurt on Ezekiel's face, realizing maybe he should go easier on the youngster. "No lie, though, I *would* like to see Africa. See where my great-grands and them came from. The old folk in the Swamp used to say we were living near like how they lived in Africa before they got kidnapped."

Harriet's fists clenched, listening to Thaddeus' intensity. She agreed with him. "Thaddeus is right, Zeke. Our fight is right here. I've got no problem if someone wants to go somewhere and be free. That's what our families did, right? I read about Delany and the Black Conventions. Saw where some folks are thinking about going to Haiti, too. Now, *that* could be sweet sure enough. I know I'd like to see Haiti! But hear me now, the beauty of Elgin is, not only that we're free and not only that we're creating a model of dignity and self-sufficiency anybody can be proud of," she continued, conscious that now she was repeating words she'd heard grown-ups use to describe her community. "The biggest thing to me is, we're not turning our backs on our people left behind in slavery. That meeting in there, and Thaddeus here ready to ride tonight, both testify to that!"

Harriet was gratified to see Thaddeus nodding. She went on, because something else Zeke had said was rubbing a sore spot.

"But back up a minute, boy, why'd you call Delany a '*smart* black man.' Smart compared to who? You calling somebody stupid? You know sometimes a man with a right smart education can't find his knife when it gets in the wrong pocket, while an uneducated man knows how to take nothing and make something from it!"

Thaddeus heard the defiance creep into Harriet's voice and listened for Ezekiel's response. A small smile playing on his lips as he thought to himself: *the boy better not mess with Harriet!*

"Well, you know," Zeke's voice shook defensively,

"Delany's got an education. He's a doctor. He even went to Africa to scout out a place for people to move to. He writes all the time. I mean, the man's brilliant, you can't deny that. So, yeah, I guess he's smarter than you or me for sure."

Thaddeus jumped in, his voice in teaching mode. "Zeke, you're not thinking you're supposed to respect a man with an education more than a man without, are you?"

"Or woman." Harriet added, nodding.

Zeke was shaking his head in confusion.

"Or woman," Thaddeus agreed. He went on with his lesson. "The other day I met a man in Detroit who was on a speaking tour in the Northern states. The man escaped from slavery two years ago, and he's been on the stump talking about his experience, raising money for Garrison and them. Now the Garrison people have started to criticize his speeches, telling him to stop sounding so smart and educated. They tell him to 'use his own voice,' like he's supposed to be an ignorant black fool with no thoughts in his thick head." Heat was back in Thaddeus' voice, and Zeke looked like he was shrinking into himself. "White folks are scared to see that black folks are just as smart as them. That man says those white abolitionists disrespect him nearly as much as his old master. Says black folks ought to be heading up *all* the abolition organizations."

Harriet was nodding vigorously. "Education is good, now, Zeke, I'm not knocking it," she continued. "You *know* I aim to get just as much of it as I possibly can. But all of us standing here right now are supposed to know that just because a person can't read doesn't mean they're not smart." Harriet was aware that she was defending her parents, Thaddeus' parents, and even Thaddeus a couple years ago. None of them knew how to read before they reached Canada.

"That man spoke the truth," Ezekiel piped up, jumping past Harriet's words to redeem himself in Thaddeus' eyes. "Black folks *should* be heading up the abolition movement.

Who would be free themselves must strike the blow." Harriet knew he was repeating the words of Fred Douglass. "We're the slaves, why should white folk be telling the man how to talk?"

"Boy, a wagon makes the loudest noise when it's going out empty," snorted Thaddeus, deciding it was time to take the boy off his high horse. "You need to use your brain before you start flapping your mouth. White folks are not leading us! Who you think is inside there?" He tilted his head sharply toward the window. "Who you think I'm taking their letter to tonight? Who you think is running the whole entire Underground Railroad? White folk? Shoot, your own daddy and mama are both better leaders than Garrison!" He snorted. "There's a whole bunch of stuff going down that those white folk haven't got the first notion about. Get your blame head out of the clouds, man, Harriet's right. Don't get carried away thinking somebody's smarter than you because they're more educated!" Then he added, "Nor you smarter than them."

Harriet started to punch her fist in the air, but then her eyes fell on Zeke, who was looking like he'd been slapped. She knew her friend worshipped Thaddeus: bigger, older and already a soldier. She pulled her fist back down, but her unexpected motion had made Thaddeus' horse jerk his head back.

"Whoa, man, easy there!" exclaimed Thaddeus, equally to Harriet and the horse. Harriet turned her face into the horse's neck and stroked it to calm him, hiding her jubilation from Zeke. Not so long ago, Thaddeus spoke to her in the same tones he had used talking to Zeke: like a teacher. But tonight he treated her as an equal, and the insides of her chest were feeling too big for her rib cage right now. How she yearned to be the one jumping on the tall chestnut's back to take off swiftly through the night! Uncle James had told her she was still too young, that she would have to swear initiation before she became a courier. She bit her lip and vowed to herself that the time would soon come.

Just then the door opened, spilling a shaft of lamplight onto the flat stones leading to the doorstep. The three young people turned toward it. William Parker walked through the door and shut it behind him.

"Zeke," he said, squinting through the dark to make out his son's profile, "the meeting's not quite over, but we need to leave now. The other items on the agenda don't need me, and we've got a long ride and a working day tomorrow." Mr. Parker nodded at Thaddeus and Harriet. Zeke, relieved to be cut loose from a tongue-lashing, disappeared behind the house to get their horses.

"Thaddeus, how you doing? Haven't seen you in a good while. You've got a long night ahead of you tonight, young man!"

"Yes sir, Mr. Parker," Thaddeus responded with a smile. "Doing fine, thank you. How's the farm coming? I'll have to stop in and see it next time I'm in Buxton. Please tell Mrs. Parker howdy for me."

Zeke returned leading their two horses and handed one set of reins to his father.

"I'll do that, son," Parker said to Thaddeus. "Ride well tonight. Good night, Harriet."

"Good night, Mr. Parker, good night, Zeke," the two of them said in chorus as father and son mounted their horses and set off toward Buxton.

The rhythmic clop-clop of the horses' feet on the night ground faded into silence, leaving Harriet and Thaddeus standing alone among the soft rustling of the leaves in the breeze. Harriet's heart started beating faster and she felt her lips and fingertips start to tingle. She stared at the ground in front of her feet as if there was something to see down there. Thaddeus took a breath, and she looked up at him. She was startled when she saw the intensity in his eyes. Her lips parted and her breath came faster.

Neither of them said anything. Thaddeus leaned in closer and reached out his arm to circle Harriet's waist. She melted into him, resting her head against his warm chest, where she could hear his heart thumping as fast as her own. She put her arm around his waist, almost holding her breath at her own daring. Her heart was singing and she was afraid to speak for fear that any sound would break the spell. She felt his fingers squeeze her waist just above her hip. Her breath caught.

"Thaddeus," she whispered.

"Sweet Harriet," he murmured. His hand moved to her shoulder and stroked her neck and back, causing the nerves of her skin to thrill in a wave from her scalp down her whole body all the way to her toes. Then he spoke with a gruff humor, "Hey, you're not a little girl any more, you know that?" She could hear his smile. She pulled back and looked up into his face, his smiling lips, his eager eyes. A shy, hesitant smile trembled on her own lips.

"I know," she said, feeling breathless and awkward. She squeezed her hand on his hip, not knowing how to move or what to say. Thank you, God, she thought, not sure if she was blaspheming, but desiring this more than anything she ever had before.

"Come, let's walk," Thaddeus shifted, taking her hand in his and starting very slowly up the road away from the house. He was suddenly aware that he had wanted to do this for nearly a year, but now that it was happening he was nervous and had no plan or idea how or what he should do. His body burned with urgency, but his heart was equally determined to be gentle, kind and respectful.

As they ambled, their arms went around one another's waists again, Harriet's head leaning against Thaddeus's shoulder. Neither one of them spoke: neither one knew what to say. Finally Harriet broke the silence.

"I wish you didn't have to leave for Detroit tonight."

The words seemed a thin trickle compared to the crashing waterfall of her emotions, but that was exactly what she was thinking at that moment. The trip to and from Detroit always took several days, and suddenly she didn't want Thaddeus gone.

"I know," Thaddeus agreed, but at the same time, he was glad that he'd soon have to take off with speed on the horse, because the intensity of his feelings scared him. "I won't be gone but a few days," he added, though that was little comfort, Harriet would no longer be in Chatham when he returned.

They fell silent until they heard voices talking over one another from inside the house, signaling that the meeting was ending. They turned back toward the house, wanting to be standing by the horse when people started coming out—especially Abiah and Thomas. But before they moved far, Harriet felt Thaddeus pull her to him by her shoulders. She looked up as he leaned down, and suddenly his warm, soft lips were on hers. She pressed her mouth to his, eyes closed, her whole body singing.

Abruptly, he straightened up, taking her hand. He pulled her quickly back to the horse, away from the shaft of light that once again reached out onto the stone walkway as the door opened. Harriet was panting, glad to know that while she could see her parents in the light, it would take a moment for their eyes to adjust to the night darkness. She felt certain if they looked now they would see the telltale glow of Thaddeus' lips on hers.

23

People's Justice

Early the next morning, Harriet came out of her sleep abruptly. She heard whispers from the place Abiah and Thomas were sleeping across the room from her in the Jones' house. That's what had awakened her—there was a strained, urgent and fearful tone to the whispering.

"What's happening?" She sat up, rubbing her eyes.

Thomas and Abiah suddenly became quiet. They looked at each other and seemed to nod, then they told her: they had just gotten word that the prisoner they'd been discussing at the meeting last night was to go before the judge today. There wouldn't be time to carry out the legal plan they'd sent with Thaddeus to the Order in Windsor and Detroit. And worst of all, the judge who would hear the case was notorious for judgments that went against black people. It seemed very likely that he would turn the man over to the slave catchers who had illegally followed him into Canada.

They told Harriet the details, although she already knew them from Thaddeus. Robert Lindsay escaped from a plantation in South Carolina and had just come across the British Canadian border when the three men caught up with him. According to law, he should have automatically been free once he stepped across the border, but the slave catchers were claiming they captured him on the US side of the unmarked border before accidentally wandering onto the Canadian side. Something would have to be done this morning if he the freedom the man had won was not to be snatched from him.

Harriet slipped out of bed, hugging her robe around her and went with her parents to sit with the Joneses and a few others who had gathered in the kitchen to patch together an emergency plan. She listened closely without speaking until they were trying to choose someone for a critical role in the scheme they had worked out.

"I'll do it," she interrupted as they were considering possibilities. They turned to her in surprise.

"No, Harriet, you're too young!" said Abiah, glancing fearfully at Thomas for support.

"That's exactly why I'm the right person to do it!" Harriet exclaimed, her heart thudding in rapid rhythm. "They won't suspect anything until it's too late!" She knew she could do this. She was grateful that Zeke had gone home with his father the night before! She was sure if he'd been there they wouldn't even have considered sending her. Zeke was a boy, after all, and he would have leapt at the chance to do this.

Harriet could barely breathe as she listened to the argument that ensued. To her great surprise, several people, including Gunsmith Jones, agreed with her.

"Let the girl do it if she's willing," he said quietly, putting one hand on top of Abiah's as he spoke. "We don't have many options, and only a few hours to put a plan into action. And Harriet's right that if one of us tries to do this, we will be stopped before we can get to him."

Harriet breathed a silent thanks, but from then on her heart continued its rapid tattoo, her breath coming in shallow gusts.

Three hours later a boisterous crowd had gathered outside the police station, where Mr. Lindsay was in jail awaiting the guards who were to escort him to the courthouse across the street. The Vigilance Committee had done a quick and efficient job of spreading the word very quickly throughout Chatham, and scores of people, black and white, were loudly expressing their anger at the fact that this man was in their town's jail. The British Empire had abolished slavery long ago! It was wrong to turn this man over to his captors! Set him free! They shouted.

Harriet stood quietly beside the door apart from the crowd. Every nerve in her body seemed to be vibrating, but she looked calm and unthreatening to the outside eye—a young girl with a basket of food over her arm, waiting for someone.

A member of the Vigilance Committee stood near the jail window, looking in every few seconds. After one last glance, in a quick movement he took off his cap and scratched his head. Mrs. Lovejoy, who Abiah and Harriet had stayed with when they first arrived in Chatham, then appeared from around the corner of the building, where she had been standing watching him. She marched determinedly up the stairs to the jailhouse without even glancing at Harriet, opened the door and strode in. Harriet slipped in behind her.

At the back of the room, Mr. Lindsay had just been brought out of his cell, a policeman gripping tightly to his arm. Mrs. Lovejoy began shouting loudly and emotionally at the sergeant behind the desk about someone stealing a harness from her horse barn. While the sergeant put out his hands in a "calm down" gesture and struggled to get her to hear that she must come back later with her complaint, Harriet walked directly toward the prisoner and the policeman holding him.

She felt bolder now. It was obvious that the judge and the police had underestimated the Vigilance Committee's information network—only two officers were in the station! With the judge having quietly called the case for this morning, they thought no one in the town would know until it was too late to mount any opposition.

The officer holding Mr. Lindsay was looking rapidly back and forth, from the loud confrontation between the sergeant and Mrs. Lovejoy on one side to this young girl approaching him with a basket. He held up his other hand to signal her to stop.

"Excuse me, sir," Harriet's nervous voice came out sounding thin, shaky and very young. "We just wanted to give the prisoner some bread and cheese to hold him through the trial."

The officer was momentarily confused at her request. He looked again at his sergeant, who by now was completely distracted by a very loud and angry Mrs. Lovejoy. Just then, Mrs. Lovejoy clutched her chest and let out a high-pitched wail, followed by a long, gurgling moan and collapsed on the floor near Harriet's feet. The officer instinctively let go of Lindsay to try to catch the falling woman. Harriet darted in and grabbed the prisoner's elbow, pulling and pointing him toward the door.

"Run, Mr. Lindsay," she whispered, continuing to tug at him. Lindsay jumped forward and threw himself through the door. Harriet ran behind him, bread and cheese flying out of the basket.

Before the confused police could react, Harriet and Lindsay were out in the crowd. One man threw a coat over him, another put a hat on his head, and in seconds he'd become invisible. Thomas appeared beside Harriet and linked his arm through hers, guiding her swiftly away from the crowd down a narrow lane between some nearby houses. By the time the police came out the door, the crowd was cheering jubilantly and the prisoner was nowhere to be seen.

◇

Back at the Jones' house, Harriet sat drinking hot tea with a shaking hand. Her body felt as though she'd been running for miles with no sleep, but her chest was filled with pride and happiness. She'd done it! Thanks to her (as well as Mrs. Lovejoy and the rest of the Vigilance Committee volunteers) Robert Lindsay was a free man! She couldn't help grinning up at Abiah and Thomas, Uncle James and Aunt Emily, who were all regarding her with a mixture of pride and relief.

Thaddeus would have to admit that she was ready to be a courier now.

24

The Order of the Men of Oppression ~ June 1854

Harriet had few opportunities to see Thaddeus that winter and spring, but a June night found them riding together. Just before they reached Windsor, when the chilly early summer night had reached its full moonless dark, Thaddeus turned Harriet over to a young man who was waiting for them in the woods alongside the road. Harriet slipped off her horse and followed Isaac to the river for the crossing to Detroit. Thaddeus and the horses would be waiting for her at Miss Peggy's house, where he stayed whenever he was in Windsor. Isaac would guide her there on her return. Tonight, Harriet was to be initiated into the secret organization, the African-American Mysteries: the Order of the Men of Oppression. She would be tested on the codes and passwords Thaddeus had drilled into her. Beyond the codes, Thaddeus had refused to tell her what to expect.

She'd never been so far from home, never been in a rowboat, never been alone with a complete stranger in a strange place. Now she held herself still and strained her eyes nervously in the dark night. A few lights flickered on the far side of the river, which seemed an awful distance away. The water was as opaque and smooth as the ink in the teacher's bottle at school, but it wasn't contained in a safe place. If she fell into it, she knew she would die.

Was the Ohio River this wide? How could her mother have crossed it with a baby in her hands? She shuddered and tried allowing herself to be mesmerized by the rhythm of the oars slipping silently and surely into the seductive blackness, then almost as silently slicing up and away from the water's sucking grasp. She kept feeling like she needed to pee. She'd never felt such utter fear, such a complete and unnerving lack of control over her own existence. Yet at the same time she felt a soaring determination and excitement that tonight, she, too, would become a soldier in the war for freedom.

The boat scraped softly on the muddy riverbank. The young oarsman jumped out, bare feet splashing in the shallow water, and pulled the little wooden vessel up into the bushes after helping Harriet scramble onto the shore. She was momentarily relieved to have earth under her feet again, but in the next moment she was overwhelmed by the knowledge that she stood on the soil of slavery. The very thought threatened to loosen her bowels. The Order was very strong in Detroit, but still, if the wrong people discovered her as she moved through this unfamiliar city, her whole life could take a horrific turn. She reassured herself with the thought that Thaddeus would not have sent her into danger, and followed Isaac silently through the strange, cramped, dark streets, peering nervously behind buildings and into alleys, passing small animals foraging behind the darkened houses, and all the while pushing back panic, until they stopped at what she hoped was the Grand Charter Lodge. It was a heavy, peeling wooden door on a level with the deserted street. Isaac knocked softly in a pattern that must be code. When a woman opened the door, Harriet looked around and realized the youth had vanished. She was trembling.

"What do you seek?" asked the woman in a hushed voice. She had a dark face on which a scar ran like the track of a tear from her left eye to the corner of her mouth. Her eyes held no welcome, her lips no smile. Her aproned body, though small, filled and blocked the half-open doorway. What if the woman didn't let her in? What if she was in the wrong place? How would she get home? Then she focused on remembering the words Thaddeus had taught her.

"Deliverance," she whispered shakily.

"How do you expect to get it?"

"By my own efforts." Harriet heard humming in her ears but felt sure these were the questions and answers she had memorized.

"Have you faith?"

"I have hope." Her voice came a bit steadier now.

The door opened wider, the woman stood aside and Harriet stepped in, her heart pounding, her spirit soaring. Silently, the woman led Harriet down narrow wooden stairs into a cellar that smelled of earth and dampness and sweat. No lamp or candle was lit down there. Harriet moved with hesitation, the woman's hand gripping her just above her elbow, guiding her forward. She could hear breathing and shuffling sounds of people moving. Suddenly, she jumped as other hands touched her face and shoulders. They put a blindfold over her eyes. She felt a heavy iron chain settle around her neck and heard a lock click solidly shut. By now she was shaking all over and wondering if everything had gone terribly wrong. Was Isaac a traitor? Had he led to her to the wrong place?

Then a deep voice asked, "Have you ever been on the railroad?"

Harriet's mind momentarily went blank. But it was a familiar question. She took a breath, and the words came back to her with a thin rivulet of relief, a whisper of hope.

"I have been a short distance," she said.

A different voice came then. "Where did you start from?"

These were the questions Harriet had been taught to expect, and slowly the humming in her ears cleared, but she still heard her heartbeat in them, a distinct, steady thumping like a hand striking cow-skin stretched taut on a drum.

"The depot."

A third voice: "Where did you stop?"

"At a place called Safety," Harriet replied quickly. The thumping sounded farther away now.

"Have you a brother there? I think I know him."

"I know you now," responded Harriet. "You traveled on the road."

A silence ensued. That was the last question, Harriet was sure. Was she supposed to say something else? Then she felt fingers untie the blindfold from behind her head. Blinking, she saw that a candle had been lit and was standing on a rough-hewn table to her left. A man wearing a minister's collar was standing before her, his hands slightly in front of him. She watched as he pulled the knuckle of his right forefinger over the knuckle of his left forefinger, his eyes steady on hers. She hesitated, momentarily forgetting which was left and which was right, and then responded by pulling the knuckle of her left forefinger over that of her right.

She licked her dry lips and realized that her mouth was open. She was panting slightly. Excitement was beginning to replace fear. But when she glanced behind the man, she gasped. The walls of the basement were made of hand-cut stones, heavy and dark in the flickering light. Along the walls stood a circle of people. Each of them had a stony, expressionless face that matched the hardness and gloom of the walls. Each of them stared at her, in each of their hands was a whip. Harriet tried to steady her breathing. No one spoke. She stood unsure, trembling again. Two men stepped toward her and she felt her body shrink into itself. But when they reached her, they unlocked the chain, carefully lifted it from her neck, and guided her to a seat at the table with the candle on it.

The minister sat on the opposite side of the table. He was stern, but she thought—hoped—that she could also feel warmth and friendliness within his poised presence. Still, her heart beat in her ears and a cold trickle of sweat made its way down her spine, as the man's rough voice commanded her to recite the official oath. She was afraid she'd forgotten the words, but she had repeated them so often under Thaddeus' tutoring that they came out almost without conscious thought.

"I, Harriet Roberson, do most solemnly and religiously swear and unreservedly vow that I never will confer the degree of confidence on any person, black or white, male or female, unless I am sure they are trustworthy. And should I violate this solemn covenant may my personal interests and domestic peace be blasted and I personally be denounced as a traitor."

She exhaled as if she'd been holding her breath. A part of her mind was trying not to imagine how these fierce-looking people meant to "blast domestic peace."

It was unlikely, since she would be operating strictly in Canada, that she'd ever be in a position to confer a degree on anyone, at least not anytime soon, but she had to swear the same oath as those who were conveying people from slavery to freedom, from South to North across the States. Her whole body was vibrating from the solemnity and weight of this night, this trust that was being placed in her and the responsibility she now would have as a member of this Order, this underground army of the oppressed.

The man she would later learn was named Lambert nodded his approval. He stood now and picked up a small bottle of pale amber liquid from the table. Taking a mouthful of it, he blew a sharp burst of mist successively in each of the four directions, much as they did at home before starting construction on a new house, and before other important events and ceremonies. He then took a swallow, and passed the flask to the next person. Harriet saw each person touch it to their lips, taking a taste before passing it along. When the last person in the circle had taken some, it was passed to Harriet, who, a bit startled to be included, put it to her lips and allowed a few drops into her mouth. When she swallowed the burning fluid, tears sprang to her eyes and she coughed. The others nodded, smiled, even laughed a little.

For a quick moment, she imagined that her father, Jacob, was proudly watching her right now.

Then a woman's voice came out of the darkness and the image disappeared. "May the Lord bless and keep us all this night and every day and night as we carry out His sacred work, and may He especially watch over the safety of our new young soldier as she carries out His work amongst our Canadian brethren and sistren."

There was a chorus of "Amens" and then she heard various voices saying things like "Girl, you're one of us now." "Welcome!" "Relax yourself and let us break bread together!"

The circle of people who lined the walls of the room, barely discernible at that distance in the dim light shed by the one lonely candle, now began to waver and break up, as each person came forward to welcome Harriet and in his or her own way said a few words about the seriousness of her commitment and her new duties. The whips had disappeared. Harriet found herself wondering if these fear-inspiring people would someday become familiar to her, and if she was really grown enough and strong enough to be worthy of them.

The room came alive. More candles were lit until the room swayed with light and the forbidding walls once again looked like ordinary stone. Food appeared, coming down the stairs on large trays, one of which, Harriet saw with surprise, was carried by a young white woman, not much older than herself, her long coppery braids partially covered by a green headscarf. The tantalizing aroma of the soup made her realize how hungry she was. She watched as two women began ladling the fragrant liquid into bowls and mugs, giving one to each person, along with chunks of bread.

Harriet gratefully accepted her portion. As she sipped the steaming soup, warmth began to spread into her body, and she became aware that she had been icy with tension ever since she had left Thaddeus in the woods. She felt relaxation begin to flow through her, accompanied by a growing sense of joy and strength. She had done it! And as she looked again at her new brothers and sisters, she felt a deep passion rising in her for their common struggle for freedom. She smiled, wishing she could hug each and every person in the room.

But by the time she had crept back through the dark streets with young Isaac, made the return trip across the river and been admitted into Miss Peggy's darkened house where a smiling Thaddeus answered the door, Harriet only felt utter, limp exhaustion. She fell into Thaddeus' hug and was asleep almost before she settled into her bed.

25

A New Courier Rides Home

When Harriet awoke the next morning, Thaddeus was moving around the room. Her eyes took in bowls of steaming oat porridge, a pitcher of frothy warm cow's milk and a small bowl of bright red strawberries on the rough table in the middle of the room. She must have woken up when the door was opened and shut by whoever brought the food into the room. Raising herself on her elbow and looking around, Harriet saw that in addition to the narrow pallet on which she had slept, another pallet was along the opposite wall, still showing evidence of Thaddeus's sleeping area: a woolen blanket pushed to one end, his leather saddle bag lying open on top of it. He stood with his back to her, rummaging in the bag. She and Thaddeus had slept in the same room. She wasn't sure how she was supposed to feel about this, but it gave her a secret pleasure.

There was a window above her bed, and another one on the side of the room that had the door in it. Each window was covered with a thin, white curtain edged with delicate, embroidered eyelets, and the low-angled rays of early morning sunlight filtered through. Harriet sat up and stretched, realizing how stiff and achy her muscles were from last night's tension. She almost expected to hear her muscles creak. Smiling self-consciously, she said good morning to Thaddeus.

Turning, he gave her a big, sunny smile.

"Ah, the courier awakens!" His eyes twinkled with pleasure. Harriet's smile broadened, pride and pleasure mingling with her self-consciousness.

"Okay, turn left outside the door and walk alongside the house. The latrine is in the back, and a pitcher of water's here," he pointed at a small table under the window, "for you to wash. Hurry back before the porridge cools off."

After trying unsuccessfully to smooth the wrinkles out of her clothes, Harriet sat on the edge of the bed and pulled on her shoes. She walked out the door into the early morning sun and looked up through the trees into the sky. Birds were calling and flitting about, getting down to their usual business of finding food. It was a normal, pleasant, early summer morning, though for Harriet it felt anything but normal.

Was it only yesterday morning she had woken up in her own house, in the familiar bed in the corner under the roof, where she had slept covered by the same worn and faded quilt since she was eleven years old? Where she had stared at the intricate designs of spider webs in the rafters and imagined this day for so long she couldn't remember?

She wished for a looking glass to examine the changes she must be able to see in herself today. Because this morning she felt transformed, as though crossing that night river had permanently divided her life into two different geographies. As though she was now in a different country, from which she would never return.

She felt a mixture of pride and awe as memories returned of the night before: the faces in that dark cellar, the sense of destiny at the realization that she was now one of them. She felt a little afraid that she was a fraud. Those were people who had risked their lives, who had lost loved ones, who had been through she could only imagine what trials and tribulations. She was young, raised in freedom, protected and sheltered. Did she deserve the confidence they were putting in her?

She had a thousand questions for Thaddeus. When she was sitting across from him, blowing on the still-hot porridge, she asked him why he hadn't warned her what the ceremony would be like so she wouldn't be so frightened. He looked up from his porridge directly into her eyes.

"Harriet, everyone in the Order went through initiation like that. I guess if a person has run away from slavery, it's not as scary for them as it was for you." He paused, remembering his own initiation. He had met some of the people before, had crossed the river before. "How could that initiation be scary when you've endured slavery and been chase by bloodhounds? I wasn't scared. Those were the people that guided me to Canada. I guess I felt a little shy and nervous. I was really young back then," he admitted, elongating time as only youth can, "and I knew I was in the presence of great people. And plus, I swore not to reveal the details of the ceremony. You too, right?" Harriet nodded her assent, feeling somewhat chastened as she thought of Thaddeus, at about the same age she was now, making his way across hundreds and hundreds of miles of unknown, treacherous country. She felt embarrassed of the fear she'd felt traveling the short distance across the river and through Detroit last night.

Looking at Thaddeus' unfocused eyes, Harriet could see he was remembering his own initiation. He continued, "I guess it was good for you to be frightened." His eyes focused again, looking sharply at her. "It was good for you to feel the chains and see the whips. It was good you weren't certain. You got a tiny little taste of what we endure in slavery. Always feeling a threat looming over us." His eyes drifted again, and again Harriet felt her inexperience. He looked back at her. "Girl, you know you're lucky you've never been whipped. You're even luckier that you've never seen someone you love bleeding under the whip, or torn from the family to sell. So it was good for you to feel that fear for a moment."

Harriet imagined the scenes Thaddeus was describing, and thought he might be right. But it felt like he was deliberately being harsh, distancing himself from her. His next words were gentler.

"Don't worry, Harriet, the people in that room, they'll give their life for you if that's called for. And you'll give yours for them, too. They're your family now. You and I are part of something great and powerful. Can you imagine? A web that stretches right across the whole continent! The Order's got organizers across Canada and the United States, and far south as Mexico. And contact with freedom fighters all over the world—Cuba, Haiti, Jamaica, Barbados, South America, England, even Africa—Sierra Leone and Liberia." His eyes sparkled. "And all of it invisible to the eyes of the enemy."

Thaddeus' voice grew more excited. He put his forearms on the table on either side of his food and leaned closer to Harriet.

"Hey, did you hear? I found out yesterday that Frederick Douglass is coming to the Dawn Settlement in August to celebrate Emancipation Day! And I think someone from the West Indies might be there, too."

His excitement was contagious. Harriet's whole being felt elevated because he had used the words "family" and "you and I" moments ago. She made a mental note to read the newspapers more, so she could know the things Thaddeus knew.

"Really?" she nearly squealed. "Boy, you don't know: I *really* want to see that man! There's two people in this world I've been wanting to meet ever since I could start reading those papers. Frederick Douglass and Mary Ann Shadd. But I never thought Mr. Douglass would come anywhere near close enough."

"I know. I hear you!" Thaddeus responded, his eyes gleaming. "But listen, girl, we better finish this food and get moving. We've got all day to talk, but we don't want to be riding in the night if we can help it."

After they ate, they carried the tray of empty dishes out the door and around to a doorway at the back of the house. Thaddeus introduced Harriet to Miss Peggy, owner of the house. She was a brown-skinned woman wearing a bright red gingham apron and matching headscarf, who greeted

Harriet with a smile and a hug. "Honey, any time you're in Windsor, you're welcome here. No advance notice necessary! Just think of this house as your home away from home." She looked over to Thaddeus, nodded and smiled again, "You all have a safe trip back home. George is in the barn getting the horses ready for you."

"Thank you again, Miss Peggy." Thaddeus' smiled. "Next time I come, I'll do my best to bring some of them sweet raspberries for you."

"Thank you, Miss Peggy," Harriet spoke shyly, immediately warming to this woman. "I appreciate the bed and the food. I hope to see you again soon." She found herself wondering again about waking up in the same room with Thaddeus. She decided that as brother and sister in the struggle, the arrangement was considered acceptable, and it came to her as a certainty that Miss Peggy was also a member of the Order.

The two young comrades relished the trip back, though it was long and tiresome. They knew that from now on they would each make the same trip often, but rarely if ever would they be making it together. As evening fell, they reached the fork in the road where they had to part, Thaddeus going on to Chatham, and Harriet turning toward Elgin and home.

Unlike the time Thaddeus rode this route at a gallop, Harriet sat slackly as her horse plodded wearily out of the woods and along the row of scattered houses towards home, horse and rider deeply tired after a long trip. A melancholy-sweet feeling had hold of her since parting from Thaddeus, which deepened into a sense of loneliness as dusk came on. Then home came into view, and the feeling vanished like the smoke easing up out of the chimney, promising food cooking in the hearth, and the welcome sound of the dog barking until he made out who was approaching.

The dog wagged his whole body around them as Harriet slipped wearily off the mare. She led the horse stiffly around back and rubbed her down. Then she climbed into the loft and threw down a pile of hay, pumped water into a bucket and left her mount munching slowly and gratefully in the barn while she trudged to the back door.

Her stepfather stood in the doorway, her mother just behind him, gladness in their eyes. Her stepfather slid his right forefinger over the knuckle of his left. Startled, Harriet looked into his eyes and saw a twinkle appear. Automatically, she slid her left forefinger over her right knuckle, but she was aware that her mouth had also dropped open. Thomas opened his arms and she stepped into his hug, then into her mother's. Zach bounced up and down behind them. Still startled by Thomas' action, she wordlessly set down her pack and went back through the door to wash up.

When she came in the second time, she had found at least a portion of her tongue.

"You...?" The rest of the question remained unspoken. She dropped into a chair and leaned her elbows on the table, holding her tired head in her hands, but looking searchingly at her stepfather. Zach's father had come into Harriet's life when she was only a little older than Zach was now. She combed her memory for any talk about what Thomas had been through before he reached them, but found nothing. He must have talked with Abiah about his past, but Harriet realized with chagrin that she had never even asked him anything about his own story.

"Well," Thomas said, "I was only a First-Degree Captive. When you're on the Railroad, to travel from one safe house to another you've got to know the signals and codes—the people have got to know they can trust you." He looked into her eyes. His voice became solemn. "I'm very proud of you, Harriet, remember that." He smiled slowly.

"I'm so proud of you, sweetheart," her mother added. "Even if I'm scared for you, too. I don't know any secret signs. When I came, they did things a little differently. I never traveled by myself, except crossing the river. They just handed me off from one Conductor to another after I got to Ohio."

Harriet was quiet, mentally confronting the courage of these two people she had always taken for granted. She remembered her fear on the boat last night, her disbelief at the thought of her mother jumping from one floating piece of ice to another across abysses of deep, black water. She felt overwhelmed, and put her head down on the table.

"Meanwhile, forget all that for a while: come eat," her mother said brightly. "You must be ready to eat a cow!"

"I am!" piped up Zachary.

"Yes, I am," admitted Harriet, looking up gratefully as her mother set a plate of steaming food in front of her. Her eyes fell on Zach, who at six years old did not really understand any of this conversation. She wondered if he would someday be looking at his parents with the same sense of wonder she felt right now.

◇

1964 - Mississippi

William and Henry Ingram, Jimmy's uncles, move silently through woods they know like the backs of their hands, their hunting rifles on their shoulders. The Civil Rights kids are out again tonight, knocking on doors, talking to people about joining the literacy class. When they first got here, the churchmen shook their heads. They wouldn't last long, these young students from the cities. They didn't know what they were getting into. Mississippi is serious business.

After the march and beatings and the jail time, several of the kids fled, as expected. But not all of them. So, William and Henry and their brother deacons decided to keep an eye on them. Can't deny they've got guts. It looks like every time white folks knock them down, they get back up, wipe off the blood, brush off the dirt, and start back to meeting, singing, knocking on doors. And people are coming out. Tired as hell of being treated like dogs, or worse. They've started attending meetings, started showing up at the courthouse to register to vote, started joining the literacy and constitution class when the registrar tests them and sends them home.

But those fool Civil Rights workers have this crazy idea about nonviolence. Do they think white folks are gonna be nonviolent? Are they fool enough to go on about nonviolence after they dug up those three kids' bodies?

"Well, if they've got the nerve to do this, we've got no choice but to protect their silly butts. Can't let them go out and get themselves all killed. They're doing what needs to be done."

And so it is decided, and now they shadow the nonviolent, foolish, courageous Civil Rights workers. The young folks don't have the sense to arm themselves for their own self-protection, so the deacons shadow them in the woods, carrying their hunting rifles. Tonight is the Ingram brothers' turn.

26

Don't Look Back

Abiah folded her hands on the table in front of her and gazed at her daughter as she ate. Harriet was her child, yet no longer a child. Dust from the long ride still coated her clothes and headscarf. Harriet was absorbed in the food and in her own thoughts; Abiah could look intently at her without being noticed. Those almond shaped eyes, turned slightly down at the outside corners, the straight, even teeth: Abiah saw Jacob in her. She felt the emptiness and pain that hid in the middle of her chest and came forward when she thought of the past. Would she ever be free of it? Abiah knew she hadn't spoken to Harriet much about her father. By the time she was old enough, Thomas was around, and Abiah hadn't resolved in her own mind how to talk about the man that had come before him in her life. In truth, she hadn't resolved how to even think about Jacob, her emotions wavering between the grief that she recognized and gave a name to, and a feeling of guilt that she buried away and tried to conceal from herself. When these feelings arose she would push them down, gaze at Thomas and Zachary, look around at her home, her community and her life, and remind herself to feel happy in the present instead of lingering in the pain of the past.

But now, looking at Harriet at this momentous crossroad in her young life, Abiah couldn't avoid thinking of Jacob. Harriet was nearly as old as she herself had been when Jacob came into her life and the two set in motion the events that led to Harriet's life being here in Buxton.

Of course, she had told Thomas a little about Jacob. But she'd never expressed the depth of their love. She'd never revealed to him that Jacob had sacrificed himself to send her and Harriet out of slavery. She had only told him that

Harriet's father had been sold away from their original home and she had no idea where he was. That she never expected to see him again.

And she'd never told Harriet much more than that, either. A few months after she and Thomas married, Harriet had asked about her father. Abiah told her again that her father's name was Jacob, and that he was a good man. That he had been a wheelwright and driver, tall and handsome, loving. That she had given Harriet his last name: Roberson. And that after they reached Canada, she learned that he had been sold. She didn't know where he was, and Harriet should not expect to ever meet him. It was sad, she had said, but it was the story of so many enslaved families. Harriet was lucky to now have a wonderful new father in her life, and she should love and respect him as her own father. And Harriet did love Thomas.

But now, looking across their own kitchen table at her hungry, weary, strong and undaunted daughter, who was fast becoming a woman in her own right, Abiah felt that Harriet should know more. Eventually, she would have to tell her daughter the whole story. Harriet was taking up the struggle to help others find freedom; she should know what her father did, how he organized to set his daughter free: how he sacrificed his own freedom for hers. For theirs. Harriet deserved to know.

Abiah looked down at her hands. Her fingers were long and slender. She turned them over and looked at the calluses on the palm side, evidence of the life they had carved out of these woods. Then a recurring daydream climbed out of some deep place in her mind. In the daydream, a friend was telling her that a man named Jacob from her Virginia home was in Chatham looking for her, and she felt a physical shock going through her body. Had she betrayed Jacob? Would her love for him reignite if she saw him again?

She pulled herself out of the daydream and looked up

at Thomas. She had to admit to herself that she didn't love Thomas like she had loved Jacob. He had brought happiness, company, comfort and financial stability into her life. Thomas loved Harriet as his own, and Abiah cared for him with a calm, peaceful kind of love. She looked at Zachary and smiled as he hungrily shoveled food into his mouth. She glanced around at this warm, familiar home they had built in the community they helped create: together, as a family — this family. She thought of the bold step Harriet had just taken. And once again, she pushed the thoughts of Jacob back into their hiding place alongside the remembered images of her mother, her sisters and the friends she'd left behind.

Look forward, she told herself. *Do not look back.*

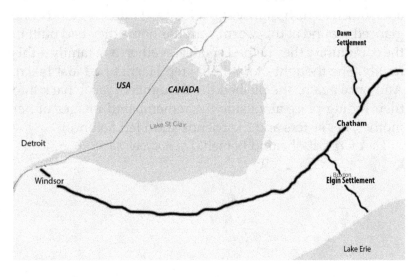

Map of the route Thaddeus and Harriet would have traveled on their courier duties.

27

The Bottom Will Rise and Create a New World ~ July 1854

Abiah, Thomas and Harriet moved everything a body could sit on into the kitchen. In addition to the four straight-back chairs already around the table, they brought in the rocker from the front porch. With a bucket turned upside down and three tree stumps, there was seating for nine people. As neighbors filed in, some took seats, while others leaned against the wall or simply stood. Harriet perched on the third rung of the ladder leading to their upstairs bedrooms, hooking her ankles under the first rung for balance. At other meetings, Harriet had listened invisibly from upstairs. Now she was a participant, though she didn't think she would speak up just yet. Except for Ezekiel Parker, she was the youngest person there.

The warm room hummed with simultaneous conversations about progress in the sawmill, a wandering cow that had been found and brought home, how a young colt was coming along and the best antidotes to the worms that were getting into the cabbages in kitchen gardens. After a while, William Parker cleared his throat and asked, "Will someone start us with a prayer?"

Slowly, the room grew quiet. A short woman stood and bowed her head. The dark skin on her round face was smooth and clear except for sagging eyelids over deep-set, tired eyes.

"Dear Lord, please watch over us as we come together again in this meeting here tonight. Please guide us to speak our minds freely and with respect for one another that we may come to an understanding. Lord, may our meeting be successful and may we continue moving forward in creating a world of unity, love and caring and free of hatred and slavery. May you bless our planning, Lord, and help it to be successful. And as always, dear Lord, remember our brothers and sisters, our mothers and fathers, and our children still in thrall in the land of slavery, and look over them, dear Lord, that they may soon rejoice in freedom. And Lord, look over all dark people who are despised only because of the color of their skin—may we all look forward to the day of true equality. Amen."

There was a soft chorus of "amen." Each person in the room was momentarily in a place of deep feelings and memories, and when they lifted their faces to look at one another again, Harriet could feel a collective consciousness of the importance of the task ahead.

Brother Parker spoke again. "Thank you, Sister Betty. If there is no objection, I volunteer to lead our meeting tonight." Heads nodded, and people murmured their consent.

"As we know, this meeting constitutes the committee assigned to plan Emancipation Day activities. Brother Thomas, could you give us a report from your trip to Chatham?"

Harriet's stepfather pushed himself upright from where he'd been leaning against the wall. He cleared his throat and began to speak. Harriet listened intently.

"Several people were at the meeting in Chatham, and we received confirmation that Mr. Frederick Douglass plans to attend the Emancipation Day celebration at the Dawn Settlement." Thomas was interrupted by an outbreak of side-comments at his mention of the famous abolitionist speaker and former slave. When it subsided, he continued, "Along with Mr. John Scoble. Mr. Scoble is Secretary of the British and Foreign Anti-Slavery Society and he came to Dawn to put in a new management system. They also expect that J.C. Brown will attend, although his illness is making some folk doubt if he'll be able to go. The celebration promises to be quite interesting."

Thomas was interrupted by several voices and some laughter. "Ain't that the truth!" said several people at the same time. And "I wonder what Mr. Douglass will have to say about it." Harriet felt frustrated for not really knowing what they were talking about.

Thomas continued, "As always, celebrations will go on in many towns and cities across the Canadas. A few people from Chatham plan to go to the Dawn on that day, but most will celebrate in Chatham where they're planning a parade, speeches and other festivities. I think the first task of this meeting is to decide if we're going to plan our own Twentieth Anniversary Emancipation celebration here in Buxton, whether we'll attend the one in Chatham, or whether to make the trip to the Dawn Settlement."

Much cross-conversation erupted at that point, and Mr. Parker rapped the table several times. Harriet sat up straighter, feeling her heart beat faster at the prospect of a trip to the Dawn Settlement. She had long heard about Dawn, a sister settlement of former slaves about forty miles away, and had heard its leader Josiah Henson, himself an escapee from slavery, speak in Chatham at last year's Emancipation celebration, which she had attended with her parents. But she'd never been there. She was excited about possibly seeing it with her own eyes.

"I want to hear what Henson and Scoble have to say about where all that money's gone!" Harriet heard Mrs. Little say loudly from her seat near the window. She was a tall, brown woman with unusual green eyes. She had arrived at Elgin three years ago with three children, and the four of them managed their fifty acres remarkably well. Mrs. Little had moved into the community like a strong wind that you couldn't ignore. She had become a good friend of Abiah's, and Harriet liked her. She wondered what money Mrs. Little was talking about.

"Yes! I've heard all kind of talk about what Brother Henson did with that money he raised over in England. I don't know what's the truth."

"Why would they bring that white man Scoble from England? That just isn't right," said Ezekiel, who had been slouching against the wall behind where his father stood and now leaned forward intently. "The people in Dawn are supposed to manage their own affairs, like we do."

"The people in Dawn aren't the ones bad-mouthing Brother Josiah, now," came the voice of one of the older people in the room in a tone of reprimand for Ezekiel.

"No, Brother James, they're not going to go against him. That doesn't mean they approve of what he's doing," replied the chairman. "Ezekiel is my son, but that's not the reason I agree with him. These young people growing up in freedom don't have the fear of the white man like some of us older folk. Sometimes we need to listen to what they have to say, even though they're young and inexperienced."

Harriet felt a moment of irritation at the look of pride that crossed Ezekiel's face, even as his father shot him an eye warning to remain silent while he was defending his son's words. Ezekiel stayed quiet and tried his best to look humble. Harriet raised one eyebrow, not that anyone noticed.

"True, true," came several voices.

Brother James spoke again, "Well, Brother William, I'm not saying you're wrong. But before we go passing judgment, we need to know the facts and hear both sides."

"I would dearly like to hear what J.C. Brown has to say about it," Thomas spoke up again. "He was a trustee at the British American Institute in Dawn for a time before he moved to Chatham, so he knows more than most, and from the inside. I'd like for us to go to the Dawn for Emancipation Day, or at least send a delegation there to try to learn the truth."

"Brothers and sisters," Mrs. Little's voice rang out as commanding as the toll of the bell on the church-school. Everyone turned to look at her. "I agree with Brother Thomas. The controversy about Mr. Henson and Mr. Scoble is the same controversy we've been dealing with for some years now: the controversy between begging and depending upon others or being self-sufficient and depending on our own selves. They call the theme of their school self-sufficiency, but the fact is, those folk *beg*." The last word felt to Harriet like it had catapulted from Mrs. Little's mouth and landed on the table for everyone to look at. Silence surrounded the word. Mrs. Little paused a moment for effect.

"Wilberforce has collapsed already, Dawn is in turmoil, and here are we. The Elgin Settlement. We are a beacon to the rest of them. We are succeeding where they are failing. And why? Because *we don't beg*." The last three words had pauses between them, and Harriet felt the hair on the back of her neck stand up. *"We work!"* Those two words cleaved the silence like the stroke of a sharp axe, followed by shouts of agreement and amen from all corners of the room. She raised her voice to continue, "We're *independent*; we stand on our *own feet*; we use *our own* muscle and *our own* sweat and *our own* brains. I agree with Brother Thomas, and I propose we start from now, in this committee, to plan our trip to the Dawn Settlement in three weeks time."

Harriet had goosebumps all over. Mrs. Little's speech filled her heart with pride, which expanded into a great feeling of love for all the people in this room, and even for the very logs in the walls, whose scars recorded the axes and hammers and sweat of her family and at least half the other people in front of her.

There was more back and forth, but Mrs. Little's words clinched their decision. The meeting agreed to send a delegation to the Dawn, and also to have a celebration at home for most of the community. The home celebration would be an afternoon and evening party, with games, food, music and storytelling, and when the delegation came back, there would be another gathering so everyone could hear from the travelers.

The meeting then addressed itself to planning and assignments. One of the jobs would be Harriet's: she was to go to Chatham to let people know their decision and arrange for word to be passed along to the organizers at the Dawn to expect them. She also volunteered for the trip to the Dawn Settlement, so when the meeting broke up, Harriet was in a state of high excitement. She was ready to ride out for Chatham that night, but she knew that wasn't about to happen. She also knew sleep wasn't about to come, so she determined to ask her parents some questions after she helped them clear up behind the meeting.

"What do they mean about begging culture?" she asked, forcing herself to overcome her embarrassment that she didn't already know. She was pleased to see that her mother and Thomas took her question seriously. Not so long ago, they would have told her not to worry about "grown folk business." The three of them sat back down at the table.

Abiah spoke first. "You were little back then, the first year we came here, so you won't remember when folks in Boston sent box after box of clothing to Reverend King for us settlers. Reverend King called a meeting and everyone came to talk about it. We all agreed to accept the gift so as to be respectful to the folk who sent it. But we also decided to let it be known that we would accept no more charity after that. We want a fair field and no favors. Black folk are just as able as white to support ourselves, and we want the world to know it. From that day to now, we've never accepted any more clothing or anything for individuals, only things for the school."

Thomas nodded. "We're different to many of the other settlements. Wilberforce and Dawn and them, they seek out donations from abroad. Giving is a good thing, but receiving not always so, because receiving causes dependence, you hear me? Instead of raising sheep, shearing sheep, spinning and weaving and sewing and knitting, a person comes to wait on somebody to give him clothes. Soon you have dissension and argument—who gets what? How much? And so on. You see? And sooner or later, someone becomes corrupt and keeps what's not rightfully theirs. And that's how it goes in most of the other settlements."

"So, what they're saying about Reverend Henson..." Harriet hesitated.

"Some folk say he went to England and raised a whole heap of money supposed to be for the school, but the money never arrived back in Dawn," Abiah answered Harriet's unfinished question. "Reverend King raises money for our school, too, but seems like everything he raises comes right back where it's supposed to go. Now, I'm not saying they're right to accuse Reverend Henson, you hear? Just telling you what people are saying."

"Oh," Harriet said thoughtfully. "So why are we in the Elgin Settlement able to do what the rest are not doing?"

"You're asking a real good question, Harriet," Thomas began. "One of the answers is what we just told you—we don't accept handouts. To go along with that, now, we work together. You see how we built the drainage ditches and the road to the Lake?"

"Everybody joins a team and we just organize and go do it," said Harriet.

"Right," Thomas nodded sharply. "And nobody's looking for any money: we're doing the work because the work needs doing! Plus, anytime we come upon a problem—like say the road is too muddy—we put all our heads together in a meeting and find the solution. We just did that now. The road is so muddy we can't use it most of the time, so we just got the Township permission to build a tramway along it. You watch, I bet you it doesn't take us a month to lay track all the way to the Lake!"

Harriet could feel Thomas' passion as he talked about this collective work, and could see the glow in Abiah's eyes as he spoke. Harriet had been so taken up with preparation and excitement for her initiation into the Order that she had only paid marginal attention to all the hubbub of cutting wood and laying rails. She looked down, once again humbled listening to her parents. There was a lot to ponder, she was realizing, not only about her new commitment to helping fugitives find new homes, but also about what sort of home and life they would be creating.

Abiah and Thomas had grown quiet. When Harriet looked up she saw that they were both gazing at her with something like pride on their faces. They were talking to her like an adult. She felt herself grow self-conscious, and as she stood up to go to bed Thomas spoke again.

"All learning doesn't go on in school, Harriet, remember that. Our people have genius, you hear me? You don't need to go learning all that Greek nor Latin to know what's important in life."

"You're right, Daddy Thomas," Harriet responded humbly. "I hear you." She repeated, "You're right. Thank you for talking to me."

Abiah got up then and took Harriet's face in her hands, planting a kiss in the middle of her forehead. "You're welcome, daughter, and thank you too. You're God's gift, you know that?"

Harriet blushed harder and mumbled another "thank you." Abiah let go of her. Harriet turned and hurried up the ladder, calling out "good night" behind her.

Sleep did not come right away, as Harriet contemplated her parents' words. She knew that much was owed to all those who had been brought to this side of the ocean as slaves, their lives and labor stolen from them for generations. The men responsible must one day be held responsible. But she also knew that debt did not excuse those whose strategy for liberation was to depend on kindly benefactors. Like the revolutionaries in Haiti that Zeke liked to talk about, oppressed people must take their lives into their own hands.

Harriet realized that her parents were continuing their

discussion. She wiggled closer to the ladder well to listen.

"It just gets under my skin that they called in a white man from England to look about their finances." It was Abiah, speaking softly but with heat in her voice. "I have the utmost respect for Father Josiah, but seems like all the money floating round him in England turned his head. The principle of the Dawn Settlement is supposed to be self-sufficiency, but seems like they've got stars in their eyes for money now. How could it be possible they used up more than 7,000 pounds and nothing to show for it at the school?"

"Money can turn a person's head quicker than a rat going down a hole," Thomas responded. "The begging culture seems like our biggest problem once we come across the border. The bloodhounds can't follow us, but greed just comes cross the river in the boat right alongside us. We're lucky Reverend King's so principled about donations."

"Thomas, I'm purely tired of hearing everybody lifting up Reverend King!" Abiah said. "Why do we need a white man directing us? I'm not disrespecting Reverend King. I love how he's dedicated, and most certainly I love his school and his teaching. But here we are, come up out of slavery, come away from the white man bossing us around, and look like we're just so comfortable moving from a bad white man to a good white man! Why do we need a white man at all? Who's doing the work here? Who is it knows how to cut trees, build houses, plant crops, make a sawmill, cut a road and build a railroad to the Lake? Who taught us barrel making? Who taught us to make pearl ash? Who teaches us to cool water, preserve food and make quilts to keep us warm, invent and build tools and machines for the house and the rest of it? *We're* the ones do all that!"

"'Biah, 'Biah, I know you're right," Harriet heard Thomas, nearly whispering now. "The way I see it, we welcome Reverend King, we know he's on our side. But we don't need him to run things. I mean, he doesn't make the decisions for us any more, does he? Without him, the Elgin Settlement wouldn't have got started, though, no way around that fact. And I just think it's a good thing how he acts about the begging culture, because if he happened to be a man like John Scoble, we surely would have some trouble on our hands."

"I know. I just get frustrated looking at how some of these folk around us acting like Reverend King is the next thing to God. Like as if we couldn't get along without him. Even my own daughter worships him. Ever since she saw him debate Larwill when she just a little girl, she made a hero out of him. But listen now, we have children coming behind us that don't know a thing about slavery. We're the ones have to set them on the right track. Just because there's no slavery in Canada West doesn't mean our children don't have a struggle on their hands, you and I both know that sure as weeds grow in these fields. I think about Harriet off riding to Chatham or Windsor now, and I get a chill just thinking about what she'll face on those streets with all them white people, specially the men. We've got to prepare our children—I don't mean just you and me, I mean all of us. We've got to prepare them to be their own boss, they've got to know who they are, and not be feeling all thankful and grateful to the white man for their lives. They're free! They've got to stand tall and respect themselves!"

Abiah's words made Harriet frown, but before she could follow that thought, Thomas said, "Let's us take Zachary with us and all of us go on to the Dawn next month. He's going on seven now. Maybe he's old enough to catch a little something. It will be an education he can't get in any school." He paused. "I'm not even worrying about Harriet anymore, that girl's got a backbone in her for real. No one's about tell her how to live her life!"

Harriet crept back into her bed, pulled up the covers and tried to think through what she'd heard.

<>

2011 - Oakland, California

Ellie Parker rubs her eyes, still smarting from the tear gas attack on the Occupy encampment. Her mind reviews the days of constant discussions about everything under the sun. She wonders where those kids, mostly white, will be in a few years. In comfortable jobs, nice homes with an SUV parked out front fitted with car seats and soccer equipment in the back? Oh, she knows they are passionate enough about injustice, but they seem all over the map in their thinking; they seem to thrive on arguing. She doesn't trust their vision to go further than youthful protests, followed by nonprofit foundations, rooftop gardens and electric cars. What is their plan for creating a world of true equality? That is what Ellie is passionate about: but how to get there?

Ellie is the namesake of a some-number-of-greats grandmother: Eliza Parker. She knows about Eliza and William and what they did at Christiana, about the amazing life they built at Buxton, Ontario. What would they think of Occupy? She wonders.

Her eyes fall once again on the quotation she found on a little book someone gave her at the People of Color booth:

"We want the people from the bottom of society to lead our struggle. We think that the people who the oppressors treat the most unfairly are the most capable to be fair; the people who have the least resources are the most capable to distribute the world's resources with equality and fairness; the people who have been the most discriminated against, left out, locked out and hated are the most capable to share and be inclusive. That is why we call ourselves 'bottom-up,' because we think the people at the bottom— poor, dark-skinned people and women—will be the most capable to lead all of humanity to create a new world based on justice."

Ellie closes her eyes: sometimes she thinks she can feel her ancestor inside herself when she does that. 'That's just who we were.' Is that Eliza? Ellie's heart aches. 'Those words describe our struggles.

Our movement. You need the same type of movement today,' the *inner voice continues. 'The thread has never disappeared. Find it and pick it up, Ellie.'*

Tears are leaking from Ellie's eyes now and it's not just from the tear gas.

28

First Mission ~ July 1854

The next morning, Harriet woke up ready to leave for Chatham, but first she had to take care of her chores and then mind Zachary while Abiah fulfilled a promise to take a turn caring for a sick neighbor. Harriet chafed at the delay. By the time Abiah returned it was afternoon already, so they agreed that she would spend the night in Chatham and return the following day. Harriet realized that she might have an evening with Thaddeus. She smiled to herself. Maybe it was true, what the old folks always said: things happen for a reason.

Harriet went to the barn and brushed down their tall, bay mare whose dark brown coat was broken by a spot of white like a full moon on her forehead. The mare turned and nuzzled Harriet's side as she worked, and then calmly accepted the bridle, eager for companionship and movement. Thomas and Abiah had bought her four years earlier, shortly after moving to the Elgin Settlement. They used her mainly for Thomas to ride across the property during his daily work and to pull logs and stumps as they cleared their land. She also pulled the buggy to take the whole family—and often others—to Chatham when they needed to go. Harriet loved her from the moment she came onto their farm, and named her Meldy. She spent her free time brushing her, riding her around the farm and carrying her treats. Now Meldy's work would include carrying Harriet on her assignments. It was Meldy she had ridden to Windsor for her initiation. Harriet wished they had a saddle, but for now she had to be satisfied with the mare's broad, well-padded back.

Harriet led Meldy through to the road, calling good-bye to her mother as she passed the front porch. She had tied a small pack onto her back containing a change of clothes, some cornbread and a couple of carrots. Now she stepped up on a tree stump and sprang onto Meldy's back while her mount tap-danced in her eagerness to get moving. Digging her heels into the mare's ribs, Harriet leaned low over her neck as Meldy took off at a canter. She loved the speed, the rushing wind on her skin, the controlled power of the animal under her. They ran past the other houses along their road and on into the woods. After Meldy had worked off her initial spurt of energy, Harriet slowed her to a trot, patted her on the neck, and then settled her into the single-foot gait she loved. In this gait, Meldy trotted so smoothly that Harriet felt like she was gliding rather than clopping. They would be in Chatham in about two hours, without either horse or rider being too tired.

It was after four o'clock when Chatham's houses began marching past on both sides of the road. Riding into town was entertaining after the quiet of the farm and the loneliness of the road. Residential areas gave way to the downtown. On every side were people going about their business. Shops doing every type of trade lined the streets, construction was in progress on several side streets as new houses went up, and workshops of all sorts raised dust, smoke and a variety of smells that mingled with the cooking smells coming from nearly every home at this hour of the day. People, mostly black people, greeted Harriet as she rode, now at a polite, sedate walk, and she responded in kind, noticing the colors and styles of clothing and bonnets, and noticing the large numbers of white people. Since moving to Buxton, where nearly everyone was black or varying shades of brown, the amount of white skin always caught Harriet's eye when she traveled to Chatham, where about two out of every three people were white.

A rough voice chopped through the rest of the sounds. "Hey nigger gal! Where you steal that horse from?"

Harriet felt a shock shoot down her spine to set her feet

trembling. Her face got hot, and she tried not to look in the direction of the voice, which came from a ruddy-faced young man and was applauded by laughter from the other youths he was walking with. Harriet saw a mother's dark hands grab the little girl and little boy walking with her and pull them abruptly to the opposite side of the street. Her mother's whispered words leaped into her mind. Meldy sensed Harriet's sudden tension and started prancing and pulling on the bit. The shock and tension became anger. Harriet wasn't sure if she should respond to the taunt or ignore it.

"Who do you think you're talking to?" Harriet said, the words coming out unbidden. Well, I guess that's the answer, Harriet thought with a little inner smile. She continued, "You jealous? Better horse than you'll ever have!"

Harriet's tension came out in a sharp laugh, and she squeezed Meldy's ribs, making the mare bolt forward a few steps. She pulled the reins up sharply and allowed Meldy to trot forward, knowing that running in town wasn't allowed and wasn't safe. But was she putting the boys in their place, or was she running from them? She wasn't sure.

As Meldy increased the distance between her and her abusers, Harriet felt her hands shaking a little. She breathed deeply to bring back control. Beneath the anger at the boys, she felt shame, and then anger at herself for that feeling. She glanced sideways at the people around her, expecting to see all their eyes on her. But, no, they were going about their business, either unaware of what had happened or ignoring it.

She shook her head and settled Meldy back to a walk as she wended her way past the crowded streets and onto the bridge across the Thames River. Uncle James' gun smithy and house were on the other side of the river, where it was quiet and residential.

When she arrived, she saw Thaddeus watching her with a smile from his seat on the low stone wall. He must have spotted her from a distance. She felt self-conscious, as if he had seen what had just happened. Of course he couldn't have, but she felt too shaky to face him yet. With a tight smile, she rode past him to the barn at the back of the property. Hidden from anyone's eyes, she slid stiffly off the mare's back and brushed the horsehair from the sweat-dampened inner thighs of the pants she wore for riding. Then she stood still for a moment, hand on Meldy's neck, and took a long, deep breath to collect herself.

She put the mare into a stall and found an armful of hay and a bucket to fill with water. Meldy indulged in a big sigh and full-body shake, and quickly stretched her neck to bury her nose in the fragrant food. Harriet turned and walked around to the front of the workshop. Seeing Thaddeus waiting expectantly, she gave him a self-conscious little wave and continued through the wide doors of the workshop to deliver her message. With a flicker of a frown, Thaddeus slipped off the wall and strolled toward the smithy.

As her eyes slowly adjusted from bright sun to the dark interior, Harriet picked out Mr. Jones working a bellows to pump air into the forge. With each squeeze of the bellows, the coals glowed whiter, briefly throwing off small fingers of flame. When they reached the heat he wanted, the smith picked up a piece of metal with a set of tongs, his hand wrapped several times in a wool cloth, set the metal into the forge and began to strike it with a heavy hammer. Harriet had been mesmerized by the flames, but now she turned to Thaddeus, who was in the doorway looking at her, and was self-conscious once again.

Thaddeus waved for her to step back with him.

"He's in the middle of work he can't interrupt right now. What are you doing here this fine day?" Thaddeus' liquid eyes smiled, but with a hint of confusion about the coolness he felt from her.

"Carrying a message," Harriet replied, and as she remembered her purpose, the bad feelings began to grow smaller in her and pride began to grow. She looked up at Thaddeus and felt a fluid warmth travel from his eyes through her whole being. She breathed. "We had an Emancipation Day committee meeting last night and decided to send a delegation to Dawn this year." She added with restrained excitement, "I'm going to go."

A different light came into Thaddeus' eyes. "Man, great decision! I plan to go, too. I want to hear Mr. Douglass, I know he's an amazing speaker. People around here are encouraging J.C. Brown to go too, because John Scoble is going to speak."

"I know, I heard. But I don't fully understand what's going on. I only know a little bit about the controversy, about Reverend Henson."

Before Thaddeus could respond, Gunsmith Jones straightened up from his work and spoke. "Hello, Harriet."

Turning back to the interior of the smithy, Harriet responded politely, "Hello, Uncle James. Hope you're doing well."

"Yes. Keeping very busy, give thanks. I have a good amount of new manufacture, plus any and everybody keeps coming in with one thing and another that needs repair. It's a good trade. My grandfather and his brother used to do metal work in Africa, I ever tell you that? I'm glad Thaddeus here finally saw the light and decided to learn the trade." He paused. "But I doubt you came here for an update on the gunsmith business." The man everyone called Gunsmith Jones smiled at the girl—now a young woman—who had visited so many times in his home, and who had heard many times about his grandfather and great-uncle in Africa. "I understand you're a messenger now," he said in a quieter voice.

"Yes, Uncle, and this my first assignment."

Harriet explained her message to Uncle James.

He heard her with interest. "Good, man, good! I'll make

sure the message gets to the Dawn. Some Dawn folk are in the market on Friday most times, but if I don't see anyone, we'll send Thaddeus. You," he nodded at Thaddeus, "ought to go deliver the message in person to Mr. Brown. He's really the right one to take it to, but now, him being sick, he would likely send word for me to take care of it. But you all should still tell him directly, and tell him I'm going to deal with it. Thaddeus knows where he lives."

Harriet nodded that she understood. Maybe J.C. Brown was the lead organizer for the Order in Chatham?

"Thank you, Uncle, I'll go there now." She glanced at Thaddeus, who nodded. "You'll see me back here later on. I'm supposed to stay the night and ride home tomorrow."

The gunsmith raised his hand in acknowledgment and farewell and turned back to his bellows, while Harriet and Thaddeus walked out of the smithy into the late afternoon sun. Turning away from the road, they made their way across a field to the path that accompanied the river to the bridge, where they would cross back into the hubbub of downtown Chatham on their way to J.C. Brown's house. For a while, Harriet was content to just know Thaddeus was beside her, fingers interlocked with hers, and to stare down at the river flowing purposefully and constantly on its way as it had done long before Chatham was built along its banks.

29

Are We in This Together?

"Thaddeus," Harriet started hesitantly, looking up from staring at the brown water of the Thames River.

"What is it, girl?" Thaddeus blinked away his own thoughts and looked down at Harriet, wrapping his arm snugly around her waist. She felt the hard muscles in his arm, and thought how much taller and thicker he'd grown in the years since that afternoon she had first set eyes on him.

"Okay," she tried to collect herself. "Okay, I want to understand about Scoble and all that. But also, something just happened." She heard her voice waver, and stopped talking.

Thaddeus heard the waver and turned from her side to look into Harriet's eyes. Suddenly she didn't want to mention the incident with the young men on the street.

"What, Harriet?" Thaddeus spoke insistently into Harriet's silence. He took hold of her arm above the elbow and squeezed lightly. "What? Tell me." He had stopped walking.

"No, no, it's nothing," Harriet looked away from him and tried to pull her arm from his grasp.

"If it was nothing, you wouldn't have mentioned it. Now you've got to tell me. I could see something was on your mind when you came to the smithy. Hey, baby girl, we're in this together, you've got to tell me."

Harriet pulled her arm away and started walking again so at least he couldn't look into her eyes. But she was softened by his words.

"Okay." She took a breath. "When I was riding through downtown, some white boys yelled at me." She looked out of the corner of her eyes at Thaddeus. He stopped walking again. "They call me nigger gal." She felt her face go hot, and to her dismay, tears came. She turned her back to Thaddeus so he wouldn't see her eyes.

Thaddeus cursed and she felt him stiffen behind her. He held her still in front of him and looked over her head toward downtown, as if to see the offenders. There was a momentary silence, and some of the hot, sudden anger from Thaddeus' body filtered into Harriet's. She felt a laugh gurgling unexpectedly up into her throat.

"They asked me where did I steal Meldy from," she giggled. "I told them they've got nothing nice as her and they're just jealous!"

As Thaddeus caught her laughter, his body relaxed a little. "You told 'em, girl! Good for you." Then the tension returned. "I hate it, man," he hissed. "I hate the bastards. Most of these white folks are sorry there's no slavery in Canada. Well, a lot of them anyway. You don't even know how lucky you are. Where you live, you don't have to put up with it every-day-every-day."

Thaddeus' words disquieted Harriet. She hadn't pictured Thaddeus walking the streets of Chatham. He would confront people like those boys nearly every day. She wondered how many times he'd had to fight with them, or if he had to swallow his anger and turn away to keep out of trouble. Either way, it would take a heavy toll on him, she realized with a jolt. When she lived in Chatham she was just a little girl. Now and then another child in Chatham had said something, but until Faith abandoned her, her mother's comforting words were enough to heal the wound. Now that she was nearly grown it wasn't childish cruelty she had to deal with. She felt much more vulnerable. Knowing that Thaddeus felt protective of her was reassuring. And in that moment, she also felt protective of him. It was a new feeling. He was a man: older than she was, bigger, stronger. Up to now she had lived with an assumption that he was strong inside and out, decisive and in charge of his own life: that she could lean on him, but he didn't need to lean on anyone.

"I know, baby," she said, looking up into his eyes. "Like you said, we're in this together. You're here for me, and I'm here for you."

She put her arm around his waist and felt his go around her shoulder. A quiet pleasure and sense of security chased away her unease. She leaned her head into the crook of his shoulder. They continued walking, each in their own thoughts, the river beside them as a silent witness.

Harriet's thoughts returned to Faith. She hadn't remembered her childhood friend in a long time. Odd that it still hurt to think about her. It occurred that she had buried the memory because she had believed Faith's insult. She remembered how fervently she had wished that her skin wasn't so dark, wished to be light-skinned, wished for long, straight, "pretty" hair. Thoughts like those hadn't plagued her so much since her family had moved to Elgin, and she had never talked to anyone about them.

"Thaddeus, you ever wish you were white?" she surprised herself speaking the thought aloud.

Thaddeus stopped dead in his tracks. He looked at her in astonishment. His thoughts were still on the white boys who had insulted her. He was still feeling the urge to go find them and punish them. Wish to be like them? What was she talking about? Anger blazed back. Long-dormant images flashed through his mind: the red-faced son of his old master tossing him to the ground, his mother submitting silently, the man's eyes reflected in the green of his little brother's own.

"Hell, no!" he spat venom, an image of the man who had so poisoned his life blocking him from seeing Harriet's troubled and quizzical face.

Harriet flinched. She was bewildered, not recognizing this face distorted by, what—hatred? She stepped back from him onto the steep riverbank and started to slip. He grabbed her arm to keep her from falling.

"Sorry, sorry!" His vision cleared quickly when he realized how he'd startled her. "It's not you, I was just thinking." Her face looked shocked. Speaking more normally, he said, "No, no, I never wished I was white. I…" He stopped, not knowing where to go, confused by his emotions.

"What, Thaddeus? What is it?" Harriet asked, her voice trembling at his sudden fierceness. There was something there, some memory, something he wasn't telling her.

"Nothing, nothing, Harriet, never mind." He couldn't talk to Harriet about what was in his mind. He didn't understand the violence of his own feelings. He felt guilt mingled with his anger. It was righteous anger of course, but the anger spilled over into thoughts of his mother, and thinking of his mother smothered him in guilt and grief. He let go of Harriet's arm and started walking again. Harriet followed uncertainly.

They emerged from the path along the river back onto the Chatham streets. There was no way to continue talking on these crowded streets. Harriet watched the rigidness in Thaddeus' back as she dropped slightly behind. They wended their way between people, animals, crates and street-side obstacles of all kinds. She felt hurt, dismayed and excluded. She wished she could think of something she could say to bring back the harmony she had destroyed with her foolish question. If only it were a few minutes earlier and she could have kept her jaws shut.

30

Pass the Torchlight in All Its Brightness and Vision

After a short walk along the town side of the river, Thaddeus led Harriet up five wooden steps onto the porch of a pretty, blue-painted wooden house shaded by a huge elm tree. A woman sat in a chair beside the door. Her face was the color and smoothness of a pecan shell, except for the worry lines etched into her forehead. Pain was barely concealed behind tired, watery eyes. But the uprightness of her back, her long, straight neck and erect head bound in a colorful, plaid fabric all spoke of strength and determination.

"Good afternoon, Mrs. Brown," said Thaddeus, "This is Harriet Roberson, up from the Elgin Settlement. She is bringing a message for Mr. Brown."

Mrs. Brown stood up.

"Good afternoon, Thaddeus. Pleased to meet you Harriet. Let me see if he's awake. Wait here a minute."

Thaddeus and Harriet nodded and sat on the porch steps. Harriet was still smarting, Thaddeus was struggling to quell the turmoil inside him. Neither of them said anything. A moment later, the woman came back, fingers tucking in ringlets of hair that had slipped out from under her scarf.

"He says he wants to see you. This movement is his life, and I won't take that from him. Just be mindful that he's sick and very weak. Don't linger too long." She led them through the house into a room at the back with windows facing to the west. The slanting rays of the sun made the sick room cheerful, as did the intricate quilt done in reds, yellows and greens and the vase of orange and purple flowers on the side table.

The remnants of unease of their previous conversation vanished when they entered the room. Mr. Brown's back and shoulders were propped up on several pillows, and he was surrounded by newspapers lying open on the quilt. Harriet recognized *Frederick Douglass' Paper* and *The Provincial Freeman.* A glass of water sat on a bedside table, along with a green-brown tea she knew would be made from healing herbs. Her confidence returned as she remembered why she was here. She was a member of the same secret order as this old and experienced man before her.

"Good afternoon, Mr. Brown," Thaddeus spoke first. "This is Harriet Roberson of Buxton. She carries a message to you from the Elgin Settlement Emancipation Day committee meeting."

"Good afternoon, sir. We had a meeting last night," Harriet spoke up, glancing briefly at Thaddeus. "Our committee decided to send a delegation to the Dawn Settlement on Emancipation Day in order that we can learn more about the controversy going on there and let our voice be heard for self-sufficiency and against begging." She spoke the words exactly as the meeting had set them out. "Our group wants to understand what happened to the money Mr. Henson and Mr. Scoble raised in England, and made special mention that we are eager to hear your own thoughts about this, sir. We know that you are sick, and we extend to you our hope and prayers for a speedy recovery."

Mr. Brown nodded, and the young people could see his glassy and feverish eyes light up. His face was flushed and his breathing rapid and hoarse. He moved as if to lean forward in his eagerness to respond, but his fatigue was too great, and he dropped back into the pillows.

"Young lady," he began, his voice raspy but his words formal and his bearing communicating great dignity in spite of his weakness: "Your message gladdens my heart. The Elgin Settlement at Buxton is a shining light for our people. It is a welcome prospect that will hasten my healing to know that a delegation of your hard-working, clear-thinking community will be at the Dawn to witness and comment upon the reports of the scurrilous Mr. Scoble and the unfortunate events that have transpired in that settlement. I can only hope that the famous Mr. Douglass will see the truth and be courageous enough to stand up for it." Mr. Brown began coughing, and soon the cough became uncontrollable. He held up one hand in a pardoning gesture, while the other reached for the water glass. He sipped several times and his coughing eased.

Harriet saw movement in the doorway. Mrs. Brown had appeared at the sound of the coughing. She made no move to enter the room, but stood watchfully.

"Mr. Brown, perhaps we ought to leave you now so you can gather your strength," Thaddeus spoke quietly. "Gunsmith Jones said to assure you that he will pass along Harriet's message. We trust you will be well enough that we will hear the whole of your reasoning a few weeks hence."

The woman in the doorway nodded. Harriet dipped her head in response. "Thank you kindly for seeing us, Mr. Brown, and I look forward to seeing you in much better health when our delegation reaches the Dawn."

Mr. Brown took a ragged breath, but smiled, saying, "Thank you, young people. It is nourishment to my soul to see people like you-all coming into adulthood in freedom and dedicating yourselves to building a world of freedom for all our people. Our future depends on such as you more than on those like myself who are now aging. I will see you at the Dawn and do what I can to pass the torchlight to you in all its brightness and vision." His voice was uneven, but somehow still formal and commanding. The strength of his words took set in Harriet's breast, making her straighten her shoulders. She noticed Thaddeus, too, standing straighter beside her. After a moment, Mr. Brown's eyes closed, and the young people turned to leave, nodding silently to Mrs. Brown as they saw themselves out.

As soon as their feet left the bottom step of the porch,

Harriet turned to Thaddeus. The encounter had reversed her mood, and she returned to the question she had wanted to ask ever since last night's meeting. "Scurrilous? Can you explain to me, Thaddeus? Mr. Scoble is an officer in a big anti-slavery society in England. To what I've heard, he's a man who has dedicated his life to freedom for the black man. I understand that the people at Dawn call him 'the white Negro.' That sounds like a truly good man to me. Why does Mr. Brown call him scurrilous? That's a strong word."

The two walked back toward downtown and the bridge as the sun's rays weakened in the early evening sky. Thaddeus also seemed to have forgotten his earlier turmoil. Their two young heads bent in concentration as they walked along the street lined with the homes of black residents.

"Well, Harriet, you know Brother Henson lived in England for a good while, speaking and raising money, especially for the school at the Dawn Settlement, the British American Institute. The British and Foreign Anti-Slavery Society is in charge of their school, I don't really understand why. I don't know, but there's a rumor that a lot of money was donated in England that never reached the school. Father Josiah used to work with Mr. Scoble in England. Then when the Dawn started to having financial troubles, Mr. Scoble came out from England to straighten things out. Some people are saying it's the fox guarding the henhouse."

"Lord have mercy! Can that really be true?"

"I don't know, Harriet, I surely don't." Thaddeus shook his head. "I have plenty respect for Mr. Brown, though. He lived at Dawn before he moved here. I know he tells it like he sees it. He's worked so hard for our people, and not only in Chatham. He works for the national conventions, he travels and speaks and organizes—all of it. I imagine he's sick now because he just plumb wore himself out. I don't know Mr. Henson, so I can't judge him. I guess you're going to have to judge for yourself."

"Emancipation Day's going to be interesting in more ways than it needs to." It was Harriet's turn to shake her head. "I don't much like this fighting among our own people." She fell silent. Back in the downtown area again, the conversation paused as they threaded their way among people doing their last shopping or plodding home from work.

"One thing I do know," Thaddeus spoke once they were on the bridge again in relative quiet. There was bitterness in his voice. "There's no way any white man from England is supposed to be coming all the way here to straighten out Dawn's finances! To me it seems like an insult for them to control the school there. Don't know how Brother Henson allows it. I don't know, Harriet, sometime I wonder if I made a mistake coming away from the Swamp. We sure never had any idea that we needed any white man to come tell us how to run our business!"

Harriet sensed that Thaddeus was heading for where he'd been when she had asked him if he ever wished he were white. She wanted to bring him back from there.

"I hear you, Thaddeus," she spoke hesitantly, in what she hoped was a calming voice. "I so do wish you lived in Buxton."

"But you don't see, Harriet?" Thaddeus' voice rose sharply and immediately Harriet knew her attempt had backfired. "Even at Buxton, you all act like Reverend King is some kind of god!"

"That's not true!" Harriet fired back hotly, feeling instantly defensive at this echo of her own mother's words from last night. "We keep our own meetings, our own government, we make our own decisions. Reverend King runs the school and he preaches. And he certainly never misused any money! Anyway, he's respectful, he doesn't boss us around." But the heat steadily drained out of Harriet's voice as she spoke. She knew defending Reverend King made her sound weak to Thaddeus. Being honest with herself, she had to admit her mother was right. She *had* nearly worshipped the man for years. But it was easier to ignore her mother's words than Thaddeus'. For the second time that afternoon, Harriet felt confused and shaken.

"Oh, Harriet." Thaddeus sounded tired now. "You know good and well that Reverend King is involved in every decision connected to money and business at Elgin. Let's just leave it for now." To soften his words, he put his arm around her waist. "Come here," he added, affection in his voice. He didn't have the energy or the desire to stay angry. She leaned into him, glad for the intimacy of his gesture, but she couldn't help feeling rebuffed, and as muddled as a child.

When they arrived back at the Jones's, Harriet left Thaddeus to go to Meldy in the barn. Her solid internal structure of knowledge and beliefs was developing cracks, and the sudden self-doubt made her want to be alone.

She took a rag and rubbed off the dried sweat imprint left by her legs and seat on the horse's warm, round back. She reached into her bag for one of the carrots and handed it to the horse. Then she leaned against the wall of the stall and stared at the big jaws crunching the treat. The quiet warmth of the big animal calmed her, the horse's lips and tongue juggling bits of carrot to keep them from falling out of her mouth. Meldy looked so serious with the effort that it made Harriet smile.

When she went back into the house, she was feeling better. A meal of Auntie Emily's beef stew amidst the chatter of the young children left her and Thaddeus both more light-hearted. Thaddeus had promised his landlord to fix a porch step before darkness closed in, so he took his leave when they had finished eating, and Harriet decided to walk with him as far as the bridge.

Instead of walking along the road, Harriet and Thaddeus once again struck off across the field between the Jones house and the river to stroll along the riverside path they had walked earlier in the day. Hesitantly, she took his hand in hers, and was happy to feel his fingers interlace with hers, squeezing gently. She looked up to find those irresistible eyes looking down at her, a smile playing around his full, soft-looking lips.

"Harriet, baby," he said softly, "please forgive me for raising my voice this afternoon."

Harriet found she couldn't speak, but she nodded, her eyes on his. They had entered the woods along the river and stopped walking.

"I..." Thaddeus hesitated, "I...well, one day I'm going to tell you some things, but I can't just yet, I don't know how. But trust me, I'm not angry with you. We might disagree, but that's okay. I want a woman with a mind of her own."

He disentangled his fingers from hers and put his hands on her shoulders. The words "not angry" and "want a woman" repeated in Harriet's mind. She felt herself trembling with relief and an overpowering surge of emotion. He wanted her! Mingled with the emotion was a physical urgency that was new to her. She wanted to press the full length of her body against Thaddeus, to merge her whole self with him. Energy pulses shot through her, going every which way. Even the soles of her feet tingled. Thaddeus was talking again, and she forced herself to listen through the ringing in her ears.

"Harriet, sweetheart." Again he paused. "I love you baby. I love you." His fingers tightened on her shoulders, and then his arms went around her and he clasped her tightly to himself. She threw her arms around him and clung to him as if to life itself. Her body seemed to be melting. She lifted her face to his and they kissed passionately, hands stroking and groping one another desperately.

"Oh, Thaddeus!" Harriet gasped when they stopped long enough to take a breath. "Thaddeus, I love you, too." Tears sprang into her eyes. "Oh, God, I love you!"

They kissed again, and then suddenly Thaddeus' hands

were on her shoulders again, pushing her gently away so he could look at her. His eyes were darting and she could feel his hands trembling.

"Harriet, you'd best go back," he said shakily. "We can't stay here in the woods so long. Uncle and Auntie are waiting for you."

Harriet's body and emotions resisted Thaddeus' words, but in her mind she knew he was right. She'd never felt such powerful desire, and she could tell Thaddeus felt the same. They couldn't stay together right now.

She nodded mutely and stepped back. They looked long and hard into one another's eyes, and then kissed each other lightly on the lips. This was so difficult! But Harriet made herself smile broadly.

"Hey, boy," she said with a forced lightness, "better watch yourself! I'm coming for you." She laughed, and Thaddeus chuckled gratefully.

"You better watch your *own* self, girl!" he came back at her with a grin, taking a deep breath. "I can see we have some serious talking and planning to do. Maybe I'll pay you a visit soon."

"Okay," Harriet said, the lightness in her voice replaced now by an almost childish delight and anticipation. "Okay, baby, bye for now." She reached out and touched his fingertips. They blew kisses at each other and reluctantly turned, Thaddeus further into the woods along the river, Harriet back towards the house. Twice as they walked, they looked back at one another and laughed. Harriet was almost hugging herself.

Grown woman now, she thought to herself, grinning without restraint now that no one could see her. *Whooee, I'm in love! Thaddeus loves me!* She shook herself in disbelief. Her whole body was vibrating with excitement and pleasure and her heart felt as if it would burst right out of her chest. How could this day have had such lows and then such highs?

Harriet moved through the Joneses' house, speaking politely to the family without really noticing them. If Mrs. Jones looked at her husband with raised eyebrows, Harriet didn't notice. She went straight to her bed in the room behind the kitchen and lay down, bathed in luminous happiness, still feeling Thaddeus' mouth on hers and carrying him into her dreams.

PRINTING PRESS USED TO PRINT THE
~PROVINCIAL FREEMAN~ IN CHATHAM IN
THE 1850ós. OSBORNE P. ANDERSON THE
LONE CANADIAN SURVIVOR OF ~THE RAID
AT HARPERS FERRY~ WAS A PRINTER FOR
THIS ANTI SLAVERY NEWSPAPER.
EDITOR - MARY ANN SHADD CARY:
PUBLISHER- ISAAC D. SHADD.

Printing press used to print Mary Ann Shadd's
Provincial Freeman.
Courtesy of the Buxton National Historic Site and Museum

31

They Built This Place Themselves ~ July 1854

When Harriet woke up before dawn the next morning, happiness and excitement awoke with her. She smiled to herself before she even threw off the covers. Feeling like she harbored a huge secret, she decided not to stay for breakfast and face having to exchange commonplace chatter with the Joneses, so she slipped out of bed, collected her things and set off on Meldy.

But she didn't go straight home. Uncle James had given her a letter that he had forgotten to give to William Parker, so when she reached Buxton she turned off on the lane that led to the Parker farm, letting Meldy walk past fields of golden-fringed wheat waving in the light breeze. The hours of riding had brought her almost back down to earth, though she still felt like she was radiating a heavenly light.

Three small dogs sniffed around her feet as she tied the horse to the Parkers' gate, which was identical to the one in front of her own house. In the space between the fence and the house, the Parkers had planted a kitchen garden. Harriet could see small green tomatoes peeking out from behind the yellow-green leaves, slender young beans hanging from climbing vines, hills of dark green potato plants and speckled throughout, marigolds and other flowers.

She shouted to announce her presence and then walked through the gate and past the garden.

Ezekiel walked out onto the porch, dressed for working. "Hey, Harriet," Ezekiel smiled, looking down to where his fingers found the catch to fasten his overalls. He settled his hat on his head and stepped down to greet her.

"Hi, Zeke." Harriet smiled, too, and stopped beside him. She felt a flash of self-consciousness, almost guilt, knowing how Zeke still felt about her: imagining that he could see what had happened between her and Thaddeus in the woods last night. She spoke quickly to dispel the feeling. "Your garden looks really pretty! I love how the flowers mix in like that—they brighten up the place."

"Yeah, they do. They have a use, you know," he said, eager as usual to tell her something she didn't know. "They're not only for beauty. Some of them are herbs for Doc Thomas's medicines. Mama learned about herbs down South, and Doc Thomas is teaching her more now. Some of them also keep away pests. And they attract the bees that pollinate everything."

"Wow." Harriet was impressed. She hadn't stopped to wonder where the stocky, grizzled old man from Mississippi got the herbs he used to doctor the people of Buxton. Now she looked at the flowers more closely, as if to detect the healing power in them. Then she remembered why she came, turning back to Zeke. "I have a letter for your father. Has he already gone out in the farm?"

"No, he's still here. Come in and sit down, we finished breakfast. Could be you didn't eat this morning? You're on the road so early."

"You're right. Thanks."

Zeke pulled the door open and held it as Harriet went through, said good morning to his parents and handed the letter to his father. Then she slipped out the back door to wash. By the time she came back in there was a plate of griddlecakes covered in berries waiting for her, along with a warm glass of creamy, fresh milk.

William Parker was sitting with his head bowed, reading the letter Harriet had given him. When he finished, he looked up at his wife with eyes shining.

"It's from William Still," he said. "He's thanking us for the letter we sent him and telling us about his work. The man is tireless! I wonder how many of our people owe their lives

and their freedom to him." He shook his head reverently.
"William Still is the man who sent warning that Gorsuch was coming for Papa," Ezekiel explained to Harriet.
His father looked at Harriet. "Yes, and he's much more than that, Harriet. He's a man you ought to know about, one of the main coordinators of the Underground Railroad. He lives in Philadelphia, and I couldn't say how many people have found refuge in his home or been passed along to safety by him and his wife. You just ask people round here how many of them stopped by Mr. Still on their way. I honestly don't know if the man sleeps. Seems like he knows everything happening everywhere. If he hadn't found out Gorsuch was coming to Christiana, I doubt you'd see us here today. Without that warning, we never would've got up our little 'greeting committee.'"

Harriet nodded, vivid images of the battle in Christiana popping into her mind. She also remembered hearing the name Still mentioned in a few other stories. Suddenly she had a question.

"Mr. Parker, that Mr. Still, is he a white man or a black man?"

"He's black." Mr. Parker looked mystified by the question. "What did you think?"

"I just wanted to know." She started wishing she hadn't asked.

"Harriet, there's no white man doing work like what Mr. Still does. Nearly all the Conductors and coordinators are black, to my knowledge. There are white folk who hide fugitives, some who are Conductors, and plenty who give food and clothing or money. There are lawyers and doctors that help us. There were even some white neighbors who helped us fight off Gorsuch. But away from that, most everyone is black in the organization." His brow wrinkled with confusion. "What made you imagine Mr. Still a white man?"

"Well," Harriet started hesitantly, "Reverend King…"

"Ah, I see." This time it was Eliza who spoke. "She grew up here, you know, William."

Despite the kindness in Eliza's voice, Harriet suddenly wanted nothing more than to be back outside, away from this conversation, back to the warm feelings that awakened her early this morning. Her question had been childish and naive, and doubly embarrassing in front of Zeke. She knew he was about to start making fun of her.

"Thank you, I have to get home now," she said hurriedly and started to rise from her seat.

Zeke took a breath to start talking, but was silenced by his mother's raised hand.

"Harriet," Mrs. Parker said quietly but firmly. The tone of her voice made Harriet sit back down. "Don't you *ever* feel bad about asking a question. The things you're wondering about are important and it's no good to be keeping them inside. Now, Reverend King is a good man, especially for a white man. But I have to say he's an exception. William and I chose to come to Buxton in spite of him, not because of him. We could see that the people here have made the place what they want it to be, and the Reverend hasn't gotten in their way. In fact, looks like he's helped. There's no denying his school is excellent, and I'm happy to have my children attend it. But there's also a danger—a danger that children growing up here are going to think they owe what they've got to Reverend King. The grown people know better, or supposed to. They all got here through the work of one *superb* organization, one *well-run* organization, one secret *black* organization that operates under very dangerous conditions. You hear me?"

Harriet nodded. "Yes, ma'am." Of course she knew this, she was a member of that organization, wasn't she? Embarrassment crept hotly up her neck.

"They all came here and put their own shoulders to the plow and their own knowledge and ingenuity to the building of this place. They never took anything from anybody. They built this place themselves. Yes, they built it to the rules set down by Reverend King and the Elgin Association directors, and sometimes that's been a problem, but mostly the Reverend is smart enough and humble enough to listen to reason and stay out of the way. He truly believes in his faith, and he truly believes in the humanity of African people and cares about our eternal souls. You have to grant him that. So that is my little sermon for you today. Respect Reverend King, but don't make him your hero. He only did what any right-minded person should do. Look around you. Each and all the families here in Buxton are heroes. You only need to listen to their stories to know that. Everything you see here in Buxton was imagined and created by your own people. Never forget that."

Zeke again took a breath, and Mr. Parker shot his son a sharp look that meant keep your mouth shut. Zeke exhaled quietly and bowed his head.

Harriet looked up at Mrs. Parker and murmured softly, "Yes, ma'am." She hesitated a moment and then stood up. "Thank you. And thank you for the breakfast." She glanced at Mr. Parker. "I hope I didn't keep you all too long from your work."

Mrs. Parker, glancing from her husband to her son, suddenly walked over to Harriet and embraced her in a tight hug.

"I'm proud of you, Harriet," she said, releasing Harriet and putting two fingers under her chin to make sure she was looking into her eyes. "You're our future, you know, young folk like you and Zeke and the rest. You all are growing up in freedom and yet you are still dedicating yourselves to our people! You just keep on asking all your questions, nobody ever learns a thing if they're afraid to ask questions! Knowledge makes you stronger. Keep studying book knowledge, and keep studying the wisdom of your elders, and you'll be both wise and tough. And God knows that's what we need!" She dropped her fingers from Harriet's chin. "You go on home now. I know your mama's looking for you. Thank you for carrying us Mr. Still's letter—it's a great day for us hearing from such a good friend."

"Thank you, Auntie Liza," Harriet murmured, turning toward the door. She was tempted to avoid Zeke's eyes, but instead she looked directly at him and smiled. She was a grown woman, she could have her own mind, and that was okay. And it was okay to question her own thinking, too. Even that challenge felt like a happy one this morning.

32

You Ever Wish You Were White? ~ July 1854

Thaddeus woke up that morning glowing, too. But he was also troubled. When Harriet had shown up yesterday, his heart had leapt with joy and anticipation. He'd looked forward to spending time alone with her. Then he'd felt guilty about how sharply he had spoken to her. He had to admit that he had overreacted to her questions and thoughts. Yes, he wished she agreed with him and didn't seem to worship Reverend King—that made him impatient with her. But if he were honest with himself, imagining the white boys taunting her had set off his emotions. Threatening her, really. Hearing her story had made him want to go after them, pulverize them, right then and there. It made him face the truth: that he had fallen completely in love with her and wanted to protect her from every possible hurt.

As he remembered the events of yesterday, he felt a cascade of relief that he'd had the good sense, or the lack of restraint, to say what he'd said in the woods last night. And also relieved and a bit proud that he'd been able to restrain himself from going too far with her in the seclusion of the forest.

That was something he was going to have to think hard about. After last night, he knew that it was only a matter of time before he and Harriet... He stopped himself from imagining them succumbing to their passion. He couldn't take a chance on Harriet getting pregnant. It would especially be a problem in Buxton, where there was such an emphasis on Christian morality. He thought that was more than a little ridiculous and hypocritical: wasn't it natural for people to love one another and make babies? Why did a church need to give its approval for that? It was another reason to be irritated with Reverend King! After all, if babies born out of wedlock were sinful, then he and Harriet—and for that matter nearly every person living in the Elgin Settlement—were doomed. But even more important to him, he didn't want to bring babies into the world without benefit of a stable family, father present. He knew from bitter experience that slavery stole black men's babies from them, denied them fatherhood, and he, a free black man, wasn't about to allow that to happen to him. If he and Harriet were falling in love, they needed to plan for their future together, not just drift along.

Then he shoved that thought into the back of his mind, because the discussion he'd had with Harriet walking to J.C. Brown's house was unresolved and kept poking at his mind like the pain of a sore tooth. He had to pay attention to it, had to stop the stabs of conscience.

When Harriet had asked her innocent question about whether he'd ever wished he were white, memories of his childhood had come roaring to his mind with an intensity he couldn't control. Like it or not, he had to look at them.

Now.

Thaddeus got out of bed and went through his morning routines without noticing what he was doing. His brain was focused on his thoughts.

He wasn't sure what was the truthful answer to Harriet's question. He didn't think he had wished to be white as a child. But when he was sent to work in the fields as a little boy while his white former playmates continued their care-free life, he had wished to be living their life instead of his. He wanted to be playing, not working. He wanted to be eating lovely, big plates of meat and delicious berry pies, not bowl after bowl of corn meal; he wanted to be wearing handsome clothes, not holey rags. He wanted to be lifted into the seat of the carriage for a ride into town to come back sucking colorful sticks of candy—not be lifted by his ears and thrown in the dirt so his former playmate's big brother could rape his mother in privacy.

His years growing up, living free in the Dismal Swamp had changed all of that and made him intensely proud to be a black man. He grew to hate everything about the white children he had once envied: the lack of responsibility, the pampering and the growing disrespect for other human beings that relentlessly turned into self-indulgence, greed and cruelty. It contrasted so sharply with the respectful, hard-working, generous people in his life: people who, for all the conflict of ordinary life, all the scandals big and small, still looked after one another selflessly. These were people who had seized their own freedom and carefully, painstakingly, built a thriving community in one of the most inhospitable environments he could imagine. A community he had chosen to leave.

He shuddered and the place between his shoulder blades and his belly felt empty. How could he bring himself to talk to Harriet about these things? They were too painful for his lips to form into words. He knew in Harriet's eyes he appeared stronger and more confident than he felt, but he wanted it to stay that way. At the same time, it seemed to him that his mother was nearby and peering right into the center of him, and he felt childish and weak—even guilty—under her penetrating gaze.

He had a recurring fantasy sometimes when he was lying under a tree and watching the leaves sway and twirl between him and the sky or sitting before a fire hypnotized by the dancing flames: he imagined his family living on their own farm in Buxton, Charlotte a young woman now, helping his happy mother, whose grateful eyes smiled on her oldest son for bringing her to this place. And he and Harriet would have their house nearby, and all of them would be working together to help build the Buxton community into a model for how the future of black people—maybe all people—

would look. His father and Nathaniel stayed in the shadows of this fantasy.

As he drank his tea this morning, Thaddeus wondered. Was the only way to settle his heart to go back to the Dismal Swamp? Maybe after the Emancipation celebration in Dawn, he would go to Windsor and talk to Henry Bibb about it.

Feeling a bit more settled, Thaddeus buttoned up his blue work shirt, soft with wear, and stepped out into the street to walk to the smithy. He wasn't sure what advice Brother Bibb would give him. Was he likely to tell the young courier to leave his important work with fugitive arrivals to go looking for his family? Bibb's own tragic story of his futile attempts to bring his family to safety came back to Thaddeus. What if his family was no longer there? Or if they were, wouldn't that mean they had decided not to come? Henry Bibb would know how to guide him and would understand how he felt.

"Son?"

His speculation was interrupted by an unfamiliar voice.

"Hello, son, you can help me a moment?"

Thaddeus blinked away his thoughts and realized there was a man on the road talking to him. A stranger. He looked up to see a tall, very dark-skinned man of his parents' generation, with uncombed hair and dusty clothes, carrying a small bag on his shoulder.

"Yes, hello, sorry," he stammered. He looked into the man's face and something tugged at his memory. This man looked familiar—a very good-looking man despite his road-worn and haggard face. Thaddeus realized the man must be a fugitive who had just arrived. Then why did he look so familiar?

"Yes, sir, my name is Thaddeus," he added, looking intently at the man's eyes: he knew those eyes. "How can I help you?"

"I just arrived in Chatham, come from Amherstburg, and before that from Virginia."

"Ah! Welcome, sir," Thaddeus smiled broadly. "I'm surprised you got here without me knowing it beforehand, because I work in the 'railroad' that you must have taken to get here."

The stranger smiled, and Thaddeus felt a quickening of his pulse at that peculiarly familiar smile. A thought began to form in his head.

"Well, I see I've come to the right person, then. When I arrived this side the river, a coach was soon leaving for Chatham, and as that's where I was heading, the good people put me on the coach and paid my fare. I've had no time to rest or bathe or eat, that's why I look like I do. I'm looking for a certain person, you see, who I've got reason to believe is in Chatham—or at least was in Chatham some years ago."

With a shock, Thaddeus knew.

"My name is Jacob Roberson, son. I'm looking for a woman called Abiah, and her daughter." His voice cracked a little. "My daughter, Harriet."

Thaddeus' throat contracted to swallow through a mouth suddenly dry and sticky. An image of Harriet laughing with Thomas, whom she adored, filled his vision. He suddenly felt as nervous and uncertain as a little boy. He moistened his lips and found his voice.

"Come with me, sir. I'm going to a man who can help you." It felt like a cowardly response, but it was all he could think to say.

33

She's Going to Want Your Support ~ July 1854

The next day, Thaddeus held the reins as the Gunsmith's horse pulled the small buggy along the rutted road to Buxton. Mrs. Jones sat at his side. Both of them tried sporadically to lighten the mood by talking, but conversation proved difficult. The topic of weather was quickly dispatched—hot, sunny, dry. They noted an interesting bird here and there, some loose cows, the spot where the Indians camped on their yearly hunting trip. In the end, most of the trip was passed in silence, both travelers pondering the difficult conversations awaiting them at the end of the journey.

When Thaddeus and Mr. Roberson had arrived at the smithy the day before, James Jones had already started the fire in preparation for the day's work and his wife was inside clearing up from breakfast. The gunsmith looked up with curiosity at the travel-worn stranger accompanying his young apprentice into the yard. He left the fire and stepped past the smithy doorway to meet them, holding his hand out in a friendly gesture to the man he quickly judged to be a newly arrived fugitive.

"Brother Jones, this is Mr. Roberson," Thaddeus said, looking at the gunsmith with a silent plea in his eyes.

Mr. Jones saw how Thaddeus looked at him. He flinched internally as the realization came. But his face gave away nothing as he smiled gravely at Jacob and shook his hand.

"Honor to meet you, Mr. Roberson."

"My pleasure, Mr. Jones," replied Jacob. Thaddeus saw it was still unfamiliar to him to be called "mister" or to call any other black man by that title. That he felt himself a stranger in a strange land. The man's weary eyes searched Mr. Jones' own hopefully. "The young man says you maybe could help me find my wife and daughter?"

Thaddeus saw the gunsmith swallow and knew he, too, had figured out who it was facing him.

Gunsmith Jones turned to bank the fire, saying over his shoulder, "You must be tired and hungry. Give me a moment and I'll take you inside and feed you. Then we can talk."

When the conversation continued inside, it was Emily Jones who had the nerve to break the news to the exhausted traveler. She sat on a chair across the kitchen table from their visitor after he had finished eating and spoke gently. Her husband stood behind her, hands on her shoulders. She said, simply and directly, that the woman Jacob was seeking indeed lived nearby, but that she had found another man after receiving news that she could never hope to see Jacob again. Thaddeus leaned against the wall near the doorway and watched Jacob take the blow.

Abiah and her husband had a son, Emily continued softly, and again Thaddeus saw a blow hit home. They had married in the church and were living in the Elgin Settlement in Buxton, a couple hours away. She knew he would be very proud of his daughter Harriet, a lovely and strong young woman who was active in the movement to assist fugitives from slavery below the border. Emily glanced at Thaddeus as she talked about Harriet.

"She favors you, Mr. Roberson," Mrs. Jones finished. "Anyone can see you all are family."

Thaddeus was amazed and relieved at Auntie Emily's courage in talking directly, yet sympathetically, to Mr. Roberson, who nonetheless now sat looking stunned. The man had perked up at Emily's description of Harriet, pride showing in his face. But when she finished, he was unable to speak, or even to nod. He put his head down, forehead resting on his crossed arms, his body looking caved in. He stayed that way for a long time, while Emily rose, put a comforting hand on his shoulder, then cleared away the plates and refilled Jacob's coffee cup.

When he finally lifted his head, he had a vacant, faraway look in his eyes that communicated a pain beyond words.

"Of course I would expect…" Jacob murmured, and then his voice failed him again. "But I hoped…" He stopped trying to speak.

Thaddeus' heart ached looking at the man, and a lump came into his throat. It had been more than thirteen years since Jacob had parted from the woman he loved, from his baby daughter. How must it feel to have searched for her with such devotion after so long a separation, and then confront the knowledge Mrs. Jones had just given him? It was unthinkable. Thaddeus found himself incapable of moving, incapable of speaking.

But Gunsmith Jones spoke. "Mr. Roberson," he began.

"Call me Jacob, please," the man responded in a dry, emotionless voice.

"Okay, Jacob, then. I know you're exhausted and you've just had some real disappointing news. Let my wife and me offer you bath and bed. Tomorrow, we'll send word to Abiah about your arrival, and leave her response in her hands. Meanwhile, you're welcome to stay with us and recover your strength."

Jacob nodded mutely at this suggestion. Emily appeared at his side, put her hand under his elbow to nudge him up and lead him past Thaddeus into the rear of the house.

Thaddeus followed the gunsmith out front and into the smithy. Before stoking the fire, Uncle James turned and put his hand on Thaddeus' shoulder.

"Thaddeus, boy, I know this turn of events affects you, too. I know your feelings for Harriet."

It was Thaddeus' turn to nod mutely. His hollow eyes beseeched Uncle James for guidance.

"It's for her mother to break this news to her daughter, but you ought to be there. If she feels about you the way you feel about her" — Thaddeus nodded again — "then she's going to want your support. She'll most likely be confused in her feelings. She maybe won't want to even talk to her mother about it. She might get mad at her mother. She might even get mad at this man here for coming into her life and disrupting it. So, it's best you drive Mrs. Jones to Buxton tomorrow when she goes to speak with Mrs. Ingram."

"Yes, sir," Thaddeus responded. He was proud to know that Mr. Jones respected him enough to give him this adult advice, to acknowledge him as a man and respect the seriousness of his feelings for Harriet. At the same time, it was intimidating to take on this responsibility. He couldn't imagine what he ought to say to Harriet. A part of him wished Mr. Jones was sending him off to the Dawn Settlement with a message instead, and he immediately scolded himself for his cowardice. Mr. Jones was expecting him to act like an adult. He brought to mind William Parker and his way of standing up to fight any obstacle without fear. He vowed to himself that the days of running from his problems were behind him. From today forward he would face them as a grown man.

Now, as he sat beside Aunt Emily in the buggy and watched the steadily trotting rump and swishing tail of the horse in front of him inexorably bringing them closer to their destination, he found himself wishing he could slow down time, give him more opportunity for contemplation. There were so many conflicting and confusing thoughts, plans and feelings going on in his head at the same time: his declaration of love for Harriet and what it implied for his future (was it just the night before last?). The upcoming trip to Dawn and all the issues it raised between him and Harriet. His thoughts of traveling south to find his family, and now this earthquake about to hit Harriet's life. Would he be able to handle what was coming? He would have to clear his mind and try to be strong for Harriet today.

◇

Harriet was coming from the chicken coop with a basket of eggs when she saw the buggy approaching with Thaddeus driving and Auntie Emily sitting alongside him. This was unusual. She'd just seen Thaddeus two days ago and knew he'd had no plan to come to Buxton. And Auntie Emily: Harriet couldn't remember when she'd last come to Buxton—plus, she was without the children. Harriet stopped, suddenly anxious, with the egg basket dangling from her arm as conflicting emotions beset her. Her whole body was excited at the unexpected prospect of time with Thaddeus, yet scared about what could have happened that would make Auntie Emily come to their house. She stood like a statue as Thaddeus brought the buggy to a halt at their gate, jumped down, tied the horse to the post and helped Aunt Emily down from the other side of the carriage. When they came through the gate toward the house, Harriet recovered herself and walked swiftly to the back door and into the kitchen.

As she set the basket down on the sideboard she saw her mother's back in the doorway greeting Aunt Emily, then saw her step aside and invite her friend in. Harriet waited while the two women walked toward her.

"Hello, Harriet," Aunt Emily said, and went on before Harriet could respond. "I need to speak to your mother privately." Then, seeing the look in the young woman's eyes, Aunt Emily quickly added, "Don't worry, it's not bad news." Emily's smile was unconvincing. Harriet simply murmured a greeting. As she walked out the back door, she heard Emily ask where Thomas was and her mother reply that he was working in the far field today.

Thaddeus was standing at the corner of the house. As she stepped through the door he reached out his hand. She took it with silent anticipation, her eyes asking, *What's happening?*

The touch of his calloused fingers exhilarated her.

Thaddeus took a deep breath. Then he smiled and pulled her closer, so he couldn't see the question in her eyes.

"Come on, let's go for a walk. They're going to be talking for a while. And now I get to see you sooner than I ever expected!"

Harriet leaned into him happily, but still asked, "What is it, Thaddeus? It's so strange to see Auntie Emily come to talk to my mother. Is everything really okay?"

"My lips are sealed," Thaddeus put as much lightness into his voice as he could concoct. He realized as soon as the words were out that they were as good as a confession that he knew what conversation was going on in the house behind them.

Harriet stiffened. "If you know, why can't you just tell me?"

Now what? thought Thaddeus. Nervously, he continued talking in a light tone.

"Well, you know, it's a grown-folk thing. Let your mama tell you about it. Meanwhile, let's keep this time for ourselves, my sweet little beauty!"

His words got the response he hoped for. Harriet relaxed and grinned up at him. They reached the cornfield and turned to walk along its edge toward the woods.

"So, you still love me today then?" Harriet said playfully, moving her hand around his waist and boldly sliding it under his shirt to rest on the bare skin of his hip. The warm smoothness of his skin set her palm aglow. He responded with a "hmmph" and put his hand around her, letting it rest low on her hip, his palm on the side of her buttock. He glanced quickly over his shoulder in the unlikely event that somehow Abiah was standing in the doorway watching them. She wasn't, and his hand slipped further back.

"Ooh, boy, you're bad!" Harriet laughed, squeezing his waist and pushing him with her toward the trees.

They tumbled to the soft, leaf-padded ground and attacked one another with breathless passion. This time it was Harriet who eventually rolled away, panting, when she felt Thaddeus' hand come up under her skirt and touch the inside of her leg. She stood up quickly to brush leaves and earth off her clothing. Thaddeus lay on his side, propped on his elbow, trying to control his breathing, among other things.

"Whoa," Harriet whispered to herself. "Whoa, boy, you better slow down," she added aloud. Thaddeus smiled crookedly up at her.

"Who better slow down? Girl, you started it! You knocked me down!"

"Me?!" Harriet tried to sound indignant but couldn't stop the giggles bubbling up from inside her.

Thaddeus got up and brushed himself off, his breathing slowly coming back to normal.

"Listen, girl, this is getting serious. We better watch out."

Harriet was silenced by the gravity of Thaddeus' voice. A small fear shot through her. He didn't want to call a halt to their newfound intimacy, did he? His touch, his kisses, the nearness and feel of his body: it was all new to Harriet and she found it completely irresistible, even though his hand on her bare thigh had startled her. When their bodies were close and their mouths together, it was like drinking honey. It was like the sun's warm rays turned to liquid and coursing through her veins. It was like…it was like nothing else she knew. She just knew she wanted more, wanted it always and forever. She couldn't think of any response, not even a joking one.

"Harriet, I want you. I love you. I can't trust myself around you. I don't know what to do." The words blurted out of Thaddeus without a thought, and the confusion he saw in Harriet's eyes made him remember his pledge to be a strong presence for her today. Saying, "I don't know what to do" did not meet that commitment. He laughed to lighten the mood.

"I don't know what to do! I don't know what to do," he made it into a little song, and grinned broadly at her, saying, "You just have me wrapped around your little finger, girl, you know that?" Thankfully, he received a coy smile in return. "So, is your whole family going to Dawn next month?"

Before she could respond to this hasty change of subject, they heard Auntie Emily's voice calling her name. They glanced at each other, and Harriet saw that Thaddeus suddenly looked nervous. Confusion overtook her again, and with one more check to make sure she'd gotten the telltale evidence off her clothes and head-wrap, she started out of the woods and strode quickly back across the field toward her house. Thaddeus followed slowly and apprehensively behind her.

34

Life's Not Easy, Life's Not Fair

When Harriet re-emerged from the house, Thaddeus was sitting under the tree in front of the barn. Her feet carried her, unseeing, across the familiar ground of her yard. She sat down beside him without saying anything. She felt a small amount of betrayal, of *How could you not tell me?* But she knew that Thaddeus could not have said anything to her before her mother did. She put her elbows on her knees and her face between her hands and looked blindly in the direction of the ants rushing about their urgent business on the earth between her feet. Thaddeus sat quietly beside her, resting his hand gently on hers. Finally she spoke, in a small and wondering voice. "I never saw Mama cry before."

Thaddeus squeezed her hand and remained silent, not having the slightest idea what to say, just trying to be a supportive presence. Harriet looked up at him, her voice now stronger.

"Thaddeus, you know that this man Jacob…my father…he…he…you know without him I wouldn't even be here—neither me nor Mama? I would…I would be a slave right now! In Virginia." Her voice carried shock and amazement, as if she had never in life recognized that possibility before. And, in truth, she felt like she had never seriously considered it before. "He…why did Mama never tell me before?" She sounded hurt, angry.

"*He's* the one found the Underground Railroad and set us up to get away. He stayed back so we'd have a better chance, and then he lost his own chance!" Her voice was indignant, awe-struck and tragic all in one. Her nose started to run and a little sob escaped from her throat. Thaddeus moved closer and put his arm around her shoulder, drawing her to him.

She collapsed against his side and cried quietly but fiercely.

Now Thaddeus was scared. What were you supposed to do for a crying woman? He started patting her like you would pat a crying baby. No words would come. He felt foolish. But Harriet didn't feel his uncertainty. She just knew he was there for her, holding her, lending her strength.

"Lord have mercy, Thaddeus," she snuffled hoarsely as the waves of sobbing ebbed into gentle swells. "Life's not easy! It's not fair. Imagine this man come to find us after all these years! And God knows what he's been through." She hiccupped and took in a sharp breath. "And then to find out his woman is with another man?" A thought suddenly struck Harriet. "Oh, sweet Jesus! Daddy Thomas! What's Daddy Thomas going to think? Daddy…" her voice faded into silence.

There were too many conflicting images and emotions. In the end, they cancelled each other out, leaving Harriet empty and flat. She collapsed against Thaddeus' chest and rested silent and motionless for a long time, as each rise and fall of his breath reassured her that her world was still there.

Thaddeus was relieved that the crying was over, but he felt he was expected to say something. "It's going to be okay, baby. It'll work out in the end." He felt Harriet sigh. He went on. "I saw him, you know."

Harriet sat up straight and looked at him sharply.

"It was me who found him…well, really, *he* found *me* on the street when I was walking to the smithy yesterday morning." He paused, looking searchingly at her. "You favor him."

An odd look flashed across Harriet's face. Her eyes lit up. "I do?" She felt a tug in her chest. "You know, Thaddeus," she said, excitement now growing in her, "I've always wondered about him. My mama never talked about him much, only to say he was a good man. I always wanted to ask her more, but I was scared, 'cause she never hardly mentioned him. I was scared to hurt Daddy Thomas, too. I think she felt the same way." She paused thoughtfully. "I love Thomas, you know. He loves me too. I know he does. Sometime I wonder if he prefers Zach, 'cause Zach is really his baby, and a boy on top of it. But to tell the truth, I don't see it. He treats me like his own daughter. But I've always wondered about my real daddy. I favor him for sure?"

Thaddeus nodded with a smile. "Yeah, I guessed who he was before he told me. He said he was looking for someone, and I just knew. You got his eyes for sure. I could tell Uncle James saw it, too. And Aunt Emily told him that he has a lovely, strong daughter and he's going to be proud of her, and she looks like him." He grinned.

Harriet suddenly threw her arms around Thaddeus and hugged him so tight he could barely breath. He choked out a laugh, and she let go and laughed along with him.

"I've got to go meet him!" Saying those words took Harriet back to the complexities of the situation. What was her mother going to do? How would Thomas feel? But no question could dampen her eagerness to meet her father.

"Come on, Thad, I'm going to go see what my mama plans on doing."

Harriet jumped up, pulling Thaddeus to his feet and half-dragging him in the direction of the house. She was glad that Zach was off with his friend this morning and not here to complicate all this. When they got to the door, Abiah and Emily were deep in conversation, and her mother's friend Ruth Little was also sitting at the table. They glanced up as the young people walked in.

"I don't know how I'm going to talk to Thomas about this," Abiah was saying, "but I know I have to go see Jacob before I do." Her face looked haunted and confused, possibly frightened, but under those emotions, Harriet detected excitement. "You know, Emily," she glanced at her daughter as she spoke, "I've had a vision of this. It comes back over and over. I've seen Jacob walking down the street in Chatham one day asking for me." She looked over at Thaddeus, and Harriet knew that Emily had told her it was Thaddeus who brought Jacob to them. "It always frightens me. And, truth be told, makes me feel guilty. The man sacrificed his freedom for Harriet and me. I used to love the man. He was my young love. I owe him."

Those last words made Harriet shiver, and she looked surreptitiously at Thaddeus. It struck her that she was about the age her mother must have been when she'd fallen in love with her father. Her mother had felt the same way about Jacob that she felt about Thaddeus. Oh, God, what would she feel if she had to be separated from Thaddeus? She suddenly saw her mother's story about running from slavery in a whole new light. Even while she was running toward freedom, she was carrying a searing pain. She had left her love behind.

Emily was nodding, her hands folded on the table in front of her.

"You do owe him, Abiah, in a sense, but you've got no call to feel guilty. It wasn't any of your fault he didn't get away to join you all. You did everything you could. Girl, you waited for him for *years*. You never even looked for a new man for yourself 'til after he was truly gone for good. That's all you could have done!"

The outspoken Ruth Little added, "Girl, if it was me, I'd be wondering if I still had feelings for him. I'd be wondering if I'd taken up my new man to keep me company, but kept my true love buried somewhere in my heart." A half-smile played on Ruth Little's lips and she raised one eyebrow suggestively. "Maybe you've got you two men now, 'Biah. Maybe you've got you a Chatham man and a home man!"

Emily shook her head sharply, "Ruth, don't be talking like that. This is no laughing matter!"

"You don't see me laughing!" Ruth spoke back just as sharply. "Plenty men keep more than one woman, I know women to keep more than one man! Abiah's going to have to look into her heart about this thing. Reverend King's not going to approve it, but he doesn't need to know. Thomas doesn't need to know, either." With that, she cut her eyes at Harriet meaningfully.

"Abiah has a happy home and family. She's a Christian wife and mother. Don't you be talking to her like that!" Harriet could see Emily was indignant, maybe even angry.

Miss Ruth's words were a shock to Harriet, but she knew her mother's friend was only describing the world as it was. In Buxton, there was *on the surface*—all God-fearing, married, family people and adultery a sin—and there was *under the surface*—the comings and goings, the rumors, the children who looked like some other mother's husband. The occasional violence, carefully hushed up. The Court of Arbitration meetings that happened without Reverend King's knowledge. The things people took care of that King wouldn't understand, as she remembered Thomas saying to William Parker, before she was old enough to know what he was talking about.

The idea that her mother might do what Miss Little was suggesting shook Harriet. She shot a confused look toward Thaddeus, who was shifting uncomfortably near the door, looking like he wanted to escape.

"You all just be quiet now." This was the firm, command-ing Mama's voice that Harriet knew, and just hearing it made her relax some. "I'll work it out. First step, I'm going to see Jacob. And Harriet's going with me." She looked across the room at her daughter. Harriet smiled. "Emily, you and Thaddeus go on back to Chatham. Tell that man he'll see us tomorrow."

Abiah spoke with such finality that the other women stood up from the table.

"Harriet, go fix some sandwiches for Auntie Emily and Thaddeus to carry with them."

As Harriet turned toward the table, Thaddeus came to her side. They gathered bread and cheese and started making sandwiches. Harriet walked out to the kitchen garden to pick a couple of tomatoes, her mind occupied with uncertainty about how she and her mother would get to Chatham tomorrow and an uncomfortable, hazy foreboding about this evening, when Thomas would be home and her mother would explain their trip to Chatham to him. And Zach.

A short while later, she stood in the road beside her mother, watching the buggy disappear into the woods, her eyes lingering on Thaddeus' broad shoulders until they were out of sight. Her mother had her arm around Harriet's waist but said nothing. Ruth Little stood behind them just inside the gate.

"Harriet," her mother finally said, turning to her, "you don't talk to anybody about this, you hear me? I don't know how I'll handle this, not 'til after I see Jacob tomorrow. Nobody needs to know about this just yet."

Harriet nodded, but felt a chill of uncertainty creeping into her belly. She wasn't going to tell Thomas? Her mother walked back through the gate, past Miss Ruth, and into the house. Harriet felt rooted to the spot. She looked vacantly toward Miss Ruth, who walked over to join her.

"Listen, now, Harriet, child," she said, putting a hand on Harriet's arm. "Don't you worry. Your mama's going through something right now and you have to let her take her time. She's going to get there, and she'll show you the way, too, you just leave her to it. You understand me?"

Harriet nodded, but felt a little rebellious bubble rise up inside.

"Yes, ma'am, but you don't think I'm going through something too? I'm no baby any more, you know! I'm nearly seventeen years old, and coming my own woman. I can't just wait for my mama to tell me what to do every minute!" The words came out with more energy and vehemence than

Harriet expected, and she feared she had disrespected her mother's friend.

Ruth Little just smiled. "You're right, Harriet. You're becoming your own woman, and you're going to make your own choices. But yet and still, you're in your mama's house, and long as you're in your mama's house you're responsible to do what she says. Besides," she put her arm around Harriet's waist now, taking a few slow steps down the road in the direction of her own house, "you've got to take *your* own time to figure this out, too. Don't be jumping into anything. Don't you make any decisions nor conclusions just yet. You just wait till you meet your daddy first. Hear?"

Harriet nodded gratefully, knowing the woman was right.

"Yes ma'am, you're right. I'm excited to meet my daddy," she paused—the word sounded foreign on her tongue and made her belly flinch. She had often used the same word to address Thomas, and wondered for a quick moment if she was being a traitor. "I love Thomas, you know," she added quickly. "He's been Daddy to me." She faltered.

"I know, sweetheart, I know. Thomas is a good man, too. A good, good man. But regardless of what your mother has to do, *you're* allowed to love the both of them if you choose! There's no reason you need to pick one over t'other." She smiled, which made Harriet smile, too. "But I know it's plumb confusing. You ever need to talk to somebody about all this, you know where to come."

Miss Little took her arm from around Harriet and faced her. Putting one hand firmly on either side of the young woman's waist, she turned her back toward home.

"You go on now. Go back to your mama. You all will be all right."

"Yes, ma'am, thank you." Harriet said, and walked back through her gate.

<>

That night, Abiah told Thomas she planned to go to Chatham the next day. There was no way that Emily Jones' visit could be a secret. People had seen her arrive and leave again, so Abiah told her husband that Emily had come to tell her that Mrs. Brown was having a hard time coping with her husband's illness and could use a visit. She saw him knit his brows at that. It was a pretty scanty reason for Emily to take the long drive when she could have sent a message with someone who happened to be traveling that way. Abiah could see it didn't sound like an emergency to him. She added that Emily had taken the opportunity for a day away from her responsibilities. Thomas accepted her explanation but didn't look entirely convinced.

Next, Abiah sent Harriet to Reverend King to arrange to borrow the buggy the next morning. She also told her to arrange with Ruth Little to take care of Zachary the next day. This caused another frown to cross Thomas' face. Why wouldn't Abiah take their son along for the outing? Abiah felt the question, but ignored it, not meeting her husband's eyes.

All evening, Abiah was distant and on edge, and Harriet knew Thomas sensed it. Her mother was trying to behave normally, but it was clear she had difficulty concentrating. Even Zach seemed to notice, he gave trouble going to bed that night, and Abiah was uncharacteristically sharp with him. Thomas finally intervened, climbing the ladder into the loft with his little son and tucking him into his bed with a soothing story.

Harriet was sitting quietly in a corner with some sewing. When Thomas came back down, he regarded Abiah silently. Abiah shook her head, saying, "I just keep thinking about Mrs. Brown. I don't know what I would do if you got sick, Thomas!"

But Harriet noticed she didn't meet his eyes. *I don't think he believes her,* she thought. She wondered about her mother meeting Jacob tomorrow. Did she even remember what he looked like? What would she feel for him? What would she say? Would this be the end of their family life with Thomas? She came close to tears, thinking of the disruption possibly in store for Thomas. For Zachary.

She realized it was different for her. She was older, she was her own person. Miss Ruth was right, Harriet could make up her own mind about a relationship with Jacob. Loyalty to Thomas swelled in her, but alongside it was excitement and yes, loyalty, too, for the father she had so often dreamed about.

35

Reunited ~ July 1854

Harriet tossed and turned that night with excitement and anticipation, but she fell asleep and slept well. In the morning, she dropped Zach off with Miss Ruth, where he was excited to play with the older children. Harriet had gotten him away from his mama easily by hoisting him up onto Meldy's wide back as she led the mare along the path to the Littles' house. Zachary had beamed down at the world from his high perch, his hands tightly entwined in the mare's long mane.

Now Harriet was alongside Reverend King's barn, hitching Meldy to the buggy. Finally, all the harness buckles were secure and the long reins ran from Meldy's bridle to the box of the buggy. Harriet led the mare to the road and climbed up onto the seat. She exchanged waves with the Reverend and Mrs. King on their verandah, her heart pumping with excitement.

◇

Meldy pulled the buggy along the bumpy road at a good trot. Abiah told Harriet to slow her down. "She keeps bouncing us around like that, we're going to churn ourselves to butter by the time we get there!"

Harriet laughed but slowed their pace. Impatient as she was to reach their destination, she also wanted this opportunity to get her mother to talk.

"What does my daddy look like, Mama?"

"Baby, it's been so long since I've seen him, I can't rightly tell you. But I always did think you looked like him." She paused and looked at her daughter, saw the impatience and excitement on her face. "Okay, well, he's tall. Taller than Thomas, taller than Thaddeus. And he's got dark skin, like your complexion. He's got eyes shaped just like your own. And he's good-looking—well, when we were young, I thought he was just the handsomest man I ever laid eyes on."

Harriet grinned. Hard as it was to imagine her mother young and in love, somehow it wasn't hard to imagine Jacob—her daddy—young and handsome and in love.

"You and him lived on the same plantation, Mama?" Harriet knew the answer, but wanted to keep her mother talking.

"Yes, baby. At first, I didn't know him 'cause that plantation was so big there was more than one living quarters. But then they moved him from the far fields to the close-in quarters where I lived with my mama." Here Abiah got quiet and looked off into the distance. "And my sisters." She fell silent.

Harriet felt a little shock as she remembered that she had a grandmother and aunts. And that they were enslaved. Of course she had always known this, but it seemed like another world. She rarely thought about it. Now she found herself wondering about the place her mother had grown up. What did it look like? Was her grandmother still alive? Were her aunts older or younger than her mother? What was life like for them? She realized how little she knew, and how little her mother had talked about her early life. Was it so horrible that Abiah didn't want to be reminded of it by the retelling?

"Mama," Harriet said hesitantly, and realized that her voice sounded like a little girl, "You must miss them, don't you?"

"Yes, baby, I miss them. When I think about them my heart pains me like somebody took a knife and stuck it in me. Still, I'm sorry I never told you much about your grandmama and your aunties. You would like them. They just loved you to death, you know." Her voice caught. "It's a hard story, but it's a relief to finally tell it to you."

And for the rest of the ride, Abiah talked to Harriet about the place where Harriet had been born, the relatives Harriet couldn't remember. She told her about working in the garden and looking out across the valley, about the buying and the selling of people, about the beatings and the rapes. She talked about the daily humiliations, the pain and the unending exhaustion. And she told her about Harriet's father: how Jacob had been the sunshine in her life. How they had planned and yearned for their escape. How, after she and Harriet had succeeded in their escape, they had written to each other for years in constant hope and expectation of being reunited, and the awful day when she had gotten the news that he was gone, sold down South, beyond reach.

Harriet listened, barely breathing, visioning in her mind's eye the place she had lived until she was a toddler, imagining that she remembered the places and people her mother described, struggling to pull an elusive glimpse of her father from her memory, or to remember the feel of being held in his hands or sitting on his shoulders. By the time the road became a street lined with houses, Harriet's mood had gone from simple excitement to something much deeper and darker. Everything her mother described was so profoundly *unfair*. She had lost all her family, everyone except her mother, and for the first time in her life she felt it deep and heavy. She was overcome by a combination of loss, tragedy and anger mingled with nervousness and hope.

Her belly began turning over as if her breakfast didn't agree with her. As they drove through the town and the horse's feet clopped across the bridge, she knew her nervousness was transmitting through the reins — Meldy started tossing her head and dancing. Harriet had to struggle with her on the last stretch of road as they both became increasingly tense.

The sound of the approaching horse and buggy brought Thaddeus and Gunsmith Jones to the door of the smithy.

Harriet was happy to have Thaddeus step up and take hold of Meldy, who settled down immediately to Thaddeus' much calmer touch. He held the horse still until the women could climb down from the buggy, then he nodded a greeting to Harriet, holding her eyes for a moment before leading Meldy to the barn to unhitch her.

Harriet and Abiah stood hesitantly where they had alit from the buggy. Then Uncle James stepped forward, took hold of Abiah's elbow and led them to the house. Harriet hadn't felt so nervous since the day she'd gone through the initiation for the Order. Her body still buzzed from the rumbling of the cartwheels, and her vision didn't seem normal—the world looked hazy and glittery. She walked behind her mother.

Abiah seemed to be holding her breath as they followed Uncle James through the door to his house, intensely aware of the man who would momentarily appear before them. Uncle James stepped to one side, and Harriet saw a man sitting at the kitchen table over her mother's shoulder. As soon as James stepped aside, the man's eyes fixed on Abiah. Abiah stopped suddenly and Harriet had to stop short to avoid bumping into her.

The man was tall and dark, familiar looking. The clothes he was wearing were clean, but worn thin and frayed. He had a grizzle of beard and a full mustache above his upper lip. Lines reached out from the corners of his eyes and a deep groove made a track from each side of his nose to the corners of his mouth. He looked old: older than Abiah. Abiah stood still for a long moment, and then she let out a long breath, her shoulders relaxing. Only then did she step forward far enough for Harriet to come through the door.

Harriet watched silently as her mother walked to the table, reached out her hands, smiled and said, "Hello Jacob."

Jacob stood up so suddenly he had to turn and grab the chair to keep it from falling over. Then he reached for

Abiah's hands and grasped them, looking into her eyes with an intensity that almost hurt.

"Abiah!" He squeezed her hands, clearly wanting desperately to take her into his arms, to hold her tight to himself and never let go. How often he must have imagined this moment! But he hesitated. She was married to another man, he wasn't sure how to behave. Abiah solved his problem by releasing her hands from his grip and stepping forward to hug him. He put his arms around her and closed his eyes.

Harriet stood transfixed. Jacob finally opened his eyes as Abiah began to pull back from the embrace. He seemed to see Harriet for the first time, and he dropped his arms from around Abiah, his eyes growing bigger, his lips parting slightly.

"Harriet?" he asked with wonder in his voice.

"Yes, sir," Harriet tried to say, but the words came out in a dry whisper. She cleared her throat and repeated herself, "Yes, sir."

Abiah turned sideways and looked from Jacob to Harriet with a proud smile.

"Yes, Jacob, this is your daughter! This is little Harriet. See how big and pretty she's grown?" Abiah's smile broadened into a grin that made Harriet relax. Suddenly she knew everything was going to be okay.

Jacob walked over to his daughter, taking her hands in his. Harriet felt like a shy little girl. She smiled at him mutely.

"Harriet, Harriet, Harriet! Praise the Lord, look at my girl! Look how you're big and healthy! You're a woman yourself now, aren't you! How old are you nowadays?" He stopped to try to figure the years.

"Nearly seventeen, sir," Harriet tried to say "Daddy" but the word wouldn't quite come off her tongue.

Jacob looked at Abiah. "She's about the same age you were when I met you! And pretty as you, too! And *you...*" He was talking about Abiah now. "You barely look a day older'n last time I saw you!" Abiah waved him off with her hand, smiling. Jacob looked so delighted that Harriet found herself grinning, too, and squeezing his hands.

"Well, aren't you going to hug her?" Abiah asked playfully.

Jacob dropped Harriet's hands and tentatively put his arms around her. She felt a little nervous at first, but suddenly yearned for the embrace. She threw her arms around him and hugged him tight. She heard Abiah and Uncle James start to laugh. Over Jacob's shoulder she saw Auntie Emily come through the doorway wiping wet hands on her apron. A vivid smile lit up her whole face. She put her fists on her hips.

"What! You let me miss it? James, what happened to you! Why didn't you call me?" she shouted with a joking aggressiveness. She walked to Abiah then and gave her a big hug. Abiah accepted it and suddenly looked shaky from release of the tension that had gripped her for the past twenty-four hours. She plopped down onto the chair Jacob had vacated. Emily squeezed her shoulder and then turned her attention to Harriet.

"So, girl, you met your daddy, eh? You sure do look like him, young lady!" she exclaimed, putting her hands on her hips and leaning back to get a better look at father and daughter.

Harriet drew back from Jacob and smiled at Auntie Emily with a mixture of gratefulness and pride. She still had no words.

"Okay, you all have got to eat something. Dinnertime now. You two," she pointed at Harriet and Abiah, "you go wash up yourselves and come back in here. And Harriet, find that boy Thaddeus and bring him here." Then she turned to the collection of children who had appeared behind her and began giving them instructions about preparing the table for dinner.

Harriet was happy to escape back outside and try to collect

herself. She nearly skipped to the barn and found Thaddeus putting Meldy into a stall. Harriet grabbed a bucket energetically and took it to the well to fill with water.

"Whoa, girl, you look like you got a whole passel of feathers tickling you!" Thaddeus laughed at her exuberance. "So, I guess you're glad to meet your daddy!"

Harriet put down the water bucket and threw her arms around Thaddeus, squeezing him till he grunted.

"Yes, Thaddeus! I don't know why I'm so happy! I used to think about him and wonder about him, but I always just put him away in a corner like somebody you hear about but are never going to meet. I can't believe it makes me so happy to see him! He seems like a real nice man, too, you know?" She couldn't contain herself.

Thaddeus smiled, happy for her, but Harriet could also see a shadow of some other emotion cross his face. She wondered briefly about Thaddeus' feelings about the family he had left behind. But as quickly as the thought came to her, it was blown out of her mind by the storm of feelings that was nearly lifting her off her feet.

Thaddeus answered slowly and soberly, hoping to help Harriet level herself out. "He does seem like a nice man. He and I talked a little this morning. I think he's been to Hell and back."

Harriet felt herself sobering up. She looked wordlessly at Thaddeus, waiting for him to continue. "I guess he'll tell more about it in time—least I think he will. Sounds like he was at some right miserable places."

Harriet's eyes darkened, her lips turned down at the corners, and Thaddeus changed his tone: he didn't want to spoil her happiness. "But girl! You can't believe how happy he is to find you, child! He told me how you were when you were a baby—round and fat and cheerful."

Harriet smiled then, reaching her hand out, "Come on inside, Thaddeus, Auntie Emily said to get you for dinner."

◇

Dinner was a boisterous affair. Gunsmith Jones got Jacob talking about his successful escape and his flight across more than one thousand miles of southern and northern states until he finally reached free soil in Amherstberg. How he'd been transported across the river and immediately shuffled onto a coach heading for Chatham and had spent the night under the trees along the river, not knowing where to go with darkness falling and no money in his pockets. The children buzzed amongst each other about this drama, while the adults talked over one another to tell Jacob about possibilities for housing and work, and places he could stay until he got himself settled. Jacob turned his attention from one to the other, but most of the information seemed to be vanishing from his mind like smoke. The only thing he could focus on was the miraculous sight of the woman he loved and his beautiful grown daughter, the only thing visible in his eyes an intense relief and wonder at being safe among friends.

After dinner, Abiah went to Emily's bedroom with her. Harriet, helping to clear up in the kitchen nearby, overheard them talking.

"You know when somebody dies and you're afraid to look at him in the coffin? You fear to see him in death looking like he looked in life? And when it doesn't look like him you're kind of relieved, 'cause it's not really him? You know what I'm saying?" Abiah's spoke slowly, thoughtfully.

"Yes, I know exactly what you mean. Like it's easier to say goodbye when you see it's not really the person you lost. The spirit is gone already and it isn't really him lying there."

"Exactly!" Abiah said. "That's how I felt when I walked through the door and saw Jacob. No, no, I don't mean he looked like he was dead, nothing like that. I mean at first, I felt relieved because he doesn't look like he did. He looks different. Older. Something."

Harriet stood quietly, wanting to hear more.

"*And?*" Emily finally spoke. "How do you feel now?"

"Oh, Em, I don't know! When he talks, and how he moves, oh God forgive me, seems like he's coming to feel like the man I knew way back. Like I can see through the oldness and the tiredness and see back to the young man. My Lord, I really was Harriet's age? Seems like I was older." Abiah fell silent.

The two women came out of the room and Harriet slipped out of their sight. They left to walk to the Brown house. Abiah's explanation to Thomas for her trip was not without a kernel of truth, and she would have to tell him how she found Mr. and Mrs. Brown. As they strolled slowly through the yard, their voices faded away.

36

Jacob's Story

After the women were gone and the plates cleared away, Harriet, Thaddeus and Jacob sat back down at the table. The children ran out into the yard, Uncle James went back to work in the smithy.

Jacob looked from Harriet to Thaddeus and back. "So, this is your man, is it?" The way he looked at him made Thaddeus unexpectedly nervous. Until now, Thaddeus had only thought about the impact of his arrival on Harriet's life. With a jolt, he realized that this man was his girlfriend's father and he would have to meet his approval. He swallowed and glanced sideways at Harriet.

"Yes, sir, he is." Harriet spoke clearly, with a lift to her chin and with a sharpness that surprised Thaddeus.

Jacob threw his head back and laughed. "Girl knows her mind, doesn't she!" he exclaimed. "Well, I guess you're your mother's daughter all right." His smile melted Thaddeus' fears.

Harriet had surprised herself with the outspokenness of her answer. She felt confusion and then relief at Jacob's response. She also felt self-conscious: she had called Thaddeus "her man," or at least agreed to it. She had stepped out of her childhood place, and her father had accepted that. Jacob was dealing with her as an adult—it was thrilling.

Emboldened, she spoke again. "Daddy, you told us how you got here. But I want to know what happened after me and Mama left. What happened to you?" Hearing herself call Jacob "daddy" made her ears hot and almost took away her breath. She was looking down at the table as she spoke, but then she glanced up at Jacob's face. She saw the intense emotion the word had evoked, and looked quickly back down as

Jacob's creased and callused knuckle went to the corner of his eye to wipe away moisture that suddenly appeared there.

After a long pause, Jacob cleared his throat and began to talk. For the next hour or more, Harriet and Thaddeus sat and listened to his voice, sometimes husky and quiet, sometimes filled with restrained emotion, sometimes choked with suppressed tears. Now and then, Harriet asked a question. She sat with her elbows on the table and her chin propped in her hands, barely moving, eyes glued to her father's face. Thaddeus leaned back in his chair, arms folded across his chest as if to protect himself from what he was hearing.

When Jacob stopped talking, Harriet was speechless. The things the man sitting across from her had experienced were unimaginable to her, despite having heard pieces of similar stories from other fugitives.

Jacob had repeatedly run away and been recaptured. Each time he was subjected to harsher and harsher torture, until finally he was sold south to Louisiana. There the story was repeated: he was sold from one sugar plantation to another, working in impossible conditions, always resisting, and frequently punished in ways so terrible he refused to describe them.

At one point, Harriet asked her father if he had fallen in love with any other woman after her mother was no longer within reach. He had snorted at the question, shaking his head. On the plantations in Louisiana, only certain men were allowed access to women: the white slave owners and their sons, plus one or two slave men selected for their size and strength. The slave owners were breeding their human stock like they bred their animals. Harriet didn't notice Thaddeus' face grow sorrowful, his eyes become round and hollow. She was shocked at her father's graphic description of his situation, and found herself applauding his own secret midnight forays to the dirt-floor shacks of women on the different plantations. She realized that none of it was about love, much less family: those were luxuries unavailable to her father. But it was about comfort and friendship and intimacy stolen from the very bowels of Hell. She also realized that if she had brothers and sisters in Louisiana, her father hadn't stayed in one place long enough to even know.

His whole story, on top of her mother's story earlier in the day, left her mind whirling with a sense of irreparable loss. Deep sorrow for her father quickly bloomed into fierce determination to defend his life and happiness now that he was here and safe. But she also couldn't shake a disturbing feeling in her gut that she likely had siblings she would never know. That her father had children left behind in the clutches of slavery, the products of hasty, chaotic connections. Nor could she shake the images of the women inhumanly used in circumstances they were helpless to control. Her skin crawled as she imagined herself in those conditions. Amid all the other emotions, she felt immensely grateful, more so than she ever had before, for her father's actions and her mother's courage that had cut her loose from that fate.

Of course Harriet had always known she had been born a slave, but it was hard to think of herself that way because she remembered nothing of those infant years. All her life she had been determined to do what she could to help fugitives from slavery, which led to her joining the Order. But now she could feel herself undergoing a profound change. She felt a deep anger—even hatred—growing within her for the people and the system that had done this to her father. To *her* family.

Four grown daughters of the real James Monroe Jones
(aka Gunsmith Jones).
Courtesy of the Chatham-Kent Black Historical Society

37

A Fire That Will Not Be Extinguished

After hearing Jacob tell his terrible story, Harriet thought again of her grandmother and aunts on her mother's side. Of course, there must also be such people on her father's side of her family, somewhere.

A fire had been kindled in her that she knew would not easily be extinguished: nor did she want it extinguished. She felt its heat pulsating through her chest, her arms and her legs, almost demanding physical action. She put her hands flat on the table and sat up straight, looking now at Thaddeus' face. She saw clouded eyes and a knitted brow. His mind was in a far and distant place. She wondered where.

For the first time since her father had started speaking, other sounds began to penetrate her consciousness. She heard the voices of the children in the yard and clanging of metal on metal coming from Uncle James' smithy. Her mother and Aunt Emily would be coming back soon. She would be leaving to go home. Everything in her rebelled at that prospect: she wanted to stay in Chatham, stay with her father, stay with Thaddeus. Her life had been suddenly and irrevocably changed. She definitely did not want to have to face Thomas and Zachary right now.

She stood up abruptly.

"Excuse me, Daddy." This time the word came more easily and was spoken with pride. "I'll soon be back. Thaddeus?" Thaddeus looked up at her vaguely. "Come outside with me, now?" Her inner urgency gave her words a new authority. Thaddeus stood up and excused himself.

Jacob nodded and leaned forward onto his folded arms. The exhaustion of weeks of running and now hours of intense emotion was making itself felt.

Outside and beyond Jacob's hearing, Harriet said, "Thaddeus, I can't to go back to Buxton right now!" The urgent tone of her words seemed to shake Thaddeus from wherever his mind had taken him. "I can't face Thomas right now! And I don't want to leave my daddy. He needs me!"

Thaddeus nodded.

"But you have to drive your mama home, don't you? Abiah can't drive, can she?"

Harriet shook her head in frustration. "No, no, she can't." Impatience at her mother's limitations, which she regarded as self-imposed, consumed her.

"I don't know, Harriet, I think you've got to go back." Thaddeus' heart wasn't in this conversation.

"Why didn't she ever learn how to drive the horse? It's stupidness!" Harriet stomped her foot in helpless frustration.

"Hush, Harriet, here she comes now." Abiah and Emily were approaching along the road, Abiah with a haunted look on her face, Emily, hands on hips and lecturing her.

As they came nearer, Harriet could make out Emily saying, "Hush your mouth, Abiah. Don't even think like that. You just put that out of your mind, hear? There's no choice in this matter. Jacob is a part of your past, Thomas and Zachary are the present. Don't you let yourself slide, Abiah, you hear me? Don't you listen to that Ruth friend of yours."

Abiah, seeing Harriet and Thaddeus were now in hearing range, put up her hand to silence anything else Emily might want to go on with. "Hey baby, you ready to go home?" Abiah smiled, not noticing the anxiety and frustration clearly visible on her daughter's face. "Where's Jacob now? I just need to talk to him a little, then we can go."

Harriet gestured toward the house without saying anything. As her mother walked toward the door, Harriet looked at Thaddeus, now leaning against a nearby tree, arms folded across his chest, that faraway look still in his eyes. She walked over and plopped down on the coarse bench under the tree and dropped her chin into her hands. Thaddeus' mind was too far away to be of any help, and she was too irritated by his lack of attention to her internal crisis to think about what might be on his mind.

The reality was that Thaddeus had been deeply moved and troubled by Jacob's story. All his fears about his family's imagined attempt to come join him in Canada West returned, flooding him with anxiety. Was it possible that they had been recaptured? Were his mother and father even now living the life Jacob had just described? And his little sister Charlotte? He trembled to imagine it. He looked at Harriet and felt that the troubles she was facing were small and easy when compared with the huge emptiness of his unknowing, especially since it was the result of his own selfish actions.

James Jones came out of his smithy, a newspaper under his arm. He stood considering the two young people under the tree in front of his barn, then he walked across his yard toward them. Harriet looked up and saw in Uncle James a possible ally. She spoke before he had a chance to say anything.

"Uncle James, I don't want to go home with my mama, my daddy needs me. I want to stay here with him. Where's he going to stay?" Her voice was urgent, rapid-fire, almost childishly pleading.

The Gunsmith paused and looked searchingly at Harriet, then over at Thaddeus, whose lack of reaction let him know that the young man's mind was elsewhere.

"Well, baby girl, I'm happy to hear you studying Jacob's well-being. Don't you worry, he'll be well taken care of. I imagine he'll stay with us a few days until the Vigilance Committee finds someplace for him. You know your Auntie Emily's not going to let him suffer for a thing meanwhile." He smiled reassuringly, and Harriet began to feel a little embarrassed by her outburst. She took a breath to speak, but Gunsmith continued.

"As to not wanting to go home: you don't know your mama needs you now, too? And what about Thomas? How do you think he'll feel if you meet your long-lost daddy and turn your back on him, eh? You forgetting everything he's done for you?" Uncle James smiled as he said this, taking the edge off what could have been harsh words. But he succeeded in nudging Harriet into remembering that there were other people she loved and cared about.

Harriet paused, remembering how grateful Jacob's story had made her feel toward her mother, and she thought about what Abiah must be feeling. Silence settled on the three people under the maple tree. Finally, Harriet nodded.

There was movement at the door of the house, and all three turned. Jacob and Abiah came out together and walked toward the road. Harriet, Thaddeus and the Gunsmith watched as they moved together, heads bowed in conversation. Emily appeared in the door, hands on her hips and a frown in her eyes. Harriet and Thaddeus were too absorbed in their own thoughts to notice the Gunsmith look at his wife with raised eyebrows, or to see Emily shake her head in evident disapproval.

Now Mr. Jones pulled the newspaper out from under his arm and opened it. Harriet saw it was the most recent edition of *The Provincial Freeman*. She was acutely interested in this militant paper with its female editor, Mary Ann Shadd, and she tried to read the headlines upside-down.

"Well, isn't this interesting," Uncle James said. Harriet figured he was merely trying to distract her. But when he went on, she listened with interest.

"It says here that Miss Shadd's going to be speaking here in Chatham this weekend, going to have a debate about the management of the Dawn Institute."

This news even shook Thaddeus out of his reverie. "Who else is speaking?" he asked.

"Looks like John Scoble, among others."

Harriet and Thaddeus looked sharply at each other. "I want to hear that!" Harriet exclaimed. "That's exactly what we've been discussing at Elgin: the reason we're sending a delegation to Dawn for Emancipation Day." She turned to Thaddeus. "I'll go home with my mother today, but I'll come back in a few days' time. Uncle James," she pivoted from Thaddeus to the Gunsmith, "I can stay with you when I get back? Maybe by that time..." Her voice drifted off as she thought about Jacob again.

Harriet had made no mention of asking anyone about returning to Chatham. She was a girl one moment and a woman the next. The gunsmith shook his head slightly, but refrained from reminding her to ask permission.

"Of course, Harriet, you know you're welcome here anytime you come to Chatham. By the way, Thaddeus," he went on, "when David brought me the paper, he told me that Henry Bibb is ailing bad. I know you've had a lot of contact with him in your travels to Windsor, and I thought you'd like to know."

◇

The Gunsmith walked back to the house, leaving Thaddeus and Harriet alone under the tree. His news about the upcoming debate and about Mr. Bibb's illness had brought both of them out of their private worlds.

The thought of Henry Bibb's illness hit Thaddeus hard. What would happen now to his plan to go to Windsor after Emancipation Day to ask Mr. Bibb's advice? He'd even hoped that maybe Bibb would be at Dawn for the ceremonies and he'd be able to talk to him there. Bibb was the only person he had bared his soul to. This news made Thaddeus feel alone, isolated and vulnerable. Suddenly, he was filled with a desire to talk to Harriet about everything. He wanted her to know what was happening with him, about his family, his history and his thoughts. He wanted her understanding and her support. He wished she wasn't about to leave.

For her part, the decision to return to Chatham within a few days brought some measure of peace to Harriet's roiling emotions. She knew Uncle James was right about her mother needing her. Her mind told her that while Jacob needed her too, he had plenty of resting and settling in to do. He'd lived without her for this long, a few more days wouldn't change anything. Harriet knew she needed to give some serious thought to Thomas and how to reassure him of her love and her loyalty. But topmost on her mind was something new that seemed pressingly urgent.

"Thaddeus," she started, hesitating and thinking as she spoke, "I want to…I feel like I need to…we got to do more."

"More what?" Thaddeus was confused. He leaned toward Harriet, wanting connection, wanting to be needed by her in exchange for needing her himself.

"I mean, I've grown up in the Elgin Settlement and had a blessed childhood. I know how lucky I am. Away from most of the ugliness, part of a community that is creating itself: it's a beautiful thing! And now being a part of the Order and helping fugitives settle into a new life? I'm so thankful to be a part of it. But when I listened to Jacob just now, to my father…" She shook her head. "You and I are a part of making history, I know. But we ought to be doing more, you know what I'm saying? I mean, it's good work to help fugitives, it's good work to build free communities. But who's going to destroy slavery! Who's going to bring justice down on the slave owners for all they've done to our people! Thaddeus," she felt tears coming into her eyes and got angry at herself for them, tossing her head, "I've got grandparents. I've got aunts, uncles, cousins, maybe even brothers and sisters and I'm never going to even know them!"

She put her hands over her face and shook her head, overcome.

Thaddeus hugged her to him, her face smothered in his chest. He pressed his eyes shut to keep the fresh tears that jumped into them from leaking out.

"Me too, Harriet. Me, too." He squeezed the words through his cramped throat, and then he could say no more.

They stood hugging each other desperately, rocking slightly back and forth, for several long moments. Gradually, each of them began to feel calmer and regain the ability to speak. They released their grip on one another and stepped back, regarding each other somberly.

"You'll be back in a couple days, Harriet. I've got things I need to talk to you about when you come."

"You do? Yes, sweetheart, I want to hear everything. And you can help me figure out my mind too, can't you?" Harriet smiled, so grateful to have Thaddeus in her life.

"Yes, baby-girl, I'll try." Thaddeus smiled, too, feeling relief wash through him. He still could barely believe this beautiful, intense woman loved him, of all people.

<>

1962

It is April, spring break, and her parents have brought her with them to the SNCC conference in Atlanta. The young girl grips the back of the pew in front of her and leans forward to sing. Some of the grown-ups' speeches go over her head, but the singing—she's right there with the singing. Most of the songs come from slavery days, when people hid the meanings in the church songs, but they were about fighting for freedom and equality. And the Movement now is taking the hiding out of them, putting it right out there point blank.

"We are soldiers
In the army

Freedom Soldiers

We have to fight although we have to die.
We gotta hold—we gotta hold up
The freedom banner,
We gotta hold it up until we die!

"I had a brother,
He was a soldier,
He had his hand on the freedom plow.
He got so old that he couldn't stand up,
He said, I'll stand up
And fight anyhow

"We are soldiers..."

Her mouth is open, she is singing with all her heart, and she knows somehow that this day, she, too, is becoming a soldier. That she has put her hand on the freedom plow and will never let go.

38

What Kind of World? ~ July 1854

Harriet hoisted herself up onto the bench of the buggy next to her mother after parting with Thaddeus and giving Jacob a tight hug and a light kiss on the cheek. She lifted the reins and slapped them down on Meldy's back. When the mare's sudden motion made the buggy lurch forward, she and her mother grabbed the seat to keep from tipping backwards. They both laughed a little and waved goodbye to the small collection of people in the Gunsmith's yard. Harriet's eyes lingered on Jacob, looking thin, gaunt, exhausted alongside Thaddeus and the healthy and energetic Jones family, but the wide smile on his face and vigorously waving hand made her smile back and wave happily.

Soon they passed through Chatham and were bumping along between fields and woods. They were silent for a time, each lost in thought. Harriet soon came to realize that talking to Thomas wasn't going to be a problem for her. She would simply be honest about her excitement at meeting Jacob, and at the same time pay attention to Thomas' feelings and reassure him of her undying love. She smiled to herself as she thought the phrase "undying love." It sounded like a syrupy sweet song. But it was true: meeting Jacob didn't make her love Thomas any the less. Miss Ruth was right about that— she could love both of them. On the other hand, thinking about how Thomas would feel about her mother made her uneasy.

She turned her thoughts to other things. She wanted to talk to Eliza Parker. Ever since she listened spellbound to the story of the battle in Christiana years ago, her respect for Mrs. Parker bordered on awe. Now, after hearing her father's story and feeling the anger and determination it aroused in her, Aunt Eliza was the person her mind jumped to.

Harriet felt she was at a crossroads in her life. She expected that her future would be partnered with Thaddeus, a prospect that made her wildly excited and happy. At the same time she was determined to devote her life to the cause of her people. But just what did that mean? She didn't want to get with Thaddeus and start having one baby after another like many of the women around her. Children were fine and she figured she would want some, but they could take up all of your time and energy. Men had more freedom to move around and do whatever needed doing for the cause. Something in Harriet rebelled against that inequality. Maybe talking to Eliza Parker would help her see her way forward, Eliza had fought with slave catchers even though she was a woman. She and the other women in Christiana had killed a man. On the other hand, she now had four children and another one coming. Harriet's thoughts continued along that jumbled line as Meldy moved steadily forward.

She started to notice that her mother seemed barely aware of her. Abiah hardly seemed to feel the bouncing of the buggy as the wooden wheels lurched roughly from one dried-mud rut to the next. Glancing sideways at her mother's wrinkled brow, Harriet wondered what Jacob and Abiah had said and felt when they went walking. Aunt Emily's words echoed in her ears. Jacob wasn't her man any more. Thomas was. What would she say to Thomas? Would Thomas be hurt? Angry? Then Ruth's words came back to her: "Chatham man and home man." But Harriet couldn't imagine her mother doing that. She had always been loyal to Thomas, and Thomas had always been loyal to her.

Her mother sighed deeply, shook her head, and seemed to come back to reality. "Harriet, you know how happy you make your daddy?" She turned to Harriet with a smile.

Harriet looked at her mother with a broad grin. "For real, Mama?" Again she felt reduced to childhood.

"Oh yes, baby. You should've seen him light up like a candle when I told him about your schooling and all like that!"

"I'm glad, Mama! I never knew what to think when we were driving in this morning. Boy, seems like last month, not this morning, doesn't it? But I was really happy to meet him! I never knew I was missing him. But seems like he's filling a hole in my life I didn't even knew was there." Harriet was surprised at her own words, she hadn't thought about it like that before.

"I can't tell you how happy I am for the both of you, sweet pea. Your daddy is a real good man, and you both deserve each other. You're going to make him real, real happy if you go see him in Chatham now and again," Abiah added hopefully.

"Oh, Mama, maybe I ought to just move there and take care of him! What do you think?"

Abiah was taken aback. "Well," she responded slowly. "I guess it's something to think about. I wasn't expecting to lose you so quick, though, baby-girl. Kind of haven't thought about the family without you in it."

"No," Harriet added quickly. "That's true, too. I wasn't thinking about everything. And I sure don't want Thomas to be feeling bad." She thought for a moment. "But you know, Mama, I'm not going to be in your house all my life." She felt heat moving up her neck. She had never called their house anything but "home" before. Calling it "your house" seemed a little treasonous. True, she had fantasies about moving out and being with Thaddeus, but so far they were nothing but fantasies. She and Thaddeus hadn't even talked about anything since they both said they loved each other. *Oh my Lord*, Harriet thought, *life is moving way too fast for me!*

Abiah only smiled. "I know you're not, my darling."

Now Harriet was speechless. Too many thoughts were running into each other in her head.

"You sure are a lucky girl. You know it? You've got your-self *two* daddies now. You know how many children haven't even got one? Girl, you're *rich!*"

Harriet and Abiah both laughed at that, and then fell silent again, but this time with less turmoil and more happiness. As they got closer to home, life seemed to be falling back into its normal, known shape, re-emerging out of the fog of confusion into which it had been thrown by the day's events. Mother and daughter sighed simultaneously, then looked at each other and laughed again. Meldy kept up her steady trot, eager to get to her barn and her feed.

<>

The next morning Harriet's bare feet carried her swiftly across familiar fields and paths toward the Parkers' house. She felt settled in her mind about Thomas and Zachary. She had handled things well. Last night, once the family was all gathered back at home, Abiah had opened the subject of Jacob with a light tone, in the vein of "you'll never believe who just arrived in Chatham." She had described their meeting with Jacob, making it sound as if it had raised no emotions in her at all— just a page out of her past unexpectedly floating down into her present life.

Thomas listened quietly, nodding and smiling at appro-priate times, but having a look of uncertainty and disbelief in his eyes. Harriet was watching him carefully and jumped in with her own story. She talked with almost childish delight, as if letting him in on an exciting surprise. While she was talking, she grabbed his hands and squeezed them, inviting him to share her excitement. Her mood was contagious, and Thomas couldn't help feeling happy for her. He laughed at her enthusiasm, reassured by the fact that she so wholeheart-edly wanted to share it with him.

Zachary caught the excitement, too.

"So he's your daddy? That mean he's my step-daddy?"
Everyone laughed together.

"No, you silly boy, Daddy is your one and only Daddy. Only I get two daddies!" Harriet announced triumphantly.

Harriet swept Zachary up and shuttled him up the ladder to bed, following him and talking with him for a long while about who Jacob was and how the relationships shook out. At one point, Zachary frowned and whispered to her, "Mama won't leave us and go live with Jacob, will she?"

Harriet hadn't seen that question coming and it jarred her. But she quickly grabbed Zach's head between her hands and gently shook it. "No, you little idiot, what've you got in your brain? Mama's not going anywhere! Where did you get that crazy idea? You mad?"

Zach looked sheepish and burrowed down into his covers. Harriet settled beside him, lost in her thoughts.

Meanwhile, after Harriet took Zach upstairs, Thomas had quietly taken Abiah's hand and led her outside. When Harriet peeked through the window, she saw them walking hand-in-hand along the edge of their farm, deep in conversation. She prayed silently that everything would be all right and Thomas would not be hurt.

This morning, though, her thoughts traveled in an entirely different direction as she approached the Parker house. She felt the determination that had gripped her when Jacob was talking. It took hold of her chest and shoulders like a physical presence.

Eliza was in the yard behind the house, sitting on a stool in front of a big wooden washtub with a pile of clothes beside it. Harriet greeted her politely. Thankfully, Ezekiel was not in sight. The younger children were in the garden, taunting one another playfully and occasionally pulling a weed or two. Harriet found another stool near the back door and moved it so she could sit alongside Eliza. She picked up a small shirt, dunked it in the water and started to rub it with the cake of hard, homemade soap.

Eliza smiled, "Morning, Harriet. How's your mama and daddy? Everybody good?"

"Yes, ma'am, everybody's fine. Everyone good your side?"

Eliza nodded, rubbing another small shirt vigorously on the scrubbing board. They were both silent for a while.

"Your garden is looking real nice, Aunt Liza," Harriet said politely. "Zeke told me you're learning the healing plants from Doc Thomas."

"Yes." Eliza looked up with a lively expression on her face. "That man is amazing, girl! He knows some of everything. I'm trying to learn some of it, but it's going to take time."

"That's real good, Aunt Liza."

Silence fell again, only interrupted by the soft splashing sounds of the water and the background sounds of the children nearby. Eliza looked at Harriet with a sparkle in her eye and said playfully, "Girl, from what I'm hearing, my Zeke's got no chance with you, does he?"

Harriet looked alarmed and embarrassed, and Eliza laughed out loud. "Yes, girl, Ruth told me about you and that Thaddeus boy from Chatham, coming into your Mama's house looking all out of breath, come from all the way across the field. Looks like you two are serious!" She laughed again. Harriet felt her face grow so hot she was sure Eliza could feel the warmth.

"It's all right child, don't let me bother you. So tell me," Eliza gracefully changed the subject, seeing Harriet's discomfort, "what called you to come here this morning? I know you're not here just to help me with my washing. Everything really okay at home?"

Harriet let out a sigh of relief and started telling Eliza about the events of the day before. She told Jacob's story in detail and watched Eliza's face react to the descriptions of the terrible things Jacob had endured. She finished by repeating the sentiments she'd shared with Thaddeus yesterday.

"Aunt Liza, there's got to be more we can be doing about slavery than just make homes for fugitives, isn't there?"

Eliza stopped moving her hands and draped a dripping piece of clothing over the edge of the washtub to quietly consider the intense face of the girl sitting beside her. Harriet wondered what she was thinking. Did her mind go back to Christiana, and before that to the many places she and William had fought smaller battles to free slaves from their mercenary captors? And then back, even further, into the memories she would never talk about, of her enslavement in Maryland? Did she have trouble imagining what it was really like for Harriet—and for her own children—growing up here in Buxton without fear, in freedom, surrounded by their own people?

Finally Eliza said, "First of all, don't use the word 'just' talking about making new homes for poor souls who've come from being somebody's farm animal. You all, we all, are making a new life for people, and it's God's work sure as you're born, you hear what I'm telling you?" There was a hot intensity in Eliza's voice.

She continued. "But yet and still, you ask a good question, Harriet. I can't rightly say I know the answer. There are many sides to every question. For me, in a sense I miss my life in Pennsylvania. We were more in the heart of the battle there, you see? Christiana is not too far from the border of slave country: Delaware and Maryland. Me myself, I come from Maryland. I escaped to Pennsylvania on the Underground Railroad.

"There were two women who used to sell in the market in Baltimore," she digressed. Her hands, which had started back to scrubbing, stopped moving again, and Harriet looked at her face. The look in her eyes told Harriet she was a long way from Buxton in her mind at that moment.

"They were slave women, but they used to carry produce to sell on market day. And they were agents of the

Underground Railroad. If you went to them, they would tell you when and where to get your start on the Railroad. They pointed the way for me and I'm forever grateful to them. I wonder if those women are still there. They were some brave and courageous people!"

Eliza shook her head and went back to scrubbing.

"William and I moved around a lot before we settled in Christiana, and the whole time we were a part of the Vigilance Committee. You know the Vigilance Committee, Harriet?"

"Tell me," Harriet responded quietly. She knew the Vigilance Committee in Chatham, which included black and some white citizens who made it their business to shelter fugitives and help them settle in to their new life. Something told her the Vigilance Committee in Pennsylvania was a different matter.

"The Vigilance Committee is kind of a branch off the Underground Railroad. William Still is one of the organizers for it, but that's in Philadelphia. My William used to organize colored men in whatever town we happened to be in at the time, and they were always ready anytime the slave catchers came. Slave catchers were common in those places, we were so close to slave country. So anytime somebody saw or heard about any slave catcher, we used to sound the horn. Same thing you've heard us talk about when Gorsuch and them came to Christiana. I used to do that most times. Blow the horn and that would be the signal to rouse up the folk from their beds or their fields or wherever they were at the time and come to a certain location. Then they would gather their information and make their plan. Most times they were successful. Either they got the person out of the way before the slave catchers could trouble them, or they ran them down and captured them back.

"It was nail-biting time every time they went out. You never knew if they were coming back alive, if they were coming back on the run and you'd have to gather up everything and clear out quick and fast. Most times, you just had to hustle and get the fugitives out of town and on to the next 'station' before the slave owner had the time to send somebody back for them again.

"It was a constant thing. Yes, it was scary sometimes, but honey, you always knew you were a part of something big, you know? You'd be surprised how many people were in the movement, you hear me? White and black, too. Whole heap of white folks looking like they were just minding their own business, and all the while having some secret room in their cellar or their barn. Used to be one farmer who built himself a special two-horse wagon to carry his crop to market, only he built in a double floor. And a trap door between the two of them. He used to be able to put to four-five people in that thing and carry them all the way to Philadelphia in it. None of the sheriffs nor slave catchers ever did suspect a thing."

Eliza sighed. "A part of me misses those days. Tell you the truth, even though I get nightmares about it sometimes, I like the memory of what they've taken to calling the Christiana Rebellion. I'm not saying I like killing, but when that man Gorsuch was on the ground, knowing he'd come to take away Abraham and them, remembering my suffering, remembering what my family and my friends had suffered in the hands of his kind, those licks I got a chance to throw, they felt real good, you hear me? You don't expect womenfolk to be violent, but girl, I can tell you, that man Gorsuch surely wished he'd never seen any of us women of Christiana!" She gave a sound that was halfway a laugh and halfway a snort. Harriet realized she had been holding her breath the last few minutes, and she let her breath out roughly.

"For me, those days we were more in the battle, you know? But yet and still, we weren't exactly fighting slavery itself. More like a coop full of chickens ready for slaughter, and one or two escape and run off. But the rest of them are stuck and just have to face their fate."

Eliza looked at Harriet, and Harriet looked back at her, stomach churning. She was about to object that something more must be possible when Eliza started talking again.

"But look at my babies over there. Free. Free as a bird flying in the sky. Not in no chicken coop!" She dropped the shirt into the laundry tub and leaned her head back, threw her arms out wide and laughed exultantly. "There's nothing that can really make me want to go back, looking at them, is there? I'm not saying life in Canada West is beautiful. I can't say that. Everywhere we look in this world, seems like we're surrounded by some evil, nasty and dangerous white folk. Chatham white folk are no different to the white folk of Christiana. Some of them are good people; a lot of them hate the sight of us and don't want us around them. I can't say I'm happy to see my children grow up amongst them. But," she paused to give emphasis to her words, "there's another way to look at it, and maybe this will help to answer your question.

"See, Harriet, there are really two questions. Slavery is but one of them. Say tomorrow they pass a law that slavery is finished and done. All the slaves are free. See? Then what? Part of our job is tearing down the old way, the other part is building up the new way. You understand what I'm saying? So, now, what is going to be the new way?"

Eliza stopped talking and looked at her young companion. Harriet had to catch up with Eliza's thoughts. Building the new way. Well, yes, she knew that building the settlement at Buxton was building a freedom community. But she never really thought about it as part of the fight against slavery, not exactly. She only thought about it as living, making life in the best way people knew how. Reverend King preached about showing the white folks that colored people can be just as smart and educated and Christian as they are, so they could accept us living amongst them peacefully. She never thought about it as a plan, a strategy or goal in a war, which is how

Eliza was now posing it. She listened again.

"What kind of world do we really want, sugar? That's the question right there. We're just going to settle down, be good Christians and beg the white folks to accept us? If you ask me, there's got to be something better than that. White folk have got no more Christian decency than we do—a good amount less, you ask me! You don't see black folk riding around terrorizing white folk, now do you? You don't see black folk saying white folk are going to pollute the race and bring down the value of their property. You don't see black folk saying white children are not good enough to be in their schools, do you?"

Harriet found herself nodding in vigorous agreement, remembering her own painful and humiliating run-ins with the kind of white folk Eliza was talking about.

"So how come they have the nerve to say they are better or more Christian than us? It isn't about if you shout and dance when you're praising God. It isn't even about if you knock drums and light candles and call out the spirits. It's about how you behave toward your fellow man, isn't it? You can attend all the church you want, sit quiet in the pews and listen to the pastor, but if you go out and disobey the golden rule, you're not doing God's work, are you? And if you're white and you don't do unto black folk like you do unto yourself, if you don't love thy neighbor as thyself, how are you going to count yourself a better Christian than me?

"No, baby girl. It's not about looking for white folk to accept us. To how I see it, when we're thinking about abolishing slavery, that means we're looking at what we want in its place. And when we're looking at *that*, we're talking about equality. Equality of all and each and every human being. You see? We're talking about every man, woman and child being treated free and equal by every other man, woman and child.

"And hear me now: when I say woman, I don't just mean

black woman and white woman being equal, I mean the woman being the equal of the man, too, you hear? In Haiti and those other French places, they talk about liberty, equality and fraternity. Fraternity means brotherhood. That's not good enough, child! Sisters are in it too, hear me? Just simplify it down: liberty and equality. Free and equal. That's what we're looking for.

"So, sugar pie, I don't know if I've answered your question exactly. Only to say that I don't care if you're in the slave South, in the so-called free North, or in so-called free Canada West, the struggle is everywhere around you. We haven't got freedom nor equality anywhere. So that means the battle is everywhere. We're in it right here, right now."

Harriet was staring at Eliza with round eyes. "Auntie Liza, you ought to be a preacher!" she exclaimed. "Your sermon would be a whole lot better than Reverend King's, and I never would have thought I'd hear myself say that! You just gave me a whole heap to think about."

Eliza smiled at Harriet. She had surprised herself, too, with her long speech. Sometimes talking made you know what was really on your mind.

"Well, all right then. But I better get back to this washing or night will catch me before I finish!" She laughed. "You go on about your business, now. I'm glad for the visit, though. Come back anytime you like, hear?"

Harriet finished rubbing the dress she found in her hands now, squeezed it out and set it in the rinsing pile. She stood up and wiped her hands dry on her own dress, then put them on her hips and leaned back her shoulders to stretch out her back.

"Thanks, Auntie, I will." She looked over at Eliza's children and shouted a good-bye to them too before starting her slow, thoughtful walk back home.

39

The Mullet and the Muskellunge ~ July 1854

Thaddeus and Harriet held hands as they joined the throng squeezing out of the Baptist Church in Chatham a few days later. The crowd was afire with loud conversation, laughter and argument. It had been a boisterous meeting, bordering on getting out of hand. The main speakers, Mary Ann Shadd and John Scoble, had been escorted out behind the pulpit so as not to be mobbed by the many people who had loudly taken one side or another in the debate, mostly the side of the shockingly outspoken young woman, whose vehement criticism of the white opposing speaker had stirred the crowd to a fever pitch.

One of the high points in the meeting came when an Indian man rose to tell a story.

"Colored people!" he shouted from the speaker's platform onto which he had jumped during a pause in the program. "I am Indian! I came from Muncey Town! I listen to this man and this woman, and I will tell you a story about the muskellunge and the mullet, two fishes who live in the water, and a four-legged creature. The four-legged thing comes to the water's edge one day, and he says, 'muskellunge, the mullet said something about you.' Muskellunge gets very angry, and says, 'I'll kill that mullet!' Now four-legged creature goes to the mullet, and says to him, 'Mullet, the muskellunge is going to kill you!' Mullet gets angry, and both fishes meet at the water's edge and fight. The four-legged thing stands off looking on. They kill each other, then the four-legged thing says, 'Ha-ha! I got my dinner!' Now, you see, the fishes are the people and your fine lady servant here, and the four-legged thing is him who calls himself the 'white friend' present today!"

A storm of laughter and shouting blew through the audience at that point and nearly ended the night's event, until Mary Ann Shadd stood to speak again and drew the attention of the crowd once more.

As the two young people struggled to get out of the church without losing one another, they were still chuckling over the story. They were nearly at a standstill as clusters of people were stalled, paying more attention to talking and laughing than to getting themselves out of the building. Finally Thaddeus, being bigger, got in front of Harriet and pushed his way through, and the two were out the door and into the warm night air. They turned left and began walking along the sidewalk. Both of them were buzzing with the excitement generated by the debate. They had both jumped up several times during the meeting and joined in the shouting.

"That woman is amazing!" Harriet exclaimed. "She's so strong! She's not afraid of anything! You see how red Mr. Scoble's face got when she accused him of stealing the people's money? He could barely speak when his turn came. She doesn't bite her tongue, does she? Just goes on ahead and says what's right and doesn't care what happens."

Thaddeus grinned. It was a new experience for him, too, to listen to a fiery woman speaker—or any woman speaker, for that matter—but what excited him the most was that Mary Ann Shadd had won Harriet around to his point of view. And he had reveled in the chance to shout his anger at the thieving white man: he was convinced that he *was* a thieving white man.

Harriet looked up into Thaddeus' smiling face, knowing exactly what was in his mind. "Yes, Thaddeus, she convinced me. You're right! White folk have no business trying to run black folks business." She grinned, too, and squeezed Thaddeus' hand tighter. "Scoble sounds like a con-man. A very educated, high-class con man, and very slick, too, but a con man yet and still. And to how Miss Shadd told it, there's more like him all over Canada West. Even your friend Mr. Bibb, God preserve him, even he sounds like he has been into the same type of thing. It all comes back to the begging culture, like they've been talking about back home all this time. It's insulting to black folk, acting like we can't take care of our own selves."

Thaddeus had winced at the mention of Henry Bibb. Miss Shadd had thrown his name into her speech several times as she attacked white missionary leadership and the practice of asking for support for fugitive communities. The Refugees Home Society near Windsor, with which Bibb was intimately connected, was one such community. Unlike the Elgin Settlement, which prided itself on self-sufficiency and refused charity donations to support its residents, according to Miss Shadd the one near Windsor was mostly sustained by collection of funds and materials from supporters south of the border, mainly white. The community was much less productive than Elgin and plagued by dissension.

Thaddeus had overheard conversations about the RHS while visiting in Windsor, but had not gotten deeply into them. He had heard about the controversy between Miss Shadd and Mr. Bibb, but his relationship with the man made him close his ears to avoid hearing the criticism. Now, as Mr. Bibb lay near death, Thaddeus felt torn as he was swept into loud support of Miss Shadd publicly flaying John Scoble. There seemed no doubt that she was right, but a part of him didn't want to admit it.

These thoughts ran through his mind before he responded to Harriet.

"She really gave him something to think about, didn't she!" he was nearly gloating. "He needs to take his white butt back to England, that's what he needs to do. Leave the people in Dawn to mind their own business. You know what I don't get, Harriet?"

They had stopped at the corner near the bridge.

"What, baby?"

"I don't get folk like Josiah Henson, going along with the Scobles of the world. Seems like people hate their own selves, or don't trust their own selves. You know?"

Harriet looked thoughtful. "I hear you. Like the white man has been telling us we're stupid for so long, we've come to believe him. Act like anything white is better than anything black. And the blacker you are, the lower you are." She felt herself becoming heated now. "You ever notice something, Thaddeus? You ever notice how many of our leaders aren't dark-skinned like you and me? Mr. Brown is light-skinned. Mr. Bibb is light-skinned. And Miss Shadd is near to white, too. And sounds like a white person when she talks. I hate to say it, because she truly inspires me, but how do you think folk would react to see me go up on that stage, black as I am, talking like I talk?" There was bitterness in Harriet's voice now. But thinking about how her heart had leaped listening to Miss Shadd made her feel ungrateful and embarrassed, and she wished she could take back the words as soon as they were out of her mouth. Thaddeus' reaction surprised her.

"I think about the same thing, Harriet, same thing." He thought again about his little brother Nathaniel. "Seems like we listen better and respect more when somebody halfway white is talking than somebody who looks like us." He fell silent, remembering Henry Bibb talking to him about people the color of himself. Of Nathaniel.

As they both fell silent, Harriet thought about her white friend from school Allison. She remembered what Allison's mother had told her mother those years ago when they were first fixing up the Elgin school, about how her father had been put out of his job, how their family almost starved before they moved to Canada. The mullet and the muskellunge story could apply to white and black, too. Divide and conquer by the rich.

She spoke that thought to Thaddeus, and he looked at her with those serious eyes of his. Putting his arm around Harriet's waist he pulled her close to him. "Harriet, baby, I need to talk to you about something. Let's go sit down the other side of the bridge."

Harriet felt her whole body respond to the close contact with Thaddeus' body, and his last words were said in a low voice that expressed so much intimacy that she felt herself get weak in his arms. She nodded silently and put her arm around his waist as they turned left and started across the river. They sat on the small section at the far end of the bridge that had no railing on it, their legs hanging over the riverbank as it angled steeply to the water. There was only a sliver of a moon, and the night had become quiet. The rest of the people who had attended the meeting had continued past the bridge to walk home, or stop in a bar here or there to continue their conversations. No black families lived this side of the bridge, except the Jones family, where Thaddeus was—eventually—walking Harriet back for the night, after which he would return across the bridge to the neighborhood where he and most of Chatham's black population lived.

Harriet sat very still. Her heart was beating quickly in anticipation of what Thaddeus was going to say. Was he going to talk about marriage? She caught her breath, trying to think what she would say. She was exquisitely aware of the touch of his hand, laid almost carelessly on her thigh, making it feel like it was on fire, and the humming warmth of his body pressing against the whole length of her side.

But Thaddeus seemed lost in his thoughts, unaware of the effect he was having on her. He took a breath as if to speak, then exhaled noisily. Taking in another breath, he held it for a moment, and started talking.

"I'm going to tell you something I'm thinking in my mind to do. Something about my family." He paused. Harriet squeezed his arm, silently encouraging him.

"I never told you about my little brother Nathaniel, how his father wasn't my father or Charlotte's." He cleared his throat, which felt swollen with the emotional effort of telling Harriet. "His daddy raped my mother. Threw me and Charlotte out of our little shack so he could have her to himself. My mother let him. Stop—I know what you're going to say, and you're right, she couldn't stop him. I know. But I could never handle the memory of it. To me it felt like she deserted us. When Nat was born my daddy threw a fit. I was mad at him for being mad at my mom. I was mad at him because he was tough with me, too. As Nat grew up I loved him and I hated him. I just started to feel like I had to get away from all of them. That's the reason I left." His voice choked now. "I left them, Harriet! I left them. Now I don't know if they're alive or dead! Oh, Jesus."

Tears were flowing down his cheeks, his face in his hands. Harriet was speechless. Before she could think what to say, Thaddeus started talking again.

"Mr. Bibb told me how his daddy raped his mama, too. And how he tried to get his wife and daughter out, but was forced to leave her to be mistress to another white man. He made me see my mother and my brother had no choice. And now I feel like *I* deserted *them*. I've been thinking, maybe I'll only give my heart peace if I go back for them."

Now he was sobbing openly. Harriet threw her arms around his shoulders, hugging his face into her bosom. She felt stunned. While Thaddeus was talking, her body cooled down. Now it was her mind that was in turmoil. All sorts of thoughts assailed her. Why hadn't Thaddeus talked about his family before? He knew everything about *her* family! Then again, why hadn't she asked him more about his family? That was shameful. She had behaved as if he had no one to care about except her. And she felt a tight fear and something else—jealousy? abandonment?—at the thought of him leaving to go to a far distant place deep in the heart of enemy territory. And disappointment: she had wanted him to talk to her about love and marriage. About them. She wanted to be able to talk to him about the conflict between a future as a wife and mother and a future as a freedom fighter. How selfish that felt now that she put it next to his need to find his mother and his father, his brother and sister. Especially when she had just been blessed with the arrival of her own father!

Her mind was spinning. She felt unworthy and incapable to say anything. Then she realized that Thaddeus had had removed his hand from her thigh and put it around her, saying, "I've never known what to do, but I woke up the other morning and I decided to go talk to Mr. Bibb after Emancipation Day, see if he could help me plan to go back and find them. And then, like a sign, Jacob showed up that same morning looking for you. When I saw you with him that made me feel it even more—how much I want to find my family!"

He shook his head like he was trying to clear it.

"And now Mr. Bibb is so sick. I don't know. I just don't know."

He went silent, Harriet mute beside him. After a moment, he spoke again. "After Emancipation Day, I'll see if I can get his advice. But Harriet," he put his finger under her chin and turned her face to him, "one thing I know for sure. If I do go, I want you here for me when I come back."

Harriet's lips had parted when Thaddeus turned her face. Now she started to take in a breath, but before she could, his lips were on hers. She closed her eyes and put her hands on either side of his face as her body caught fire once again. Thaddeus pulled away.

"Harriet, will you wait for me? I can't imagine living without you. If you want to marry, I'll marry you."

Harriet shocked herself then by bursting into tears. She

grabbed his head and pulled his mouth back to hers, kissing him fiercely. He lifted her up and put her on his lap, without their mouths separating from each other.

"I'll wait for you," Harriet said breathlessly moments later. "I don't want you to go. I'm scared to death, but yes, baby, of course I'll wait for you. But not tonight. Tonight I can't wait." She stood up and grabbed his hand, pulling. "Come on away from this road, baby, come with me!" And they hurried off the road and into the woods.

◇

Sex was no secret to Harriet, though she hadn't tried it yet. No child growing up on a farm could be unaware of how sex worked. Harriet had seen cats, dogs, cows and even horses at it, plus numerous chickens and other birds cooing and chirping and fluttering on top of one another.

Harriet had even watched her mother and Thomas on more than one occasion. When they lived in Chatham, she would pretend to be asleep and keep one eye cracked open to see them start hugging and kissing and touching one another. They would go into the other room after a while, but she would hear the movements and the sounds. Then when they moved to Buxton and built the new house, there was a knothole in the floor that she and even little Zach used to put their eye to. A couple times, Abiah seemed to be looking right up at them, and they drew back. Sure enough, one night the hole had a rag stuffed in it. They were afraid to take it out. Soon after that, their parents put up a wall to separate off their bedroom downstairs and their bed was no longer in the room below that hole. But when William and Eliza Parker stayed with them, Harriet pulled the rag back out and watched some more. It was quite clear to her that there was exquisite pleasure involved in the whole unattractive-yet-irresistible, noisy, grunting activity.

And of course, she had also been warned away from it over and over again by her parents and other grown people in her life. "Now, Harriet," they would say, "don't you be chasing boys, hear? And don't you let any boy be touching and feeling on you, you hear? One thing leads to another, and you're not ready to be making any babies, you understand? We ever hear or see of any mess like that, your backside is going to be so tore up you won't sit for a week!"

But tonight, tonight Harriet was her own woman. Her parents' threats were no longer prevention, she was beyond their reach now. She knew what she wanted, and even though it scared and intimidated her, nothing was going to hold her back.

◇

The two young people pulled their clothes back together and lay alongside each other on the forest floor. Both of them were smiling, each one's face turned toward the other. Thaddeus chuckled deeply.

"I guess we shouldn't have done that, but I'm not regretting it!"

"I know, me neither," Harriet responded and sighed deeply.

She smiled to herself, feeling a sense of accomplishment and gratitude. She had some soreness, and she hadn't experienced ecstasy, but that would come in the future. So people said.

Each of them thought very briefly in the back of their heads of the complications pregnancy could cause, but both of them dismissed the possibility just as quickly, with a passing idea that they would be married anyway. For the moment, Harriet's inner conflict about how to weigh motherhood against freedom fighting was forgotten.

Thaddeus had been introduced to the delights of sex in an

on-and-off relationship with an older woman in Windsor, but this with Harriet was a different thing. He didn't understand what had come over him, but Harriet had become the most precious thing in his life. He'd been a part of enough male huffing and puffing, bragging and storytelling about sexual prowess, but he knew he could never talk about Harriet like that.

After a while, the ground started to feel cool and damp through their clothes. They got up and brushed each other off, trying to erase the unmistakable evidence that they had been rolling around in the leaves and soft earth. They giggled and shoved while they were doing it, until something made them remember how long ago the meeting had ended. Auntie Emily and Uncle James would certainly suspect something, maybe even be worried about Harriet. Suddenly it was urgent to get to the Gunsmith's yard.

When they reached the house, there was no candle light in the windows. Harriet opened the door as quietly as possible, still holding Thaddeus' hand. The door squeaked. Emily's voice called out sharply, "Harriet, that you?"

"Yes, ma'am," Harriet whispered back.

Emily was making no attempt to be quiet. "Well, you get your butt in this house and get to bed. There's no excuse for you being out so late."

"Yes, ma'am," Harriet replied quietly, knowing she should feel remorse but not feeling it. She grinned over her shoulder at Thaddeus.

"Thaddeus with you?"

"Yes, ma'am, I'm here," Thaddeus responded with a full voice. "Sorry we stayed so late. The meeting went long and then we got to talking. That Miss Shadd is a mess! You should have heard her!"

"Oh, you stop your lying, boy," Emily said in a no-nonsense voice. "You get yourself on home now, leave this young girl be."

"Yes ma'am, good night Miss Emily," Thaddeus said, no hesitation or regret in his voice.

Harriet drew her hand from his and waved it lightly at him with a sly grin on her mouth that she was careful to conceal when she turned back into the house and shut the door.

Mary Ann Shadd Cary, who debated John Scoble.
Shadd was the first woman in Canada to publish a newspaper,
the *Provincial Freeman*.
The statue stands in Chatham, Ontario, where she lived.

40

Turkey Buzzard Laid Me and Sun Hatched Me ~ July 1854

A few days later, Harriet was sitting on the porch steps of the little house where Jacob now had a room. Jacob sat behind her on a chair. Harriet was shucking some early sweet corn. She was taking pleasure in staying with her father for a while, showing him around Chatham and listening to him talk.

Right now, he was trying to answer her question about his family.

"Well, darling, far as I could testify, turkey buzzard laid me and sun hatched me. I don't know anything about my parents. They told me that my momma was sold off when I was only about two years old, and my daddy was from another plantation and long gone before I was even born. Said I have a little brother who was sold off with my momma, but I've got no idea his whereabouts nor hers. It's like my own self—I don't know if I have nary a child excepting you. Could be I have few babies across Mississippi, but I don't know about any of them."

Harriet swallowed hard, silenced by her father's words. At least her mother had grown up around her family. At least there was a tiny possibility that some day Harriet might know some of her cousins. That she might in some distant future when there was no more slavery get to see her grandmother and aunts that used to know her when she was a baby. But his story left her feeling an emptiness that immediately began to fill up with anger and bitterness. How could human beings calling themselves Christians treat their fellow man in such a heartless way?

She realized she must have asked the question out loud, because she heard her father talking again. "Some people look like they have a gizzard instead of a heart."

"White folks are just evil, Daddy Jacob!" she blurted out, feeling anger, but at the same time some guilt, acknowledging her care and respect for Allison, Mrs. Lovejoy and Reverend King.

"A lot of them are that, sweetheart," Jacob responded. "Best thing that ever happened to me was getting away from them. Truth be told, I don't feel any comfortableness at all even walking by them on the street out here. Guess I'll be getting used to it after time."

"What I can't understand," Harriet mused as she picked the fine, golden hairs from between the rows of plump kernels, "I can't understand why some folk are so worried about getting white folks to accept us. Seems like they want us to come close as possible to *being* white. And you know that can't happen!"

"What do you mean, baby?"

"Well, even like Mary Ann Shadd—now, don't get me wrong, she's a great lady—great lady! But you read her paper, she always writes about *'uplifting'* the black man. Now, I understand where a person like you, just come from deep in the heart of slavery, you need work, you need money, you need to learn to read and write because slavery kept it from you. So you need to up-lift, true. But then they talk about 'moral and spiritual uplift' of the fugitive slave. What do they mean by that? Are they saying that you're *im*moral? That you don't have decency?"

Harriet's voice had risen and become indignant. The corn lay untouched in her lap. These days she had spent with her father, she felt like a veil was lifting off her face, like her eyes could see more clearly. Her indignation was as much at herself for the ideas she had accepted all her life as it was for the words in *The Provincial Freeman* and the other newspapers she read.

Mary Ann Shadd had inspired her with her bold speech,

her fearlessness in standing on stage confronting what she knew to be wrong. But at the same time, much of what she said sounded just like Reverend King. Harriet could no longer deny that Reverend King must think that the people of Elgin wouldn't get along without him as their guide, though he was not a thief like John Scoble. He was a principled man who opposed the begging culture and truly devoted his life to the people of the Elgin Settlement. But sometimes he seemed to think the thing they needed most and above all was to be accepted by their white neighbors.

Something about the events of the last few weeks, from the day she had ridden into Chatham and had that conversation with Thaddeus, from the arrival of her father, and from listening to Mary Ann Shadd—something in that combination had vaulted her from her easy, accepting childhood into an angry, determined young womanhood. Her father was talking again.

"I don't know who those people are you're talking about, nor truly what they mean about moral and spiritual. All I know is the white folks I knew don't have anything they could rightfully call moral or spiritual. That is excepting the ones that are part of the Underground Railroad, they are God's people, for true. I guess it's kind of hard to be an honest man when you've got to steal to eat, though. I had to do that plenty of times. Kill the master's chicken, or even hog sometimes. They call it stealing, but the master stole my life and my labor ever since I was a boy, so I guess taking a little back is maybe my right."

Harriet nodded thoughtfully, considering "sin." Stealing was a sin. Having babies out of wedlock was a sin. In that moment she questioned everything she had been taught about morality in Reverend King's church and school. Her father was a good man! If he had fathered babies out of wedlock, if he had stolen from his master, how could those things be sinful when *his* father had been stolen from his African home, and Jacob was forced to work for the slave owner without ever getting a plug nickel for his work. Was he to accept a life of starvation, treated like a castrated ox pulling a plow, instead of a man? That couldn't be God's will! If he'd had any choice in the matter, she was sure he would now be married to her mother and would have been a father to her and probably some sisters and brothers. He would be a hard-working farmer in Elgin. It was not through any wrongdoing of his own that he ended up committing those "sins"! And how could a system where some human beings owned others like cattle be anything but sinful? How could a person who owned other people preach to them about "thou shalt not steal?" Or any other sin?

Jacob cleared his throat, and the sound took Harriet out of her reverie.

"You think it was immoral for me to steal food, Harriet?" Her father's question was almost plaintive, and Harriet realized that she hadn't responded to his conversation.

"No!" she almost shouted in her vehemence. "Far as I can see your master stole *you*! Stealing from him doesn't seem like a sin. Doesn't seem like stealing. Seems like setting something to right." She shook her head and went on.

"That's just exactly what I'm talking about, Daddy Jacob. If you haven't done anything wrong, why do you need to lift up? Sounds to me like what they really want is for black folk to act more like white folk. Like, don't shout and sing in church, don't talk loud, don't play the dozens. White folks are free to act like they want, but we're supposed to sit all quiet-like in church and school, tiptoe around on the street, and bow and curtsy in white business places. Shoot—that's not about morality, it's just about pleasing white folks. Seems like some of the people who call themselves our leaders—black folk just downright embarrass them!"

"Funny, Harriet," said Jacob slowly and thoughtfully, "to hear you talk, it reminds me how we had to behave to white folks on the plantations. It's the biggest sin when a slave talks back to any white person. Got to always, always be polite and quiet-like. And don't let them catch you shouting or singing! One of the places I was, a big plantation, hundreds of slaves, we used to keep secret prayer meetings—they call it stealing the meeting. Used to sing and shout into a big washtub to keep the master from hearing. And don't let them hear any drums—they're sure you're plotting violence if you beat drums—not even if you're burying somebody. Truth is, mean as they are and powerful as they are, they're scared of us! You hear me? Scared to death."

Thaddeus had told Harriet the same thing—that white people were scared of black people. Harriet saw it in little things, sometimes, but it seemed they were more afraid of black men than black women. Thaddeus had told her how white folk often crossed to the other side of the street when he was walking with friends through Chatham. He laughed about it, but she knew the laughter was hiding anger and hurt.

Harriet nodded at her father again, imagining slave owners and their families frightened by people who had to hide in the woods and shout into washtubs to praise God. The thought made her smile. She thought about all she had heard and read about the need for moral and spiritual uplift, and compared that to her experience sitting here, learning at the feet of her own father, fresh from slavery and unable to read or write a single letter. She felt anger well up in defense of the morality of this good and loving man whose blood flowed in her veins—whose selfless courage had set her free.

It occurred to her to wonder why she hadn't noticed all of this before. But being honest with herself, she realized that she had known most of it all along but refused to face it, because it conflicted with what she had been taught in school and at church.

"Yeah, Daddy J, you're right. Something's got to be done

to change this back-ways world we live in. I'm happier than I can tell you that you're here and not back down in Louisiana, but you're right about the white folks here. Thaddeus has told me more times than one, plenty of these white folks are sorry there isn't slavery here in Canada. It's a sad state of affairs, sir!" She stood up, holding the clean ears of corn in her apron and picking up the bowl with the husks in it.

"Let's get this corn to Miss Percy so we can eat something after all this philosophizing!" she grinned cheerfully as she walked around to the bushes to dump the husks. On top of the confusion, anger and hurt, happiness inflated her chest as she looked at the man sitting on the porch, the man whose face looked like hers.

"Sure enough!" her father grinned right back at her.

<>

Harriet stayed in Chatham with Jacob for the few days remaining before the trip to Dawn for Emancipation Day. The hours were filled helping get her father settled into his new life. She had gone back and forth with the Vigilance Committee to find the room he was now in, and to get some initial supplies of a few clothes and some basic foodstuffs. She collected fresh vegetables and eggs from the gardens and coops of the Joneses and other friends in Chatham to give to him and his landlady. She also got some leads for possible jobs. Jacob had spent several days resting, sleeping much of the time to recover from the profound weakness of his body. He had allowed himself to relax for the first time after years of abuse followed by months of running, fear and uncertainty. Harriet could see that for some time he would be a deep well of exhaustion. It would also take him time to get his bearings in his new, foreign surroundings. Harriet was glad that he had arrived in the middle of the warmest time of the year, at least he didn't have to adjust to the freezing Canadian winter yet. She found his bewilderment sometimes funny, sometimes embarrassing. There was so much he didn't know about simple things she took for granted, which made her feel all the more protective of him.

Thaddeus was working at the smithy, but he managed some few hours with Harriet here and there, much of it spent answering what seemed like hundreds of questions Harriet had about his family, his childhood and his trip from the free African community in the Great Dismal Swamp across half of the United States and into Windsor nearly five years earlier. She seemed to have an endless appetite for the details of his life. Thaddeus was deeply grateful. He knew it was an act of generosity for her to be willing to accept their possible separation before they had even really gotten together. A part of him didn't want to leave her, and he tossed and turned in his bed at night, wondering whether or not he should go.

He talked about it with Mr. Jones while they were working. The older man listened with single-minded focus. Black family unity was disrespected and discouraged by the system of slavery. He was supportive of the young man's desire to pull his family back together. At the same time, he asked difficult questions. What if he couldn't find them, what then? Or then: Thaddeus' family knew where he was, right? Hadn't they said they might come? What if they had decided to stay where they were? Would Thaddeus stay with them in order to unite his family? Or was he only interested in unity if it was here in Canada? Thaddeus had to admit that he would not stay at his old home, he had a life here now. He had important work. He had Harriet! Mr. Jones only succeeded in making him more confused.

Meanwhile, Harriet cherished the hours she managed to carve out to spend with Thaddeus. She felt lucky to have a reason to stay in Chatham for a while. Jacob's room was not too far from where Thaddeus was living, but by the time he got back from work and she finished her daily tasks, it didn't feel like much time was left for the two of them. She wanted more. Part of her deeply wished that Thaddeus wouldn't leave, because she was desperately afraid that something terrible would happen and he might not come back. But she knew this was something he had to decide. She imagined to what lengths she would go to reunite with her family if they were separated—even Jacob, whom she had just met! If she loved Thaddeus, it meant she had to support him in his quest. It would be pure selfishness to stand in his way.

41

Emancipation Day ~ August 1, 1854

When day dawned on July 31, Harriet arose from the quilt she had been using as a bed on the floor of Jacob's room. Excitement seeped into her with the rays of the rising sun and she came awake quickly. Yesterday, the delegation from Buxton had arrived in Chatham. Today she and Thaddeus would join them to complete the journey to the Dawn Settlement and set up camp. Tomorrow was Emancipation Day: the anniversary of the day slavery had ended in the British Empire! For much of her life, Emancipation Day had been the most festive holiday of the year. Harriet was in a state of happy anticipation about this gala event and all that it represented.

It would be such a major gathering. She would see the famous Frederick Douglass in person, after hearing so much about him for years and hungrily reading whatever issues she could find of his newspaper. Mary Ann Shadd might be there. She would hear Josiah Henson speak, and hopefully J.C. Brown, who was on the mend. And she heard that a speaker might be in attendance from Jamaica, a country where formerly enslaved people had been building a new life for twenty years, longer than she had been alive. And there would be the exhilarating freedom of being amongst a large and festive crowd of strangers from all around the countryside, with food, music, storytelling, the excitement of camping.

And the prospect of slipping away with Thaddeus.

◇

Thaddeus came awake that morning in much the same

state. The energy that pumped through his body with each heartbeat was mingled with trepidation. Would this be the end of the stable and predictable life he had known for the years of his maturing into manhood? Life had fallen into a pattern. Between the trips to Windsor that brought him the satisfaction of helping fugitives begin their new lives, he worked hard in the smithy to learn from a master the challenging but fascinating trade of metal work. And the sweetness and promise of his new love made him feel almost complete. But after Emancipation Day, he would decide whether to leave all that behind for an unpredictable and dangerous journey.

The future made him nervous, even the next few days. They might be the last he would spend with Harriet for an unknown amount of time. They would be with her mother and Thomas, which also made him feel jittery. The thought of Abiah and Thomas brought memories of the day before, when the Buxton delegation had arrived in Chatham in preparation for today's trip. The Ingrams came to the Jones' house in mid-afternoon while Thaddeus was still at work. Brother James sent him to help them.

Taking their bags from the buggy to the room where they would sleep, Thaddeus overheard Abiah talking to Aunt Emily as the two stepped into the house. "Thomas wants to meet Jacob," Abiah said in a hushed voice. "I'm worried, Em. He says he wants to meet Harriet's daddy, but I know it's not about Harriet. It's like Jacob is his rival. I can tell he doesn't trust me, especially since I came to Chatham without telling him Jacob was here. That was a mistake. I've never known Thomas to be a violent man, but I've seen what jealousy can do. I'm scared, Em!"

"Don't you worry, Abiah," Aunt Emily responded confidently. "Nobody is going to harm another person in this yard!"

Thaddeus, who had paused just around the corner, hurried to the back room with the bags. When he walked back toward the smithy, Thomas was talking to the Gunsmith. Thaddeus could see the smokiness clouding Thomas' eyes, saw the tension in the man's back and shoulders. He heard Thomas say he wanted to meet Harriet's father, but his attempt at sounding welcoming failed completely.

James squinted at Thomas, one eyebrow going up slightly. James turned to Thaddeus, who was now close by. "Thaddeus, Thomas and Abiah would like to see Harriet and Jacob. Go fetch them for us, now."

Thaddeus nodded and set off at once for Jacob's room. Harriet greeted him with excitement that was quickly shadowed by concern when she heard the message. Thaddeus grasped Harriet's forearms and gave her a quick kiss. "We'll soon be on our way," he said encouragingly. She smiled back, excitement once again her main emotion.

Thaddeus returned to the smithy. When father and daughter arrived an hour later, he watched them approaching the gate through Thomas' eyes, Harriet holding the elbow of a tall, slender man, fatigue furrowing his face and slowing his step. He could see that Thomas was disarmed by the smile on Harriet's face and the pride in her eyes. Harriet's evident happiness at introducing Jacob to Thomas would not permit Thomas to spoil this moment for the girl who had been his daughter for so many years. Thaddeus saw his body relax a little, a tight smile appearing on his face in response to Harriet's wide grin. Then Thomas glanced at Abiah, and he saw the tension run up Thomas's back again, the smile abandoning his haggard face.

"Daddy..." Harriet undid Thomas with the first word out of her mouth. "Meet my father, Jacob Roberson!"

Jacob spoke first, holding out his long, thin arm to offer his large, calloused hand to Thomas. "I'm so happy to meet you, Mr. Ingram. I want to thank you from the depths of my heart for taking care of Harriet when I could not." He didn't mention Abiah, nor did he look at her.

Thomas hesitated a moment, then took Jacob's hand. "You're most welcome, Jacob." Thaddeus noticed that Jacob had called Thomas "Mr. Ingram," but Thomas had called Jacob by his first name. He seemed to hold onto the other man's hand a little too long. "I'm happy you found your way out of hell and have lived to see her again," Thomas added, still pressing Jacob's hand, his eyes boring into the other man's like a drill.

Jacob slowly withdrew his hand, but he returned Thomas's gaze steadily, without hostility. Thomas dropped his hand. The two nodded at one another.

Harriet, distracted by Zachary running across the yard, failed to see the unspoken communication between the two men. But Abiah saw it, and she shivered slightly, though the day was hot.

"Daddy Jacob, this is my little brother, Zachary." Harriet smiled, catching Zachary. "Zach, say hello to Mr. Roberson!"

"Hello, Mr. Roberson," Zachary murmured politely, looking slantwise up at this tall stranger.

Jacob bent down and held out his hand with a quick glance at Thomas.

"Hello Zachary, glad to meet you."

"Shake his hand, Zach!" Harriet prompted the suddenly shy little boy.

Zach timidly put his little hand into the vast one offered him, then giggled, turned around, and ran back to the safety of the house and the Jones children.

Jacob didn't stay long. Harriet explained that they had a lot to do before her departure the next morning for the Dawn settlement. While Thomas went into the smithy to see the Gunsmith's work, Abiah walked with her daughter and Jacob to the gate. Thaddeus hurried to catch up with them to say goodbye. Harriet turned to Thaddeus. Holding hands, the two made plans to meet up the next morning at the bridge. Glancing at Jacob and Abiah, Thaddeus saw their eyes lock for a long moment with what seemed like hunger. Then Harriet turned back and took Jacob's arm, not noticing the moment when her parents' eyes unlocked.

◇

That next day, Harriet left Jacob at home and met Thaddeus by the bridge for the much-anticipated journey. After many long miles, the delegation from Buxton arrived at the Dawn Settlement with time enough to set up camp and build cooking fires in the designated area.

Thaddeus and Harriet, young enough to have energy left after their trek, spent the early evening scavenging for firewood and walking the neighborhood to see the sights. Several big tents were set up to protect the Buxton folk from any weather that might develop, and when night came, they laid their bedding alongside Harriet's parents, Harriet next to Zachary, and Thaddeus on the other side of Abiah and Thomas.

On Emancipation morning, everyone in the tent rose with the sun, the atmosphere humming with expectation. While fires were laid and breakfast cooked and eaten, the delegation took turns bathing in the nearby river. The sky was blue and cloudless. Early in the morning, the heat of the sun was already on them. By mid-morning, everyone had carefully dressed in their Sunday best. They strolled over to the large, grassy lawn where the event was to happen.

The residents of the Dawn Settlement were busy hammering together the speakers' platforms, one on either side of the lawn, while others, mostly young, were carrying chairs and benches from all around and setting them in rows.

Thaddeus offered to help the platform-builders, but they had too many volunteers already, so he rejoined Harriet and the others. Realizing that their help wasn't needed, the group resumed walking past scattered farms toward the school-house where the parade would start. They passed the church and saw the nearby sawmill, in front of which sat a pile of logs growing moss.

"Wonder why the sawmill is not working," Thomas said to William Parker, who was walking alongside him.

"I wonder the same," William responded, raising his eyebrows questioningly. Both men worked at the sawmill in Buxton, which rarely paused its feverish activity, producing boards that were quickly used in construction or sold to more distant markets. There was certainly no time for moss to grow on their logs!

"Isn't that Reverend Henson yonder in that doorway?" Eliza Parker said to Abiah, not so discreetly pointing toward a nearby log house. "I've never seen him, but from how people describe him, it looks so—see the big beard?"

"Could be," Abiah nodded, "the man looks old enough for Reverend Henson."

Another man appeared briefly in the doorway behind the bearded elder, and Harriet gasped, recognizing him.

"That's Frederick Douglass!" Her first word came out almost as a shout, but she quickly lowered her voice as she excitedly said the name. "I've seen his picture in the papers: that's him!"

Thaddeus turned to look.

"Wonder what he's going to say today. I wonder if he knows about the controversy going on over this side."

"He must be having a second thought about emigration, though," Harriet said. "I mean, he's here in Canada, isn't he? Even though he always writes against emigration."

When they reached the schoolhouse, people who had come from other places were already milling around. Everyone was dressed in colorful clothes and polished shoes or boots. Some people carried banners celebrating emancipation in the British West Indies and the whole of the British realm. British flags flew. Some wore badges they had made for the occasion. From behind the schoolhouse the sounds of musical instruments and drums tuning up and practicing, all at odds with one another, added to the excitement. To the side several young women were practicing with batons to lead the parade.

Harriet put her arm through Thaddeus' and squeezed with excitement, bouncing a little on her toes. Thaddeus squeezed her closer with his elbow and reached his other hand across to grasp her forearm. He grinned down at her, feeling the same excitement, suppressing his own urge to jump up and down.

After what seemed like an eternity, the two young people and the rest of the gathering found themselves being directed into formation by young Dawn volunteers as the band emerged from behind the schoolhouse, while the baton-wielders took their places at the front. The squeaks and random drumbeats of the musicians fell silent, the crowd followed suit. The bubble of restrained eagerness burst when, at a signal from the bandleader, the fifes, horns and drums blasted simultaneously, starting a lively tune with the band marching off smartly. The crowd jumped to follow, their feet moving to the rhythms of the music. The banners and flags unfurled, the marchers burst into talk, laughter and song. It was a bouncing, dancing, hand-clapping caterpillar of humanity, weaving its way toward the lawn.

When the parade reached its destination, the band continued to play, drawing an even bigger crowd of people clapping hands, swaying, dancing to the music. Then the band fell silent and people began filling seats, which proved far too few for everyone to rest their legs. Thaddeus, Harriet and several other Buxtonites wove their way through the crowd to get near the speakers' platform. They wanted to hear clearly in order to understand the controversy they expected so they could bring an explanation home with them as promised. Chairs were scarce, so the pair sat on the grass between the stage and the first row of seats.

A man walked out onto the platform and in a booming voice introduced himself as George Cary. He greeted all the assembled and shouted a proposal that Father Josiah Henson be accepted to preside over the day's activities. A cheer of agreement came up from the crowd, and the bearded old man they had seen in the doorway of his house stepped up onto the platform. Thaddeus and Harriet, eyes focused on the stage, reached their hands out and fumbled until their fingers found each other's. They were intent on hearing every word.

Reverend Henson welcomed and congratulated the crowd with humor and charisma. A few brief speeches followed, marking Emancipation Day and celebrating freedom from slavery in the British Empire. Then the promised speaker from Jamaica was introduced. Harriet and Thaddeus listened keenly, straining to understand the accent. The man talked of the Free Village movement, which sounded a bit like the self-sufficiency movement in Canada West.

He finished with words that resonated: "As we celebrate here today, let us remember the struggle that forced emancipation on the British government! Let us remember the heroism and sacrifice of Sam Sharpe and the sixty thousand people who rose up in the Christmas Rebellion and burnt down the whole of western Jamaica in their bid to end slavery! It was not out of the goodness of their hearts that the British Parliament declared emancipation. Let us never forget!"

Harriet and Thaddeus leapt to their feet to join the shouting and clapping that accompanied the speaker's retreat from the stage. Henson came to the front again, and as people gradually quieted and resumed their seats, he introduced another foreign guest. As Frederick Douglass ascended the stage, Henson and a white man Harriet and Thaddeus quickly recognized as John Scoble set up a loud cheering and clapping, which Harriet joined. But the crowd, knowing Douglass' reputation as an adamant opponent of emigration to Canada, responded only with polite applause.

Douglass was a powerful-looking figure. A large beard and a fluffy halo of soft curls framed his light-brown face, reminding Harriet of pictures of a lion's mane. His penetrating voice commanded attention, his words flowing hypnotically. He spoke about emancipation in the British West Indies and mentioned the first free black republic in the Americas—Haiti—where the slaves had risen and claimed their own freedom, where today the government was in the hands of the descendants of those slaves. He went on to talk about how the pro-slavery forces in the United States were plotting to spread slavery to all the states of the union, and how one plan to accomplish that was to convince or force all free people of color to emigrate. While congratulating the people here assembled on the success of their communities, he asserted that a mass migration of blacks from the US to Canada could overwhelm the progress they had made. He went on to congratulate Father Henson, John Scoble and the Trustees at Dawn for their hard work on behalf of the black citizens of the area.

Harriet nearly fell asleep at several points during the talk, despite her best efforts. Douglass seemed to go on forever, and the sun beating down on her head made her drowsy. By the time he finished talking, nearly two hours had passed. While the crowd was polite, his presentation was greeted coolly. She noticed many others who were dozing, talking to one another, or wandering around at the edges of the lawn. She looked at Thaddeus, and he merely shrugged his shoulders, wondering the same things she was. Why had the famous abolitionist come to speak to emigrants when his message was against emigration? Why did he support Mr. Scoble?

John Scoble then took the platform. He was greeted coldly. People were willing to give the famous black abolitionist Douglass their respect, but Scoble was known locally and many people seemed hostile toward him. Harriet and Thaddeus, after hearing him trounced by Mary Ann Shadd so recently, felt a similar antagonism.

Scoble also spoke about emancipation in the British West Indies and went on to give credit to the abolition movement in England, led by many famous men, whom he named, including himself. He spoke about a variety of speeches he had made and meetings he had attended, helping to convince England's government of the moral and economic necessity of ending involuntary servitude.

Someone sitting close behind Harriet and Thaddeus leaned to his neighbor, saying loudly enough to be heard by many in the audience, "The man makes it sound like Emancipation was down to white folk in England. What about this Sam Sharpe and the Christmas Rebellion just a year before they 'saw the light?' My friends, you are listening to the man rewrite history!"

There was a loud response to this man's words, as people shouted "Amen, brother!" and "tell it, son!"

Scoble paused momentarily, confused by the sounds of the crowd, but then continued congratulating himself for his role in British abolition, pausing frequently for applause that never came. People muttered loudly that Scoble was supposed to be reporting to them about finances and plans for the land and school at Dawn Institute, but he never touched on those topics in his speech. Finally, he stepped down as the audience grumbled its dissatisfaction.

A recess in the program was announced for dinner. A row of food sellers lined the edges of the lawn, but Harriet and Thaddeus, along with the rest of the Buxton group, had little satchels with them that they had packed at breakfast time, containing large chunks of cornbread, dried meat, boiled eggs, tomatoes and early peaches. As they spread this out between them, they noticed J.C. Brown sitting not far away. They both called to him and waved, and he responded with a weak smile and gestured for them to come closer. They gathered up their picnic and moved closer to the man, who looked to be still not quite free of the grip of illness, though thankfully not feverish like when they had last seen him.

"These are two very promising young people," Brown said to the ones around him. "They are with a delegation that came all the way from Buxton hoping to understand the problems at the Dawn. I look to young people like these, growing up in a community free of the begging culture, to become future leaders of our people." The people sitting with him nodded and greeted Harriet and Thaddeus, who felt embarrassed at being called future leaders.

Mr. Brown went back to his previous conversation. "I'm afraid I'm really not feeling well at all. I think it may be best to leave shortly so I can return to my bed before nightfall."

A woman near him responded with some urgency in her voice, "J.C., I understand that you have made a great sacrifice to come here. But we expect that the moment you leave, Scoble will bring forward his proposal with no one here to object. You used to live here, you've been a trustee, and you can set the record straight. You don't think you can manage to stay just a bit longer?"

The several men and women standing close by nodded vigorously. Harriet and Thaddeus looked on curiously. Mr. Brown bowed his head in assent and sighed deeply.

"All right, my sister, I will try. You people came all the way from Dawn to Chatham with your wagon to fetch me. I'll do my best to meet your expectations. I imagine I can sleep in the wagon on the way home if need be. But I must impress upon you that you, yourselves, need to take it on yourselves to learn to speak out on your own behalf! There is nothing I know that you don't know, you must learn to stand up for yourselves." The group around him looked at one another self-consciously and remained silent. Brown smiled weakly, then started coughing. He lacked the energy to argue. It was easier just to stay and do what they wanted. The woman who had spoken earlier came forward with a small bottle of tawny-gold liquid, murmuring "honey and herbs," and Brown swallowed it gratefully, his cough subsiding.

Harriet and Thaddeus returned to their food, thinking about Mr. Brown's words to the Dawn people and about what he'd said about them as future leaders. They were more encouraged by his words than by those of the speakers, who, except for the Jamaican, had been disappointing. The crowd seemed to feel the same way. The celebratory energy of earlier in the day had become diluted.

Harriet worried that the day would all be for nothing.

42

Controversy

Around five o'clock, as people at the Emancipation Day celebration finished their meals, there was a commotion on the opposite side of the lawn as someone stepped up onto the smaller platform there. Harriet was excited to see it was Reverend King. She stood up to see better. Thaddeus reluctantly rose beside her.

"I ask the permission of the assembled to speak from this side of the lawn!" called out the familiar, confident and straightforward voice so familiar to Harriet, "because I refuse to speak from the same platform recently inhabited by the previous speakers."

A huge roar of approval burst forth from the crowd, their energy instantly revived.

Shouts of "Speak, Rev! Speak!" and "Amen!" came simultaneously from many places in the audience. Hoots of approval and clapping went on for some time.

Harriet grinned so broadly, shouting and hooting, that Thaddeus started to laugh. She elbowed him in the ribs and he raised his hands over his heads and clapped loudly. "Yes, man! Speak!" he shouted. Despite his misgivings about Reverend King, he was impressed by the man's audacity and forthrightness in challenging the famous men who had spoken from the opposite platform. It was particularly interesting to see a white man challenging John Scoble. The two young people moved closer to the speaker.

The crowd stayed on its feet for most of Reverend King's speech, which they constantly interrupted with "amens" and shouts of approval. He was in the best form Harriet had seen him in a long time, talking in loud and animated tones about the evils of the begging culture and detailing the successes of the free black people of the Elgin Settlement. He talked about their logging and sawmill, their farms, grain mill and gristmill, the schooling of the youth in the classics (huge shouts of approval here), the brickyard and pearl ash factory, the digging of drainage ditches, the several churches that had now been established, and the hotel and post office, shoe store and carpenter shop that anchored the village of Buxton. He congratulated the hard-working, self-sufficient people of Buxton as proof of the humanity and intelligence of former slaves given the chance at land ownership and independence, challenging anyone to compete with the success that had come from a rejection of dependence on handouts. As he detailed the accomplishments of her home community, Harriet's heart swelled with pride. By the time he stepped down from the platform, the crowd was once again in high celebration.

Harriet put her hands on her hips and glared with a smiling challenge at Thaddeus, daring him to say anything negative. Thaddeus shrugged, saying, "Well, baby, I've got to admit, he hit the nail on its head, for sure! Whew! I see why you like him. But —"

"But nothing! Not now Thaddeus! You know I agree with you, anyway. But he's good, isn't he?"

"Yeah, girl, he's good. I just want to hear it from a black man is all."

Harriet nodded thoughtfully, remembering the words of J.C. Brown about them being future leaders, about people speaking out for themselves.

"You are a black man, Thaddeus," she said gently.

Thaddeus paused, his eyes widened, reminded too of Mr. Brown's words.

Nodding, he said softly, "Yes, I am, Harriet. And you are a black woman." She nodded. Then they put their arms around one another, pondering the responsibility they were beginning to realize was on their shoulders.

Meanwhile, the crowd was milling aimlessly. Another recess had been called. The couple decided to wend their way back to their original sitting spot. Harriet saw someone pleading with Scoble over to the side of the main platform. He was shaking his head vigorously. She could just make out his angry words. "No, I will *not* read it. These colored people are all prejudiced against me. I'll have nothing to do with them!"

The enthusiastic response to Reverend King was highly insulting to Scoble. Harriet began to suspect that the purpose of the recess was to allow the crowd to cool down from its excitement in the wake of the Buxton man's speech. Reverend Henson, who sat on a chair alongside the rear of the platform, looked rattled and uncomfortable. Scoble walked over and began talking to him, but not loudly enough for Harriet to hear.

After a while, Frederick Douglass again mounted the stage and began saying congratulatory things about the Dawn Settlement, trying—unsuccessfully—to rouse the crowd. When he finished, Mr. Scoble took the stage again. Harriet guessed that the hour or more since Reverend King had finished speaking was enough for him to get back his courage to face the people he thought were prejudiced against him. Clearly, he was feeling pressure to advance the proposal everyone was expecting from him.

Scoble announced once again his support for integrated education, saying that the Dawn belongs as much to the white man as to the colored. The words shocked Harriet. The school at Buxton admitted white students, which Harriet had no quarrel with. She and Allison were still friends. But no one at Buxton, including Reverend King, would ever say that the Elgin Settlement belonged to white folk equally to black! In fact, no property owner in Elgin was permitted to sell to a white person for at least ten years after purchasing their land. What was Scoble really about? Now he was saying he had submitted his proposal, but there would be no approval or disapproval, as he had sole authority to execute the decisions. By then most people in the audience were shaking their heads, protesting openly, or turning away.

"Mr. Chairman?" came a hoarse voice from near them. Harriet realized it was Mr. Brown and her pulse quickened in anticipation. Thaddeus turned around sharply, then looked quickly up at Mr. Henson, who was pretending not to hear. "Mr. Chairman, may I have permission to make a few remarks!?" Brown asked more loudly.

The people within earshot of Mr. Brown's voice shouted their support. Josiah Henson glanced around uncomfortably. "Yes, Mr. Brown," he finally said, "but you must restrict your comments to the theme of the day, which is the emancipation of the slaves of the British Empire!"

The crowd, hearing this, began to hiss and shout its disapproval. A moment later, George Cary, who had been in close conference with Henson and Scoble all day, surprised Harriet and Thaddeus by objecting to Mr. Henson's restriction. "Mr. Chairman, the speaker should be permitted to say whatever he thinks best, as others have been doing today!"

By this time, helped by his friends, J.C. Brown was ascending the platform. With each step, he seemed to gain energy, and by the time he got to the front, his voice was loud enough to be heard across most of the crowd.

"Seeing as there are broad axes here cutting out large abolition chips, I hope you will not think hard of seeing my small hatchet cutting at a small knot."

The audience, eager to hear his words, quieted their voices in response to seeing his ill health. They realized that here was a man, former resident and Trustee at Dawn, who was about to stand up against John Scoble. And a black man at that, Thaddeus and Harriet wordlessly communicated with one another: or at least brown.

"My friend Mr. Douglass," he went on, "I think that your

298

memory has grown short, sir. Perhaps you should keep your notes closer for reference. Did you not state on this platform that the first abolitionist came out in 1829? When in truth, three came out a full nine years before that, sir! Those three went to Texas to look out a location for the colored people. As a member of that party of three, I consider myself evidence of that fact, sir!"

The audience laughed and leaned forward in their seats.

"And Mr. Scoble, sir. I contend that you are not proposing to carry out the objectives intended by the settlement at Dawn. And I, as a trustee, will not submit to *any* proposition advanced by *you*!"

At this point, the audience interrupted with loud cheers and whoops.

Then there was a fast back-and-forth between Brown and Josiah Henson, who was loudly claiming that Brown was not a trustee. Several others joined in the shouting, and it became clear that Brown, indeed, was a trustee. He then pressed his advantage.

"I can prove that Mr. Henson himself is guilty of the grossest falsehoods of anyone here on this ground today! He went to England three years ago and there printed and published a book, expecting the lies within it to gain him great profit. In this book..." Brown paused for effect and the audience hushed. "In this book he claimed that he colonized *seven thousand souls* to Dawn!" Brown paused again as the audience reacted with shock, amazement, loud boos and guffaws.

John Scoble jumped up onto the platform, advancing toward Brown. The crowd began shouting and pointing. One of the organizers standing in the wings put a firm hand on Mr. Scoble's arm, restraining him while telling him that no gentleman would behave in such a way. "I consider you no gentleman, sir," he finished, and Scoble retreated toward the stairs.

Brown faced the audience once more, and with visible effort raised his voice even louder. "I call upon anyone in this audience to record the fact, if he should know of even *three* persons Mr. Henson has moved into Dawn, excepting his own family, to please stand up on your feet now and let the fact be known!"

Another pause, as people looked around to see if anyone was standing. Several people standing because they had no chairs folded their bodies as if to sit down. On the platform, Josiah Henson sat down heavily, looking around him with an expression that was somehow simultaneously hunted and indignant. People laughed and pointed at this unintended gesture. J.C. Brown turned to look at him, looked back at the audience, gave a sharp nod that became his farewell bow, and walked unevenly off the stage. When he reached the stairs, the group who had been with him reached out to support him as his legs buckled. They led him toward their wagon on the edge of the lawn, patting him on the back and thanking him as they made him comfortable.

Harriet and Thaddeus watched the whole exchange in silent amazement.

◇

Though the program was over, people were slow to leave. Lively conversations and arguments continued all across the lawn. Music could be heard in various venues around the edges of the lawn as after-parties got organized. Thaddeus and Harriet had begun walking back toward the Buxton camp when they overheard a conversation that made them stop. One of those speaking was a man who closely resembled Mary Ann Shadd. Perhaps her brother, thought Harriet.

"This has been going on for years, you know," that man was saying. "Scoble attended the Toronto Convention in '51: he and his little group of henchmen, including Henson. For years before that there was talk about what happened to six thousand, two hundred and fifty pounds—that's twenty five thousand dollars in American money—that Reverend Henson raised in England for his school. They acknowledged they had collected the money, but up to today, it has not been accounted for. They accused this same J.C. Brown of starting a false rumor that Henson had squandered it, but they never to this day came forward to explain why the money never reached the school! So at the convention in '51 Henson and Scoble got on the nominating committee for delegates. They put Brown's name on the list so they could publicly accuse him, on record, of making false charges against Henson. This enabled them to display that record in England, which lay the groundwork for them to collect more money in Dawn's name over there. They proposed Henry Bibb for president of the convention, knowing he would take their side."

Thaddeus flinched at the reference to Bibb, but worse was to come.

"Ah, you mustn't speak ill of the dead," someone in the little group said.

"What do you mean?" asked the man they thought was Shadd.

"I have just heard of Henry Bibb's death in the early hours of this morning."

At those words, Thaddeus gave a visible start. Harriet grabbed him. They walked a few steps away, then Thaddeus stopped, his eyes gone hollow. In his mind he was once again a teenaged youth with his head between his knees, tears flowing as he learned from the wrenching experience of the older man, offered generously to him despite what the words cost their speaker. However wrong this man may have been in the controversy raging among the black fugitive communities of Canada West, Thaddeus would always keep him in his heart.

"Oh, baby, I'm sorry," Harriet started, not knowing what

to say next. Realizing that words were unnecessary, Harriet put her arms around Thaddeus and simply held him. The scattering crowd drifted around the motionless couple.

At this moment someone tapped Harriet on the shoulder. She looked up and, much to her surprise, Isaac the boatman stood there, all the way from Windsor. She let go of Thaddeus and turned to him. "Isaac! What are you doing here?"

Isaac smiled brightly. "Well, for the longest time I've wanted to leave the Detroit River for a few days and see a bit more of the world!" He laughed. "And see Frederick Douglass and the rest. So when Miss Peggy had an urgent letter to get to Thaddeus, I volunteered and they let me come!" He reached into a pocket and drew out a somewhat crumpled envelope.

Thaddeus was shaken out of his reverie by Isaac's unexpected appearance. He blinked as his brain registered the words "urgent letter to get to Thaddeus." When Isaac went into his pocket Thaddeus felt a quick, intense curiosity that chased away thoughts of Henry Bibb. He reached for the letter and stared at the envelope, which simply said "Thaddeus Childs." He didn't recognize the handwriting.

"Open it, Thaddeus!" Harriet squeezed his shoulder.

His hand shook as he pulled the envelope and drew out the page. His eye flew to the signature: "your sister Charlotte." Hot tears blinded him. He began to tremble. Harriet took the paper from him.

"Sit down, Thaddeus," she pulled his arm. "Sit down! Isaac, help him."

Isaac and Harriet sat on either side. A few people still milling looked at them with curiosity.

"Read it to me, Harriet," said Thaddeus through shaky, nervous laughter. "I can't see anything." Tears were rolling down his cheeks.

Harriet smoothed the paper and read.

"My dearest brother Thaddeus. I know You must have

given your Family up for dead, not hearing from us all these Years. The Truth is, soon after you left us, Father had a problem with some other men in our Village and we moved deeper into the Swamp. We had no commerce with the Canals as we did when you were working in the Shingles. Only recently did I return to the Home you knew and then did my old friend Janey tell me the many Times they received word of your Letters. I have followed your Footsteps and write this from the Home of Miss Peggy! I am much exhausted from my Journey and she will not allow me to continue until she has "fattened me up" as she says. Oh Thaddeus, you will soon see me! I will be in Chatham with you before you know."

Harriet's voice was shaking by the time she finished the letter and her own eyes blurred the last few lines, while Isaac beamed a smile that looked like it would split his face.

From despair to soaring joy in a moment, Thaddeus sat stunned. While Henry Bibb was on his deathbed, his own sister Charlotte was sipping soup at Miss Peggy's house a few streets away. It was too much to take in. They all sat in silence for some time until Thaddeus was ready to move again.

The ditch was a canal filled with water when Thaddeus
would have worked there.

CAMP MFG CO
SINCE 1881

WASHINGTON DITCH

SURVEYED BY GEORGE WASHINGTON IN 1763.
A CART ROAD WAS BUILT FIRST ALONG THIS
4½ MILE DITCH AND THE CANAL DUG ALONG-
SIDE BY SLAVE LABOR FOR TRANSPORTATION.
GRESHAM NIMMO, UNDER THE PERSONAL
DIRECTION OF GEORGE WASHINGTON, DID THE
SURVEYING AND KEPT THE NOTES.

Photos taken at Great Dismal Swamp National Wildlife
Refuge in 2010 by the author

43

The Covenant

A few hours after Thaddeus received the letter from his sister Charlotte, the rose and gold of dying sunlight found Harriet and Thaddeus sitting beside the river. After a dinner accompanied by the family celebrating Thaddeus' news they had walked along the riverbank until they found a grassy spot with bushes around it that hid them from the view of any passersby. As the light waned and stars began to appear, they lay side by side looking into the sky, reverently, silently, each heart responding to the other's nearness while both minds attempted to comprehend the transformation that had taken place in them that day.

They needed few words. Their joy at Charlotte's letter flowed golden, soothing, in them both. The knowledge that Thaddeus would not be leaving left them free to ponder their future. Together. Here.

It was clear that on this day they had grown up. Issues that they had until now considered the domain of the older generation had become their responsibility. They began to confront their duty to plan for the future of their communities, the safety of the fugitives and even the movement to destroy slavery. They felt the mature weight of this obligation on their young shoulders for the first time.

J.C. Brown's words rang in their ears. His illness and the death of Henry Bibb lent them a solemn gravity. They remembered that Frederick Douglass joined the abolitionist movement when he was just a year older than Harriet, and younger than Thaddeus. Each of their minds relived the oaths they had sworn in the ceremonies of the Order, and felt their profound significance once again.

Thaddeus rolled onto his side and propped his head on

his elbow so he could look into Harriet's face. His nerves hummed with the combination of many emotions. He put his free hand on Harriet's warm, flat belly. She looked up at him with a gentle smile and put her hand lightly on top of his.

"Harriet," he spoke softly, but with determination, "I hardly need say how happy and content I am to have word of my family and to anticipate reunion with my sister. I can finally release the years of guilt and accept my decision to come here. But even more, today I have come to see that my commitment to the Order—to the refugees and to the fight against slavery—is my life and what I re-dedicate myself to. And Harriet," he continued, a swelling in his throat making his voice hoarse, "I want you to marry me. I want us to be united in the struggle as a family." He closed his eyes for a moment.

Harriet took in a sharp breath and rolled onto her side to face him. A surging tide of emotion took her, a combination of love, happiness and determination, washing over the joyous relief she had felt from the moment she read the letter. She closed her eyes and sighed.

"Oh Thaddeus, yes, I want that too!" She brought her face to his and they kissed, their arms encircling one another and pulling their bodies close. After a while, Harriet loosened her grip and sat up, her back straight, her eyes serious.

"But Thaddeus, I don't want to marry only to turn wife and mother, tend a garden and make a comfortable home." The conviction that had taken root in her from the afternoon she had heard her father's story had grown during today's events. "Our responsibility isn't only to each other. It is to the freedom of our people. I want to be a woman more like Mary Ann Shadd than my mother, God bless her. I'm a soldier for my people. I'm a sworn member of the Order. I want us to stand side by side in the freedom army." She took a breath and searched Thaddeus' eyes. "Are you willing to have that kind of wife, Thaddeus Childs?"

Thaddeus leaned back and stared at the remarkable

woman facing him, her eyes flashing, her body tense with determination. Why had he asked her to marry him? He had little regard for the rules and expectations of the church, had no real desire to live in the narrow confines laid down by the likes of Reverend King in the Elgin Settlement, but he had assumed Harriet did. His proposal of marriage had been an offer to compromise with what he assumed were her desires in the name of love.

He shook his head in near disbelief, remembering the hesitant girl with whom he had argued as they walked to and from J.C. Brown's house less than a month ago. A powerful person seemed to have appeared in place of that girl, like a formidable young hawk taking its first strong, graceful flight after awkwardly and hesitantly testing its wings only moments before. His face broke into a grin. He felt overwhelmed by love, respect and awe.

"Yes, yes, YES!" he shouted. Both of them flinched at his loudness and looked around, glad that no one was near. Harriet laughed merrily, joyously, her voice like the fifes running up and down the tunes in today's parade.

"Yes! Baby, sweetheart, yes," Thaddeus said a little more quietly but no less fervently, "together we'll take up the light the elders are passing to us."

They sat encircled in each other's arms, joy and optimism combining with a solemn sense of covenant. Their fingers intertwined and they leaned against one another, gazing across the river into the future.

The bird they call Fire Lantern lands in the bush,
Folds its flame-hued wings into its black body.
Its mate flutters to perch beside it.
They have come a long way:
They are ready.

The End

Dear Reader,

Novels are full of imaginary people and happenings. But what about novels like this one, that seem to be about the real past? You probably wonder: what is real and what is imaginary? I'd like to answer this question and also let you know how to find out more.

The main answer is, this is real history and very much true. Before I wrote it, I read everything I could find, and I visited the site of the Elgin Settlement in Buxton, Ontario. I also went to Chatham, Ontario and the Great Dismal Swamp on the border of North Carolina and Virginia. I owe a great debt to **Gwen Robinson**, a modern **griot** (a griot is a person in Africa whose job is to preserve history by memory) and founder of the Chatham-Kent Black Historical Society. Gwen graciously allowed me to twice interview her. Later she read the draft of my book, corrected it to make sure the history was accurate, and strongly encouraged me to get it published to help set the record straight.

I also owe a debt to **Shannon Prince and Sterling Alexander of the Buxton Museum**, who gave me much time and information, and who have kept their ancestors' history alive. **Delores Freeman of the National Fish and Wildlife Service at the Great Dismal Swamp** also shared her deep knowledge.

One of my main hopes for *Freedom Soldiers* is that readers will learn that African-American and African-Canadian people and organizations were the true backbone and leadership of the Underground Railroad and the anti-slavery movement. They worked in secret and mostly without leaving a written record—written records would have been a dangerous paper trail. Since then most history books and novels have intentionally or unintentionally left them out, making it seem—falsely—as though white abolitionists led the struggle to abolish slavery.

That said, the idea of an historical novel is to use real history to create a story, and in doing that many small things are changed to fit the story. The main characters in my story are made up. Harriet, Thaddeus, Abiah, and their family members all came to life for the first time on the pages of this book. But there are also plenty of real people, as you will see below. And Abiah's crossing of the Ohio River on ice floes with baby in arms is from the true story of Elgin settler Eliza Harris, who also inspired a character in Harriet Beecher Stowe's famous 19th century novel, Uncle Tom's Cabin.

Below is information about real characters and events from the book. Each topic is in bold type, so you can easily find the parts you're interested in. If you look in the **Bibliography** printed after this letter, you will see books, articles and websites where you can learn more. If you do a web search on any of them, you'll dig up fascinating information.

The **Great Dismal Swamp** is a real place, and you can visit the National Park there today. They have good information about the Underground Railroad. The canal where Thaddeus and his coworkers brought cypress to sell is still there. It was dug by slaves who "belonged to" George Washington, the first President of the United States. For decades, *tens of thousands of people* escaped slavery to live, farm, work and raise their free children there.

Gunsmith and Emily Jones were real people. Mr. Jones was the grandson of a metal tradesman from Africa who was forced into slavery in America. He graduated from Oberlin College in Ohio before he moved to Chatham and met Emily. Later he advised John Brown, who led a raid that helped ignite the US Civil War and end slavery. Here's a link to an article about him: http://www.chathamthisweek.com/2014/02/13/gunsmith-jones-saw-opportunity-in-chatham

Edwin Larwill really did and said the racist things in the book.

Reverend William King was a founder of the Elgin Settlement, just as he is in the book. He wrote a short autobiography, which you can read.

Isaac Riley was the first settler at the Elgin Settlement.

The attack on the Elgin school we do not know about for sure, but there was a rumor that it would be attacked. You can read about this in Donald G. Simpson's book *Under the North Star*. We don't know what happened in the woods that day. We also don't know for sure if girls attended the school in those early years.

William and Eliza Parker led the **Christiana Rebellion** in Pennsylvania and then fled to the Elgin Settlement. Mr. Parker wrote about it in *The Atlantic Monthly*, Volume XVII, in 1866. You can find this document and plenty of other information if you search for his name and Christiana online. You will find that the story Mr. Parker tells in *Freedom Soldiers* is the same thing he said in his autobiography. However, I made up the other conversations they had with their neighbors. Ezekiel and the other children are made up; the Parkers had three much younger children when they moved to the Elgin Settlement. The story about the conflict in Detroit was invented, although many similar events actually happened.

Henry Bibb was another former enslaved person who wrote his autobiography, *Narrative of the Life and Adventures of Henry Bibb, an American Slave, Written by Himself*. The story of his life that he told Thaddeus in the book is taken straight from his autobiography and even uses some of the same words. The other conversations with Thaddeus were made up, but his role and opinions in the controversies among Canadian settlers are accurate.

Harriet's initiation ceremony comes from an 1887 interview in The Detroit Tribune with the real William Lambert, an organizer of the **African-American Mysteries and the**

Order of the Men of Oppression, which was reported to have thousands of African-American members and a few white members. Lambert was a leader of the Detroit Vigilance Committee, a friend of Frederick Douglass and an advisor to John Brown.

The two market women in Baltimore who Eliza Parker says were agents of the Underground Railroad really were. This shows how extensive the black organizing was: people who were still enslaved were an active part of it.

Mary Ann Shadd was a real person and a very influential leader. She debated **John Scoble,** but the debate was at Dawn, not Chatham. An Indian man told the story of the **mullet and the muskellunge** during that debate.

The white birdwatcher Alexander Ross traveled to plantations and equipped enslaved people to make the journey North with the Underground Railroad, though not quite at the time depicted in the novel.

William Still, a leader of the Vigilance Committee in Pennsylvania, along with his wife helped hundreds of refugees like the Parkers along their road to freedom and unusually *did* keep written records, which he hid in his well. You can read these online.

J.C. Brown, Frederick Douglass, and **Josiah Henson** were all real people.

All the real people in the book took the type of actions and had the type of opinions that they have in the novel. The verbal conflicts that happened at the Emancipation Day celebration were real. Look for the **letter from J. C. Brown to The Provincial Freeman, August 26, 1854** for his description of the day's events and the content of his speech that day

There are museums and historical sites you can visit at the sites of the Elgin and Dawn Settlements staffed by descendants of the people who lived there during the time of this novel. Check out **The Buxton Museum** online or in person. There is a reunion of descendants of the Elgin Settlement every Labor Day, and it is open to the public.

<>

History is mostly written by the people in power. Most historians have neglected to, or chosen not to, write the truth about the role of black people and black leadership in the movement to overthrow slavery in the Americas, whether that be in South America, the Caribbean or North America. I hope this story about one small but important portion of that vast, intercontinental movement will help people to know the truth. I hope it will help a new generation of young people, who feel the fire in their bellies, to 'take up the torchlight in all its brightness and vision.'

Like anything worthwhile, this book is the product of many people, not just one. A friend did some of the early research with me and helped me to more fully understand the history and experience in its proper context. He and several other brothers and sisters in the struggle taught me to understand the need in today's world, just as in the time of the Underground Railroad, for humbly respecting and accepting the guidance of the poorest and most exploited black women and men in the movement for social justice, as well as in the writing of this book.

Several people from many walks of life read early drafts and gave suggestions that helped the book along. I especially thank my dear friend Barbara Foley, who critiqued the first draft and made excellent suggestions for rewriting it; my publisher, Tim Sheard, who also made significant suggestions for revision; and several young readers in my community in Jamaica. I incorporated all of this input, but any errors are mine and mine alone.

I especially thank the novel's characters, Harriet, Thaddeus and Abiah, who, in the magical process of story-telling used my fingers and keyboard to tell their story.

And Jacob, the namesake of the grandfather I never met, whose own escape in a different time and place made my existence possible.

Finally, I would love to hear from you. My email address is: katherine1854williams@gmail.com

With respect, Kathy Williams

Bibliography

These are some of the websites, articles and books I read to put Harriet and Thaddeus into the real history of the times they lived in.

Aaron   Fugitive Slave Narrative   http://docsouth.unc.edu/neh/aaron/aaron.html

Anderson, Osborne P., *A Voice from Harper's Ferry: A Narrative of Events at Harper's Ferry; with Incidents Prior and Subsequent to its Capture by Captain Brown and His Men,* Boston, 1861

Beecher-Stowe, Harriet, *Dred, A Tale of the Great Dismal Swamp,* Phillips, Sampson and Company 1856, Electronic edition, University of North Carolina at Chapel Hill

Bibb, Henry, *Narrative of the Life and Adventures of Henry Bibb, an American Slave, Written by Himself*

Bristow, Peggy, coordinator, *'We're Rooted Here and They Can't Pull Us Up',* University of Toronto Press, 1994

Breen, Thomas, Associated Press, Monday, July 4, 2011, "Southern swamp holds clues about runaway slaves"

Brown, John, et al, "The United States League of Gileadites" from Sanborn, F. B. ed., *The Life and Letters of John Brown.* Boston: Roberts Brothers, 1891, pp. 124-27

Brown, John, and Chatham Convention, *Provisional Constitution and Ordinances for the People of the United States,* 1858 (Constitution of Harper's Ferry raiding party)

Buxton Museum website: www.buxtonmuseum.com

Coffin, Levi, *Reminiscences*

Daily Detroit Post, February 23, 1875: "Death of George DeBaptiste", Clarke Historical Library http://clarke.cmich.edu

Delany, Martin R., Chief Commissioner, *Report of the Niger Valley Exploring Party,* Chatham, Canada West, July 30, 1861, New York: Thomas Hamilton, No. 48 Beekman Street

DuBois, W.E.B., *John Brown,* Free Press, George W. Jacobs & Co. 1909.

Farmer, Silas, City Historiographer, *The History of Detroit and Michigan, Past and Present,* Chapter 48 "Slavery and the Colored

Race" Detroit, Silas Farmer & Co, 1889, http://clarke.cmich.
edu/resource_tab/bibliographies_of_clarke_library_material/
underground_railroad/pdfs/farmer.pdf

Freeman, Delores, presentation at the Great Dismal Swamp
National Wildlife Refuge, September 2010

Grandy, Moses, *Narrative of the Life of Mose Grandy; Late
a Slave in the United States of America,* University of North
Carolina at Chapel Hill, Electronic Edition, 1996

Henson, Josiah, *Autobiography*

Hochschild, Adam, *Bury the Chains: Prophets and Rebels in the
Fight to Free an Empire's Slaves* Houghton Mifflin, Boston, 2005

Hodges, Willis Augustus, Willard B. Gatewood, Jr., editor, *Free
Man of Color, the Autobiography of Willis Augustus Hodges,*
University of Tennessee Press, Knoxville, 1982 (written 1849)

International School for Bottom-up Organizing, *The Bottom Will Rise
and Create a New World* 2011, http://www.peoplesorganizing.org/
book2.html (for passage quoted on page 179)

Jones, Thomas, *Experience and Personal Narrative of Uncle Tom
Jones; Who Was for Forty Years a Slave. Also the Surprising
Adventures of Wild Tom, of the Island Retreat, a Fugitive Negro
from South Carolina,* Electronic Edition, University of North
Carolina at Chapel Hill, 1999

King, William, *Autobiography of Reverend William King, Written
at Intervals during the Last Three Years of His Life;* January, 1892

Landon, Fred, "From Chatham to Harper's Ferry", *The Canadian
Magazine,* Toronto, October 1919, Vol LIII, No. 6

Leasher, Evelyn, "William Lambert, An African American
Leader of Detroit's Anti-Slavery Movement", http://clarke.cmich.
edu/resource_tab/bibliographies_of_clarke_library_material/
underground_railroad/underground_railroad_index.html in which
is found an interview with William Lambert from the *Detroit
Tribune* of January 17, 1887 entitled "Freedom's Railway

Libby, Jean, editor, *John Brown Mysteries* Pictorial Histories
Publishing Co., 1999

Longfellow, Henry W, "The Slave in Dismal Swamp"

Oates, Stephen , *The Fires of Jubilee*

Parker, William, *Autobiography*, Atlantic Monthly, Volume XVII, 1866

Pease, Jane H. and Pease, William H. , *They Who Would Be Free;* University of Illinois, 1974

Ibid. *Black Utopia, Negro Communal Experiments in America*; State Historical Society of Wisconsin, 1963

Prince, Bryan, *A Shadow on the Household* Emblem: McClelland & Stewart 2009

Ibid. *I Came as a Stranger* Tundra Books, 2004

Renehan, Edward J., Jr., *The Secret Six; The True Tale of the Men Who Conspired with John Brown,* University of South Carolina, 1997

Ripley, C. Peter, ed, *The Black Abolitionist Papers, Vol II; Canada 1830-1865,* U. North Carolina Press, 1986

Shadd, Mary A., *A Plea for Emigration; or, Notes of Canada West, in its Moral, Social and Political Aspect: with Suggestions Respecting Mexico, W. Indies and Vancouver's Island, for the Information of Colored Emigrants.* Detroit: George W. Pattison, 1852

Siebert, Wilbur H., *The Underground Railroad from Slavery to Freedom*, The Macmillan Company, 1898; republished by Dover Publications, 2006

Simpson, Donald G., *Under the North Star*, Africa World Press, New Jersey, 2005

Smardz Frost, *I've Got a Home in Glory Land: A Lost Tale of the Underground Railroad,* Farrar, Straus and Giroux,

Still, William, *The Underground Rail Road, a Record of Facts, Authentic Narratives, Letters* 1872

Tobin, Jacqueline L. and Jones, Hettie, *From Midnight to Dawn: The Last Tracks of the Underground Railroad*

U.S. Fish and Wildlife Service Great Dismal Swamp National Wildlife Refuge, *The Great Dismal Swamp and the Underground Railroad*

About the Author

Katherine Fischer Williams is a retired public school teacher who grew up on Chicago's South Side, where she was active in the Civil Rights Movement and went on to a lifetime in the struggle for a world of equality and freedom. She now lives in rural Jamaica, where she writes and participates in community organizing.

TITLES FROM HARD BALL PRESS

A Great Vision: A Militant Family's Journey Through the Twentieth Century, Richard March

Caring: 1199 Nursing Home Workers Tell Their Story, Tim Sheard, ed.

Fight For Your Long Day, Classroom Edition, by Alex Kudera

I Still Can't Fly: Confessions of a Lifelong Troublemaker, Kevin John Carroll (Winter 2018-19)

Love Dies – A Thriller, Timothy Sheard

The Man Who Fell From the Sky – Bill Fletcher Jr.

Murder of a Post Office Manager – A Legal Thriller, Paul Felton

New York Hustle: Pool Rooms, School Rooms and Street Corner, A Memoir, Stan Maron

Passion's Pride: Return to the Dawning – Cathie Wright- Lewis

The Secrets of the Snow –Poetry, Hiva Panahi

Sixteen Tons – A Novel, Kevin Corley

Throw Out the Water – Sequel to Sixteen Tons, Kevin Corley

We Are One: Stories of Work, Life & Love – Elizabeth Gottieb, ed.

What Did You Learn at Work Today? The Forbidden Lessons of Labor Education, Helena Worthen

With Our Loving Hands: 1199 Nursing Home Workers Tell Their Story, Timothy Sheard, ed.

Winning Richmond: How a Progressive Alliance Won City Hall – Gayle McLaughlin

Woman Missing – A Mill Town Mystery, Linda Nordquist

The Lenny Moss Mysteries – Timothy Sheard

This Won't Hurt A Bit

Some Cuts Never Heal

A Race Against Death

No Place To Be Sick

Slim To None

A Bitter Pill

Someone Has To Die

CHILDREN'S BOOKS from HARD BALL PRESS

Joelito's Big Decision, La gran Decisión de Joelito:
Ann Berlak (Author), Daniel Camacho (Illustrator),
José Antonio Galloso (Translator)
Manny and the Mango Tree, Many y el Árbol de Mango:
Alí R. and Valerie Bustamante (Authors), Monica Lunot-
Kuker (Illustrator). Mauricio Niebla (Translator)
The Cabbage That Came Back, El Repollo que Volvió
Stephen Pearl & Rafael Pearl (Authors), Rafael Pearl (Illustra-
tor), Sara Pearl (Translator)
Hats Off For Gabbie, ¡Aplausos para Gaby!:
Marivir Montebon (Author), Yana Murashko (Illustrator),
Mauricio Niebla (Translator)
Margarito's Forest/El Bosque de Don Margarito:
Andy Carter (Author), Alison Havens (Illustrator), Sergio
Villatoro (Graphic Design),
Artwork contributions by the children of the Saq Ja' elemen-
tary school
K'iche tranlations by Eduardo Elas and Manuel Hernandez
Translated by Omar Mejia
*Jimmy's Carwash Adventure, La Aventura de Jaime en el
Autolavado:*
Victor Narro (Author), Yana Murashko (Illustrator), Madelin
Arroyo (Translator)
Good Guy Jake/Buen Chico Jake,
Mark Torres (author), Yana Murashko (illustrator), Madelin
Arroyo (translator)
Polar Bear Pete's Ice Is Melting!
Timothy Sheard (author), Kayla Fils-Amie (illustrator),
Madelin Arroyo (translator)

HOW TO ORDER BOOKS:
Order books from www.hardballpress.com, Amazon.com,
or independent booksellers everywhere.
**Receive a 20% discount for orders of 10 or more, a 40% discount for
orders of 50 or more when ordering from www.hardballpress.com.**

CPSIA information can be obtained
at www.ICGtesting.com
Printed in the USA
LVHW051600310719
626020LV00016B/788